Praise for *The Christie Affair*

"*The Christie Affair* is a genuine marvel. An astonishingly clever novel that manages to be both a deeply satisfying mystery and a profoundly moving story about lost love and the many ways in which grief can shape one's character. Full of unexpected twists and written in beautiful prose, *The Christie Affair* brilliantly answers a question that has haunted readers for years: What happened to Agatha Christie in the days she was missing? Nina de Gramont takes this thread of a story and weaves it into a rich and vibrant tapestry."

—Kristin Hannah, author of *The Four Winds*

"This story is all about murder and lies and love and discovery. I loved it so much. I could not put it down. I read it in one sitting."

—Reese Witherspoon (A Reese's Book Club Pick)

"Sizzles from its first sentence." —*The Wall Street Journal*

"Expect delightful Christie-like plot twists." —*People*

"The author weaves a clever, highly original, mesmerizing tale filled with strange and unexpected turns and concludes it in an unexpected but wholly satisfying manner. With its superb writing, strong characterizations, and wonderfully imaginative plot, this is a must-read." —*Booklist* (starred review)

"Dare I admit I haven't read any Agatha Christie or know about her disappearance? I feared this might somehow diminish *The Christie Affair* for me. But Nina de Gramont's skillful storytelling is exceeded only by her tenderness for her characters, and I was swept up, turning the pages and savoring them, too. This is a cracking good read!"

—Therese Anne Fowler, author of *A Good Neighborhood*

"Historical kinda-fiction, a thriller wrapped in romance, mystery, and some fascinating conjecture."   —*Goodreads*

"Ingeniously plotted . . . gorgeously written. An accomplished author, de Gramont takes a page from the great mystery writer herself and makes swift work of tying up loose ends as the story reaches its boiling point, leaving readers marvelously entertained and breathlessly connecting the dots."

—*Shelf Awareness*

"A superior thriller . . . gripping."   —*Publishers Weekly*

"A meta delight for fans of crime writing, *The Christie Affair* is a fictional murder mystery woven around the real-life disappearance of Agatha Christie. This enduring conundrum from 1926 is not so much fictionalized as creatively reimagined. Whether you know much about what happened then or not, you'll find this delicious whodunit totally irresistible."

—*CrimeReads*

"*The Christie Affair* deserves all the hype it's gotten . . . [It is de Gramont's] most mature and polished work to date, with rounded characters and a smooth-running, steel-trap plot that the author of *The Mousetrap* could admire. Actual historical details are mixed with authorial invention into a smooth, tasty puree. Lovers of mystery, romance, and literary fiction should be equally pleased." —*StarNews*

"Refreshingly thoughtful and inventive." —*Air Mail*

"[*The Christie Affair*] unfolds as if it were one of Christie's mysteries, rewarding the reader with the thrill of discovery over and over.... And in true Agatha Christie fashion, when all is finally revealed and the full picture comes into focus, the result is unexpected, exhilarating, and enormously satisfying." —Amazon

"*The Christie Affair* is a pitch-perfect hat trick of a novel, delivering a fascinating glimpse into history, with the sensational and unexplained disappearance of Agatha Christie, a layered and completely satisfying murder mystery, and a moving, emotional rendering of love, loss, revenge, and redemption—all with effortlessly stunning prose. I loved every page, and will be recommending this to everyone I know!"
—Paula McLain, author of *The Paris Wife* and *When the Stars Go Dark*

"This novel about the eleven-day disappearance of Agatha Christie, told from the point of view of Christie's husband's mistress, is such a delight: intriguing, fast-paced, and elegantly written. Nina de Gramont takes you on an adventure through the English countryside with as many twists and turns as, well, an Agatha Christie novel. The unlikely alliances, complex motivations, and jaw-dropping surprises will keep you riveted until the very last page."

—Christina Baker Kline, author of
Orphan Train and *The Exiles*

"Immersive, reflexive, and propulsive, *The Christie Affair* is an extremely impressive literary novel, which reveals its hidden themes and secrets through a narrative dance brilliantly done. This tale of two very different women who want the very same things in life forges surprising bonds both with its characters and the reader, deliciously subverting our notions of what makes a heroine, mother, writer, and wife."

—Natalie Jenner, author of *The Jane Austen Society*

"*The Christie Affair* is my favorite kind of story: a fresh take on a real-life event, layered with mystery and filled with breathtaking plot twists. Toss in the windswept English countryside and a tragic past, and I'm done for. Nina de Gramont's novel shines on so many levels, it's hard to keep count: as an ode to Agatha Christie's legacy, as a dashing love story, and as a tribute to complicated, determined women. Magnificent."

—Fiona Davis, author of *The Lions of Fifth Avenue*

"I read in a single sitting *The Christie Affair* by Nina de Gramont, who weaves a captivating tale around the real-life disappearance of mystery writer Agatha Christie from the point of view of her husband's lover. The story combines dark pasts, dangerous liaisons, and unforeseen twists into a masterful work reminiscent of one of Christie's enigmatic works. *The Christie*

Affair is both enthralling and beguiling and will keep readers guessing until the very last page."

—Pam Jenoff, author of *The Lost Girls of Paris*

"Rooted in fact and reason but charged throughout with emotion and imagination, this is an extraordinary murder mystery novel that dares to invoke the spirit of Dame Christie and succeeds." —*CriminalElement*

The
CHRISTIE
AFFAIR

Nina de Gramont

ST. MARTIN'S GRIFFIN
NEW YORK

Published in the United States by St. Martin's Griffin,
an imprint of St. Martin's Publishing Group

THE CHRISTIE AFFAIR. Copyright © 2022 by Nina de Gramont. All rights reserved.
Printed in Canada. For information, address
St. Martin's Publishing Group, 120 Broadway, New York, NY 10271.

www.stmartins.com

Designed by Michelle McMillian

The Library of Congress has cataloged the hardcover edition as follows:

Names: de Gramont, Nina, author.
Title: The Christie affair / Nina de Gramont.
Description: First edition | New York: St. Martin's Press, 2022.
Identifiers: LCCN 2021039239 | ISBN 9781250274618 (hardcover) |
    ISBN 9781250282132 (international, sold outside the U.S. subject
    to rights availability) | ISBN 9781250274625 (ebook)
Subjects: LCGFT: Novels.
Classification: LCC PS3557.R24 C48 2022 | DDC 813/.54—dc23
LC record available at https://lccn.loc.gov/2021039239

ISBN 978-1-250-79263-1 (trade paperback)

Our books may be purchased in bulk for promotional, educational,
or business use. Please contact your local bookseller or the Macmillan Corporate
and Premium Sales Department at 1-800-221-7945, extension 5442, or
by email at MacmillanSpecialMarkets@macmillan.com.

First St. Martin's Griffin Edition: 2023

10 9 8 7 6 5 4 3 2 1

For Liza Jane Hanson

Part One

"She cares too much, that little one.
It is not safe. No, it is not safe."

—Hercule Poirot

Here Lies Sister Mary

Along time ago in another country, I nearly killed a woman.

It's a particular feeling, the urge to murder. First comes rage, larger than any you've ever imagined. It takes over your body so completely it's like a divine force, grabbing hold of your will, your limbs, your psyche. It conveys a strength you never knew you possessed. Your hands, harmless until now, rise up to squeeze another person's life away. There's a joy to it. In retrospect it's frightening, but I daresay in the moment it feels sweet, the way justice feels sweet.

Agatha Christie had a fascination with murder. But she was tenderhearted. She never wanted to kill anyone. Not for a moment. Not even me.

"Call me Agatha," she always said, reaching out a slender hand. But I never would, not in those early days, no matter how many weekends I spent at one of her homes, no matter how many private moments we shared. The familiarity didn't feel proper, though propriety was already waning in the years after the Great War. Agatha was upper-crust and elegant, but perfectly willing to dispense with manners and social mores. Whereas I had worked too hard to learn those manners and mores to ever abandon them easily.

I liked her. Back then I refused to think highly of her writing. But I always admitted to admiring her as a person. I still admire her. Recently, when I confided this to one of my sisters, she asked me if I had regrets about what I'd done, and how much pain it caused.

"Of course I do," I told her without hesitation. Anyone who says *I have no regrets* is either a psychopath or a liar. I am neither of those things, simply adept at keeping secrets. In this way the first Mrs. Christie and the second are very much alike. We both know you can't tell your own story without exposing someone else's. Her whole life, Agatha refused to answer any questions about the eleven days she went missing, and it wasn't only because she needed to protect herself.

I would have refused to answer, too, if anyone had thought to ask.

The Disappearance

I told Archie it was the wrong time to leave his wife, but I didn't mean it. As far as I was concerned, this game had gone on far too long. It was time for me to play the winning hand. But he liked things to be his own idea, so I protested.

"She's too fragile," I said. Agatha was still reeling from her mother's death.

"Clarissa died months ago," Archie said. "And no matter when I tell her, it will be beastly." *Fragile* was the last word anyone would use to describe Archie. He sat at the great mahogany desk in his London office, all pomp and power. "There's no making everybody happy," he said. "Somebody has got to be unhappy, and I'm tired of it being me."

I faced him, perched on the leather chair usually reserved for financiers and businessmen. "Darling." My voice would never achieve the genteel tones of Agatha's, but by then I had at least managed to wash away the East End. "She needs more time to recover."

"She's a grown woman."

"A person never stops needing her mother."

"You're too indulgent, Nan. Too kind."

I smiled as if this were true. The things Archie hated most in the world were illness, weakness, sadness. He had no patience for recuperation. As his mistress, I always maintained a cheerful demeanor. Light and airy. The perfect contrast to his not-quite-fooled and grief-stricken wife.

His face softened. A smile twitched the corner of his mouth. As the French like to say, "Happy people have no history." Archie never inquired after my past. He only wanted me now, beaming and willing. He ran a hand over his hair, putting back in place what had not been disrupted. I noticed a bit of gray at the temples. It made him looked distinguished. There may have been a mercenary element to my relationship with Archie, but that doesn't mean I couldn't enjoy him. He was tall, handsome, and in love with me.

He stood from his desk and crossed the room to kneel before my chair.

"Archie," I said, pretending to scold. "What if someone comes in?"

"No one will come in." He put his arms round my waist and laid his head in my lap. I wore a pleated skirt, a button-up blouse, a loose cardigan, and stockings. Fake pearls and a smart new hat. I stroked Archie's head but gently pushed it away as he pressed his face against me.

"Not here," I said, but without urgency. Cheerful, cheerful, cheerful. A girl who'd never been sick or sad a day in her life.

Archie kissed me. He tasted like pipe smoke. I closed my hands on the lapel of his jacket and didn't object when he cupped his hand around my breast. Tonight he would be going home to his wife. If the course I'd planned so carefully was to continue, it was best to send him to her thinking of me. A sponge soaked in quinine sulfate—procured by my married younger sister—stood guard inside me, protecting against pregnancy. Never once had I encountered Archie without preparing myself in this way, but for the moment my precautions proved unnecessary. He pulled my skirt modestly back into place, smoothing over the pleats, then stood and walked back round his desk.

Almost the moment he returned to his chair, in walked Agatha. She rapped lightly on the door at the same time she pushed it open. Her sensible heels made the barest sound on the carpet. At thirty-six, Agatha's auburn hair faded toward brown. She was several inches taller than me, and nearly ten years older.

"Agatha," Archie said sharply. "You might have knocked."

"Oh, Archie. This isn't a dressing room." Then she turned to me. "Miss O'Dea. I wasn't expecting to see you here."

Archie's strategy had always been to hide me in plain sight. I was regularly invited to parties and even weekends at the Christies' home. Six months ago, he would at least have made an excuse for my presence in his office. *Stan's loaned Nan to do some shorthand,* he might have said. Stan was my employer at the Imperial British Rubber Company. He was a friend of Archie's, but never loaned anybody anything.

This time Archie didn't offer up a single word to explain me, perched where I didn't belong. Agatha's brows arched as she realized her husband couldn't be bothered with the usual subterfuge. She gathered her composure by addressing me.

"Look at us." She pointed to her outfit and then mine. "We're twins."

It was an effort not to touch my face. I was blushing furiously. What if she had come in two minutes earlier? Would she have pretended ignorance against all evidence, just as doggedly as she did now?

"Yes," I said. "Yes, it's true, we are."

That season nearly every woman in London was a twin, the same clothes, the same shoulder-length hair. But Agatha's suit was authentic Chanel, and her pearls were not fake. She didn't register these discrepancies with any disdain, if at all. She wasn't that sort of person, a virtue that backfired when it came to me. Never once did Agatha object to the daughter of a clerk, a mere secretary, entering her social circles. "She's friends with Stan's daughter," Archie had told her. "Excellent golfer." That was all the explanation she ever required.

In photographs from this time Agatha looks much darker, less pretty than she really was. Her eyes were sparkling and blue. She had a girlish sprinkling of freckles across her nose and a face that moved quickly from one expression to the next. Finally Archie stood to greet her, taking her hand as though she were a business associate. I decided—the way someone who's doing something cruel can decide—it was all to the good: she deserved better than Archie, this pretty and ambitious woman. She deserved someone who would collect her in his arms with unabashed adoration and be faithful to her. As guilt crept in to discourage me, I reminded myself that Agatha was born on her feet, and that's how she'd always land.

She told Archie, likely for the second or third time, that she'd had a meeting with Donald Fraser, her new literary agent. "Since I'm in town, I thought we might go to luncheon. Before your weekend away."

"I can't today." Archie gestured unconvincingly toward his empty desk. "I've a mountain of work to get through."

"Ah. You sure? I've booked a table at Simpson's."

"I'm certain," he said. "I'm afraid you've come by for nothing."

"Would you like to come with me, Miss O'Dea? A girls' luncheon?"

I couldn't bear seeing her rejected twice. "Oh, yes. That would be lovely."

Archie coughed, irritated. Another man might have been nervous, faced with this meeting, wife and lover. But he'd moved past caring. He wanted his marriage over, and if that came about from Agatha walking in on us, so be it. While his wife and I lunched, he would keep an appointment at Garrard and Company to buy the most beautiful ring, my first real diamond.

"You must tell me about your new literary agent," I said, getting to my feet. "What an exciting career you have, Mrs. Christie." This was not flattery. Agatha's career was leagues more interesting to me than Archie's work in finance, though she wasn't well-known at this time, not in the way she would become. A rising star not quite risen. I envied her.

Agatha put her arm through mine. I accepted the gesture with ease. Nothing came more naturally to me than intimacy with other women. I had three sisters. Agatha's face set into a smile that managed to be both dreamy and determined. Archie sometimes complained about the weight she'd gained over the past seven years, since Teddy arrived, but her arm felt thin and delicate. I let her lead me through the offices and out onto the busy London street. My cheeks went pink from the cold. Agatha released my arm abruptly and brought a hand to her forehead, steadying herself.

"Are you all right, Mrs. Christie?"

"Agatha," she said, her voice sharper than it had been in Archie's office. "Please call me Agatha."

I nodded. And then proceeded to do what I did every time she made this request—for the bulk of our time that afternoon, I didn't call her anything at all.

Have you ever known a woman who went on to become famous? Looking back, you can see things in memory, can't you. About the way she held herself. The determination with which she spoke. To her dying day, Agatha claimed not to be an ambitious person. She thought she kept her intensity secret, but I could see it in the way her eyes swept over a room. The way she examined everyone who crossed her line of vision, imagining a history she could sum up in a single sentence. Unlike Archie, Agatha always wanted to know about your past. If you didn't care to reveal it, she'd create something of her own and convince herself it was true.

At Simpson's Agatha and I were escorted upstairs to the ladies' dining room. When we were seated, she removed her hat, so I did, too, though many other ladies wore theirs. She fluffed her pretty hair back into place. The gesture seemed less vanity than a way to comfort herself. She might have asked me what I'd been doing in Archie's office. But she knew I'd have a lie at the ready and didn't want to hear it.

Instead she said, "Your mother's still living, isn't she, Miss O'Dea?"

"Yes, both my parents."

She stared at me frankly. Assessing. One is allowed to say it in retrospect. I was pretty. Slim, young, athletic. At the same time, I was no Helen of Troy. If I had been, my relationship with Archie might have been less alarming. The modesty of my charms indicated he might very well be in love.

"How's Teddy?" I asked.

"She's fine."

"And the writing?"

"It's fine." She waved her hand as if nothing mattered less. "It's all a parlor trick. Shiny objects and red herrings." A look crossed her face, as if she couldn't help but smile when thinking of it, so I knew despite her dismissal, she was proud of her work.

An enormous bang erupted as a white-coated waiter dropped his tray full of empty dishes. I couldn't help but jump. At the table next to us, a man dining with his wife covered his head with his arms as reflex. Not so long ago loud crashes in London meant something far more ominous than shattered dishware, and so many of our men had seen the worst of it.

Agatha took a sip of tea. "How I miss the calm before the War. Do you think we'll ever recover, Miss O'Dea?"

"I don't see how we can."

"I suppose you were too young to do any nursing."

I nodded. During the War, it was mostly matronly types who tended the soldiers, by design, to avert the bloom of un-suitable romances. Agatha had been assigned to a hospital dispensary in Torquay. It was where she learned so much about poison.

"My sister Megs became a nurse," I said. "After the War, as her profession. In fact she works now at a hospital in Torquay."

Agatha did not ask more about this. She wouldn't know someone like my sister. Instead she asked, "Did you lose anyone close to you?"

"A boy I used to know. In Ireland."

"Was he killed?"

"Let's just say he never came home. Not really."

"Archie was in the Flying Corps. Of course you know that. I suppose it was different for those in the air."

Didn't that sum up the whole world? Always the poor ones carrying the world's scars. Agatha liked to quote William Blake: "Some are born to sweet delight, some are born to endless night." In my mind, even at that moment—lunching at Simpson's while her husband shopped for my engagement ring—I considered Agatha the former and myself the latter.

An expression kept rising to Agatha's face that I could see her actively pushing away. As if she wanted to say something, but couldn't bring herself to. She had brought me to luncheon, I'm sure of it, to confront me. Perhaps to ask for mercy. But it's easy to postpone the most unpleasant conversations, especially if confrontation is not in your nature.

To do so, and because she meant it, Agatha said, "What rubbish, war. Any war. It's a terrible thing for a man to endure. If I had a son, I'd do whatever I could to keep him away from it. I don't care what the cause is, or if England's at stake."

"I think I'll do the same. If I ever have a son."

Our meat was carved tableside and I chose a piece that was rarer than I liked. I suppose I was trying to impress Agatha.

The richer the people, the bloodier they liked their steak. As I sawed into the meat, the red oozing made my stomach turn.

"Do you still think of the Irish boy?" Agatha asked.

"Only every day of my life."

"Is that why you never married?"

Never married. As if I never would. "I suppose it is."

"Well. You're still young. And who knows? Perhaps he'll turn up one day, recovered."

"I doubt that very much."

"There was a time during the War I thought Archie and I would never be able to marry. But we did and we've been so happy. We have, you know. Been happy."

"I'm sure that's true." Clipped and stern. Talk of the War had steeled me. A person who has nothing might be excused for taking one thing—a husband—from a person who has everything.

The waiter returned and asked if we wanted a cheese course. We both declined. Agatha put down her fork with her meat half-eaten. If her manners had been less perfect, she would have pushed her plate away. "I must start eating less. I'm too fat, Archie says."

"You look just fine," I said, to soothe her and because it was true. "You look beautiful."

Agatha laughed, a little meanly, derision toward herself, not me, and I softened again. It gave me no pleasure to cause anyone pain. The death of her mother was dreadfully timed, too close to Archie's leaving. I'd never planned on that. Agatha's father had died when she was eleven, so in addition to the loss of her mother, she now found herself in her family's oldest generation at far too young an age.

We walked outside together after Agatha insisted on paying

the bill. On the street she turned to me and reached out, curling her forefinger and thumb around my chin.

"Do you have plans for this weekend, Miss O'Dea?" Her tone insinuated she knew perfectly well what my plans were.

"No. But I'm taking a holiday next week. At the Bellefort Hotel in Harrogate." Immediately I wondered why I'd told her. I hadn't even told Archie. But something about sharing a woman's husband makes you feel close to her. Sometimes even closer than to him.

"Treating yourself," she said, as if the concept did not appeal to her sensible nature. "Lovely for you."

I was thankful she didn't ask how I could afford such an extravagance.

She let go of my chin. Her eyes held something I couldn't quite read. "Well, goodbye then. Enjoy your holiday."

She turned and walked a few steps, paused, then walked back to me. "You don't love him." Her face had utterly changed. From contained and still to wide-eyed and tremulous. "It would be bad enough if you did. But since you don't, please leave him to the person who does."

All my edges disappeared. I felt ghostly in my refusal to respond, as if I might dissipate, the pieces of me floating off and away into the air. Agatha didn't touch me again. Instead she held my face in her gaze, examining my response—blood leaving my cheeks, the guilty refusal to move or breathe.

"Mrs. Christie." It was all I could manage to say. She was demanding a confession I did not have permission to make.

"Miss O'Dea." Clipped, final. Returning to her usual self. Her name on my lips had prefaced a denial. My name on hers was a stern dismissal.

I stood in front of the restaurant and watched her walk away. In my memory she vanishes into a great cloud of fog, but that can't be right. It was broad daylight—crisp and clear. More likely she simply walked around a corner, or into a crowd.

I was due to return to work but instead headed toward Archie's office. My secretarial job no longer meant much to me as Archie covered more and more of my expenses. I knew he would be worried about my lunching with Agatha, and if he really did tell her tonight he was leaving, she might level the charge that I didn't love him. So it was important to leave him feeling as though I did.

On my way I passed a bookshop that displayed a mountain of copies of a pink children's book, a little teddy bear clutching the string of a balloon and flying off into the air. *Winnie-the-Pooh*. It looked so whimsical, I went in and bought a copy for Archie to give Teddy. For a moment I considered giving it to her myself, as a Christmas gift. By then her parents might be living apart. Perhaps Teddy would spend Christmas with her father and me. Cozy, the three of us, exchanging gifts beneath a Christmas tree. Sometimes one did hear of children living with their father after a divorce. And Archie always claimed Teddy loved him better. Though that was like Archie, wasn't it, not only to say such a thing but believe it.

When I returned to Archie's office, I gave him the book to give to Teddy himself. He locked the door and drew me into his lap, unbuttoning my skirt and pulling it up around my waist.

"It won't be like this much longer," he breathed into my ear, shuddering, though I did believe he liked it like this. Didn't all men?

I stepped off him and smoothed my skirt. My hat was still on my head, it had barely budged.

"How did she seem?" he asked, returning to his desk.

"Sad." If she ever told him she'd confronted me, I'd deny it. "And worried."

"You mustn't go soft on her. It's kinder to plunge the knife quickly."

"I'm sure you're right."

I blew him a kiss and headed toward the door, hoping none of my protestations had made a dent in his resolve. My conversation with Agatha made his leaving her all the more urgent. I unlocked the latch.

"Nan," Archie said, before I could step through the doorway. "Next time you see me I'll be a free man."

"Not at all," I told him. "You'll belong to me."

He smiled, and I knew there was nothing for me to worry about, at least in terms of Archie breaking the news to Agatha. The man had a mission. Once he decided to do something, he did it with the coldness required of a pilot releasing bombs to cause death and havoc below. All the while sailing through the sky, untouchable.

The Disappearance

In the history of the world there's been one story a man tells his mistress. He doesn't love his wife, perhaps never loved her at all. There's been no sex for years, not a whisper of it. His marriage is absent passion, absent affection, absent joy. A barren and miserable place. He stays for the children, or for money, or for propriety. It's a matter of convenience. The new lover is his only respite.

How many times has this story been true? Not many, is my guess. I know it wasn't true of the Christies.

That evening Archie made his usual commute from London to Sunningdale. The couple had named their home Styles after the manor in Agatha's first novel. It was a lovely Victorian with substantial gardens. When Archie came through the front door, Agatha was waiting for him, dressed for dinner. He never told me what she was wearing, but I know it was a chiffon dress the shade of seafoam. I imagine the cut emphasized the swell of her bosom, but Archie only said she seemed so distracted he decided to wait till morning to tell her he was leaving. "Emotions do run higher at night, don't they?" he said.

Agatha, who knew the news was coming, resolved to do silent battle. Usually her little terrier, Peter, never left her side, but for tonight she sent the dog to bed with Teddy so he wouldn't be an annoyance. She tried to exude the cheerful countenance her husband required.

I've sometimes thought Agatha invented Hercule Poirot as an antidote to Archie. There was never an emotional cue Poirot missed, nor a wayward emotion for which he didn't feel sympathy. Poirot could absorb and assess a person's sadness, then forgive it. Whereas Archie simply wanted to say *Cheer up* and have the order followed.

Having decided to postpone the inevitable scene, Archie sat down to a quiet dinner with his wife, the two of them seated at opposite ends of the long dining table. When I asked what they discussed, he said, "Just small talk."

"How did she seem?"

"Sullen." Archie spoke the word as if it were a great personal affront. "She seemed self-indulgently morose."

After dinner Agatha asked him to adjourn to the sitting room for a glass of brandy. He declined and went upstairs to see Teddy. Honoria, who doubled as Agatha's personal secretary and Teddy's nanny, was in the midst of putting Teddy to bed.

The little dog dashed out the door as soon as Archie stepped inside, and Teddy let out a wail of protest. "Mother promised Peter would stay with me tonight!"

Luckily Archie had my gift, *Winnie-the-Pooh*, to offer as consolation. Once Teddy had excitedly torn away the wrapping, he read her the first chapter. She begged him to go on reading, so that by the time he retired, Agatha—never knowing this was her last chance to recover him—already slept. "Like the dead," Archie told me.

But the following Saturday I arrived at Styles to return Archie's car from Godalming and saw *Winnie-the-Pooh* on a table in the vestibule, still in its brown paper wrapping. And at Simpson's Agatha had had the vague and scarcely animated look of an insomniac, feeling her way through the day after too many sleepless nights. She loved her husband. After twelve years of marriage, she loved him blindly and hopefully, as if in her thirty-six years of life she'd learned nothing about the world.

I know she wouldn't have gone to sleep before Archie came to bed. Here's what I think really happened:

Agatha was there to greet Archie when he arrived home. That much would have been true. The color in her cheeks was high and determined. She'd resolved to win him back not with anger and threats but the sheer force of her adoration and so had dressed carefully. I know exactly what she wore because on Saturday morning it still lay crumpled in a heap on their bedroom floor, the maid having been too upset to collect and launder it. When I saw it there, I knelt and picked it up, holding it against me as if trying it on. It was much too long, seafoam chiffon flowing past my feet. It smelled of Yardley perfume, Old English Lavender, light and pretty.

A silly garment to wear in the middle of winter but still. How lovely she would have looked, there to greet him. Freckles sprinkled across her nose, and across her breasts, high and visible. Perhaps she had a drink in her hand, not for herself (she almost never drank), but to hand to him, his favorite Scotch.

"AC," she said, stepping close to him, placing one hand on his chest, letting him trade his winter coat for the drink. Since their wedding night they'd called each other that, AC.

"Here." Archie did not return the endearment. Along with his coat he handed her the wrapped children's book. "It's for Teddy." He didn't tell her I had bought it but she likely suspected. Archie wasn't one for books—he hadn't even read the novels she'd written, not since the first was published. Agatha slid the package unopened onto the table.

In the sitting room she poured water for herself. She was good at waiting things out. She'd waited years to marry Archie, then she waited out the War for them to live together. She sent her first book to a publisher and waited two years before they accepted it—so that by the time she received word, she'd almost forgotten she'd written a book. She signed a miserable contract with Bodley Head for her first five novels, realized her mistake almost immediately, then waited it out instead of accepting their many offers to renegotiate. Now she was free and had moved on to a far superior publisher. A person *had* to put her mind to something and hope for the best. A person had to be willing to bide her time.

The house was too cold. Goose bumps rose on her bare arms, propelling her to stand closer to Archie. He had a hale and impenetrable mien, radiating warmth, not of the personal kind, but actual heat.

"Where's Teddy?" he asked.

"Upstairs with Honoria. Having a bath and then to bed."

He nodded, inhaling the lavender. A man does like it when a

woman tries, especially when she's foreign to him, as his wife had become the moment he'd decided to tell her he was leaving. Agatha had instructed the cook to prepare his favorite meal, beef Wellington, a good winter dinner. She lit candles. Just the two of them and a bottle of good French wine. Agatha poured herself a glass to be companionable but didn't take so much as a sip. She sat, not all the way across the table as Archie told me, but just beside him. He left-handed, she right, their elbows bumping against each other with the intimacy of people who'd passed so many hours living in the same home, sleeping in the same bed. Archie was only human, and worse than that, only a man. A kind of melancholy overtook him. It wasn't true that he'd never loved her at all. In fact his determination to marry me brought to mind the last time he'd felt such urgency, to marry Agatha, even though the War was raging, and they had no money, and both their families—especially his mother—insisted they wait. Now in the candlelight she looked much as she had on their wedding night. Their anniversary approached, Christmas Eve. Impossible not to dwell on memories such as that, this time of year.

He finished his meal and did not stop in the nursery to bid Teddy good night. It was late, after all, and she would already be sleeping.

I know it was Archie who removed his wife's dress and left it crumpled on the floor. He liked a naked woman while he was fully clothed. And this was his last chance with this particular woman. Alone in their bedroom, his wife shivered with relief and joy as much as the cold. The maid had lit the fire in their bedroom. In the dim and flickering light, Agatha looked vulnerable with adoration.

Marriage. The way two lives intertwine. It's a stubborn thing, difficult to let go. Archie was not an unfeeling man, and on this last night with his wife, after so many months of damming his feelings toward her, he let the floodgates open one final time.

"Agatha," he said to her, over and over. I suspect he also said, *I love you*. So that she would have returned the words, tears running down her cheeks as though she'd won him back for good. Not realizing, as they stayed up late, the sheets increasingly tangled as they made love again and again—that for this one night she was the mistress, never again to be his wife.

The Disappearance

Agatha opened her eyes to find herself alone. Archie had risen before dawn, leaving their night behind him as only a man can. He bathed, washing away the scent of his wife, whatever emotions he had for her already abandoned in the bedroom. Whereas Agatha stirred, the irregular discovery of her nakedness beneath the sheets immediately reminding her of all that had happened. She smiled victoriously and stretched. Archie was hers again. She had won him back.

Humming to herself, she dressed in what she would have slept in, a long silk nightdress. Before she went downstairs, she added a flannel dressing gown. A quick glance in the mirror showed all she needed was quick fingers through her fading red hair. Even she, critical of herself, could see she looked lovely. Flushed with happiness. *Happiness.* The aspect Archie admired most. Today his first glimpse of her radiant self would fill him with love, visible love. She hurried downstairs to catch him before he left for the office.

Imagine her dismay as she reached the bottom of the stairs to find Archie, dressed, his weekend valise packed, his attitude hardened.

"Surely you're not still going on your weekend?" Her face paled, the flush left. All the delight and joy vanished before Archie could see it.

"Agatha." His voice was full of warning. A scold. As if she were a misbehaved child.

"Agatha," she echoed. Her voice rose, high-pitched, spiraling up the stairs. Perhaps it traveled through the door of the nursery, where Teddy lay, asleep or awake; neither parent had gone in to check on her. "*Agatha,*" she said again. "You sound as if *I'm* the one doing something wrong. As if *I'm* the one causing trouble. I say it's you. It's *you.* Archie. *Archie. Archie.*"

He sighed and glanced toward the kitchen, where the cook was preparing breakfast. Honoria would bring Teddy down any moment. He didn't want anyone to overhear Agatha, whose hysteria would only grow once he'd said what there was no longer any way to avoid. He had a plan and nothing would derail it. My engagement ring sat in his valise, its hefty price tag paid in full.

"Come here." He maintained the tone of a father scolding an unruly child. "We can talk in my study." He stepped forward and grabbed her by the elbow.

Agatha didn't have an office of her own. She wrote her books wherever she found herself, so long as she had a table and a typewriter. Really, she didn't even think of herself as an author. Her primary occupation and identity was Married

Lady. That's who she was. Married. To Archie. Who would she be if that was no longer the case?

She took a seat on the silk sofa in Archie's study. Peter trotted in and jumped up beside her. Archie didn't like dogs on the furniture, but he had more important matters to address, so he held his tongue and pulled the door closed with a click.

Agatha once told me that upon her first heartbreak, thrown over by a boy she adored, she'd run to her mother with quivering lips. Clarissa Miller had handed her daughter a handkerchief with one hand and raised the other with forefinger pointed, moving it up and down to mark her syllables. "Don't you dare cry. I forbid it." Obedient by nature and wanting nothing more than to please her mother, Agatha had shuddered once, swallowing the tears as they threatened to fall.

But there hadn't only been heartbreaks. In her youth she had been gay and lively, turning down one marriage proposal after another. When Archie pressed his hand upon her, she was already engaged to another young man, Tommy, who was diffident and kind and never—she felt sure of it—would have brought her to this moment, struggling to follow her mother's erstwhile advice.

Archie didn't sit beside her on the sofa, but settled into a wingback chair close enough that she could reach for him. It was a natural gesture after the night they'd spent together, and she gave in to it, holding out her arms.

"Agatha," came the hard reply, and then the words she'd been dreading for months. "There's no easy way to say this."

"Then don't say it," she pleaded, dropping her pathetic, outstretched arms and pulling Peter into her lap, stroking the dog to calm herself. "Please just don't say it at all."

"I'm only telling you what you must already know. I love Nan O'Dea and I'm going to marry her."

"No. I won't have that. It can't be. You love *me*." The memories of last night hovered so clear, so close, it might still have been happening. Unlike Archie, she hadn't bathed. His scent clung to her, drowning out the lavender perfume. "I'm your wife."

"A divorce," Archie said. It was easier to just burst out with the word as a simple statement of fact. An end goal so obvious it needed no context, not even a complete sentence. What a triumph over emotion. Archie felt nothing, not even worry about his wife collapsing in front of him, only a commitment to the word. *Divorce.*

Agatha sat silent. Her hand ran faster and faster over the terrier's soft fur, her expression unchanging. Archie, unwisely emboldened, began to talk. He admitted our relationship had been going on nearly two years.

("You needn't have told her that," I said, though I knew he hated to be chastised.

"You're right," he admitted. "I was fooled by her silence. It was the last thing I expected. It was almost as if she couldn't hear me.")

Turning too quickly to detail, he instructed Agatha to file for the divorce. "It will have to be adultery." In those days that was the principal claim the courts allowed. "I've spoken to Brunskill—"

"Brunskill!" Mr. Brunskill was Archie's solicitor, addled and mustachioed. A new outrage, that he should know this assault lay in wait for her.

"Yes. Brunskill says you can just say 'unnamed third party.' The important thing is to keep Nan's name out of all this."

Agatha's fervent petting of Peter halted abruptly. "*That* is the important thing?"

Archie should have realized his mistake but instead he pressed on. "This might be in the papers, because of your books. Your name. A bit known, these days."

She stood up, Peter falling to the floor with a reproachful yelp. Usually solicitous of the dog, she barely seemed to notice.

Archie remained seated. As he told me later, "There's never any point trying to reason with a woman once she's become unhinged."

Agatha's husband was in love with someone else. A life-changing transgression stated simply as the time of day. Now she was meant to receive this information with calm and dignity. Archie had broken rules with passion as his excuse, and she was asked to rationally pick up the pieces. She was to take measures to protect her rival's reputation. It was more than she could bear. She clenched her fists and let out a scream, loud and full of rage.

"Agatha. Please. The servants will hear you, and the child."

"The child. The child! Don't you talk to me about the child." Because he refused to stand, she had to bend from the waist to pummel him, fists balled up, raining down upon his suited chest. The blows caused Archie no pain. He told me he had to watch himself to keep from laughing.

"How cruel you are," I said, but let the words fall lightly, as if cruelty bothered me not one whit.

Poor Agatha. She had woken from her fondest dream into her worst nightmare. And nothing she said or did could wrest any emotion from her husband.

Finally Archie stood. He grabbed her wrists to stop the blows. "Enough of this. I'm leaving. After work I'll be headed to weekend with the Owens. We can sort the rest next week."

"I suppose she'll be there, too?"

"No," Archie said, because it was the reply he thought would cause the least reaction, and lying had become second nature to him since he first got tangled up with me.

"She *will* be there. I know she will. A house party, a couples' weekend. Only you won't be with your wife, you'll be with her, that harlot. That nasty little harlot."

A common mistake wives make as they watch their husbands go. The road back to Archie's affections was not paved with insults to me. He was that most impenetrable of creatures, an infatuated man. The darkest scowl crossed his face and he tightened his grip.

"You mustn't talk about Nan that way."

"You. Telling me what I shouldn't do. *You* shouldn't go away with a woman who's not your wife. *You* shouldn't be leaving me now, when I need you most. I will talk about Nan any way I like."

"Calm down, Agatha."

She kicked him in the shins. As she only wore slippers, it barely made him flinch. How maddening her own ineffectual strength must have been. She twisted her wrists out of his grasp so furiously that when he let go, she fell backward. Archie noted welts already beginning to form as Agatha stroked each wrist in turn, but he wasn't able to regret it, so firm was his conviction that she had brought this on herself. He had one goal and one goal only, and that was to be rid of her.

The night before, Archie had succumbed to nostalgia and carnal longing. But today he returned to his mission. Like any good zealot he would not allow himself to be dissuaded. With long-legged strides he crossed the study to return to the front hallway. He picked up his valise and walked out to his car, the secondhand Delage Agatha had bought for him with money from her new contract. It was rather a grand car and Archie preened in its presence, as if its ownership were something he'd achieved entirely on his own. It had an electric-starter motor, no cranking necessary, he could just hop in and escape. How galling it must have been, as she flung herself through the doorway, seeing him drive away in that extravagant gift.

"Archie!" she cried, running down the long drive. "Archie!"

Dust flew up from the tires, a cloud in front of her. Archie didn't even turn to glance through the back windscreen. His shoulders were set, firm and determined. He was gone from her, unreachable in every possible way.

Unreachable is same the word Honoria used later, to describe Agatha. It was Honoria's job to wake Teddy and ready her for school, and after Honoria had risen, she heard loud voices from inside Mr. Christie's study, a marital squabble and a bad one at that. So she went to the nursery, where Teddy sat in a corner, already awake and playing with her dolls. That was the sort of child Teddy was, a seven-year-old who could climb out of bed and set to amusing herself, troubling no one.

"Hullo there, Teddy."

"Good morning." Teddy pushed dark hair out of her eyes. She was not surprised to see Honoria. Often Teddy awoke to find both parents already gone for the day. Before she was five her parents had left her an entire year, to travel round the world. Agatha herself had been raised largely by a beloved servant she called Nursie. In her experience, it was a perfectly reasonable way to bring up a child.

"Come," Honoria said, reaching out her hand. "Let's find you some breakfast. Then it's dressed and off to school."

Teddy got to her feet and slipped her hand into Honoria's. The two of them reached the top of the stairs just as Archie was escaping Agatha's histrionics in his study. Teddy reached out, as if to wave in greeting, but Archie didn't see her. He closed the door behind him. It stood closed only a moment before Agatha emerged, the air around her so thick with urgency that for an instant Honoria thought Agatha had been attacked. Honoria stepped forward as Agatha flung the door open and ran outside. Teddy grabbed the edge of Honoria's cardigan, keeping her there with her, and Honoria hugged the child to her ample hip, patting her in comfort, as Agatha cried, "Archie! Archie!"

Honoria waited inside, politely pretending none of this was happening. She heard the car drive away, but Agatha didn't return. So Honoria shepherded Teddy downstairs and into the kitchen. Then Honoria went back into the front hall. Styles boasted great windows at the front and back of the house. Through the former, Honoria could see Agatha standing in her dressing gown and slippers, her hair moving in the slight wind, the dust around her settling in the flat morning light. Honoria had never seen a person stand so still and yet emanate so kinetic a sense of disarray.

"Agatha?" Honoria said, stepping outside. The two women were intimate enough to put aside the formality of employee and grand lady. Honoria reached out and touched her shoulder. "Agatha, are you all right?"

Agatha stood as if she couldn't hear, looking after the long-gone car in disbelief. When Honoria spoke again, Agatha didn't answer. Honoria didn't feel right going back into the house, leaving her alone, but it felt so odd, the two of them. One fully clothed and ready for the day, one still as a statue, dressed as an invalid with a long road to recovery.

The spell didn't last too terribly long. Agatha roused herself and headed into Archie's study, where she sat down to write a letter to her husband. It may have been a plea. It may have been a declaration of war. Nobody would ever know, except for Archie, who read it once, then threw it in the fire.

I wonder now if Agatha had a plan. A writer, after all, she would carefully have considered every line of prose she wrote and every possibility to spring from her next movement. When I picture her at the desk, I don't see a woman in a fugue state or person on the verge of amnesia. I see the kind of determination you only recognize if you've felt it yourself. Determination born of desperation transformed into purpose. Soon afterward, when I learned of her disappearance, I wasn't the least surprised. I understood.

I had disappeared once, too.

Here Lies Sister Mary

Perhaps you're finding it difficult to feel kindly toward a home-wrecker such as me. But I don't require your affection. I only ask you to see me on a wintery day in Ireland, riding in a borrowed milk wagon. I was nineteen years old.

A sorrowful Irishman—old by my standards at the time—held the reins of two shaggy horses who pulled the cart. My coat wasn't warm enough for the damp chill. If Finbarr had driven me instead of his father, I could have cuddled beside him for extra warmth. But Finbarr never would have driven me where we were headed. Mr. Mahoney, though, was not entirely without kindness. Every now and then he would let one hand go of the reins and pat my shoulder. It may have made him feel better, but it did nothing for me. Empty milk bottles clanged as we rode over rutted dirt roads. If the bottles had been full, I expect the milk would have frozen by the time we reached the convent. It was a long road to Sunday's Corner from Ballycotton.

"I won't be here long," I said, allowing my father's brogue into the rhythm of my words, as if anything could endear me to Mr. Mahoney. "Finbarr will come for me as soon as he recovers."

"*If* he recovers." Mr. Mahoney's eyes were grim and looking anywhere but at me. Which would be worse? I wondered. His only son dying? Or recovering and claiming me and the shame I'd brought? As far as Mr. Mahoney was concerned, the best outcome would be Finbarr's getting well, then forgetting he'd ever laid eyes on me. For now what Mr. Mahoney wanted was me safely locked and stored away so he could get home and see his son alive at least one more time.

"He *will* recover," I said, fierce with believing the impossible as only the very young can be. Beneath my coat the dress I wore held a faint spattering of blood from Finbarr's coughing.

"You sound like an Irish girl. Not a bad idea to keep that up. The English aren't so popular these days, round here."

I nodded, but I only understand his words in retrospect. If he had said *Sinn Féin* aloud, it would have meant nothing to me. I wouldn't have been able to say what IRA stood for. My Ireland was the ocean, the shorebirds, the sheep. Green hills and Finbarr. Nothing to do with any government, its or my own.

"You're a lucky girl," Mr. Mahoney said. "Not so long ago the only place for you would have been the workhouse. But these nuns look out for mothers and babies."

I thought it would be better if the workhouse *were* the only place for me. Surely Mr. Mahoney would never have had the heart to deliver me to a place meant for criminals, so he'd have to let me stay with his family. As it was, I'd spent my last penny on the journey to his door. I suppose I went along with him voluntarily, but that doesn't seem the right word when you've nowhere else to go.

Finally we arrived at the convent in Sunday's Corner. Mr. Mahoney jumped from the wagon and offered a broad, calloused hand to help me down. The building was beautiful. With red bricks and turrets, it loomed and rambled, looking like a cross between a university and a castle, both places I never expected to see inside. On the grass out front stood a statue of a winged angel, hands clenched at her side rather than raised in prayer. Over the convent's door, in a vaulted nook where a window should have been, stood another statue, made of plaster—a nun wearing a blue-and-white habit, her palms at her side face out, as if offering sanctuary to all who entered.

My parents had never been religious. "Sunday's for resting," my father used to say, explaining why he didn't go to Mass. My mother was Protestant. I'd mostly only been to church with my aunt Rosie and uncle Jack.

"That must be the Virgin Mary," I murmured.

Mr. Mahoney let out a joyless chuff of a laugh, a sound that derided how little I knew about everything in the world. I'd come to Ireland hoping to live in his modest, dirt-floored house. Mr. Mahoney had deep circles under his faded eyes, but I could tell they'd once been just like Finbarr's. I looked at him, willing him to see me and change his mind.

"The sisters will take good care of you." He may have believed this was true. His voice was gentle, almost regretful. Perhaps he'd go a little ways down the road, then turn around to come back for me before I could even unpack. "We'll send word to you about Finbarr. I promise that."

He lurched my suitcase from the back of the wagon—my mother's suitcase; I'd stolen it from her before I left. She would have given it to me if I'd asked. Better yet, she would have begged me to stay or run away with me herself. "How could you ever have thought otherwise?" she would ask me, too late. "I would have done anything, fought anyone, including your father, to keep from losing another daughter."

If I'd known in that moment what I do now, I would have trudged off on my own two feet, away from the convent. I would have walked down its long drive, over the hills, and swam across the freezing Irish Sea back to England.

Inside, the nuns traded my clothes for a drab, shapeless dress that wouldn't need replacing no matter how big my belly grew, and a pair of ill-fitting clogs. A young, sweet-faced nun took my suitcase. She smiled warmly and promised, "We'll take good care of this for you." I never saw it again. An older nun sat me down and cut my hair so that it barely covered my ears. I'd only ever worn it long and worried what Finbarr would think when he came to get me.

I didn't follow Mr. Mahoney's advice and speak with an Irish brogue. Once the nuns had explained the rules of my new home, I barely spoke at all, not for weeks.

A young person can't know her life, what it will be or how it will unfold. When you grow older, you gain a sense that hardships occupy particular moments in time, which by and by will pass. But when you're young, a single moment seems like the whole world. It feels permanent. Years hence I would go on to live a bigger life. I would travel all over the world. But that winter I was scarcely more than a child. I knew exactly two places: London and County Cork, and only tiny pockets of both. I knew I was young but I didn't understand *how* young, or that youth was a fleeting condition. I knew the War had ended but I didn't yet believe it. The Great War had seemed not so much an event as a place, unmovable as England but nowhere near as destructible. In London my father's favorite pub had been blown to rubble, kegs of ale rolling out onto the street as more bombs fell. For the rest of his life my father would say the world lost its innocence during the Great War.

The first task I was given at the convent—my hair shorn, my own clothes taken away—was tending the nuns' graveyard. With two other girls, both of them heavily pregnant, I went out to sweep and rake and clean the headstones of lichen. The cold air might have tasted like freedom if not for the iron bars extending around the perimeter, as far as I could see. To the right was a high stone wall. Thin sounds carried over it, which I didn't realize were the voices of small children, brought out for a breath of air before their supper. Visible through the iron bars lay the road that led away from the convent, no sign of Mr. Mahoney returning for me with a change of heart. Neither of the other girls spoke to me. We weren't supposed to speak at all or even know one another's names.

The nuns' headstones were thick crosses, each one etched with the words HERE LIES SISTER MARY. As if only one woman had died but she somehow needed fifty graves. I ran my coarse cloth over the stones, dipping my fingers into the carved gray words. And I knew in that moment. The world had never been innocent.

But I had been innocent.

Let's go back a little further. Before the War, this time. See me at thirteen—skinny and nimble as a cricket—the first time my parents sent me to spend a summer at my aunt Rosie and uncle Jack's farm.

"Nan likes to run," my father said, formulating the plan. "She wasn't meant for the city, was she." He worked as a clerk at the Porphyrion Fire Insurance Company and often said these same words—*not meant for the city*—about himself. It pained him to stoop long hours over a desk for little money. I always suspected Da would have regretted leaving Ireland if that wouldn't have meant regretting us. His wife was English and that meant his family was, too. Except, apparently, for me.

My sisters Megs (elder) and Louisa (younger) were proper girlie girls, interested in clothes and hair and cooking. Or at least that's what they pretended to be interested in. My sister Colleen (eldest) only cared about books and school. I liked books, too, but I also liked kicking a football with the neighborhood boys. Sometimes after dark my father would come find me with them, sweaty and filthy in an empty lot.

"If she were a boy, she could be a champion," he boasted.

"She's too old for that now," my mother complained, but my father took pity.

"Those other three are yours," he said to Mum, "but this one's my Irish girl."

My father had grown up on a farm just outside the fishing village of Ballycotton. Since I'd been born, he'd gone back to visit a time or two when his brother paid the way. But there'd never been enough money for us all to travel there. The thought of my going at all, let alone for a whole summer, was thrilling. I knew it was a modest house but much roomier than our London flat, which only had two bedrooms, one for my parents and one for us four girls. Uncle Jack had done well with the farm. His wife, Rosie, had inherited a small amount of money when her father died, and they'd added solid wood floors and lined the walls of the sitting room with bookshelves. They kept the grass near the house cut short for lawn tennis. ("Tennis," my father scoffed, when he told us. "Now that's an idea above his station.")

The landscape existed in my mind, the most vivid green. Rolling hills and low stone walls—uninterrupted miles for me to kick a football through the meadows with my little cousin Seamus. I clasped my hands together and fell to my knees beside my mother, imploring her to let me go, only partly joking about the fervor.

My mother laughed. "It's just I'll miss you."

I jumped to my feet and threw my arms around her. She had a dear, freckly face and wide green eyes. Sometimes I regret losing my East End accent because it's meant losing the sound of her.

"I'll miss you, too," I admitted.

"It won't be a holiday," my father warned. "Jack'll pay your passage, but you'll be doing plenty of chores to pay him back."

Most of the chores would be outdoors, with horses and sheep, a joy to me. I was grateful my uncle would hire a girl to do them.

And so we come to the Irish boy. Finbarr Mahoney was a fisherman's son. Two years before we met, he came upon a wizened farmer at the village docks, about to drop a puppy—the runt of a litter of border collies—into the freezing sea.

"Here." Finbarr hoisted a bucket of mackerel. "I'll trade you."

Nobody would have known there was anything urgent in the transaction. Finbarr had the lightest, smiling air about him.

As if everything—even life and death—were easy. He hoisted the puppy under his chin and handed over the bucket, knowing he'd have to pay his father back for the fish.

"The man was about to throw the puppy away," Finbarr's father scolded. "Do you really think he expected to be paid for it?"

Finbarr named the dog Alby, first bottle-feeding then training him. Uncle Jack was glad to hire Finbarr to bicycle over to the farm on his days off the boat, to help move sheep from one pasture to the other. Jack said Alby was the best herding dog in County Cork.

"It's because of the boy," Aunt Rosie said. "He's got a way with creatures, hasn't he. He could turn a goat into a champion herder. You can't tell me another handler would have the same results with that dog."

My uncle's collie was a passable herder but nothing to Alby. I thought that dog—small, slight, and graceful—was the most beautiful thing I'd ever seen. I thought Finbarr—hair black and silky, gleaming nearly blue in the summer sun—was the second most beautiful. He had a way with creatures, as Aunt Rosie had said, and after all, what was I? Finbarr was a few years older than me. When he rode by, he'd pretend to tip the hat he wasn't wearing. I have never liked people who constantly smile, as if they think everything's funny. But Finbarr smiled differently, not out of amusement, but happiness. As if he liked the world and enjoyed being in it.

"It seems a wonderful thing," I said to my aunt Rosie that evening, while we did the washing up, "to always be happy."

Right away she knew whom I meant. "He's been like that his whole life," Aunt Rosie said with deep fondness. "Sunny. Proves rich or poor doesn't matter, if you ask me. Some people are just born happy. I think that's the luckiest thing. If you're sunny inside, you never have to worry about the weather."

One evening after supper Finbarr bicycled over to the house when Seamus and I were playing tennis. I'd learned to play my first week and now won every game. "I don't know where you get the energy after a full day of work," Uncle Jack had said to us, shaking his head in fond admiration.

"Where's Alby?" Seamus called to Finbarr. He was ten then and dazzled by the dog as I was.

"I left him home. I thought you'd be playing tennis. He'll chase the balls and spoil the game."

My uncle's collie, Brutus, lay under the porch, tired after a day of herding, uninterested in playing.

"You can play with Nan," Seamus said, handing over his racket. "Win one for me, will you?" His red curls drooped from the failed attempt to best me.

I bounced the ball on my racket, recognizing it as showing off but not able to help myself. Finbarr smiled as usual, blue eyes turned gray by fading evening sunlight. "Ready then?" I hit the ball over the net before he could answer. We goofed like that a bit, sending the ball back and forth to each other. Then we played in earnest. I won two games before Alby came crashing over the hills. Running straight for Finbarr, then changing course, leaping to snatch the ball from the air.

We threw our rackets down and chased him. There were other balls but it seemed the natural thing to do. Laughter filling the sky. Uncle Jack and Aunt Rosie came out to the porch to laugh along with us. Finally Finbarr stopped running, stood stock-still, and yelled, "Alby, stop."

The dog halted so immediately, so precisely, it was clear Finbarr had had this power all along.

"Out," Finbarr commanded, and Alby spat the ball onto the grass. Finbarr approached him with measured steps, scooped the ball up, and held it in the air. "Nan. Make a wish."

"I wish I could stay in Ireland forever."

He threw the ball, a long arc, and Alby went rushing for it, catching it midair, paws miles above the ground.

"Granted," Finbarr said, and turned to me. Magical enough to make it so.

A few days later he came by the house after helping Uncle Jack. I had finished mucking out the stables and lay on the hill in a pocket of clover, still reeking of manure, reading *A Room with a View*. Brutus lay beside me resting his head on my stomach.

"Your uncle will need a new dog before long," Finbarr said. Alby stood at his side, ears perked. "You can tell they're getting old when they're tired at the end of the day."

"Doesn't Alby get tired sometimes?" I shaded my eyes to see him.

"Never." Finbarr said it with a confidence so firm it had to be wishful.

"Well, Brutus will never get old," I said, also wishful, patting the dog's narrow tawny head. From somewhere nearby a skylark chirruped, continuous and complaining. Of course there were birds in London but I'd never noticed them much. Since coming to Ireland, I'd learned the sky was its own separate universe, just above our heads, teeming with its own brand of singing life.

"I brought you something." Finbarr held out a four-leaf clover.

I reached for it without sitting up, and straightaway the fourth leaf fluttered away. He'd been holding it there with his finger. "Fake luck." I flicked it away with a laugh, still delighted.

Finbarr flopped down beside me. He never minded being contradicted, just as he never minded my winning game after game of tennis. He never minded anything.

"I hope I don't smell like fish," he said.

I thought about lying and saying no. Instead I said, "Well, I smell of sheep and horse shite, so we're a good match."

"I smell of those things, too." He wove his fingers together, arched his arms over behind his head, and made a pillow of his hands. "You like to read, do you?"

"Yes."

"I could read that book when you're done." He stared straight up at the sky, not at my book. "Then we can talk about it."

"Do you like to read?"

"No. But I could start."

"This one's mostly about a girl."

"I don't mind reading about girls."

I turned my head and stared at him, and he tilted his head toward me. Long black eyelashes framed eyes of layered blue. Soon Uncle Jack would come up over the hill, and he wouldn't like to see us, lying side by side, even though we were a good two feet apart.

"I think I'd like to be a writer," I said. It was nothing I'd ever thought of before. I liked to read but had never tried my hand at stories or poems.

"You'd be a grand writer," Finbarr said. "You'd be grand at anything."

He put a strand of grass between his teeth and turned his eyes back to the sky. Legs crossed at the ankles. Alby tugged at his pant legs, dissatisfied with a full day of running, or else eager to get home for the evening meal.

"Nan O'Dea," my aunt called from the house. "You get up this minute please, and wash up for supper."

I knew the sternness in her voice was over me and Finbarr, lying down together, not my need to wash. We jumped to our feet, both of us with mussed hair, sun from a day working out-doors rosying our cheeks.

"Stay for supper, Finbarr?" Aunt Rosie called, forgiving him, as no one could ever help but do.

"I'd love to, Mrs. O'Dea."

With as much energy as the younger of the two dogs, we raced each other to the house. Finbarr won. He jumped on the porch with both feet, raising his arms up in the air. Victory.

Sometimes you fall in love with a place, dramatic and urgent as falling in love with any person. I started begging to return to Ireland almost the moment I arrived back in London. My sisters belonged to my mother and England but Ireland was where I belonged. I had an ancestral memory of those green hills. The place lived in my bones, so they ached when I was away from it. At that age, when I thought of Finbarr, it was as another part of the landscape.

"I'll only send you back if you promise never to stay," my mother said. "I don't want any of my girls living off far from home. Not even you, Colleen."

Those last words were spoken with a loving tone, but Colleen didn't answer. She sat sprawled at the kitchen table, her green eyes fixed on the pages of a book by Filson Young about the *Titanic*. Her wild blond hair spilled onto the table, curtaining her face. The rest of us had brown hair and brown eyes like our father.

Mum laughed and shook her head. "The roof could fall in around that one and she wouldn't notice."

Louisa, the most practical of us all, pushed her hand against Colleen's shoulder. Colleen sat up, blinking as if just woken. "She's already living off far from home," Louisa said, tapping the pages of the book.

Oh, let me pause for a moment here. Colleen, seventeen years old, with her life ahead of her. All of us together and hopeful for the future, in the tiny, run-down kitchen that was the heart of our home. Our mother still able to believe her four girls would transition seamlessly from providing her a house full of children to one full of grandchildren.

My father stamped in, breaking the merriment as he sometimes did, carrying his heavy day with him. "That Jones boy was hanging about outside waiting for you," he said to Colleen.

She put her book aside and lifted her heavy hair to knot it on top of her head. Years later I'd read a poem by William Butler Yeats and chafe at the lines "Only God, my dear, / Could love you for yourself alone / And not your yellow hair." It brought my sister to mind, and how boys who didn't know a thing about her loved her in an instant. My mother worked a few days a week at a haberdasher, Buttons and Bits. One time Colleen covered a shift for her, and the owner forbade her from ever working there again because she drew too many boys, leaning on the counter with no interest in buying anything. Colleen's hair was like a siren, screaming out to the city streets, drawing attention, and not from God. I hated that poem.

Every night when we sisters settled into our beds in the room we shared, Colleen would tell us stories, sometimes recounting the book she was reading and sometimes making up her own. Some mornings all four of us woke with a stoop in our back, our stomachs aching, from having laughed so hard the night before. I would have loved Colleen if she had no hair at all. So would Megs and Louisa. And my mother.

"That Jones boy can wait all he likes," Colleen said. "I never said I'd see him."

"There must be something you do," my father said, shaking off his coat. "To lead those blokes on."

Colleen let out a quick, outraged laugh. Just yesterday Derek Jones and two other boys had dogged Colleen and me on our way to the Whitechapel Library. "You're spoiling our walk," she'd finally told them, sharp and firm, and they drifted off with longing glances over their shoulders. Colleen wore a knit wool hat and pulled it down over her ears. Much as she liked to disappear into books, when she returned to the world, she was direct and no-nonsense. "Lucky me with such admirers, eh, Nan?" she'd said.

"Hush with that," Mum said to our father. "She does nothing but live in the same world with them. Do you want me shaving her head? Leave the girl be."

Colleen snapped up her book and disappeared into our room while the rest of us worked on dinner. Mum patted my back because I was nearest, and it always soothed her to touch one of her children. Perhaps she was thinking what she must already have known. Sometimes living in the same world with them was all it took.

The next summer Finbarr came to the farm for tennis almost every night. He trained Alby to lie absolutely still no matter what happened. I think Alby would have expended less energy running ten miles than it took to fight his every instinct and stay frozen in the face of that bouncing tennis ball. But stay frozen he did, never jumping to his feet until Finbarr gave him the command.

"Ready. Ball," Finbarr would say, and finally the dog could catapult into the air.

In autumn, back home at my family's dinner table in London, I listed the tricks Alby could do.

"Finbarr tells him to sidestep one way and then another. He tells him to stand still until he gets the command to move."

"Not so impressive for that breed," my father said, from the looks of him remembering the dogs of his youth.

"I'm not done. Alby can do all the usual tricks—sit, sit pretty, cover. Uncle Jack says he's the best herding dog he's ever seen." This would mean he'd be the best my father ever saw. "And Finbarr taught him to catch a football and balance it on his nose. He taught him to jump on a horse's back and sit pretty."

"You make it sound as if Finbarr's the clever one," said Megs. "I'd say it's the dog."

"They're both clever." But I knew Finbarr could do the same with any dog. He had a gift.

"Perhaps I'll go next summer, too," Megs said.

"Give your sister some competition for this clever Mahoney boy," my father said.

My sisters and I had a particular look we exchanged when my father said something ridiculous. We would never fight among ourselves over a boy.

Mum ended the conversation by saying what she always did, speaking to me but looking at Colleen. "Don't you go marrying that Ballycotton boy. I don't want to have grandchildren I only see but once a year."

"Why do you always look at me first?" Colleen objected. "I'd be the last one to ever leave you, Mum." She stood up and collected our plates, stopping to give Mum a kiss on the cheek.

That night in our room Colleen said, "What if I go with you next summer? Get out of the city. Do you think I'd like it?"

Colleen and I slept in one bed, by the window, Louisa and Megs in another, pressed against the wall.

I sat up. "Oh, you'd love it." I started to spill into my usual paeans for Ireland.

Colleen clapped a hand over my mouth. "Yes, I know. It's sheer heaven. But even heaven's not for everyone."

"Heaven may not be. But Ireland is."

The following summer I was fifteen, Uncle Jack's farm was going strong, but not strong enough to pay passage for two of us.

"I wonder if Colleen should have a turn," Mum said, when Da got Jack's letter. She was tying a bow at her collar, trying to look smart on her way to work at Buttons and Bits.

"Oh, I'd never take Ireland away from Nan," Colleen said quickly, before I even had a chance to turn pale with loss.

"Just as well," Da said. "I want this one here where I can see her." He tapped her chin fondly, but from the way Colleen bit her lip I could tell she knew he was only half joking.

The exchange occurred so fast I only realize in the telling of it the debt I owed my sister. Traveling back to Ireland on my own. I must have had my share of doubts and forebodings, during this time in my life, as we do in all times of our lives, even childhood. But what I remember is a beautiful ignorance of everything the future held. Ignorance of the looming war, and how it would permeate all our days to come. Reality wasn't the newspaper making my uncle's face crease with worry. Reality was the way the ocean carried through the air I breathed. Reality was clean white sheets we hung on the clothesline to dry in the sun, so that by the time they got to our beds a hint of brine stayed with them, filling our dreams with waves, rocks, and seals. Reality was the black-haired, blue-eyed boy and his dog, traveling over green hills to see me.

"Nan," Aunt Rosie called. It was morning. I had just come downstairs and was tying my apron on to help her with the boxty. "Finbarr Mahoney's out front. He's wanting you to ride with him."

"May I go?"

"Sure you may." As much as my mother hated the idea of my one day moving to Ireland, her sister-in-law loved it. "Jack's got errands in town so there's no work with him today. You can ride Angela. Let Finbarr take Jack's horse. Be home in time to help me with supper. And take Seamus with you."

The three of us rode half a mile down the road, toward the shore. Alby trotted beside us. Finbarr drew his horse to a stop and pulled tuppence from his pocket. He sailed the coin over to Seamus. It was a good toss but Seamus missed it. He had to struggle down from his horse to collect it off the road.

"There's a good lad," Finbarr said. "Go off on your own, will you? We'll meet you here in a few hours."

Seamus tossed the coin back to Finbarr. Seamus was only twelve but knew he'd been sent along as my chaperone. "I think I'll be staying," my cousin said, and climbed back on his horse.

Finbarr laughed. He clucked and his horse took off, galloping toward Ballywilling Beach. I understood I was meant to follow, the two of us outrunning my cousin, but Seamus was a stalwart sort and saw through this plan. He had also practically been born in the saddle and was a much better rider than Finbarr, who'd never had his own horse, or me, who'd only learned to ride two years before. So as Aunt Rosie envisioned, it was the three of us, riding in a group, sandpipers and plovers rising into the sky to get out of our way. Clouds overhead moved aside to let sun through. I would have betrayed my mother in an instant, taking myself and future children away from London, across the sea, to live on these shores forever.

"The tide's out," Finbarr said, as my horse came to walk abreast of his. "We can pick across the tide pools from one beach to the next."

Horse hooves clipped over tiny pebbles and dipped into the salty water. Alby splashed through the waves, porpoising through the deeper shallows. We climbed off the horses and Finbarr showed me some whistles he'd been working on as commands. Seamus stayed on his horse, a polite distance, eyes on us.

"Here," Finbarr said, trying to teach me to whistle. He cupped his hand around my chin, pushing my lips into a pucker.

I tried to release the same sharp-noted whistle that had made Alby run forward, then backtrack in a wide circle. But the saddest little bit of breath came out.

"Try with your fingers." Finbarr put both forefingers into his mouth and let out a noise so loud it made me jump. Alby raced forward and came to a sitting stop at our feet. Finbarr took a small rubber ball from his pocket and cocked his arm to throw it.

"Make a wish," he said.

"I wish this day would never end."

The ball and the dog flew.

"Granted," Finbarr said when Alby caught it.

Alby trotted back to us and spat the ball at our feet. I knelt to embrace him. "Thank you, Alby. You're beautiful. You're perfect."

"Just like you." Finbarr knelt beside me and pushed my hair behind my ears.

"None of that," Seamus called. His voice hadn't changed yet.

"Thank you for joining me, Nan," Finbarr said, when we'd returned the horses to the barn. "There's always work to be done, but I hope we can go for another ride together before the summer's end."

"I hope so, too."

August came and with it the War. Finbarr appeared at our farm. That's how I'd come to think of it. Not just Jack, Rosie, and Seamus's farm. Mine, too.

From the window in the kitchen I could see Finbarr walking over the hill, Alby at his heels. The boy and dog with matching strides, at once purposeful and carefree. There was no conscription, Finbarr joined the British forces with his parents' blessing because in those days that's what patriotism meant, to a certain kind of person. *Britons never, never, never shall be slaves* and *Come and do your bit.* My uncle Jack would join, too, once the efforts were under way. But we didn't know that yet. For now war was a young man's business.

"Go on out," Aunt Rosie said, when she caught me watching through the window. This time she didn't send Seamus with me. She knew what Finbarr had come to say. We make special dispensations for soldiers, even when it comes to girls.

"I'm sorry to leave." Finbarr's voice was somber, but the lightness hadn't left him. None of this was real. War was nothing but a ruined summer. "This wasn't how I imagined things would go."

Tears clouded my eyes. At first this embarrassed me, but Finbarr reached out and took my hand.

"Are you frightened?" I asked.

"Sure, I think I am. Though I don't quite know what to be frightened of. I can't hardly imagine what it'll be like." The world around us stood green and untroubled. "Do you know what I *can* imagine? After it all. The War won't take long. Six months tops and it'll all be over. And you'll come to Ireland to stay, and we'll have a farm of our own, and I'll train dogs, and you'll write books."

My face broke open into a smile that nearly cracked my body in two. He hadn't said the word *married*, I was too young for that, but everything else he'd said spelled it out, didn't it? I could marry Finbarr. I could marry Ireland. My future was sealed, just one quick war to get out of the way.

"Will you pray for me?" Finbarr asked.

My father had left his religion when he left Ireland. I had never prayed in my life, not even when I went to church with Rosie and Jack, but I promised I would.

"May I have a picture of you?" he said, another soldierly request.

"I don't have one here." My parents had exactly one picture of me, with my three sisters, taken and framed years ago. "But I'll get one made. I'll send it to you. I promise."

Finbarr gathered me in his arms and held me a long while. He didn't rock or sway or move. He just stood, his arms tight, our bodies together. I wished we could stay inside that stillness. No moving forward into the future, nor ever leaving that precise spot. Finbarr's lips rested in the curve of my neck. I could feel Aunt Rosie watching from the window, but I didn't care, not even when Finbarr finally pulled away and kissed me a long time, until Rosie knocked on the window loud enough for us to hear and pull apart.

"You're my girl." He held me by the shoulders. "Isn't that the truth, Nan?"

"Yes. It is."

He pulled a claddagh from his pocket and slipped it onto my right ring finger, crown pointing toward me. I was taken. In the crown was a tiny emerald, no bigger than a crumb from a slice of soda bread. Terrible to admit, the main emotion I felt was joy, crackling through my body. How many girls that summer felt the same callow happiness, a boy admitting his love and bestowing a ring before walking off to war? We didn't know what it meant. None of us did.

The Disappearance

Sometimes a life is so entirely disrupted, on such a large and ungraspable scale, all one can do is face the ruined day. After Archie drove away, Agatha tried to pull herself together. She briefly placed her hands on the keys of her typewriter, then gave up at once. Nothing she wrote would be any good. Nothing she did would be any good until she could sort things out with Archie—until she could rectify this mess. She would find a way to do this today, and then she would write tomorrow.

Despite what was widely reported only days later, Agatha never contemplated suicide. This was not in her nature. The idea affronted her. When hearing of someone else's suicide, she always felt enraged. Wasteful and cowardly. As long as there was life there was hope.

Hope. She could crank up her beloved Morris Cowley and follow Archie to London. She could march into his office and grab him by the lapel and insist he see the necessity of working things out. She could shake his love for her back into him. He would remember she was flesh of his flesh. He would not go away for the weekend with his mistress but end things with her and return home where he belonged.

All of that would involve a scene. Agatha had not been raised to cause scenes or display emotions in public. She was raised to keep busy, so she bundled up in her fur coat and accompanied Honoria and Teddy on their walk to school. "Here," she said to Teddy, handing the little girl her hoop and stick. "You can spin this along the way."

Teddy obliged till the end of the drive, then tossed the hoop on the grass to skip ahead. Peter followed her. He was a wonderfully companionable dog, there was never any question of a leash. Agatha reclaimed the hoop and rolled it herself as they walked along the dirt road.

"My mother didn't believe in schooling for a girl," Agatha said to Honoria. "She thought it was best to let my mind develop naturally."

Honoria knew this perfectly well but listened attentively as if hearing it for the first time. A person in despair likes to visit the past. Agatha's past had included her beloved Nursie, and a governess here or there. She'd spent occasional months in proper schools in Torquay, and overseas when she was older. And she'd gone to finishing school, one couldn't do without that. Honoria nodded, as if finishing school would have been an option for her.

"But mostly I ran wild in Torquay, all over the grounds at Ashfield." Agatha stared after Teddy, a pretty child whose brown hair seemed to grow richer and darker by the day. Agatha's eyes glazed over with the past, remembering how she used to roll her hoop in the gardens at home, through the dark ilex, past the elms, around the big beech tree, making up imaginary friends to keep her company. Did Teddy have the same goings-on in her private thoughts? Did she entertain herself with endless stories and invented companions? Or was she only concerned with the tangible world, the real friends that would preclude a need for pretending?

"Oh, Honoria," Agatha said. The hoop calmed her but slowed them down. It was child size and she had to stoop to make it work. Teddy ran ahead down the road, in sight but out of earshot. Agatha gave up, tossing the hoop to the side to collect on their way home.

"You'll have to face it, Agatha." Honoria was weary of the way Agatha believed the game was still on, when so clearly it had already been won by someone else. "I know it's hard, but face it you must. He's gone for good."

"I simply can't believe that." Agatha would never speak of intimate things between herself and her husband, so she didn't tell Honoria about the night before. Instead she rattled off a list of examples, friends she knew whose husbands had a lark with some other woman but then got over it and returned home. She thought again of waiting out her contract with Bodley Head so she could settle handsomely at William Collins. The strategy had worked with her career and now it would work with her marriage. All one needed to get through these things was patience and a plan.

Honoria listened, but it sounded to her like desperation. She could tell by the way Agatha wrung her hands, she knew it was desperation, too. Sometimes hard truths needed to be stated plainly.

"Colonel Christie won't get over it," Honoria insisted. "I'm sorry to say so, but it's no use painting the lily. I see it in his face. And why would you want to stay married to a man who prefers that little tart? Better to face facts. He's gone from you."

"Gone from me," Agatha echoed. Her cheeks stung from the chilly air.

Her mother had warned her only last summer—the summer that turned out to be her last—not to spend too much time in Torquay, away from her husband: "If a woman spends too much time away from her husband, she loses him. Especially a husband like Archie."

At that time Archie was indeed already deeply embroiled with me, and somewhere inside her Agatha knew it, and all the same she *refused* to know it—refused to see she could lose her mother and her husband in so brief a time. So she had squeezed her mother's frail hand and ignored the death rattle in her voice and promised, "There's no man more loyal than Archie. He's faithful to his core. You can bet your life on that."

Perhaps her mother *had* bet her life on it. And lost.

By this time Teddy, always bold and impatient, had gained a considerable distance ahead of Agatha and Honoria. Sunningdale, in Berkshire abutting Surrey, was an easy distance to London by train. The houses were far apart from one another, and private, with lovely gardens. The roads weren't paved, and dust flew up when the occasional carriage or bicycle or automobile went by. The two women were not hoverers by nature and were happy to let Teddy meander ahead. They didn't worry when she crested the hill and disappeared.

As Honoria and Agatha caught sight of her again, a good way down the road, they could also make out the figure of a man, kneeling on the ground, talking to her.

"Do you know him?" Agatha asked Honoria. For all Agatha knew this was someone the two ran into regularly, part of their daily routine.

"No. I don't believe I do."

Both women brought hands to shield their eyes from the sun. Strangers always seemed to take to Teddy. Once on the beach at Torquay a woman had scooped her up and hugged her.

Agatha could see the man patting Peter's scruff with both hands in a way that made her feel he must be the right sort. Then the man stood. He was tall—taller than Archie—and young. Seeing the women, he raised his hand to his forehead in a salute. Instead of heading toward them or away from them on the road, he stepped into the hedgerow.

"How peculiar." Agatha watched the spot where he'd stood, as if he'd been a mirage she could make reappear by squinting into the sun.

"Teddy," Honoria called. "Stay where you are now, you hear me?"

By the time the two women reached her the man was no-where in sight. Teddy waited, shifting from one foot to another. "It's too cold to stand still," she said. In her mittened hands she held a little figure, carved of wood recently enough that Agatha caught the scent of sawdust as Teddy held it up to show her.

"How lovely," Agatha said, though her brow furrowed in consternation. "Is it a dog?"

"It is. Mr. Sonny gave it to me."

"Is that who you were talking to? Mr. Sonny?"

"Yes. He said I could call this dog Sonny, too, if I like."

"Well, then you shall." Agatha took the little girl's hand.

"He says in America all dogs are named Sonny."

"That hardly seems likely, does it? Was he American?"

"I don't know."

"We better get a move on," said Honoria, "if we're to get to school on time."

"I think I'll go home," Agatha said. "See what I can get done."

"You won't go anywhere," Honoria cautioned, meaning, *You won't go to Archie.* "Promise?"

"Promise."

Agatha stood in the road as Honoria and Teddy walked on. She watched them until they disappeared, Teddy with a jolly skip in her step, holding the hand-whittled dog high in her hand. Agatha found herself racked with inordinate worry, and regret. She should have taken the dog herself, put it in her pocket, to make sure it wouldn't be lost.

Perhaps Archie will come home, she thought. Perhaps during the day he'd remember all that had passed between them last night—and all these last years—and return to his senses. Become, once more, the man who'd pressed so urgently for her hand in marriage. When dinnertime came round, he would march through the door, suitcase in hand, no use for it now, as he'd decided to come home to stay.

You may well wonder if you can believe what I tell you about things that occurred when I myself was not present. But this is as reliable an account as you can ever hope to receive. Think for a moment. Don't you know about events that pertain to you, but which you didn't witness? Don't you find yourself, sometimes, recounting them? There's plenty we remember that we never saw with our own eyes or lived with our own bodies. It's a simple matter of weaving together what we know, what we've been told, and what we imagine. Not unlike the way a detective pieces together the answers to a crime.

For example, Inspector Frank Chilton—who's not yet important to this story but will soon become so. The two of us have stayed in touch, written letters to each other about the different ways we remember this time, re-creating for each other what little we didn't already know. And then there's everything Archie and Agatha have told me. And what I know about both of them.

Some reports of this day, the one that would turn into the night Agatha disappeared, claim Agatha paid a visit to Archie's mother. But Peg—who meted out admonishments in her thick Irish brogue—was the last person Agatha would have wanted to see. Peg had never been on Agatha's side, not a single time. Like my father, Peg hailed from County Cork. Her answer to all ills was a dismissive admonition: "You must get over it." Why visit someone who'd tell Agatha what she already knew? There was no choice but to get over her mother's death and the defection of her husband. Agatha was brought up to get on with things, to keep her head and never make a fuss.

But that evening. As the clock's chimes persisted, one after the other, and her husband didn't return, how she lost her head. How the fuss rose up inside her.

Agatha locked herself in Archie's study, feeling torn to pieces over the battle between what she wanted to happen (Archie striding through the door), and what was proving to be true (Archie somewhere else, gathering me in his arms instead of her).

No, no, no, no.

Who hasn't heard that word, ringing through the body, rebelling against events unfolding against our dearest, most desperate wishes? No matter what happened in Agatha's novels, her characters always reacted with admirably low affect. "It's a bad knock," one of them might say, upon discovering their loved one's murder. In my experience loss is seldom taken so lightly, even by those who pride themselves on cool heads and unquivering lips. When something unendingly dear to you is taken away, with no hope of return, wails can't help but ensue.

Somewhere in the midst of her sorrow Agatha stopped to make an inventory. The things she couldn't live without. Her car—the wonderful car she'd bought all on her own. The typewriter that had made it happen. Her child and her dog. What if she did lose Archie? Given all the pain he was causing her, might Nan in fact be taking Agatha's biggest problem off her hands?

The idea returned her to *no*. That wouldn't do. It couldn't be borne. Archie was hers. Her own husband. She would never give him up, *never*.

"The only person who can really hurt you in life," she would write, many years later, "is a husband."

Agatha's wails recommenced. Honoria, and the cook. The butler. And Anna, the new parlor maid. All of them lived at Styles with the Christies, but none reported hearing these wails. Still I know they occurred. She must have stifled them somehow. Her sleeve. A pillow from one of the chairs.

This was not a bad knock. This was a demolition. Agatha's pretty face grew puffy, her blue eyes narrowed to slits. Peter covered her face with kisses in attempt to console. She pushed him away, then grabbed him tightly to her chest. Tears wet his wiry fur. The sobs that could be contained but not halted ravaged her throat. *No, no, no, no.* This *mustn't* be her life. This *mustn't* be how events unfolded.

She tried to muster up the resolve her mother would have demanded, but it was not to be achieved, any more than Archie's return. The night stood stubborn and dark outside the windows. Agatha gave herself over to utter collapse—falling into red-faced, sobbing, wounded pieces.

By now Archie and I were fully ensconced in our weekend away with Noel and Ursula Owen at their cottage in Godalming. After a lovely dinner we'd adjourned to the drawing room for brandy. Earlier, upon his arrival, Archie had taken me aside to announce he'd ended his marriage.

"We'd best lie low for a bit," I said. "After this weekend. We should stay out of each other's way, to give you a chance to sort out the details, let the dust settle." If Archie hadn't left Agatha as promised, I would have fabricated a trip to my sister Megs so he wouldn't question my upcoming absence.

"Don't you know I'll go mad without you?" The kiss that followed was furtive and triumphant, but I could tell he accepted my reasoning. I'd have the next week, at least, to myself.

Noel Owen was a ruddy-faced man who'd inherited a good-sized fortune from a titled relative. He had the air of someone who'd rather be outdoors shooting doves and always spoke loudly, as if his voice had to carry across a great distance over the sound of popping rifles. He and Ursula claimed to be fond of Agatha, but this did not intrude upon their willingness to accept me as a fourth in golf, and at weekend house parties.

Ursula and I sat together on a lilac settee, talking about an article she'd recently read about a new term in psychology called lucid dreaming.

"The idea," she said, "is that in a dream a person might be able to control events. And I thought how much better I'd like it if there were such a thing as lucid living. Much better to control what happens in life than what happens in your dreams."

She laughed and so did I, though it brought me back to summers in Ireland, which always hit me with a kick in the gut. Those days when the whole world had seemed like lucid living, and I could summon a boy cresting the hill to visit me as if out of thin air.

Noel poured me another brandy, then grabbed my hand and bellowed to Archie, "Can't you give her any better jewelry than that, Mr. Christie?"

I wanted to snatch my hand away but smiled instead, letting him examine the ring. From this company's point of view it must have looked inexpensive and insignificant, like something a child might wear, turning the skin beneath it faintly green.

"It's sentimental," I said.

Noel did not let go. Ursula's smile looked waxen. She was bespectacled and too thin, but as far as I could tell, her husband adored her almost as heartily as he seemed to adore Archie.

"She'll have something better than that soon enough," Archie said. He stood smartly, holding his snifter, elbow resting on the mantel. He had the something better in his suitcase and planned to present it to me before the weekend was out. He smiled at me over the rim of his glass. He wasn't one to worry over past romance and had never asked me a word about the claddagh. In his presence I always wore it with the crown pointed away from me.

A little while later Archie and I stood upstairs in the hallway between our rooms. If he fretted at all about his wife's well-

and dark of color. Why, you would think they belonged to an old lady.

She walked outside expecting to find a carriage waiting for her. Instead there was only a car, a black Bentley, sitting unused and forlorn in the drive. Very well. She preferred horses to engines but was used to doing for herself. Not entirely appropriate for a young lady to arrive at a party alone, but if she didn't show up, her hosts might worry. She rolled up her sleeves, cranked up the car, and sat herself behind the wheel to drive off into the night.

Miss Oliver didn't at the moment remember that the car, like the house, had belonged to her brother. She did remember how to drive, and so she did, away from her house, lurching down the dark roads with no particular direction, only her phantom destination.

Goodness it was hot. She lifted the back of her hand to her brow. It was almost pleasing, the pulse of heat, skin on skin, proof that she was alive, and heading somewhere exciting, where many loved ones awaited. With only one light hand on the wheel the car swerved a bit to the left, one wheel skittering on pebbles and brush. She grasped the wheel and righted herself on the road, peering through the windscreen at the road ahead of her.

An awful pain seared, sharp enough to snap her into a moment of clarity. The car lurched and she slammed on the brakes, slamming her head into the windscreen.

Now a new pain, and blood trickling into her eyes. She pushed the door open and stepped out of the car. Terribly cold. Head clearing. And terribly lonesome—a dark country road in the dead of night. For a moment Miss Oliver could understand.

She was not a young girl on the way to a party, but a confused old woman who had driven miles from home and then off the road. The car sat there, looking whole and well. Not even needing a push. If she could just crank it back up, she could turn around and drive on home to her own bed.

"What was I thinking?" Miss Oliver said, crossing her wrists and pressing her hands to her chest. "I might have been killed."

Oh, it was hot. The fog descended upon her again. She took off her wool coat and threw it upon the driver's seat. "I must get to the party. My hostess will be so worried if I'm late."

She walked off into the night, leaving her car by the side of the road, not heading back toward home, but straight into the brush and brambles. Nettles scraped across her wrists. Still she kept walking, even when her feet began to sink into murky water, icy enough to feel as if something were biting her about the ankles.

"I might lie down a bit," she said to no one, and sank to the ground, feeling not at all well, and rather cold, and wondering where on earth her coat had gone.

The Disappearance

The sun had been up for hours when a maid knocked on Archie's door. I lay in bed across the hall reading *The Great Gatsby*. This, I thought, turning another page, was the kind of book I would write if I were an author. Not detective stories.

Despite the thickness of the walls I could hear the maid's voice clearly: "Colonel Christie. There's a telephone call for you. The lady says it's urgent."

The rush of air that followed indicated Archie used too much force opening the door. Then I heard his sure-footed steps, following the maid down the hall. I could guess the words going through his mind. No doubt he thought—as I did—that the call must be from Agatha, in the midst of unbearable torment, longing for him to come home and calling it urgent. I shivered under the covers, glad I wouldn't be the one to hear her tears and pleas.

I closed my book and rose to dress. At least Agatha hadn't

shown up on the Owens' doorstep. There's no telling what some-one will do in a true state of bereavement. Especially a woman.

The Owens kept their telephone in their sitting room. When I got downstairs, Archie was just emerging, wearing a dressing gown, a broad scowl on his face.

"Was it Agatha?" I whispered.

"It was Honoria." He tightened the sash around his trim waist. "She claims Agatha has gone missing."

"Oh, dear. I hope she's all right."

"I'm certain it's just histrionics. A ruse to get me back to Styles. I'm ashamed of Honoria, that she'd go along with it."

"But, Archie." I reached out my hand to touch his elbow. "Shouldn't you find out? Make sure everything's all right? There's Teddy to think of."

He frowned at my misstep, my sounding like an admonishing wife instead of a mistress. I stepped closer and placed my hand on his chest. "Indulge her. She's hurt. Badly hurt."

Archie's face softened. He nodded. I felt a pang of humiliation on Agatha's behalf. That kindness from her husband should be directed by me. He jogged up the stairs, and I went to join the Owens in the dining room to take breakfast. I'd already finished my jam and toast when Archie bustled in, fully dressed and holding his pocket watch. I looked on impatiently while he poured himself a cup of coffee. It seemed important that he hurry off home and make sure all was well.

The doorbell chimed. After a few moments a maid came in, looking puzzled. "So sorry to interrupt, but there's a policeman here."

Noel got to his feet. "I'll see what this is about."

"He's asking for Colonel Christie."

"Well then," Noel said with the confidence of a man who

rules the police, and not the other way around, "I suppose you best show him in."

"I'm on my way out," Archie said. "I'll see what he wants as I go."

He nodded to me, and I took this as instruction to stay where I was. The men went into the hall, and when Ursula followed them, I decided I might as well, too. By the time I reached the foyer Archie had gone rather pale.

Noel was scolding the police officer. "This is preposterous, Thomas. Surely you can trust the man to see to his business on his own."

"A lady's missing." The policeman was young—still spotty across his chin—and the effort it took to contradict Noel Owen was evident in the quaver of his voice. "I've been told to bring Colonel Christie back to Sunningdale."

"I'm sure it's all a mix-up." Archie recovered himself, willing color back to his cheeks. "I'm happy to go home and clear it up, obviously that's what's needed, but if I could just drive my own car, so I don't have to send someone round for it . . . ?"

"Sorry, sir." The officer looked pained to say it. He wasn't looking forward to a drive with Archie. "I do have my orders."

"I'll drive your car to Styles," I said.

Everyone turned toward me at once. The police officer raised his brows. I could see his eyes dart about the hall, searching for a husband to go with me. A husband who didn't already belong to someone else.

Archie had taught me to drive on the country roads through Berkshire and Surrey, but this was the first time I'd done it alone. The novelty of driving solo chased other thoughts from my head. I was not especially worried about Agatha, not yet. I sympathized with her impulse to run away, and I also believed that one way or another the world protected people such as her. I drove slowly enough that I saw the young police officer from Godalming heading home, no doubt relieved to be rid of Archie from his passenger seat.

By the time I arrived at Styles, the local constable's car was parked in front of the house, so I drove around the back and walked inside through the servants' entrance. In those days, doors were seldom locked anywhere outside London. Since the War ended, there was little to fear. I tiptoed through the house into the front hall, where I saw the new parlor maid, Anna, her ear pressed to the sitting room door. Archie must have been in there with the police. The book I'd bought Teddy lay on a little table by the stairs, still wrapped in its package. I retrieved it and tucked it under my arm.

Anna turned toward me. She was a plump, pretty, freckled girl who blushed easily. Archie claimed she flirted with him, and I had no patience for such girls, who preyed on husbands—or even available men—simply to better their own circumstances. I regarded her sternly as she stepped back from the door, blushing at being caught eavesdropping.

"Oh, Miss O'Dea." There were people, at the time, who regularly came and went from Styles, and I was one of them. "I didn't know you'd come round. Is there anything I can get you?"

"No, thank you. I have a gift for Teddy. Is she nearby?"

"I believe Teddy's upstairs in the nursery. Would you like me to take it to her?"

"May I take it myself? You do look busy." I said this in a way that promised I wouldn't say a word about her eavesdropping, so long as she didn't stand between me and the nursery.

"Yes, that would be fine." Anna gestured toward the stairs.

I made my quick detour into Archie and Agatha's room and observed her dress still on the floor. Then I went to the nursery. The door stood just a bit open. Teddy sat cross-legged, playing with toy soldiers and a little wooden dog. At the sight of me she jumped to her feet, ran to the doorway, and threw her arms round my waist.

"Miss O'Dea!" she said, the delighted sort of greeting only a child can perform.

I returned the hug, happy to find her alone, without Honoria hovering. Teddy was small for her age, with delicate bones. She raised her little face up toward me. Her cheeks were pale and she had violet marks under her eyes, as if she hadn't slept well.

"Look at you, you little beauty." I took her chin in my thumb and forefinger, the way Agatha had mine the other day. "Everything all right?"

"Everything's fine." Teddy sighed in the tentative way of a child who knows things are amiss but doesn't want to say so.

"I brought you a present."

She stepped back to expend some effort untwining the string. When she'd manage to unwrap the book, she tossed the brown paper to the floor. At her age I would have found a proper place to discard the wrappings, but this was the life Teddy lived. Not aristocratic, but posh enough that clothes and rubbish were simply flung aside for someone else to clear away. Once I became her stepmother, I'd encourage her to be the sort of person who folded her clothes and put them away, who attended to her own discarded wrappings. But for now it wasn't my place to say a word.

"Oh." Teddy smiled at the cheerful pink cover. "What a funny little bear."

I sat myself down on the round woven rug and leaned against the wall. Teddy climbed into my lap. Her hair tickled my chin and I leaned my cheek against the crown of her head as I read. It was a lovely book, inexplicably touching, Christopher Robin wandering off to find the Hundred Acre Wood.

"But don't you ever wander off like that," I said to Teddy. "Your mum and dad would miss you terribly."

"I won't." Her mouth opened into a great yawn. "Thank you for this book, Miss O'Dea. I do like it."

Teddy read one page to me herself, then I continued reading it aloud even as I could feel Teddy's breath slowing down, her little head tilting forward. I hoped the evenness of my voice and the sweetness of the prose might help her continue with the sleep she so dearly needed. And before long I found my eyelids fluttering closed, my head resting on the top of hers as I fell asleep, too.

"How dare you."

Honoria spoke in a furious hiss, designed to wake me while allowing the child to sleep. Peter trotted into the room, tail wagging, and for the first time I felt alarm. Agatha took the dog with her almost everywhere.

Teddy stirred sleepily, and Honoria scooped her up and laid her on her cot. Then Honoria gestured furiously with her head. I kissed Teddy on the forehead, then followed Honoria into the hallway.

Just at that moment Archie crested the stairs. "Good Lord.

This won't do, Nan. We can't have your name wrapped up in all this." He'd said this repeatedly, about the divorce. Now that police were afoot, it seemed to have become doubly important—getting me out of the way.

"Wrapped up in all this what?" I asked. "Where is Agatha? Is she all right?"

"Of course she's not all right," Honoria said. "This is all owing to you, Nan O'Dea. Don't pretend it's not."

"That will do, Honoria," Archie said.

She refused to retreat, crossing her arms defiantly. Archie took me by the elbow and led me downstairs to his study, where he closed the doors behind us. The room was cold. Someone had allowed the fire to go out.

"Agatha drove off late last night and nobody's seen her since." He didn't look at my face as he told me the rest. Her Morris Cowley had been discovered in the wee hours of this morning, at the lip of the chalk pit below Newlands Corner. Off the road, its lights shining until the battery ran out. The bonnet of the car rested in the shrubbery. In the back seat was a fur coat, a packed suitcase, and a driving license. Frustratingly lacking of clues, and disturbing to think she might have wandered into the cold night without her coat.

"Honoria says her typewriter is gone." Archie lay his hands flat on his desk, where Agatha sometimes wrote during the day while he was at work. His hands looked as though they were trying to absorb her last moment of industry, as if her work above all else would hold a clue to her whereabouts.

Despite the chill a fine layer of sweat formed on Archie's brow. He mopped it with his handkerchief. When he returned the cloth to his pocket, he drew out a folded letter. After staring at it for a moment, he ripped it into bits and threw it on the fire.

"What was that? Was that from Agatha?"

"This is all some damnable stunt. To punish me. To punish *you*. To get your name into the papers."

"That doesn't sound like her."

"That's the point, isn't it? She's not herself. This whole bloody business has made her not like herself."

Me. I was the whole bloody business. I didn't know what to say. Certainly this was no time for the smiles Archie always craved. He clapped his hands, as if he had a task to complete but first had a few things to get out of the way. In the corner of the room, on the floor, I saw light glint off a band of gold. Agatha's wedding ring. I pointed to it and Archie bent, reddening, to scoop it up and bury it in his suit pocket.

"The important thing is for you to get out of here fast as possible."

I stood, unsure of what to do. In a way this was perfect—an added excuse to be out of touch over the next several days. At the same time it was unnerving, what seemed like Archie's momentary defection. That wouldn't do, not at all.

"Nan, are you listening? You mustn't be here. It doesn't look right." He reached out and drew me to him. When I pressed my head against his chest, I could hear his heart, knocking away at an alarming clip. For a woman, a damaged reputation could bring about all manner of horror, in those days. But I knew it wasn't concern for me making his heart erratic.

"Agatha," he whispered into my hair as he held me tight. "Where are you?"

◆ ◆ ◆

On the ten-minute walk to the Sunningdale station, the bitter cold stung my face. Unlike Agatha I did not own a fur coat. I wondered how she managed now, wherever she was, having left her warmest garment in her car. What if I wandered by New-lands Corner and helped myself to it? The thought made me both laugh and frown, pulling my wool coat close around me.

With luck Agatha would turn up by the end of the day. At this very moment police searched through the brush all around Sunningdale, but certainly she wouldn't be found there, but return, perfectly hale and well, on her own steam. It wasn't for me to worry about. My knuckles burned with the cold. I blew into my hands. They smelled like Teddy's soap and I wondered what they'd tell her about Agatha's whereabouts. If anything happened to Agatha—anything permanent—I would become the little girl's full-time mother. That is, if Archie wasn't too traumatized to go ahead with our plans and didn't blame me for whatever happened to his wife. A certain kind of man does tend to blame a woman.

But if he didn't, I could take over. I could be the one walking Teddy to school in the morning, and stealing into Archie's study while he was at work to scribble down stories. Even Honoria would have to change her tone, wouldn't she, if she wanted to stay on at Styles.

I shook these thoughts away. I didn't want any harm to come to Agatha. I wanted her to be found, whole and healthy. But there was nothing I could do to help, and I needed to turn to my own affairs. I needed to focus on the week ahead, leaving the Christie family behind for just a little while, before coming back to join it forever.

The Disappearance

DAY ONE

Saturday, December 4, 1926

Wherever you may sit reading these pages, however much time has passed. You know Agatha Christie did not stay missing. You know she didn't die in December of 1926. She survived to a ripe old age and wrote many more novels and stories. At least one book a year—Christie for Christmas, her publisher used to say, banking on those December profits. Agatha moved past Archie and her shattered marriage, not only to become the bestselling author of all time, but to find a love much better suited to her, the way a woman with a little life under her belt will, once she's clear-eyed about her past and can see what's best for her future.

Nobody could know any of that when the police fetched her car back to the road. Plenty of petrol was in the tank; the engine looked to be in fine working order. No signs of any trouble. No explanation readily discernible. A little ways away another group of policemen, perhaps six of them, stood on the edge of the Silent Pool. Over the years more than one corpse had been dredged from those spring-fed waters.

One of the policemen said, "We'll have to drag it if she doesn't turn up by morning."

At Styles the police gave Archie a brief rundown about what little they'd discovered, and what they planned next. Archie imagined nets cast into the Silent Pool. He envisioned them returning to shore, his wife's body snarled in their threads, and covered his face with such sincere horror that for a moment the police stopped suspecting him of having done something criminal.

In the nursery Teddy said bedtime prayers as usual, Agatha's absence regular enough, Archie's agitation far removed. Outside, night had fallen but still policemen spread out, along with volunteers from the town, scouring and searching all over the countryside. Bodies of water glimmered ominously. By now everyone in Berkshire and Surrey was developing a theory about where Agatha might have gone, what might have happened. Not one of them anywhere close to correct.

I didn't have a telephone in my flat, but there was a call box on the corner. In the evening I walked out to it, pressed the A button, deposited my pennies, and waited for Archie to answer.

"How are you?" I spoke low, as if the passersby might hear. "Is there any word?"

"No." If I hadn't known it was him, I'm not sure I would have recognized his voice. Its tremor, uncertainty, seemed wholly out of character. "The police are involved, Nan. They are highly involved."

"Well. That's good, isn't it? They're serious about finding her."

"Frightfully serious. They mean to find her as quickly as possible. She'll be mortified when she finds out about all this fuss."

I nodded, imagining it, the crack in her dignity. It did seem alarming that she wouldn't immediately rush back to prevent exactly that. I could tell from Archie's voice, it terrified him. He'd take more comfort if the police had dismissed the whole thing as nonsense.

"I've been searching through her papers. There's a story about you, I think."

"Is there?"

"Yes. I'm quite sure it's you. An adulteress. The main character pushes her over a cliff in the end."

I drew in a breath that was half inhale, half laugh. Perhaps Agatha really had gone mad. Though one could argue her wanting to kill me was perfectly reasonable.

"Perhaps I should be looking over my shoulder." I made my voice sound light, but Archie had already moved on to other worries.

"Oh, Nan. Why did I have to be so callous with her? You were right. I should have waited."

"No. There never would have been the right time." It was disconcerting to hear him so distraught, his voice strangled by what seemed to be real grief. "She'll turn up. She's just upset. The moment she realizes what a fuss has started she'll run right home."

But cheering up didn't seem to be what Archie wanted. I could hear someone come into the room and he told me he needed to ring off. Quickly, I asked what he'd told Teddy about Agatha's whereabouts.

"I said she went to Ashfield to see after her mother's things."

"Might she really be there?"

"The Torquay police have already looked into it. She's not there. She's not anywhere."

I didn't know how to reply.

"Look." His voice hardened. "Better if we don't communicate till this is all sorted out. We don't want your name in all this."

"No. We don't."

He rang off the line without saying goodbye.

I placed the earpiece back on its rung and opened the door to the box, stepping out onto the street. The sky had gone dark, streaked with the last colors of a sunset I'd managed to miss. My breath tumbled out, visible in the frigid air, and I didn't realize until I'd walked halfway home that I'd been examining the face of every woman, to see if it was Agatha.

She would be all right. I felt sure of it. She was far more practical than I. And it wasn't as though she were a desperate young girl, with no resources or place to go. The whole world stood with its arms out, holding a net to catch her once she fell. She might be distraught, but I knew she would never commit suicide. Nor would she endure discomfort, the way I did, walking a while instead of returning straight home, past the point of shivering, without gloves, teeth beginning to chatter.

When you don't see someone, standing right before your eyes. When you don't know where she is. You imagine all manner of horror befalling her. By now the number of people were increasing—the minds picturing Agatha struggling through the brush. Running off into the wood, stumbling into a freezing-cold lake.

I shook my head. She had taken my chin in her hand. She

had chastened me. *You don't love him.* As her Inspector Poirot liked to say, "One must respect the psychology."

Agatha was a rational, practical, contained Englishwoman. How fond her novels were of categorizing people. A woman does this, an American does that, Italians are just like this. Perhaps she felt comfortable with these generalities because she fit her own so splendidly. Stiff upper lip, a fine English lady.

Now she had abandoned her natural character, thanks to me. At the same time, what she did best was spin stories. Plot. All of this had the air of a plot, a way to remind Archie how much she meant to him. Indeed, how much he loved her. Worry tends to give way to such emotion, doesn't it.

I gave in to the cold and went home. My flat was tidy like a barracks. No decorations, no photographs, no mementos. My quilt was the same color as the walls, not quite white, not quite ivory. The landlord had rented it to me on the condition that I entertain no men. My neighbor, Mrs. Kettering, an ancient widow, was supposed to keep an eye out for misbehavior, but she liked me and hadn't revealed the rare occasions Archie had come to my door. You'd think he might have noticed, even from standing on the threshold: this was no home, but a station, for someone on a quest, who doesn't have time to adorn the present day, only to plan for the future.

I packed for my trip to Harrogate, my mind unwelcomely focused on Agatha. I folded a pair of knickers and thought, *She's gone off to a swank hotel to nurse her wounds, not even realizing anybody's worried.* But that didn't explain the abandoned car. So I thought, *She left the car so we* would *worry,* which would serve us right, and then she'd gone off to a swank hotel to laugh at us or wait for Archie to find her, his worry rekindling his love.

But what were the chances she'd pull off something like that with no help? Honoria—the most likely accomplice—seemed worried as the rest of us.

"Agatha's an emotional sort," Archie once said to me. "Don't let the manners fool you."

An emotional sort. As if there were any other kind of human. Show me an unemotional sort and I'll show you someone dangerous. How can emotion be avoided when life careens in its unexpected directions? During the War, Agatha had written to her new husband, exhortations for his safety like incantations upon the page, fountain pen flying over paper. Now in Sunningdale, it wasn't Archie in danger but Agatha. Archie realizing he was rather an emotional sort himself—not allowed to join the search. He paced the floors of the house, fit to climb the walls. He regretted tossing her letter upon the fire so hastily. What clues might she have hid in those words that could have been useful to the search? How dear the evidence of her being alive and vital and forming sentences, so recently, heat and heart upon the page.

I took the claddagh off my finger and put it back on, crown pointing toward me. The last time I saw Finbarr, years ago by now, was when he came to find me in London, after our child was lost to us. He'd gathered me up in his arms and cried, soaking the hair at the crown of my head.

"Was she beautiful?" he asked when I told him I'd had his baby.

"Yes." I was past the point of weeping, my hands clutching his collar. "More beautiful than you can imagine."

The memory of our child's beauty had no healing power. None of it was Finbarr's fault, and still I sent him away. With

Ireland embroiled in its war for independence, he left Great Britain for Australia, where nobody would expect him to fight for any country, and he could work training herding dogs. He had wanted me to go with him, but I refused. Just this past September I had written him at the last address I knew, to tell him about Archie, the marriage I believed was impending, and my reasons for stealing another woman's husband. I owed him that much, but I never heard back. Perhaps the words I wrote repulsed him, written by a woman he'd never imagined I could become. Or perhaps he'd simply moved again, to America, or back to Ireland. Beyond it all. A place I could never reach.

It was too soon for Agatha to move beyond anything. I packed my warmest clothes, boots and hats and gloves, so I could go for walks while I was in the country. Perhaps if I found a deserted road, I would even run. I tried to picture Agatha running beside me, the two of us invisible to the outside world and finally equals.

I folded a skirt and thought, *She headed to Godalming so she could confront Archie and me, make a great scene in front of the Owens.* In her unaccustomed Sturm und Drang she'd driven off the road, then left her car and wandered out into the frigid night. First thing tomorrow morning I'd hear the news: her body had been found frozen in the hedgerow, or in the nets they used to drag the Silent Pool.

I folded a cardigan, a gift from Archie, the softest cashmere I owned, and thought, *Right now, Teddy might be playing upstairs at Styles.* She might be reading *Winnie-the-Pooh*. Not knowing Agatha had gone.

Do you ever think about the Irish boy?

Only every day of my life.

I wrapped a pair of walking shoes in a scarf. She'd boarded

a ship to America and now sat snug in a first-class cabin. The whole world and a new future ahead of her. Me having provided the impetus she needed to escape.

I snapped my suitcase shut. That was that. No more thoughts of my lover's wife, or even Finbarr, could intrude. Whatever happened next, in its aftermath my life with Archie would begin. I had one week to myself before then. I planned to immerse myself fully.

Here Lies Sister Mary

I might have stayed in Ireland during the War if Colleen hadn't died. Soon as I received word, I knew the exact moment it had happened. I'd been walking with Brutus up from the barn, my hair loose, clapping my hands together to rid them of saddle soap. Daylight was waning while mist descended as companion to the coming dusk. And a chill came over me out of nowhere, as if I'd been plunged into icy water. "Someone walked over my grave," my mother used to say.

When I received the telegram days later, nothing could keep me from home.

"It doesn't say how," I sobbed to Aunt Rosie, holding up the wired letter, a few lines, pennies saved. "She's only nineteen. Why doesn't it say how?" And of course I thought, *If she'd come to Ireland instead of me, she would have been safe.*

Rosie thumped my back in comfort, looking solemnly at Uncle Jack. It had to be grave indeed for someone so young to die of something that couldn't be told in a telegram.

"You ought to stay here with us," Aunt Rosie said. "There's nothing you can do to fix this. And you'll be safer here than in London."

Perhaps I would not have rushed back to England if only I'd been told how Colleen died. But it was the kind of news, posing the kind of question, that prevented sitting still. The only thing I could bear was being on the move. On the boat from Dublin I stood on deck gripping the handrail, refusing to smile at soldiers. "Come now, lass," an old woman hissed at me. "It's your duty to send them off with happy memories."

All I could think about was getting home to Colleen. I knew this was illogical, yet I felt determined to see my sister. At the same time I had this sense, a vision, that as I headed to England, she was on another boat headed to Ireland, both of us on the choppy Irish Sea, traveling in opposite directions, sailing past each other without so much as a wave.

When I arrived home, my mother was in bed. She sat up and hugged me close but wouldn't say a word.

"What happened?" I asked my father.

He took me by the shoulders, his fingers digging in, in a way that made him foreign to me. "She ran wild."

"Colleen? Wild?" I'd never heard something so absurd.

"I won't have my girls running wild. None of you, do you hear, Nan?" He let go of me. His face looked changed and would be forevermore. As if someone else had stepped into his body, taken it over. I felt a tug of fear that once I knew Colleen's story, the same would happen to me.

Megs came and took me by the elbow, her dark eyes and

pointed features much like my own, the exact same height as me. Colleen had been the tall one. Megs and I walked through London in the summer fog, from the East End to the Waterloo Bridge. "Walking's the thing for grief," Megs said.

These were my mother's words. "Walking's the thing for grief," she had told us. And Colleen had looked up from her book and said, *"Solvitur ambulando."* At Mum's blank expression Colleen translated the Latin: "It is solved by walking." And Mum laughed and said, "My clever girl."

Now, faced with the worst grief of her life, our mother didn't walk. She was unable to move. Louisa, too, had taken to her bed and refused to leave. Colleen's death could not be solved by anything.

But Megs and I walked just the same. "Da won't let us have a funeral," she told me.

"Why ever not?"

By the time we reached the bridge, I knew the story. Colleen had been pregnant. The fellow had gone off to war and never answered her letters.

"Who was he?" All I could think of was the boys she'd turned away, without ever seeming remotely tempted.

"He told her he was a philosophy student. She met him at the library. Perhaps he was a cad or perhaps he was killed in the war. Either way, when Da found out about the baby, he turned Colleen out of the house." Megs's face was pale, dark eyes lusterless. Hating to tell me there was something we could do—we girls—that would rob us of our father's love. I'm not sure I ever saw my father smile again after Colleen died, but it may be I just stopped looking at him. When he hardened himself against one daughter, he hardened the rest of us against him. His wife, too.

Under a dull sun on the Waterloo Bridge I stood arm in arm with the one older sister I had left. "It was only love," Megs told me. "That's what Colleen said. Da told her it was a sin and a disgrace. She said, 'No, Da. It was only love.'"

"How could he?" I never thought, *How could Colleen?* I knew about love by now. Easy to imagine taking the same path as Colleen. But my father's? I closed my eyes and tried to picture the young man clever enough to enchant my smart and beautiful sister, then callous enough to abandon her. He must have been killed, I decided.

Megs kept her anger focused on our father. "I suppose he figured he had one to spare." Her voice sounded empty and resigned. How many of us would Da go through before there wasn't one to spare?

Megs and I let go of each other and leaned forward, staring down into the water. Colleen had walked here, taking the south-bank route, I knew that's how she would go, and still nothing had been solved. Megs and I had walked the same way and still our sister was gone forever. As I look back now, with my view from the future, I see two young, brown-haired girls, small in the scope of things, and all around them machines of war, galvanizing themselves from every corner of the globe to encroach upon their world. But in that moment Megs and I didn't see it. Never in living memory had a war touched English soil, and it still seemed impossible, the way it wouldn't years later, when the second one came along.

All I had at the time was the view from behind my own eyes. A foggy summer day in the city. Megs and I, exhausted from our walk, and from our loss, leaned against each other. I wished I could cry, but my insides were leaden with the same flat, hollow ring of Megs's voice. If I'd had flowers I would have tossed them, to flutter down into the water, the same spot where Colleen had flung herself into the Thames.

Years later I would see a film, *Brigadoon*, and it would remind me how I held Ballycotton in my head during the War: protected, perfect, untouchable. Safe from the ravages of time and progress. Hiding in the clouds, waiting for my return.

In London the world was empty of its young men. My mother finally got out of bed and took me to have my portrait made. I was surprised when she walked into the kitchen, dressed for the day.

"Put on your best dress," she told me. "We're going to have a picture made in Forest Hill, to send to your Irish soldier." She finger curled my hair and gave me Vaseline for my lips and eyelashes.

On the bus my mother blinked and blinked, unaccustomed to natural light, which poured through the windows. She'd stayed inside so long.

"Oh, Mum," I said.

"Never you mind." She grabbed onto my hand. "We're going to take care of you, Nan. My darling girl. And you mustn't be crying. He doesn't want to see tears in his picture, I'll tell you that."

I thought Finbarr wouldn't mind seeing tears. I'd never known him to mind anything. Still I smiled dutifully at the camera, sitting on the photographer's stool, sincere in my happiness as I imagined looking at Finbarr's cheerful face. Some days later

I went on my own to collect it, a pretty picture, so much prettier than I was in real life, I worried he'd be disappointed when he saw me again. My smile showed off the good luck of my straight white teeth. In the letter I sent along with the picture, I wrote in tiny, crowded print. Paper was scarce during the War and I wanted to tell him the truth about everything. Over the next four years I wrote to him regularly and dutifully. I wrote about what had happened to Colleen and how I couldn't look at my father anymore, nor he at any of us. I wrote simple things about school and my friends. I wrote how the War had reached us in London with the zeppelin bombing, and how Megs wanted to work as a nurse but Da wouldn't let her, and in this case Mum agreed. I admitted I knew Finbarr's danger was much greater, but I was terrified of the aerial attacks: "Nothing could be crueler than attacking from the sky." As my pencil moved carefully, sparingly over the page, I held in my head the same Finbarr from peacetime. In my mind his smile broke open easily as ever. He wrote back, saying he hoped to get enough leave, and save enough money, to come to London. He kept the picture of me tucked into his sleeve during battle and tacked beside his bunk at night. I imagined the edges frayed and worn. He'd touch my cheek before sleeping and tell me good night. I wished I had a picture of him.

Two men had failed my sister. First the philosophy student and then our father. But I knew Finbarr would never fail me. He would crouch in the trenches with my smiling face tucked into his sleeve, and he would think about the day on Ballywilling Beach. He'd remember our goodbye kiss and put his fingers to his lips.

"I love you, Nan," Finbarr wrote. The letters were a celebration on the page. I'd never heard him say it aloud. "Wait
for me."

As if I'd ever do anything else.

Four years of war. Four sisters turned to three. I wrote a poem
about Colleen that won a contest, a five-shilling prize. It was
printed in the newspaper, but my father refused to read it. One
morning after he went to work, Mum called Megs, Louisa, and
me into her bedroom.

"Look here." She opened her bottom drawer and pulled out
a tea tin. She twisted off the lid to show us where she'd been
squirreling away the money she earned at Buttons and Bits. I'd
been working there myself, a day or two a week, and knew it
would take considerable time to amass what Mum was showing
us. "None of you will go the way of Colleen, do you hear?" Her
voice sounded as stern as I'd ever heard her. "If ever you're in
trouble, come to me. We'll take this money and run away." She
showed us she'd put her mother's wedding ring in the tin along
with the bills and coins. "We'll go to America or Australia and
say you're a war widow. And then we'll come back and say you
got married there, and he ran off or widowed you. Your father
be damned. You promise me, now. I can't lose another of you."

We promised, all three of us. I handed over the five shillings
for my poem, to add to her cache.

When news of the Hundred Days Offensive began, I worried myself sick, especially when letters from Finbarr ceased

with no warning. "There might not be any post coming from the front," my mother tried to soothe. "Let's not fret till there's cause."

There was plenty of cause. Bad news arrived for girl after girl, mother after mother, father after father. By now I was nineteen, but I think in my heart I may have been much younger. The world quaked around us. One minute my mother would be her old self, brisk and loving. Then she would fade away, pale and still, staring out the window.

"What are you watching for, Mum?"

"Nothing," she'd say, and go back to some busywork. But I knew what she was watching for. Colleen headed toward home, a small child's hand in hers. Love and reason have never been well acquainted.

On Armistice Day I had never seen so many people in one place as there were on the streets of London. With Megs, Louisa, and our friend Emily Hastings, I went out into the celebrating throng. What noise and joy. We couldn't stand shoulder to shoulder, everybody moved sideways.

Megs, Louisa, Emily, and I tried to hold hands as we made our way through the streets, but it was impossible. It should have been frightening, trapped in the midst of so thick a crowd, but the happiness was even thicker. You can't imagine the joy and goodwill. If you tripped, a hundred hands reached out to catch you. If you sneezed, a thousand people said, "God bless you." A soldier caught Megs's arm as she tripped over a curb, then tipped his hat and reveled on with his mates. I searched the crowd, as if there were any reason for Finbarr to be held within it, as if—being lucky enough that he loved me—I could be lucky enough to summon him before my eyes.

Somewhere out in the masses, Agatha Christie was walking, too. During this stretch of time, a lonely married lady with her husband off to war, she'd occupied herself by taking a course in shorthand. When the Armistice was announced right in the middle of class, everyone stumbled out into the celebrating day, marveling at the crowd just as we did. Englishwomen—Englishwomen!—dancing in the street. For all I knew, Agatha and I were shoulder to shoulder, at one or many times during that heady day.

I'm not sure when Megs and I were jostled apart, but somewhere I lost hold of her fingers, a laughing matter and not a frightening one. We'd all catch up eventually. I made it as far as Trafalgar Square. A delivery truck rumbled up Northumberland Avenue with soldiers draped over every inch of it, so I couldn't make out the advertisements written on its side. Just as the truck came to a halt, not able to go a single bit farther because of the crowds, a soldier jumped off the bonnet and landed up ahead of me, his peaked army cap covering cropped black hair.

It was such a swift and lighthearted movement. Seconds earlier the world had been only the throng, no individuals, just one great mass of human life. I had barely existed myself except as a part of it. Now, though, even though a good fifty bodies were jammed into the space between us, there were exactly two people in all of London. Finbarr and me. Facing each other with joyful eyes. Oh, as if I'd conjured him. *Make a wish, Nan.* The sort of miracle that convinces us life on earth has meaning. His black hair shone blue in the London gray as it had on his own emerald island.

"Is it you?" he shouted. He held a bottle of champagne in one hand. "Am I drunk? Am I dreaming?"

"It's me." My voice rasped with the shouting of it.

"Step aside," Finbarr commanded the crowd. "That's my girl. I see my girl."

Could the Red Sea refuse Moses? Could the throng refuse this handsome, blue-eyed soldier, home from victory safe and sound?

In his khaki uniform and army boots, Finbarr made his way through the cleared path and swept me up in his arms. When the crowd closed back in, he hoisted me onto his shoulders, and I saw multitudes spreading all over London, as if an ocean of people had washed into the city, flowing through its undammed streets. All of them beaming, the sky above us free of danger.

"You didn't tell me you were coming to London," I shouted down to him.

He slid me off his shoulders and into his arms. "I only found out day before yesterday. There was no time. Anyway, I knew I'd find you." As if London were Ballycotton and he only had to wander the docks, asking fishermen where Nan O'Dea lived. "It's like a miracle, isn't it? You're like a miracle, same as ever." His voice had changed. Deeper, raspier, as if something had broken inside his throat, which indeed it had. In that moment I owed it to the shouting but would learn later it was a permanent alteration, brought on by mustard gas.

He kissed me, deeply, and I kissed him back. Everyone around us cheered. Celebrating not just the end of the War but our reunion. Nan and Finbarr, together as we should have been had the world never cut us apart. Victory was ours. The world had been righted. Now we could return to our happy old selves.

We moved sideways through the crowd, hand in hand, and I feared we'd be cleaved apart as Megs and I had. I could scarcely see which direction we were headed or which shops we passed. When Finbarr pulled me into the lobby of a grand hotel, it was as if falling into a bubble of quiet emptiness. There were no guests anywhere, and nobody stood behind the front desk. All who should have been here had abandoned their posts to celebrate in the streets. The lobby was unbearably grand—a pocket of silent extravagance I could never imagine affording. Welcoming us. Beside imposing stone columns, great potted palms reached their velvet fronds toward the ceiling. The marble floors felt cold through the soles of our shoes. If we whispered, it would have echoed.

So we didn't whisper. Finbarr still had hold of my hand, and we rushed up the wide, grand staircase. At the door to each room Finbarr turned the knob, until one fell open for us, and we stepped inside with a sharp slam, a bubble inside the bubble. Here was a talent of Finbarr's I hadn't yet discovered but would come to know well: finding places to hide amid any manner of excitement or turmoil.

A little while later there would be the barest bit of time to talk, hastily, as we dressed. Finbarr suggested marrying before he returned to Ireland, but I couldn't leave before I had my mother's blessing. He would promise to send money for my passage to Ireland. The next day I would meet him at the train station to kiss him goodbye. We agreed we'd be married inside mere months. Even if my mother forbade it, I'd give her a kiss and a thousand apologies and say my farewells. No hurry. The War was over. We had all the time in the world.

But first. Just us. How many couples faced each other in that same moment, all across the world? An entire generation with only moments to reclaim their lost youth. In our stolen hotel room there was no time to spare for words. All Finbarr said was "I have to be back to my regiment before sundown." So we took a long moment to inhale the sight of each other, and the nearness. The aloneness and the quiet. He offered me the champagne bottle and I took a swig, warm bubbles burning my nose. I'd never had so much as a sip of champagne before that moment.

We gathered each other up and fell into a wide bed the likes of which we'd never known. But the only luxury we reveled in was the two of us, unchaperoned and unfettered and together at last after all this time.

In any moment during that afternoon did I recall my sister Colleen as a cautionary tale? I did not. There was no comparing her disappeared man to the one present and before my eyes. This was Finbarr. I knew he would never forsake or abandon me. He would never break a promise or say an untrue word.

And he never did.

The Disappearance

Missing person notice sent to police stations through-out England:

> Missing from her home, Styles, Sunningdale, Berkshire, Mrs. Agatha Mary Clarissa Christie, Age 36, height 5 feet 7 inches; hair red, shingled part grey; complexion fair, build slight; dressed in grey stockinette skirt, green jumper, grey and dark grey cardigan and small velour hat; wearing a platinum ring with one pearl; no wedding ring; black handbag with purse containing perhaps 5 or 10 pounds. Left home by car at 9:45 p.m. Friday saying that she was going for a drive.

Inspector Frank Chilton rode in the third-class smoking carriage from Brixham to Harrogate. He was glad to make the trip. It had been a mistake to move back to his mother's seaside cottage during the chill winter months, when the wrong breeze from off-shore could climb into your bones, stirring up the cold from those nights in the trenches, the cold that still lived there and always would.

"They want police officers searching in every county," Sam Lippincott had told him. "I'm shorthanded since you left, and with Jim off on his honeymoon."

Within half an hour of receiving Lippincott's telegram, Chilton had bicycled over to the Cooke estate to borrow their telephone. "Every inch of England scoured, as if the queen herself were missing," said Lippincott, his voice crackling through the wires. The words were scornful but his tone was jolly. Chilton's old police chief was happy to have an excuse to summon his friend back to Yorkshire so soon. "Out of retirement with you. You can pass the lady's photograph around and take a motor through the countryside. You'll never have an easier job than searching for someone who's surely someplace else."

"Nor a more frustrating one." But Chilton had already decided to join in the probably fruitless search. Busywork was better than no work at all. He'd left his position with the Leeds police three weeks earlier, to be closer to his mother. He hadn't yet found new employment, and his old outfit was short of inspectors. Now this lady author was missing—famous enough that every police force in England was in on the hunt, spread out over the entire country—but not so famous Chilton had ever heard of her. Yorkshire headquarters already had men searching Huddersfield and Leeds. They didn't have a man to spare for Harrogate and Ripley. Except the one who'd only just left.

"We'll put you up at the Bellefort," Lippincott had said.

"My cousin and his wife own the place, you know. They say they'll be glad to give you a room free of charge"

Chilton certainly did know about Lippincott's cousin. Simon Leech had married a girl from Antigua. Isabelle Leech was a lovely person, possessed of the rare combination of flawless manners and her own strong mind. But the marriage had scandalized the family and also jeopardized Simon's hotel and spa. It was one thing to have a dark-skinned woman working the front desk, another to discover her married to its English owner. No doubt in addition to needing an extra man searching for Mrs. Christie, Lippincott's cousin needed more guests. Empty rooms tended to breed empty rooms. The cousins were as close as brothers, and this was a chance to help both the hotel and Chilton. As for the missing lady, nobody expected her to turn up in Yorkshire. But Chilton would search all the same. He wasn't the sort to shirk, even when assigned a hopeless task.

"It can be a working holiday for you," Lippincott said, clearly pleased to be able to offer such a thing. "Won't get a better offer than that anytime soon, will you?" Chilton and Lippincott had been in the same regiment during the War and fought together all the way to the end. Lippincott was one of the ones who had come out all right. Not too all right—any man with a heart would be altered by battle in some way—but fine enough to do his job, love his family, hear a door slam without jumping through the roof.

On the train north, Chilton stared out the window at the passing wych elms and hedgerows, the landscape nearly empty of people, wind whipping, everyone hunkering indoors. He was as likely to find Agatha Christie wandering beside the train tracks as anywhere.

Chilton's left arm had gone limp since taking shrapnel in the shoulder. His good hand shook as he lit his cigarette. You might think detective work wouldn't suit a man whose one working arm still trembled from war memories. You'd be right. Which is why Lippincott's calling him out of retirement after less than a month was likely a way of giving him a parting gift, rather than expecting a crime to be solved.

"Have a soak while you're at it," Lippincott had said, once all was agreed upon, proving Chilton's suspicions. Harrogate was famous for its natural hot baths, a luxury Chilton hadn't even considered partaking in when he lived nearby. "It'll do you good."

Smoke from Chilton's exhale rose to mingle with the other passengers'. If a fool's errand was all he was good for, at least it was something more than wandering the beach by his mother's house, an old man at forty. For much of his life Chilton had two brothers. Now he had none. The youngest, Malcolm, had died at Gallipoli. The second youngest, Michael, died in the labyrinth at the Battle of Arras, where Chilton had fought beside him. From that day forward, for the sake of their mother, Chilton had committed to staying alive, even as the stench of rotting bodies followed him from the trenches and refused to ever leave.

Once their mother was gone, though, Chilton would be free and clear. Perhaps then he'd follow the lead of this Christie woman, who from the sound of it had committed suicide. The place they'd find her was at the bottom of a lake. Chances were they'd have found her corpse closer to home by the time he arrived at the hotel. He'd spend one night there and turn around, back toward home.

Suicide. The word had a way of hounding Chilton. A hard thing for a woman to do when she had a child. But then from what Lippincott had said—and the fact that police all over England were being mobilized for the search—the Christies were of the breed who had enough people to look after the child so that she might not even notice her mother was gone. Chilton's mother had been there for her sons every bedtime, every meal, every skinned knee.

The train whistle blew for a stop. There *were* some pleasures left in this life, things he would miss when he left it. Chilton did like the sound of a train whistle. A time away, train travel was. A chance to gather your thoughts or have no thoughts at all. Nobody would be looking for him and nobody would find him either, here on a train. Perhaps that's what this Agatha Christie was doing. It's what he would do if he wanted to get away from the world. Board a train and ride it all over England. Never get off at any stop. Everything you needed, from privies to dining cars to shelter from the rain and a place to rest your head. If he wanted to escape, to disappear, he'd simply ride on and on to nowhere. Which was, now that he thought about it, close to what he was doing—searching for someone in a place she surely wouldn't be found.

After a while Chilton fell asleep with his head lolled back, mouth slightly open, cigarette still burning in his hand. The woman across the aisle, old enough to be his mother, hadn't wanted to ride in the smoking carriage, but no seats were left in the nonsmoking. She looked at the sleeping man kindly. He had that particular look about him, so many did nowadays. And he was a handsome fellow if you looked beyond the edges, a little squidgy and rumpled, but a good strong chin. Nice broad hands. She reached across the aisle and took the cigarette from his fingertips, sneaking one small puff before grinding it out in the ashtray.

In Surrey and Berkshire, a hundred policemen continued to search through the brush and hedges in the damp cold. They walked through the villages handing out circulars. Archie was shown a copy of the missing person notice and registered the description like a blow to his heart. *Slight. Fair.* In their youth he had seen her in ballrooms. Peach silk and pale freckles. Twirling and smiling. Once at a house party, on a gallop around a field with their hosts, she hadn't bothered with a riding outfit, simply worn a pink dress. Her hairpieces—all women wore them in those days—flew off her head and into the wind. The long curls that had looked fetching when attached to her now seemed ghastly as any discarded body part. Agatha slid from her sidesaddle to retrieve them. Archie held tight to his reins, participating in this ride out of duty rather than pleasure. His father—a judge in the Indian Civil Service—had died after a fall from a horse, the blow to his head turning into a brain infection. To watch Agatha you'd never know riding could result in injury or death. Just mirth. What a sight she'd been, holding her skirts in one hand, scooping up the errant hair in the other, roaring with laughter all the while, yet controlled enough to accomplish the task at hand, then hoist herself back onto her horse. What a good sport. What a delight.

Archie thought, *I can't imagine Nan handling such a situation—*

hair flying right off her head—with the same mirthful gales of laughter. Does she even know how to ride a horse? Different manner of upbringing altogether.

In truth it was hard for Archie to imagine me at all, at this time. What he thought about was his wife. The things he once loved about her. Slight and fair. Is that what she looked like? Somehow he had forgotten to notice.

He had noticed when they first met, at a ball in Chudleigh. A week later he had ridden a motorbike all the way to Torquay to see her. He knew she was engaged to some other bloke but that hardly seemed an obstacle. When Archie made up his mind to have something, he had it. Agatha would have registered this trait with a writer's eye. Attaching it to him in quick strokes. She wasn't interested in romances, she placed them in her books because that was the fashion. She especially disliked romance in detective novels. It was a distraction.

Oh, what a distraction she had been, to Archie, at one time. With her vanishment it all came back to him, as if the corporeal had left and all these memories—all these feelings—had erupted exactly as she herself departed the plane. Now what distracted him was the inability to see her. As if the sight of her would solve everything—certainly the way Deputy Chief Constable Thompson and his minions looked at Archie, as if they might see blood dripping from his hands. He calculated who knew about him and Nan, versus who suspected. The Owens. That pair he could trust to remain discreet. Then there was Honoria, who would have told the cook, who was married to the butler. Perhaps the new maid didn't know, but the rest of the staff did, and even now the police were interviewing them, one by one.

"A nervous breakdown," Archie had told Deputy Chief Constable Thompson, at once, before the officer got the chance to pose a single question. He saw Thompson's eyes narrow, clearly finding the outburst suspicious, but Archie couldn't help himself. "She's been suffering terribly from nerves." As if the rephrasing could abate the hole he was digging himself.

"I see." Thompson had a full, protruding chest of the sort particularly athletic men develop when they get on in years. An impressive gray mustache and an eternally scolding countenance. *Give me no nonsense,* Thompson's bearing seemed to say, *and I'll spare you further ruin.* "Had she consulted a doctor?"

"Goodness, no. Neither of us believes in that sort of thing. Fresh air and a firm bearing, that's what restores a person's mind."

Thompson nodded. Approving of the philosophy, if not the man.

Honoria watched this exchange, arms wrapped round herself as if to keep all she knew inside. Agatha had written two letters—one to Archie, which nobody else ever saw, and one to Honoria, saying, "I'm off to Torquay for the weekend." Honoria had handed hers over to the police, but hadn't yet mentioned Friday morning's fuss, or Archie's affair. Fond as she was of Agatha, if her employer never returned, that would leave Archie in charge of her livelihood. The man was a cad but certainly (likely?) not a murderer. Honoria hoped to stay on at Styles, tending Teddy, even if the lady of the house never returned. And weren't the letters proof that Agatha had planned all this, that she had *left* rather than *vanished*? Nobody would have batted an eyelash over her absence or checked to see if she really was in Torquay (she was not) if it hadn't been for that abandoned car: ominous evidence of something terribly amiss. Telegraphing that whatever Agatha's destination, she surely had not arrived there.

When I stole away to Ireland, I left no letter for my parents. My mother found her tea tin empty of every last penny she'd hidden. That was all the information she needed. I imagine her holding it to her bosom, lamenting the part of her plan I'd omitted—bringing her along with me.

When I went missing, just after the War, there weren't a hundred policemen to be found in England. They'd all gone off as soldiers and took their time returning to duty. And I hadn't been an author, or a wife. Just a disgraced girl from a family that barely scraped by, the kind who went missing every day. There weren't enough police in the world to set out looking for all of us.

But for Agatha Christie: thousands of men—policeman and locals. Hounds. Even airplanes. Combing every inch of every forest. Spread out, even after dark, carrying torches. Searching and searching. The great mass of them in Surrey and Berkshire, but inspectors dispatched all over the country. As if the sheer force of her anguish had made her, inexplicably, the most important person on earth.

The Disappearance

DAY THREE

Monday, December 6, 1926

Special cable to THE NEW YORK TIMES

MRS. AGATHA CHRISTIE, NOVELIST, DISAPPEARS IN STRANGE WAY FROM HER HOME IN ENGLAND

LONDON, Dec. 5—Mrs. Agatha Clarissa Christie, the novelist, daughter of the late Frederick Miller of New York and wife of Colonel Archibald Christie, has vanished from her home at Sunningdale, in Berkshire, under mysterious circumstances, and a hundred policemen have searched for her in vain during the weekend.

Late on Friday night Agatha packed an attaché case with clothing and went out alone in a two-seater automobile, leaving a note for her secretary saying she would not return that night.

At eight o'clock yesterday morning the novelist's car

was found abandoned near Guildford on the edge of a chalk pit, the front wheels actually overhanging the edge. The car evidently had run away and only a thick hedge growth prevented it from plunging into the pit. In the car were found articles of clothing and an attaché case containing papers.

All available policemen were mobilized and have conducted an exhaustive search for miles around but no trace of Agatha has been found.

Colonel Christie states that his wife has been suffering from a nervous breakdown. A friend describes Agatha as particularly happy in her homelife and devoted to her only child.

The grounds of Styles had been bustling with police officers throughout the weekend. Now the reporters arrived. Fleeing from their persistent questions, Anna, the new parlor maid, broke down and told one of the handsomer policemen that Archie and Agatha had had a terrible row the morning of the night she disappeared.

"She didn't seem herself after," Anna said tearfully. "And what woman would? He spoke so cruelly to her."

The officer patted her shoulder clumsily. Anna stepped closer to him and he put his arm around her. "There, there," he said. "Men are dogs, aren't they."

She lifted her fetching, tearstained face. "You seem nice."

"I think I am," he said, as if deciding just in that moment.

After a rather pleasant interlude (they would be married the following February) Anna and the officer headed back to Berkshire Police Headquarters to deliver the new information to Deputy Chief Constable Thompson. He frowned that such news would only come to light after a full weekend of intensive searching. Bad enough the press had to get hold of the disappearance. Now this.

"You think the colonel killed the old girl?" asked the young officer.

Thompson snorted. Young people think anyone a minute older than them is old, don't they? This poor fellow didn't know thirty-six would be upon him before he could blink. Thompson had a daughter Agatha's age, born the same year and month. How he hated the thought of anything happening to her.

"Can't know yet, can we?" Thompson said.

"But, Constable." Anna, flush with the situation's drama, spoke in almost a whisper.

"If you've got something to say, might as well be loud enough to hear." Thompson didn't mean to snap but he did hate a mutterer.

"I think there might be a lady involved. A different lady."

She hadn't raised her voice one whit, but Thompson heard her loud and clear. His face darkened. If his daughter's husband were ever to do anything of the kind, Thompson would wring his neck. He got to his feet. "I better get back to Styles and have a chat with Colonel Christie."

"Oh," Anna said. "He's left. Gone off to London. Says he's going to get the Scotland Yard involved."

"The Scotland Yard!" As if they were for hire at the snap of a rich man's fingers. Worse, as if the Berkshire police couldn't handle it themselves. Thompson had already known Archie Christie was arrogant. Now he knew he was an arrogant cad. Nothing put a cloud of suspicion over a man like a strumpet on the side. Thompson feared more than ever for Agatha Christie's life.

Archie was as yet unaware that his dalliance had been revealed. All he knew was the Berkshire and Surrey police were useless, not turning up so much as a strand of Agatha's hair. He was glad enough they didn't seem to know about his extramarital relations, but then what did that say about their investigative prowess? Archie had his solicitor arrange a meeting with the Scotland Yard, but that proved another dead end.

"Sorry, Colonel." The young inspector—so thin he looked as if taking nourishment would be an exhausting business—gave a shake of his head. He might not have been on the job long, but marital spats and women who stormed off because of them were beneath his purview. "If the local police ask for our help, then we're all-hands-on-deck. Until then?" He raised his hands in the air, indicating them not on deck in the slightest.

Archie hated to betray emotion but he was afraid he did. A hand, raised to his brow, shading his eyes. He pulled it away at once, horrified the inspector might think he was crying. Archie thought—the way he wouldn't have otherwise—of his last night with his wife. Why had he indulged himself so? Mightn't she have taken it better if he'd left well enough alone? Or what if he'd never been enticed by Nan in the first place, when he saw her from a distance on the golf course, best swing he'd ever seen from a woman. That same afternoon there she was again, drinking a gin and tonic on the patio. He had strode over as if he had every right to her, and she had blinked through the sunlight as she offered her hand, looking both demure and knowing, a smile twitching the corner of her lips. As if she knew everything that was about to happen. *How do you do, Colonel Christie.* Her voice was so low, so beautifully modulated, he couldn't believe when she said she was Stan's secretary.

What a mistake. What a bleeding, terrible mistake. Nan had used her acquired manners to befriend her employer's daughter and gain entry to the country club. He ought to have let her remain their guest and never become his own. Agatha didn't need to acquire manners, she was born with them. She was from Archie's world. AC and AC. They fit. In the midst of this family emergency, Nan seemed a foreigner, someone who'd elbowed her way in. Troublesome at worst, irrelevant at best.

Out on the street, Archie blinked into city daylight. Crowds bustling about as he stood on the pavement, undecided. Across the street, a tallish woman with a particular stride caught his eye. He knew it wasn't his wife but, all the same, found himself crossing. The woman wore a dark fur coat, surely Agatha had one just like it. She turned down one street, then another, then rounded a corner. When he turned the same direction, she was gone. As if she had melted into thin air.

Nonsense. She'd probably just gone into one of the buildings. With no one to chase, Archie reclaimed his car and navigated the streets to my flat. He sat parked on the street, staring up at my window. No sign of life. It could be I had gone to work. Work! In the midst of all this mess. What a luxury it would be, to pretend to business as usual. Perhaps he should go straight to his office. Perhaps if he behaved as though everything were normal, it would become so. Agatha would return—breeze right in without knocking as she had last week, fashionable and cheery and trying too hard. This time she'd find him alone. He'd gather her in his arms and give her a proper kiss. *Of course I'd love to have luncheon with my beautiful wife.*

How had he missed it, what she'd been on the brink of? Or was it that he'd seen it but simply hadn't cared? Once upon a time he'd been so protective of Agatha, so jealous, he couldn't bear seeing even a waiter talk to her. He'd told her he never wanted to have a son because he never wanted to see her doting on another man. Her doting belonged to him and him alone.

He got out of the car. Hands in his pockets. Staring up at my window as though waiting for a sign. If he saw any movement, he'd run up and knock. And if I opened the door, he knew—despite all his very real feelings, and the desire to find his wife and change the course he'd so rashly set upon her—he would gather me up in his arms and lose all this terrible commotion for a while. He deserved that. No matter what, a man deserved that, to forget his troubles. Until Agatha came home, nothing could change what he'd done, and if he'd known that night at the Owens' was the last time he'd make love to me, well then, surely he'd have savored it a bit more. The way he had with Agatha.

A pretty young woman bustled by in a worn winter coat. She scowled at Archie as if she'd read every one of his thoughts. He looked away from her, up toward my window, watching for any passing shadow.

Nothing. Did he know I didn't love him? No. Archie wasn't the sort of man to know such a thing.

He turned and walked to his car, brim of his hat pointed toward the pavement. The thought of Agatha, dead somewhere, or injured and alone, was too much to suffer. How lucky he'd felt, in the old days, when she turned her light on him. How long it had been since he'd felt lucky, rather than simply believing the world should belong to him, without ever requiring so much as a thank-you.

That night, home at Styles, Archie did something he had never done in all the seven years since she'd arrived. He put Teddy to bed.

"What's wrong, Father?" It was more disruption than treat to have him sitting on her bed, wearing his shirtsleeves, eyes glassy with whiskey and remorse. Peter nestled in beside her; the dog was always a comfort. She closed her hand into his wiry fur.

"Nothing's wrong, darling." Archie stroked her forehead with the particular fervor of a distant parent who might have lost everything but his child. "I just want to say good night to my little girl. Is there anything wrong with that?"

"No." Teddy had her covers pulled just under her chin, blinking through the darkness, wishing he would go away and take the strangeness with him. A child does not like to feel responsible for an adult's emotional state. If he hadn't been so bleary, an uncomfortable volatility brewing, she might have asked him to read more *Winnie-the-Pooh*. Honoria had already finished it once for her, but Teddy wanted to start over, and reading herself was a painstaking business.

"Is Mother coming back?"

"Of course she is," he said, too sharp. "Mother always comes back, doesn't she?"

"I meant tonight."

"Sorry. No. No, I don't think tonight." There were no machinations to keep Teddy from knowing the fuss kicked up around her was a search for her missing mother. Only straight denials of the truth. Not a ruse that could be maintained for long when all of England was searching.

"Well, then." He kissed her forehead. "Sleep well, Teddy."

She closed her eyes tightly, pretending the kiss had put her straight to sleep.

For me the same day began far away from all that clamor. The previous night I had arrived at the Bellefort Hotel and Spa, low-key and cozy, the perfect place for anyone who needed to lie low for a bit. The woman at the front desk—West Indian from the look and sound of her—greeted me warmly.

"I am Mrs. Leech," she said with her lovely Caribbean lilt. "You just be sure to let me know if there's anything you need. Anything at all."

She handed me a fountain pen to sign the registry. I paused for a moment. I'd made the reservation under the name Mrs. O'Dea. It wouldn't have been proper for a young unmarried woman to stay on her own at a hotel. Now I found myself adding another name. "Mrs. Genevieve O'Dea," I wrote, a painful scrape forming in my throat. Genevieve was the name I'd given my lost child. Perhaps I ought to have written Genevieve Mahoney, if only to have seen it written one time.

"Thank you, Mrs. Leech. Would it be possible to take dinner in my room?"

"Of course it would. I'll send up a lovely tray for you."

A woman who'd been approaching the stairs wearing a hotel dressing gown—likely just returning from a spa treatment—bustled over to the front desk. "Dinner in our room!" she said to Mrs. Leech. "Why, that's just the thing, isn't it. We'll do the same, if you please."

"Yes, Mrs. Marston."

Mrs. Marston turned to me. She was about Agatha's age—perhaps a year or two older—with a round, jolly face. Roses in her cheeks. "We're on our honeymoon, Mr. Marston and I," she told me, looking right into my face without—I suspected—really registering me. "Have to keep our energy up, you know!"

Mrs. Leech and I exchanged a quick glance to share our aversion to thinking further on that matter.

Morning came quickly and I knew I couldn't stay in my room forever, so I headed down to breakfast. The Bellefort was comfortable but not particularly posh. It wouldn't have done for a setting in one of Agatha's novels. But E. M. Forster would have liked it—the chairs comfortable to sink into but worn about the arms. I made my way to the dining room, took a seat, and asked the grandmotherly waitress for extra cream.

"Mind if I join you?" an American girl asked.

I looked up. She was my age or thereabouts, with bobbed blond hair and an intent, intelligent face. Other seats were available at empty tables, but instead of pointing this out I nodded. She sat across from me and smiled.

"My name's Lizzie Clarke," she said, louder than was necessary, typical American. "I'm here with my husband. He's still asleep, the slugabed. The hot waters are knocking it right out of him." She laughed, again too loudly.

I glanced around the room to see if the other diners seemed bothered.

Lizzie took this as a request to fill me in on our fellow guests.

She pointed out a fantastically pretty woman, young enough to have been a child during the War, with hair so blond it was nearly white. "Her name's Mrs. Race."

Mrs. Race sat alone, staring out the window forlornly.

"How pretty she is," I said, warmly enough that Lizzie herself might take it as a compliment. "She can't be here on her own. Can she?"

"Oh, no. She's got a husband with her. They're on honeymoon."

"I met another woman here on honeymoon."

"Yes, I've met that one, too. Much more pleased about it than the one over there."

I glanced again at the young bride. The poor thing's lower lip trembled.

Lizzie said, "She and her new husband seem to do nothing but argue. So the old honeymooners are jolly, and the young ones are not. Pity anyone shouldn't be jolly on their honeymoon. Isn't it?"

I smiled. "You like people watching, do you?"

"It's my favorite hobby," Lizzie admitted with a self-deprecating laugh that made me feel fond of her.

Who should enter just then but the older honeymooners, Mr. and Mrs. Marston. They sat on the far side of the dining room and I indulged in a bit of people watching myself. Mrs. Marston had dark hair, just a few strands of gray, and a broad, ample back. I stared over her shoulder, directly at her husband. Mr. Marston was a jowly, red-faced fellow who didn't seem to notice me, eyes only for his new wife. How sweet.

"Say," Lizzie said, when we'd finished eating. "Are you heading to the baths? Would you like a walk before? We could get good and chilly so the hot water will feel that much better."

Lizzie was already on her feet. I pushed my chair back. We left the dining room together, then went to our rooms to collect warm clothes before meeting outside to venture down the frigid road, cold gray skies settling in around us. It was a good idea to get ourselves nice and cold before a soak back at the Bellefort Hotel, and cold we would get, despite our coats, hats, and gloves.

"What's your husband like?" I asked as we walked. If she could be direct, so could I.

"He's lovely. I recommend American men. They're different from British. More emotional and expressive." Away from the gaze of our fellow guests she slipped her arm through mine as if we were old friends.

"It's nice that you speak so kindly of him. Not all women do, of their husbands. They complain about them and malign them, and then they're surprised when they run off with someone else."

Lizzie laughed. She stopped and lit a cigarette, shading the flame of her match with gloved hands. "If the husband deserves his wife's complaints, the person he runs off with will complain about him one day. Probably about the very same things. True?"

I patted my hat back into place. I'd taken pains to look respectable and put together. A proper married lady on holiday. Composed, running away from nothing, simply taking a little time for myself.

Lizzie's gaze turned away from me, focused down the road. A young man came into view, walking toward us. He was tall, with a graceful step. Even at this distance, more than a hundred feet, he was clearly fixated, coming directly toward us as if he had something urgent to relay.

"He doesn't look quite right," Lizzie murmured.

I didn't look at her, but remained focused on the man. My impression was precisely opposite to Lizzie's. He looked quite right to me. Almost nothing in my life required the sudden control and presence of mind to keep my voice neutral when I spoke. "Funnily enough, I happen to know him. Would you mind excusing us a moment?"

"Not at all." She gave a pretty little shiver. "I'm about ready for some hot water. Perhaps I'll see you in the baths?"

"Perhaps." But I had already started moving in the opposite direction.

"Remember not to trust strangers too quickly."

"Thank you." I spoke without looking back at her. "Thank you for the reminder."

My feet moved swiftly, as they used to when I was young. Carrying me toward the man. It was like hurrying toward the best part of the past. A shift had occurred in the atmosphere. Skies opening up to bestow a gift when I least deserved one.

He wore an Aran sweater and a peacoat, open and unbuttoned despite the cold. Black hair fell across his brow. The smile had been stamped out of his eyes, but they were still the loveliest layered blue. My heels were chunky, fine for walking, but ill-suited to the run I couldn't help but break into. I couldn't get to him fast enough. My coat blew open, too. If I ran into his arms, I knew he would pick me up and spin me around, but for some reason I stopped just short of them. Looking at him, making sure this was real, felt more important than embracing him.

"Finbarr," I said. "Upon my word."

"Hello, Nan." He reached out and took my hand. Brought my palm to his lips, three beats of a kiss. "I've missed you."

In Berkshire and Surrey, they searched as though for a dead woman. The Silent Pool, the brush, ditches. Hounds bayed, noses to the ground. If Agatha Christie was found near her home, it would be because she'd died there, by her own hand or someone else's.

Elsewhere in England authorities searched for a live person in hiding. Police officers from Land's End to Coldstream were showing Agatha's photograph to hotel guests and proprietors. *Have you seen this lady?* Chilton was one of many, going through these motions. He'd been charged to search for her, so searching was how he planned to conduct himself. On his arrival the day before he'd acted an ordinary guest, checking in and eating dinner in the dining room with the sparse assortment of guests. Simon Leech's wife ushered him to a table and sat him opposite a pretty young lady with abundant dark hair whom Mrs. Leech introduced as Miss Cornelia Armstrong.

"Surely you're not here all on your own," Chilton said to Miss Armstrong, before he could stop himself.

Miss Armstrong smiled as if she found his incredulousness a compliment. "Why surely I *am*," she said, with no small note of good-natured reproach. "It's 1926, or haven't you heard? Men went to war at my age. Surely I can manage a spa."

Chilton smiled, and the innkeeper patted the table as if pleased the conversation was off to a rousing start. "Be sure to tell all your friends which is the best hotel in Harrogate," Mrs. Leech trilled, before bustling off with an industrious smile. The rest of Chilton's evening passed agreeably as he learned more about suffrage from Miss Armstrong than he had ever known before.

On Monday morning, first thing after breakfast, Chilton caught a ride into town with Mr. Leech. Leeds Police Headquarters was much as he'd left it. Lippincott always kept his door open. He waved Chilton into his office.

"Quite a time to take your retirement, just as the crime of the century's been committed."

They laughed, having agreed this was no crime at all. Just a lady with a tiny bit of renown, missing when nothing else was occurring in the world, creating a silly season in winter. The papers were going wild. Lippincott gave Chilton some police bulletins and a photograph of Agatha from her publisher, the same one being placed in countless other hands across England.

"If she's not dead, she'll be frightfully embarrassed at all this fuss," Chilton said. Looking at Agatha's photograph—wistful and lovely—he regretted his laughter. It was a stark business, suicide, but he understood that when you had to go, you had to go. Surely she'd had her reasons.

Lippincott revealed his more cynical but less tragic theory. "What she'll do is sell a lot of books. A handful of English readers knew her name on Friday. If she doesn't turn up by the end of the week, she'll be a global sensation."

"Publicity stunt, you think?"

"Some sort of stunt. But that's why I wanted you back, Chilton. I knew you'd treat it like it was real, either way. And we must take it seriously. No one yet knows where this woman's gone. She might as well be here as anywhere."

Chilton saluted in agreement, half in jest, but it took them both grim for an instant. They'd seen a lot together, the two of them, when saluting was an everyday business.

"Look here, though, Chilton. Thanks to my cousin I can put you up at no expense. And I've got a police auto for you to use to conduct your searching. You retired too early for us to give you a fancy watch, or anything of that sort. So take this as a bit of a holiday, won't you? Search for Agatha Christie, but take the waters, too. Enjoy the hotel. Eat well. Have a massage, for goodness' sake."

Chilton could not begin to imagine submitting himself to a massage. "Do you know I lived in Yorkshire seven years and never put so much as a toe in the baths?"

"Well then," Lippincott said, even though Chilton was sure the same stood true for Lippincott. He might wish his dear cousin's establishment well but was unlikely to ever frequent it. "High time."

For me the cold of the day had disappeared, along with the clear blue sky. All I could see was Finbarr. He put a gentle hand on my elbow and steered me away, looking over his shoulder to see if Lizzie Clarke was still there.

"You needn't worry about her," I said, but he didn't seem to hear me. He led me off the road, through a hedgerow, into a stand of silver birch trees.

"Finbarr." When we were young in Ireland, this sort of detour might have been playful, testing how game I could be. "What are you doing?"

"I might ask the same of you." His raspy postwar voice sobered me.

"I'm on holiday. How on earth did you find me?"

"Never mind that. The important thing is what happens next. You and me, leaving this plot of yours behind, and going home to Ballycotton."

"Ballycotton is not my home." I pulled my arm out of his grip. At first sight of him my brain had gone to atoms. Now those atoms started to swirl and sharpen, forming a clearer picture. "It never was and it never will be."

"It was and it will. My father died, Nan." From the way he said it, I gathered his mother had died, too, perhaps a good while ago. "I've saved enough money to buy a small place, where I can raise and train dogs. We can go home. You and me."

I pictured the home he meant, and the road to Sunday's Corner. I knew I should say I was sorry for his parents' deaths. But I wasn't sorry and never would be.

"Nan, you can't go through with this. It's wrongheaded, and wrong besides. You belong with me, not with a man already married."

So he *had* received the letter I'd sent him. And this was his answer. It had been a mistake to write to him, a moment of weakness.

"It's too late." I hoped my voice sounded more sad than reproachful. "You're too late."

He put his hand around my wrist, firm but gentle, and pulled me farther into the wood. My hat had started to fall and he pulled it back onto my head, down over my ears, which must have been burning red from high dudgeon, and the chill. Finbarr didn't want me to be cold. After the Armistice celebrations, when we had lain together in London, in the midst of a passion that had been building for years, he'd paused to adjust the pillow beneath my head.

This was the third time I'd seen him since that day. The first was in Ballycotton, when he lay delirious with influenza. The second was nearly a year later, after I'd left Ireland forever, and he finally came to find me in London. He had pleaded with me to go away with him to Australia. But I didn't.

The Finbarr who'd made love to me on the day of the Armistice celebration had seemed his old self. Or it could be that was just what I'd wanted to see—a blissful, fleeting illusion. By the time he came back for me, neither of us were ourselves. I was wrecked by loss. And he was just wrecked. Twenty pounds lighter. No trace of the joyful air that had been his salient trait. His voice, ruined by the mustard gas, didn't sound a bit like the boy I remembered.

("Sometimes," Agatha Christie wrote, years later, "one cannot help a tide of rage coming over one when one thinks of war.")

"No," I'd told him then. "I can't go away with you. I can't go anywhere."

Now, six years later, in Harrogate, Finbarr and I might not have returned to our original selves. But we could at least face each other calmly. I could look at him and feel no recrimination. None of this had ever been his fault.

"What we need"—he gathered my hands up in his—"is to get away from here. We can start over. You and me."

"Oh, Finbarr. That's not what I need. Not at all."

I pulled away from him. There was a considerable amount of brush to crash through, to get back to the road. The winter sky opened wide above me and I hugged myself tightly. *Breathe in, breathe out.* That's how I'd get through these next days. One breath followed by another.

Finbarr was just behind me. He put his hand on my shoulder and I shrugged it off. The last time I'd seen him, my insides were melted to gray. There was still so much to be reckoned with. And then there was the change in him. A few days from this moment Inspector Chilton would say something to me about going to war. How the world seemed one way beforehand. Then afterward you had seen the Big Sadness and you couldn't ever unsee it. Finbarr had not a single line on his face. He owned the same tall, spare, and agile form. But the sun had left him. Like the rasp in his voice had replaced the old clarity, the Big Sadness had replaced his joy. If it hadn't made him seem like a ship that had lost its anchor, it might have made me love him even more. I had seen a measure of that sadness myself.

He reached out and pulled me back into his arms. Three beats. Then he let me go, turned, and trudged off down the road, the same way he'd come. Perhaps he thought I'd follow him, but I didn't. I just stood watching him go. He knew I was still there because while I was still in earshot he raised one arm, without looking back, and called, "You'll see me again soon, Nan. Very soon."

More than an hour later, just before entering the baths with Lizzie Clarke, I asked myself the logical question Finbarr hadn't answered: How had he known to find me in Harrogate?

"Are you all right?" asked Lizzie, as I settled beside her in the hot water.

I nodded, a gesture that didn't say *Yes* so much as *I'll tell you later*. I was wearing the knee-length bathing dress I usually took to the beach, with matching shorts underneath. Although Lizzie was in water up to her chin, I could tell her outfit was considerably more daring, not least because it was the color of a ripe tomato. All the women wore caps, our hair completely covered, a kind of uniform no matter how different our bathing costumes.

Steam settled around me, and my brain felt suddenly light. Perhaps I had managed to conjure Finbarr. Lucid living. Or perhaps the very opposite, and I'd imagined his being here. I almost wanted to ask Lizzie for confirmation. *Did a black-haired man walk down the road toward us? Did you leave me alone with him? Did you say he didn't look quite right?* Would it be better or worse if it hadn't happened at all, me back in Finbarr's arms?

The natural baths at the Bellefort were beneath the hotel in what felt like steamy caves. Low stone ceilings, so even the smaller of us had to bend our heads until we were neck-deep. One needn't be staying at the hotel to use them, for a small fee, but on this day it was mostly our fellow guests bathing with us. Sitting across from us, immersed up to her chin, was the older of the newly-wed brides, Mrs. Marston. She observed Lizzie and me cheerily through the steam. We stared frankly back at her, but she wasn't the sort to examine others. There was something shallow about her gaze. I supposed if she was asked about Lizzie and me later, she wouldn't be able to name a single trait—hair color, eye color, nothing. Only our sex and approximate age. We existed as an audience for what she had to tell us.

"How are you two dears?" Mrs. Marston said, with a warmth that sounded genuine.

"We're just fine," Lizzie said, with her direct American syllables.

"We met last night," I said, before Lizzie could announce my name. I could tell Mrs. Marston had no recollection of this. "I'm told congratulations are in order?"

The woman laughed, large brown eyes twinkling. "Indeed. Six days of married life and counting. It's bliss, I tell you. Bliss."

"How wonderful for you," Lizzie said. "And where did you two lovebirds meet?"

"Oh, we've known each other a long while, Mr. Marston and I. Star-crossed you might say. Pain and drama, ladies. Mark my words. It makes it all the better when the stars finally align."

"I can't say I agree." Lizzie kept her eyes firmly on Mrs. Marston. "My husband and I had our share of pain and drama. I could have done without all that. Well and truly."

"Well, then you know," Mrs. Marston said, casting off the disagreement.

I thought of Agatha, all of her current pain and drama, and hoped she might one day be happier than she'd ever been, by virtue of the pain I was causing her now. I refused to consider Agatha's death as a possibility. We were connected, Agatha and I. If anything happened to her, I would feel it in my bones, the same way I had when Colleen died.

Mrs. Marston settled more fully in the water, letting it cover her chin, bright eyes sparkling away as if to prove her happiness. Then she lowered her head closer to the water and said, "I was rather dismayed to find out this hotel was owned by a colored person. Don't know if we would have booked it had we known."

"Mrs. Leech? She seems perfectly nice to me." Lizzie's voice was clipped and firm, putting an end to that.

To her credit or else an inability to broach dissent, Mrs. Marston obliged by changing the subject. "Do you have any children?" she asked Lizzie.

"We had one. He died shortly after he was born."

"Oh, my dear," Mrs. Marston said, all motherly comfort. "But you're young. You'll have another? And then another, and another. Won't you?"

"I hope so." Lizzie's expression was hard to read. "But that doesn't mean I'll ever forget the first."

"Of course not. Truth be told I'm hoping it's not too late for me. To have a child. Stranger things have happened. And that's all I've ever wanted, really. A baby. Well. A baby and Mr. Marston."

I stood and grabbed a hotel dressing gown to cover my bathing dress. "I feel a bit light-headed. Perhaps I'll see you at tea."

Mrs. Marston said to Lizzie, as if I had already left, "A morose one, your friend. She needs to find a husband, that's all, isn't it?"

"Who says I haven't found a husband." I pulled the belt of my dressing gown tight, my voice too baldly irritated.

"Now, now," Mrs. Marston said, as if she was used to being in charge. "Keep your head, dear, I was only japing." As if to prove it, she let out a merry laugh, trilling through the cavern, reverberating, the least happy sound I could imagine.

Here Lies Sister Mary

All over the world girls waited to hear from soldiers they'd never see again, but I was lucky to love a man who kept his promises. Finbarr folded a pound note into the first letter he sent.

He wrote, *I thought I'd grown dead inside till I saw you standing there in the square.*

He wrote, *It wasn't just Armistice that swept me away.*

He wrote, *We should have waited for our wedding night, it's true, but I know in my heart there never will be a more perfect moment. And our wedding night will come, Nan, never you doubt it.*

And then his second letter arrived, empty of money. It only said, *I love you* and *I'm afraid I've come down with a fever.*

I didn't feel too well myself.

My father received word from Ireland. Uncle Jack had survived the War—remaining unscathed in battle. But he came home from the front with influenza and gave it to his wife and child. Aunt Rosie recovered. Uncle Jack did not. Nor did Seamus. It had seemed such a mercy that my sweet cousin was too young to fight in the War. And now he was dead all the same. It seemed the tides of this war would never stop lapping our shores. I wept for my lost second family, my beloved farm standing empty. My mother comforted me, not able to stop herself from pressing her palm against my forehead.

When Emily Hastings got sick, Megs, Louisa, and I were forbidden to visit her. "It'll be a miracle if it passes you girls by," my mother said at dinner, wiping tears away. "Did you know Andrew Pennington died just yesterday? All these young people. Boys who came home safe from the War, only to be killed by the flu."

The giant and kindly crowd that swept Finbarr and me together had been teeming with invisible sickness. My mother gave up her job at Buttons and Bits and insisted I do the same.

"No, you don't," my father said, when he caught me trying to leave our flat. "It's not safe to be out and about just now."

"Megs thinks we already had it last spring," I said. All three of us girls had come down with mild fevers and recovered quickly.

"Thinking is different than knowing," he snapped. "And knowing's what I'd need before letting you into danger."

For years there had been little warmth between us. But in that moment I could see in his face the loss of his eldest child, and his brother, and the nephew he'd scarcely known. Da had aged a hundred years since I last allowed myself to really look at him. So I hugged him tightly. I thought of Finbarr's letter. Would there be anyone left in Ballycotton who'd know to write me if he died? We didn't have a telephone. Certainly the Mahoneys didn't, there was hardly even electricity in Ballycotton.

"You look green around the gills, Nan," my mother said that evening. She checked my temperature again. She couldn't keep her hands away from our faces. "You better rest. I'll bring you a plate."

I sequestered myself in my room, both hands spread across my belly. I didn't have the flu. I had something else. My mother's fear of influenza had replaced, at least temporarily, her fear of pregnancy. It made her blind to what really ailed me. She couldn't know that for this brief span of time, whenever she touched me or held me, she touched and held her grandchild, too.

Colleen had been my age, almost to the day, when she tossed herself into the Thames. I wouldn't ever let that happen to my mother again. I didn't tell Megs and Louisa I was pregnant because I didn't want them fearing what would become of me. And I wouldn't give my father a chance to thunder me away. I'd get myself across the Irish Sea and marry Finbarr. Even if he was dying, it was better to be a soldier's widow than a soldier's fool. The small detail of I dos and a priest's or vicar's blessing would render the difference between heroine and pariah. All I had to do was get myself from my island to Finbarr's.

The only place my mother went these days was the grocer's. As soon as she was out the door, I went to her room and pulled out the tea tin she'd shown us. Between the money she'd secreted away and the pound note Finbarr had sent me, I'd have just enough to get to Ballycotton. I shook my grandmother's ring into my hands and considered slipping it onto my finger. Instead I put it back in the tin. I didn't need to disguise myself as a married woman. I'd be the real thing soon enough.

◆　◆　◆

The last of my money went to the fisherman who carried me in his mule-pulled cart from the train station to the Mahoneys' white clay cottage in the village. Masts from the harbor dinged and gulls swooped and sang. I knew Alby was not allowed inside but slept underneath the house and was disappointed he didn't bound out to greet me. But perhaps that meant Finbarr had recovered and was off making a good wage herding.

Mrs. Mahoney opened the door. I'd met her before, at Sunday church services. But then she'd been smiling. She was a tiny woman, with shoulders so bony I could see the sharp *V* of them through her cardigan.

"You can't see him," she said before I could even remind her who I was. "It's not safe for you." Still she stepped aside to let me in, then lit the stove to make a cup of tea. It was cold in the house, and I wanted to pull my chair closer to the fire, but didn't want to insult her. The floor beneath my feet was dirt. At another time the sight of boats through the window might have been cheerful, but just then they looked to me like everything in the world Finbarr didn't want. Noticing my gaze, Mrs. Mahoney stood up, went to the window, and drew the shutters closed.

"I'm Jack O'Dea's niece."

"I know who you are."

I could tell she wanted to say something about Seamus and Jack. Perhaps offer condolences. Perhaps blame them—Finbarr would have gone over there, wouldn't he, before they'd fallen ill. She slid the cup of tea in front of me without offering milk or sugar.

My eyes roamed the small kitchen. There were two doors— the one I'd come in, from the outside, and the one leading to the rest of the house, firmly closed.

"Is Finbarr here? Is he all right?"

"He's here and he's not all right and he doesn't need you upsetting him." She sat down to her own tea. From the way she refused to let her eyes rest on me longer than a few seconds, I could tell it was an effort to refrain from kindness. Did she know? About me? Or was her coldness due to worrying over her only child?

"Is it the flu?"

"It is and you mustn't catch it. We must get you out of this house straightaway. I've been tending him day and night, I could be carrying it myself. I'm sure I am."

"If I could just see Finbarr . . ."

"You can't."

"I could stand in the doorway."

"Are you deaf, girl? I said no."

"Nan. My name's Nan. Finbarr wants to see me. I know he does."

She looked away, toward the shuttered window. She had black hair like Finbarr's, streaked through with gray. As his would be one day. I'd thought at first her rosy cheeks were caused by the cold, but up close I saw little broken blood vessels along her cheekbones. Careworn. She would have been beautiful once. Finbarr told me she wished she'd had a hundred children. Now here I was offering her one more.

"Where's Alby?"

"Traded off for provisions during the War."

Would they have written to tell him? Or had Finbarr arrived home and found Alby gone? I imagined him whistling round the house till his father finally gathered the strength to admit what had been done. Finbarr would have worked extra hours at every farm near Ballycotton, first to earn my passage home and then to buy his dog back.

I reached into my bag and pulled out one of Finbarr's letters. "Look." I held it toward her. "He wants to marry me. He sent me money to come here. So we could be married." I pointed to the words on the page. "He promised."

She stared at me, unmoved. I shook the letter under her eyes. A horrible feeling when something you think holds power turns out to be useless.

"And don't you know, that's what a man says, to get a woman to do what he wants. The trick is in saying no. That's how you get a man to marry you. Before. Not after."

How did she know? It must have been my urgency that gave me away. I was thin as I'd ever been. Still there was no use arguing. "He wrote this after," I said simply, then put my head down on the table. I was so tired. And suddenly horribly, horribly hungry.

"Don't you cry."

As if it hadn't occurred to me until I heard the words, that's exactly what I did. Great, guttural sobs, filling the small house. For a moment I felt embarrassed, but then I thought, if Finbarr heard me, perhaps he'd will himself out from wherever he was and come into the kitchen. He'd tell his mother the truth. He'd insist on marrying me that very day. But no matter how I sobbed, he didn't appear, and his mother didn't soften. I cried until I fell asleep, my head resting on my arms.

"At least let me give her something to eat," Mrs. Mahoney said to her husband, willing to expose softness when she believed I couldn't hear.

I opened my eyes to see Finbarr's parents, standing by the door that led to the rest of the house as if they meant to guard it from me. If Finbarr had inherited his joyful air from either of them, it was gone from both now. Still they had made him, these two people, they had made Finbarr and raised him in this small, dirt-floored house. *I love you* rose in my throat, and *Thank you*, but I choked the words back. They wouldn't want to hear them from me.

"Let me give her a glass of milk and some bread," his mother said. "And there's stew left over from last night. The poor girl, in the way she is, she must be famished."

I lifted my head, feeling the creases in my face. My eyes felt swollen from sleep and crying. *The poor girl.* I recognized Mrs. Mahoney's new sympathy as a bad sign. If she no longer needed to steel herself toward me, my fate was no longer in her hands. Somebody else had taken over.

Mr. Mahoney sat in the chair beside me. He wore an oilskin coat and smelled of fish and salt air. His wife set to bustling, making me a plate.

"If you'd just let me see him for one moment. All I ask is one moment." Then it would all be clear to everyone. They'd never seen us together. They couldn't know. If they did, they would understand.

Mr. Mahoney put his hand on my arm. Slim like his wife but much taller, with a full, ruddy face, hard-bitten by years on the sea. When he spoke, it was with the brogue that still sounded like music to me.

"Listen. Nan is it?"

I refused to nod. Shouldn't he know by now it was Nan? Of course he knew.

"I know you'd like to speak with Finbarr. But he's not in a way for that now. He can scarcely lift his head from the pillow."

"I don't mind."

They looked at me, the two of them, as if I'd lain with every soldier home from the War and landed on their doorstep to trap their son's eternal soul.

"You don't understand," Mr. Mahoney said. "The poor boy, he might not live to see tomorrow morning."

"Please."

They looked at each other.

"You promise you won't touch him?" said Mrs. Mahoney. "We don't need you getting sick, too. You've more to think of than just yourself now."

Perhaps she cared about me and my baby after all. It was impossible to think of being anywhere near Finbarr without touching him, but I nodded.

The door swung open with a creak to reveal a dark room hanging heavy with despair, the curtains drawn. My nostrils filled with a sad, pungent odor, like mushrooms and sweat. The figure on the bed barely made a rise in the covers.

I walked to the side of the bed and knelt down to see his face. "Finbarr," I whispered. "It's me. I've come to you." I reached out my hand to stroke his hair off the feverish head, but his mother was behind me now and caught it before I could touch him. Finbarr's eyes, open, did not land on me or focus. Though I hadn't touched him, I could feel heat emanating from his body, almost as warm as the stove. A stale, awful scent as if he'd soiled himself settled around us. He moved, and a damp cloth that may have been cooling his forehead fell to the dirt floor. It was crusted with blood and so were his ears. His lips had turned an odd dark blue, and they didn't move or say my name. He didn't see me. I struggled to tear my hand out of his mother's so I could touch him. Surprisingly strong, she increased her grip.

"If you let me stay," I whispered, "I could take care of him for you."

"And where would the sense in that be?" Mr. Mahoney put his arm around my shoulders. He pressed me to my feet, turned me around, and gently pushed me out of the room.

They fed me dinner and made me a pallet by the stove in the kitchen. When I was sure they'd be sleeping, I crept into Finbarr's room and lay down beside him. "Dogs and books." I whispered, the words scratching my throat with despair. "We'll get Alby back and it will be dogs and books and you and me and the baby."

His body moved and for a moment I thought he'd answer, but instead he coughed, shaking, dry coughs that didn't bring him to consciousness. I froze, worried his mother would hear and run into the room, but she didn't. Finbarr's body quieted. I stayed beside him, awake all night, so before dawn I could be found on my pallet, a good girl.

"Might I say goodbye to him," I said, before we left.

"You must think of what's best for the baby, dear," his mother admonished.

I nodded, not yet realizing that as far as the world was concerned, what was best for the baby could mean something entirely different from what was best for me.

The Disappearance

Perhaps it's only hindsight, rearranging memory. But it seems to me that evening at the Bellefort Hotel when I first saw Inspector Frank Chilton, I knew he was searching for Agatha. Not that I knew his name yet—that discovery was moments away. He stood at the front desk, talking to the Mrs. Isabelle Leech, our Caribbean proprietress. My senses were heightened from being held in Finbarr's arms. I might have turned and headed back to my room to avoid Chilton, if he hadn't glanced my way. Once he spotted me, a retreat would only garner suspicion. I kept my eyes down and tried to head past him to the dining room.

"Pardon me," Chilton said. "Miss."

"Mrs.," I corrected him, then smiled too stiffly. I could feel the edge of my lips stretch unnaturally. "Mrs. O'Dea." After escaping the baths I had walked to another hotel to clear my head and bought a new shawl at their gift shop, as well as some paper and a fountain pen. Perhaps I'd write a story while I was here, or a poem. I pulled the shawl close around me, and its price tag tumbled from the dark threads.

Chilton reached out and touched it. "Is that what you're worth, then?"

It was the sort of jest I loathed, but something in his face made me relax. He looked embarrassed at making such an easy joke. He looked mild, even kind. It was bad luck to have a police inspector at the hotel, but I saw at once it was good luck that it happened to be this one.

"Here you go." Mrs. Leech passed me a pair of shears. "Inspector Chilton's here looking for a lady gone missing from Berkshire."

"Goodness. Missing from Berkshire and you're searching for her in Yorkshire?"

"All of England's in on this hunt," he explained. "Inspectors and police officers dispatched to every county."

This news set my teeth on edge. I smiled to conceal it. "My, my. She must be ever so important."

Chilton intercepted the shears and cut the tag off for me. "If I could trouble you just a moment, Mrs. O'Dea." He placed the snipped price tag in my hand. His fingers were chapped and tobacco stained, his clothing rumpled. He held out a photograph with his right hand. His left dangled at his side. "This is the lady. Have you seen her?"

"May I?"

He nodded and I eased the photograph out of his hand. Agatha stared back at me, hair swept off her face, head tilted, wearing pearls and a suit jacket. I thought of my mother, wresting herself out of her grief over Colleen to help me have the little picture made for Finbarr, to send to him at the front. I had worn my best dress, no jewelry at all, nowhere near so glamorous.

"Pretty. But, no, I haven't seen her in Yorkshire." I hoped he'd remember my precise words if any connection between the two of us was drawn later. "I do hope she'll be all right." I handed the photograph back to him.

"Ah, well," Chilton said, as if he hadn't expected any other reply. "Thank you for looking."

As I entered the dining room, I saw that Mrs. Race—the beautiful blond bride—was now joined by her handsome, scowling husband. The two of them sat by a window, too absorbed in their silent unhappiness to notice my probably obtrusive stare.

My new friend, Lizzie Clarke, waved me to her table, and her husband stood to offer me a chair. He was a lanky fellow, charmingly inelegant the way Americans can be, with dark eyes and a sweet, earnest expression.

"Donny Clarke," he introduced himself.

"Hello, Mr. Clarke."

"Please. Call me Donny. Thanks so much for entertaining Lizzie this morning. Fun to make a fast friend on vacation."

I'd scarcely unfolded my napkin before I heard merry, unmistakable laughter as Mrs. Marston entered the room with her husband. She looked quite a bit different from when I'd last seen her at the baths. Her hair was curled, and she wore a smart jacket and faux pearls.

"Well, look who it is," Mrs. Marston said, stopping by our table. "The chummy young ladies."

The husband, Mr. Marston, stood by her side. He was decades older than she, a weathered, ruddy faced man in his sixties. He placed a hand at the back of Donny's chair, his smile the indulgent sort a certain kind of man likes to bestow upon young ladies. I turned my eyes back to our table. Lizzie stared back at him more frankly.

"How do you do, Mr. Marston," Lizzie said. "I trust married life is treating you well?"

"Sure and it is," he said, thickly Irish. A change came over his face and he seemed suddenly eager to return to his table. "Are you ready to eat now, Mrs. Marston?"

She trilled with delight at the sound of her married name. Mr. Marston put his wide, meaty hand at the small of her back and guided her hastily to an empty table.

"You all right, Lizzie?" I asked.

She nodded emphatically.

The waitress came to take our order. We had a choice of fish pie, roast beef, or chicken stew, and we all chose the roast beef. The room had great, tall windows and I found myself staring through them, one at a time, expecting Finbarr to be standing on the other side, watching me. The sun had long since set; even if he'd been there, he wouldn't be visible. Where was he spending the night? Would he have a hot meal, or any meal at all? Just this morning it had been years since he'd last held me. Now it was merely hours.

I glanced over at the Marstons, busily unfolding their napkins. Mrs. Marston appeared cheerful as ever. Her husband was harder to read.

"Don't bother yourself with those two," Lizzie said. "There's much better people watching over there." She jutted her chin at the beautiful young couple. Mr. Race looked peeved and arrogant, Mrs. Race stubbornly tearful.

Almost as if Lizzie had known exactly what was about to happen, a commotion erupted.

"I don't care," Mrs. Race cried, loud enough for every diner to not only hear, but fall silent. She jumped to her feet nimbly, throwing down her napkin. "I don't care how much the wedding cost or what people will say. I can't go on. I simply can't!"

"See here," her husband said in a whisper that was no less audible but far more chilling than his wife's outburst. "Sit down and stop making a scene."

The young bride turned as though to storm out of the room. Her husband reached out to grab her wrist. Before I had a chance to worry about damage to those slim, delicate bones, she picked up her foot and stomped his foot, hard enough to make him let go.

"What will you do?" she asked. "Hit me? In front of all these people?"

There was a scuffle as most of the men in the room—including Donny and Inspector Chilton—rose to their feet and approached the Races' table, ready to intervene. Lizzie stood, too, and stepped toward the scuffle for a better look. Her bravery impressed me, but I remained seated, my view of the scene obscured by the crowd of concerned onlookers.

The door to the dining room flew open and in marched the owner of the hotel. "Look here," Simon Leech said. "That's quite enough of that."

"This is nobody's business but our own," Mr. Race announced to the room at large.

"In that case best not to have rows in public." The last thing Mr. Leech needed was trouble at his struggling hotel.

He kept his voice stern but kind. "Let me buy you a bottle of champagne. You're newlyweds, after all. It's a time for celebration, not arguing."

I looked over at Mrs. Marston, who was still twisted round in her chair, away from her husband, so as to watch the spectacle. A look of consternation crossed her face, as if she—also newly wedded—deserved a bottle of champagne, too. Mr. Marston rose to his feet, but his purpose was not to request equal treatment. He had his hands to his throat and sputtered wildly as if he wanted to gasp but couldn't.

"Darling!" his wife cried, turning back toward him. "Oh, my darling. Help him, please, somebody help him!"

Mr. Marston fell to the floor. His eyes bulged, his hands clasped his throat, and his feet kicked like a freshly landed fish. Almost everyone—the hotel staff as well as the guests—headed over to the scene of distress.

Young Mrs. Race reached him first. "Stand back," she commanded, seeming a different person from the one who'd just done battle with her husband. "I'm a nurse." She loosened Mr. Marston's tie and shirt collar, then took his pulse. By now she had his head pulled into her lap, and something about that pretty young girl balancing his wide, red, froggish face so close to her body was grotesque to me.

By now Lizzie had returned to her seat; she and I did not move from our table. We sat, quietly watching everything unfold. Lizzie took a sip of wine and said, "Too many cooks."

"If you ask me, it's too late," I said. The violence in Mr. Marston's body had come to rest. His eyes stared glassily at the ceiling.

The doctor who performed massages had gone for the day,

but there was another one, a guest staying in room 403. Someone ran to fetch him. All poor Mrs. Marston could do was crouch beside her husband, staring in shock at the scene before her. The doctor arrived half-dressed. He was youngish but prematurely white-haired and looked elegant and purposeful despite his indecent state.

"It's no use," the doctor said, after a swift examination. He looked around the room, addressing all of us with an appropriately solemn expression. Then with practiced fingers he pulled Mr. Marston's eyelids closed.

The sound that emanated from Mrs. Marston was altogether unholy. She clutched at her throat as her husband had done earlier, and for a moment I thought she might also fall to her death.

"Come now," said Inspector Chilton, stepping forward. He put his arms around her shoulders. She accepted his embrace, her screams giving way to sobs. Chilton led her across the room to another table and seated her with her back to her deceased husband.

"A hefty dose of brandy will do for her," the doctor said. "And perhaps a sheet for him, while we wait for the coroner to arrive. Best go ahead and call the authorities."

"Oh, you've no idea," Mrs. Marston was sobbing. "How long we waited, what we've been through, what we've given up. Oh, my poor dear darling. It can't be. Just like that? It can't. Where will I go? What will I do?"

She pushed herself up from the table and rushed back to her husband, throwing herself upon him and weeping. The force of her ministrations startled the body enough that his eyes popped open. Mrs. Marston gasped, a pathetic and hopeful moment, then commenced to weep again as she realized he hadn't come back to life, and she'd lost him for the second time.

"I believe I'll take this plate to my room," I said to Lizzie and Donny. I'd barely taken a bite.

"Yes," Lizzie said. "We'll talk later. Will you be all right?"

"I believe I will. And you?"

She nodded but her eyes brimmed. We'd witnessed a shocking thing.

As I passed the grandfather clock in the front hall, I saw Mr. and Mrs. Race by the stairs, no longer scowling or arguing. The tragedy seemed to have subdued them. Her head was lowered, and though his hand was on her arm, it did not seem to be an aggressive grip. Their foreheads pressed together. Perhaps he was apologizing, or even comforting her. I paused a moment, and when neither of them looked toward me, I continued on.

My room had a wide four-poster bed and a little writing desk. I sat down at the latter and used it for my dinner table. It pushed up to a window, and again I looked out into the darkness, as if for all the world I were fourteen years old and back in Ireland, knowing Finbarr might arrive any moment for lawn tennis.

The death I'd witnessed had not spoiled my appetite, not for food and not for love. I cleaned my plate, having learned during the War never to waste food. Sleep was another matter. The bed was comfortable. Eventually the ruckus downstairs quieted. I lay still, trying to clear my mind, unable to close my eyes, staring up at the canopy. I must have fallen asleep eventually, because by the time sunlight poured through the drapes I'd forgotten to close, I was awakened by a scream.

The Disappearance

DAY FOUR

Tuesday, December 7, 1926

I donned my dressing gown and peered into the hall, making myself one of several faces dotting the corridor, all belonging to women. I could hear the doctor's voice inside a room not far from mine, presumably the origin of the scream, trying to calm someone down. Mrs. Leech, I surmised. The door directly across the hall from me opened with an urgent audible whoosh, bespeaking great confidence. There stood Miss Cornelia Armstrong, the young lady traveling on her own.

"That was Mrs. Marston's room," she announced for the whole hotel to hear. Miss Armstrong was barely nineteen, with impeccable posture and thick black hair spilling down her back in astonishing quantity. She had a way of lifting her chin as she spoke, daring the listener to contradict her.

"Oh, dear," I said.

"I'm going to see what's happened."

There was no stopping her. Miss Armstrong marched

down the hall toward Mrs. Marston's room. Miss Armstrong had her dressing gown loosely belted and was showing more of her décolletage than she likely intended. When she returned, her face was pale, and her voice shook as she reported, "Mrs. Marston is dead. I saw the doctor pull the sheet over her face."

By now more guests had gathered in the hall, including a painfully thin spinster who covered her mouth with one slim, freckled hand and gasped, "How dreadful."

"I suspect she died of a broken heart," Miss Armstrong announced to the bleary-eyed gatherers with an air of diagnostic expertise. She had delicate white skin and eyes almost black as her hair. "They'd been star-crossed, you know, Mrs. and Mrs. Marston. Before they married."

I wanted to say I was thankful I shouldn't have to hear that phrase—*star-crossed*—ever again in my life. I wanted to say if it was possible for a broken heart to kill, I'd have been dead long ago. Instead I closed my door without another word. Given the situation, the usual manners did not apply.

Chilton was downstairs using the telephone to call Lippincott. He heard the scream but, muffled as it was, did not pay it particular notice. Perhaps one of the ladies had come upon a spider.

"Will you be sparing a man to investigate?" he asked Lippincott, referring to Mr. Marston's death.

"There's no man to spare, that's why you're here in the first place. Probably nothing to it. A heart attack is my guess."

Of course this was likely right. Why would anyone want to harm the old Irishman?

Just as Chilton rang off, Mrs. Leech came rushing down the stairs, looking most discombobulated. "Mrs. Leech?"

She held up her hand, too weepy to answer, and rushed to the kitchen, where her husband oversaw breakfast preparations. After a moment the doctor came downstairs, no more fully dressed than he'd been the previous night, sweat gathered on his brow despite the season. Chilton gave him a handkerchief. The two had chatted last night while they shared a cigarette and waited for the coroner to collect poor Mr. Marston and had already established battles in common.

The doctor mopped his brow. "Damn it all. I'm supposed to be on holiday."

"What's happened now?"

"Another death. The wife. Mrs. Marston. What a honeymoon they're having, eh?"

"Gads. Well. Perhaps now they're having the ultimate honeymoon. Reunited in the hereafter." Chilton didn't believe this for a moment, but he had an inkling the Marstons would have liked the idea. They had that look about them, a smug religiosity, as if happiness were owed, in this life and whatever followed. He hadn't had a chance to chat with Marston before the old man keeled over, but even though plenty of older men had signed up to do their bit in the War, Chilton could tell Marston hadn't been one of them.

Because jocularity could be soothing under the most dire circumstances, Chilton thought about saying something such as *Who'd you think would want to off that pair?* Certainly the odds of the first death being suspicious were elevated now the man's wife was dead.

"Any ideas about the cause?"

"Not a mark on her, at least at a glance, nor anything else disturbed. Young for it to be heart failure, though she'd certainly had a shock."

"Did she take anything? Last night?"

The doctor bristled. "I gave her a simple sleeping draft. Perfectly harmless."

"Of course. Damn shame."

"Indeed. I might be cutting this holiday short. Hardly seems right. Or restful, for that matter."

Chilton nodded and took his leave. He felt a little guilty for having disliked the Marstons at first sight. For now he'd take care of his primary order of business, searching for Agatha Christie. He'd canvas the hotels, keep an eye out on the roads. Carefully doing his duty.

After the unfortunate ruckus I skipped breakfast, instead bundling up in my warmest clothes. As I passed the front desk, Mrs. Leech greeted me with frantic cheer. "Off for a walk, are you? Lovely day for it, cold air will do you good. Terrible about the Marstons, him dying of a heart attack and her of a broken heart."

"Has the coroner made his conclusions already?"

"Well, then, what else could it be? So sad, so sad, but could have happened anywhere! Nothing to do with us!"

I gathered more than one guest had already checked out, the hot baths not seeming much of a cure in the wake of two sudden deaths. The last thing the Leeches' hotel needed.

Walking down the dusty road, I thought of my conversation with Ursula Owen at Godalming on the night of Agatha's disappearance, about lucid dreaming. And how lucid living would be a lovely corollary. As a girl I'd had that very ability—to think of Finbarr and suddenly he'd appear. On this day in Harrogate, for the first time since the Armistice celebration, I knew I'd regained the power. Nothing else supernatural was afoot. I felt confident the ghosts of the Marstons were well and truly departed. But I knew that if I walked the same direction Lizzie and I had done yesterday, Finbarr would appear.

Sure enough, when I rounded just the corner I'd envisioned, there he was: hands in his pockets, breath gusting out before him, cheeks rosy. This time I didn't run to him but walked and kept walking as he held out his arms, straight into them.

"Are you all right?" I asked. "Are you eating? Sleeping?"

"Yes," he said into my ear. His hand at my back was steady, no tremor. "Are you?"

"Me?" I pulled away from him. "I'm staying in a hotel. Luxury. Food. Roof and hearth fires. Where are you staying?"

"Where there's a roof and a hearth. You're not to worry about us, Nan."

"Us?"

Someone walked over my grave. I had the most illogical, most glorious vision: Finbarr beside a wide hearth with a crackling fire, holding our child in his lap.

Chilton drove over rutted roads in the car Lippincott had provided. He slowed down as he passed a couple, young if not tenderly so, the man old enough to have been in the War and with the look of someone who had been (Chilton could tell at a glance from almost any distance). Sometimes it seemed he himself still lived in the tunnels at Arras, under the shaking ceilings, roots and rubble falling. The claustrophobia, and the knowledge that if you followed your instinct and broke free, you'd find yourself in an onslaught of enemy fire. Then you'd find yourself dead, riddled with machine-gun bullets. If only Chilton had known at the time how he'd come to long for that outcome.

This young man must still want to be alive, judging by the way he held the girl by the elbows—with such fervor Chilton slowed down to make sure the embrace was a willing one. Both were so caught up in each other's face they didn't seem to notice the car, or Chilton's scrutiny. The girl was small and dark haired, her face so full of emotion that she might not be British. French, perhaps. Whatever her nationality, she clearly wasn't in peril—at least from the fellow who held on to her. From her own emotions, well, that was another matter.

Chilton changed gears and motored on, the girl's face still in his mind. He had met her. Yes, she was staying at the Belle-fort Hotel; he'd shown her the picture of Agatha Christie and she'd examined it dutifully. No wonder he hadn't immediately recognized her. She had seemed perfectly contained in that moment—a good English lady after all. *Mrs.* O'Dea, she'd said. The young man wasn't her husband, and he wasn't a guest at the hotel, Chilton was sure of both. What secret lives people do lead.

Chilton's reveries took him on one wrong turn, then another, down a particularly dim country road. He pulled over to take out the map Mrs. Leech had given him. As he turned off the motor, he noticed a house, shut up for winter, the windows boarded, but with smoke rising from the chimney in a steady swirl. He stepped out of the car. The air smelled like firewood and mulched leaves. As he got closer to the house, he saw an automobile was parked beside it. Somebody had meant to hide it, from the looks of the way it was left toward the back, with low elm branches obscuring it from the road. Dragged there, not grown. The car was large and black. Chilton couldn't say the make of it, he wasn't much for cars. The front stoop of the house was caked with frozen dust. No footprints. Chilton put his ear to the door, which was made of thick wood—a modest but well-built country house, sturdy and generous with space and materials. Lovely gables. From inside he heard a clattering that it took a moment to identify as typewriter keys. A cheerful, industrious sound, *clackety clack clack clack*. He used the heavy brass knocker and felt almost sorry when the noise abruptly stopped, followed by irritated footsteps. He stepped back as the door flung open.

The woman was on the tall side, with red hair and lively eyes. Her face rearranged itself the moment she saw him, from expectation to dismay to the kind of courteous mask people use to protect themselves from the truth. She wore a man's clothes: trousers, and a thick cardigan over a collared shirt. Then, just barely visible, pearls.

"How do you do," she said in smooth, posh tones. Her hair fell to her shoulders in loose waves. She brushed both sides self-consciously behind her ears, then held out a hand as if he'd been invited for tea.

Chilton took her hand. She was prettier than in the picture he'd left on the passenger seat of the automobile. Fairer and more youthful, with the kind of movement in her face—even as she tried to appear unmovable—that no picture can properly capture. Eyes not dark, as they'd seemed, but bright blue flecked with green. At the same time, unmistakably the same woman.

"Mrs. Agatha Christie. My goodness. We've been looking for you."

Part Two

"There are more important things than
finding the murderer."

—Hercule Poirot

The Disappearance

Agatha drove away from Styles just past midnight, hardly caring if she ever saw it again. The house was unlucky, she'd felt it from the first day she set foot inside. Archie had been the one who wanted to buy it, so he could be nearer to his golf club. Damn golf. Damn Archie. Clearly there was no reasoning with him. Perhaps she'd have better luck with me.

She had left the house earlier for a short while, at 9:45. The reports were correct on that account. Agatha headed out, driving awhile to clear her mind, then turned round and came home, letting herself inside while the household slept. The house felt dark and quiet and empty. Bad luck clung to the ceilings like billows of smoke. Her skin was too small to contain the rage and sorrow and anxiety; she wanted to claw at herself to escape it. She wanted to burst, splattering herself and all her misery over the walls. She yanked off her wedding ring and threw it hard as she could at the wall, so that it dinged the paint and then fell to the floor, spinning several times before wobbling to rest. Let it be swept up with the dust tomorrow.

It wouldn't do. It couldn't be borne. If she were a drinker, she would have polished off a bottle of something, but she wasn't, so she gathered up her typewriter and some things to carry her over for a few days. She would go to Ashfield to get her mind straight. But once she had loaded her things into the car and climbed behind the wheel, she changed her mind. She would not politely allow that monstrous little hussy to upend her life entirely. Not without a fight. Instead of slinking away to her childhood home to brood, she would drive directly to Godalming and march into the Owens' cottage and cause an unbearable scene. So what if it was past midnight? So what if she woke every last person in the house? It wouldn't endear her to Archie, but what did that matter? She'd already thrown herself on his mercy and found he had none. But his mistress might be a different story.

Agatha regretted the genteel approach she'd taken with me on the pavement in front of Simpson's. Now she imagined grabbing me by the shoulders, perhaps with a measured shake, and demanding I give up her husband. If that didn't work, she'd fall to her knees and beg. She'd let all the anguish pour out, visible and audible. *Angoisse*, her mother would have said—she'd liked to use French when discussing emotion, on the rare occasions she determined emotion had to be discussed. But Agatha would not allow any mollifying translation. Imagining it, she thought, *Nan might take pity*. The girl was a slut, not a monster.

It was difficult to see beyond the windscreen, between the darkness and her eyes, puffed to slits from crying. Otherwise she might have seen him earlier, the man who walked down the middle of the road, trying to flag her down, his long arms waving in and out over his head in X formation. As it was, she nearly ran him down to his death. It felt to her as if the last moment, when she swerved to miss him, realizing—again at the last moment—that if she didn't put on the brakes, she'd fly headlong into the chalk pit.

Not something she longed for, death. Not one bit. The sort of thing you realize, in the instance after an accident almost kills you. And after all, she knew a good bit about poison, between her stint in the dispensary during the War, and research for her novels. If she'd wanted to be dead, she already would be.

There was a knock on the driver's-side window. The man she'd swerved to avoid killing leaned down, staring at her with unnerving calm, as if all this were perfectly normal. Perhaps now he'd kill *her*, but she rolled down the window anyway. Black hair fell into his eyes, and his breath gusted in the cold air. From his coat and black hair she recognized him as the same fellow who'd given Teddy the whittled dog.

"Are you quite all right?" He had a raspy Irish brogue and soulful blue eyes.

"I believe I am."

"I'm sorry if I startled you."

"Startled me? My dear, you ran me quite off the road."

He opened the door to her car, so she could get out. She felt it again, the awareness that perhaps she ought to be afraid of him. The car wobbled precariously, and she saw its front wheels were hanging over the pit. It struck her again with the force of averted tragedy, how very much she wanted to be alive.

"I've come to talk to you about Nan O'Dea," the young man said.

Oh, the impudence. The way the world was unfolding before

her. An awful dream. *Wake up*, she commanded herself. *Wake up, wake up.* She closed her eyes, determined to open them and find herself home in bed with her husband. Even as the cold air insisted she was out on the road in the dead of night, confronted by a stranger wanting to discuss the most intimate horror of her life.

"Mrs. Christie, I think we might be able to help each other. You and I." He had a nice face. *Très sympathique,* her mother would have said. A handsome young man with an aura of kindness about him, if sadly lacking any humor. She raised her hands and placed them over her face.

"There now," the Irishman said. She removed her hands and he gently touched her cheek just below her eye, where a tear would have fallen. "We'll have time for tears later, won't we? It's cold and there's some traveling to do."

"I don't know if my car will start." As if this were the reason not to go with him. Not even considering that she'd be traveling with this stranger. Not even worrying that she must have gone mad not to at least try to back up and drive away, fast as possible.

"We'll leave it. That'll give them something to worry about, won't it? As luck would have it, we're both up and about after dark. And I've recently come upon a vehicle nobody seems to be using."

"Stolen?"

"Abandoned not far from here, on the grass by the road. I've borrowed it."

"So you'll be returning it then?" Her voice was skeptical and pointed.

"If I can."

His voice had a melancholy that pinched Agatha's already-vulnerable heart. "How lucky." She suddenly wanted to be forgiving. "The luck of the Irish, I suppose."

A rasping sound, the sad echo of a laugh that never was. "I'm afraid to say I've not found much truth in that expression."

Ah, she thought, the light dawning. This was Nan's young man. Agatha had scarcely paid attention to what the girl had said about her past the other day at Simpson's. Now Agatha narrowed her eyes, unsure of what to do. The last thing she needed was another man in love with Nan O'Dea.

Still, she stepped out of the car and placed her hand in his. He nodded, as if proud of her for making the right decision, and she decided to let herself be convinced and give herself over to his care. The scene she'd planned in Godalming would be of no use. But this fellow could be.

"You gather what you need," he said, "and I'll bring the other car round."

Dazed enough to forget her hastily packed suitcase, Agatha transferred the most immediate necessities—her sponge bag, her typewriter—into a roomy Bentley. Before getting into it, she stopped a moment and stared longingly at her own car. You must understand how she adored that vehicle. How proud she was at buying it herself, with money earned from her writing. Perhaps right now someone was sitting in front of a fire, unable to sleep, turning the pages of her latest novel, *The Murder of Roger Ackroyd*. The embodiment of that, to her, was the wonderful little car, now teetering on the brink of destruction, just like her life.

Very well then. She'd leave it behind for another.

The Irishman drove. It always seemed right to Agatha, when

a man and a woman were in a car together, that the man should drive. The road lay ahead of them, empty and bleak, stars shining down, the moon a waning crescent. The barest wind snuck through the windows, shaking in their frames. This car was not so well kept as her own.

How rarely she ever found herself awake and about in the darkened world. The man sitting next to, driving, was such an entirely different presence from her husband. And just in that moment, only half-awake, only half believing in the ruin her life had become, Agatha realized her skin fit again. She found herself thinking or, more accurately, feeling:

What an adventure.

Here Lies Sister Mary

Years after my stay at the convent—years after my stay at the Bellefort Hotel—I had another baby, a girl whom I named after my aunt Rosie. I would have liked to have more children, but for Archie one child from each of his wives was enough. He never wanted too much of my attention taken from him. Committed to being the wife he wanted, I found it easy enough to spend the days lavishing love on my child, and the evenings lavishing love on my husband. Unlike Agatha, I never became a writer. For me that possibility fell away.

It's all right. I loved being a mother and I loved my little Rosie. But a hundred babies, a thousand, would never make up for the loss of the first.

Fallen away. That's what the nuns told us we'd done. Fallen away.

Mr. Mahoney called the convent a charity. *The sisters will take good care of you.* But to me it felt awfully like the workhouse I was lucky to have avoided. Later I learned the history. Somewhere between 1900 and 1906, Pelletstown, the first special institution for unwed mothers, had been established in County Dublin. Not long afterward the convent at Sunday's Corner followed suit. In exchange for what they called our safe haven, we would labor without pay until our babies were born. Then we would stay on another two or three years, working. Our children would remain in the convent—first in the nursery and then on the other side of that high cement wall—until they were adopted, fostered out, or moved to an orphanage. We were meant to go to the county hospital in the City of Cork to deliver two weeks before our babies were due, but that spring a girl's water broke during lawn duty, when she swung a heavy scythe to cut the grass. She gave birth on a mattress by the laundry room with no doctor or nurse, only a few other girls in attendance. Afterward the nuns drove her and her baby to hospital in their farm truck. Ten days later she was back on the front lawn, pulling daisies and weeds, and wielding the scythe where needed.

Some girls worked the convent farm—tending ducks, milking cows, and digging potatoes—under the close watch of the nuns. But I was kept inside the gates. Perhaps the nuns saw escape in my eyes. I tended their graveyard and did laundry and scrubbed floors on my hands and knees. Each night I fell onto my bed exhausted to the core of my being. From growing a child inside me. From worry. From being so far from home. From waking each day at five for prayers and Mass, then laboring till six-thirty in the evening. And perhaps most exhausting of all, from loving Finbarr. From waiting for him to recover, return to consciousness, and come fetch me. A rumor persisted among the girls that a few years ago, someone's beau had shown up and paid the Mother Superior for her release. Father Joseph had married the couple in the parish church. Not all the girls were pregnant by boys they loved. But those who were, me included, counted on this fantasy as our only hope. I refused to consider Finbarr's death a possibility. We weren't allowed to send or receive letters, but surely his parents would tell him where I was, and he'd come for me. I didn't start wishing for him to come for *us* until the first day my baby kicked.

Bess, Fiona, Susanna, and I were working in the base-ment laundry over boiling, soapy cauldrons. The floor was tiled, a pattern of large gray squares and smaller blue and pink squares, a cruel commemoration of the babies most of us wouldn't be allowed to keep. Heat from the fires kept my forehead slick with sweat as I stirred sheets and napkins with a long wooden stick. All of a sudden my child moved inside my body: unmistakably, distinctly, gracefully. I froze with the magnitude of falling in love. Children have moved in the womb since the dawn of man, but never had any child moved in just this way. A somersault, toes grazing my insides, send-ing up a fountain of bubbles. I stopped, startled, and put my hand on my belly.

Bess stopped stirring and smiled. "It's like magic, isn't it?"

We weren't supposed to become friends or talk to each other or even know each other's names. But of course we did. Girls thrown together find friends sure as night follows day. I'd in-sisted Bess and Fiona memorize my family's address in London, so we could write to one another if this ever ended.

"Was it real?" I asked Bess, rubbing my hand over the spot where I'd felt the movement.

"Sure and it was." Bess was further along than me, but so

narrow and slight you could barely see the pregnancy beneath her apron and shapeless dress. "Did you think you were in all this trouble for the sake of a mirage?"

I laughed. The sound startled me, it had been so long since I'd heard such a sound from myself or anyone around me.

"Can't you be quiet?" Susanna snapped. She hated breaking rules. Susanna was the oldest girl in the convent, somewhere in her thirties. This was her second stay here. Last time her baby had been adopted at six months, and she'd remained another year before being released as a maid to a local family, only to return, pregnant again, five years later.

Sister Mary Clare, the youngest and kindest nun, came in to check on us. She was lenient enough not to chastise us for talking. The room filled with her humming, a haunting Gaelic tune that trailed her like a mist wherever she went. Unlike some of the other nuns, she didn't have a strop attached to her habit. Also unlike the other nuns, she was not Irish but English. The sound of her voice was a comfort to me. On one of my first days at the convent I had asked her how she came to Ireland.

"My father was Irish. When I was a girl, he sent me here to work for relatives."

My heart jumped with recognition.

The nun said, in a sad and dreamy voice, "It didn't go as I'd thought." It was the only time I ever saw her look anything but jolly.

Since that day I'd thought of her less as a nun and more like one of the girls. Sister Mary Clare, I was sure, had arrived at the convent by means of hardship. When she came into the laundry room, I didn't hurry back to work but stood exactly as I had been, hands out of the sink, fingers spread wide over my belly.

"Did the baby move?" Sister Mary Clare stepped close, putting one arm around me, and one soft hand on my stomach.

"Yes."

"Good work, Mother." She took out her own handkerchief and wiped my brow. She was only about ten years older than me, with a clear, unlined face, plain but made bright by smiling. None of the other nuns would ever call us "Mother." They only called us girls.

I set straight back to work. My baby rustled again, and all of a sudden I was not, as I'd thought, alone. Someone else was here with me, a member of my family, the closest person to me there had ever been in the world. Bess turned her eyes back to her washing, but I could see a little smile at the edges of her lips. The two of us, keeping each other company in the love we had for our babies.

Another nun, Sister Mary Declan, poked her head into the room. "Father Joseph's asking for you, Bess." Unlike her younger colleague, Sister Mary Declan *did* wear a strop tied to her habit and seldom hesitated to use it, no matter how young or pregnant the girl. We cast our eyes downward. Bess's smile disappeared, but she wiped her hands on her apron and dutifully followed the nun. Sister Mary Clare went along with them.

"Poor dear," said Fiona, watching Bess leave. "But I suppose the Father knows what's best for us, doesn't he?"

I couldn't glean from this whether Fiona knew why Father Joseph had summoned Bess. Fiona had grown up in an orphanage, then been released at the age of thirteen to work for distant relatives. A few months later their parish priest brought her here. I never heard Fiona say a word about the boy responsible. The convent burgeoned with girls who'd welcomed young men back from the War. Now the same men were dead from the flu, or fighting the Irish War of Independence, or simply gone on with their lives without a backward glance.

And of course some of us—such as Susanna and Fiona, I expected—had not been disappointed by boys we loved, but subjected to something far worse. Fiona's child was a year old now. He had just been moved from the nursery to the other side of the convent. She took comfort in the large raspberry birthmark on his forehead, which she thought would prevent him from being adopted. She never seemed able to think past their time here, and what would come afterward.

Fiona never questioned the nuns or the priest. *They know best*, she continually muttered to herself. *They know best.*

"Bess will be just fine," she sang now, stirring her cauldron like a young, harmless, and hopeful witch. "Her beau will come to get her and they'll be married. I know it, Nan." Even though I didn't argue or ask how she knew, she added pointedly, "I just do."

The joy of my baby's movement faded. Fiona had red hair and freckles; her fair skin was flush and sweaty from the steam.

"Bess's beau is American," Fiona told Susanna. "She met him when she was nursing wounded soldiers at a field hospital."

"Her mother should never have let her near the soldiers," Susanna said through clenched teeth. "And I do wish you two would stop talking."

"I think her man will come for her," Fiona said, ignoring the plea for silence. "I'm praying for it. From what she says, he sounds like a good lad." Fiona let go of her stick. "Let's take just a moment and pray for Bess. The sisters can't get mad if they see that, can they? A little prayer break? For Bess and her child and their happy ever after?"

"The sisters can get mad at anything they like," Susanna said, not budging from her station. "If you don't know that by now, you'll never know anything."

Susanna was right, but still Fiona and I clasped our hands and pressed our foreheads together. I didn't pray so much as worry. That Father Joseph would turn his attentions from Bess to me. I tried to pretend not to know what happened when he called her to him, but today, thinking of Bess's baby moving inside her same as mine, I couldn't move my mind away from the horror of it. I worried Finbarr had died, which I knew was all that would ever prevent him from coming to get me.

Magical Finbarr. If anyone could get me out of here, it was him. I closed my eyes, leaning into Fiona, and pictured him, tennis ball high in his hand.

Make a wish.

The two of us—no, the three of us—leaving this place safely, and together.

Granted.

Sister Mary Frances blustered in and cracked Fiona across the back with her cane.

"None of that," the old nun said, as if prayer were something that didn't belong to us anymore, except at the nuns' discretion. "It's only hard work that will wash your sins away."

Fiona straightened, smiling instead of wincing. "You're right, Sister." Fiona's voice sounded sweet and pure. "I know you're right."

I returned to my cauldron. Fiona rolled a cart of soaking sheets up to dry on the rooftop. This time of day she might catch a glimpse of her little boy in the yard. She worried because he wasn't walking yet. *Shouldn't he be walking,* she was sure to ask me, when she returned.

I tried to think of Bess, off with Father Joseph, as if prayers had done any good. As if I had it in me, despite all my sympathies and fondness, to pray for anyone except my baby, and myself.

The Disappearance

A gatha removed her hand from Chilton's the moment he said her name. What a fool she'd been to open the door. Finbarr had told her to keep her head low. He hadn't said not to answer the door because it likely hadn't occurred to him that anyone would come knocking, or that she'd be silly enough to answer if somebody did. But that's what she'd done, instinctively, obedient as ever. Somebody knocks and in the absence of your butler a polite lady is obliged to answer. *What power these customs do have over us,* Agatha thought, and steeled her spine ramrod straight, as if that could undo the mess into which good manners had propelled her.

"I'm afraid you're mistaken. I don't know anyone by that name."

"I have a photograph of you. It's there in the automobile. Shall I show it to you?"

"A photograph." She waved her hand in front of her face as if moving smoke out of the way. "One face in a photograph looks very much like another, doesn't it?"

Had they really sent police all the way to Yorkshire to search for her? What a needless fuss. She felt a terrible flurry in her stomach. If they were looking for her here—where no one had any reason to imagine she'd go—where else would they search? Who else would know she'd run off, and why? Oh, she hated to think of her stalwart new benefactors—her new agent and publisher—learning of this whole humiliating mess.

"Mrs. Christie," the man said gently. "My name's Inspector Frank Chilton. I'm representing the police department in Leeds. I've been charged with looking for you, though I daresay I never thought I'd find you."

He had a pleasant face and manner. Mild and kind. Agatha saw at once he'd be easy to dismiss. "I beg your pardon, Inspector Chilton. But I expect you didn't hear me. My name is not Agatha Christie."

She saw Chilton look past her, to where she'd stationed herself at the long farm table, notebooks piled on it, and her typewriter. She closed the door against herself, blocking his view.

"And your name, then?" He kept his tone kindly, but firm enough to remind her he was a police inspector.

"I don't suppose that's any of your business. My husband will be along shortly. Ah. There he is now."

She felt herself smile as Finbarr came up the walk, hands in his pockets and color in his cheeks. An entirely involuntary reaction. They'd been apart very little these last four days. She found herself very much wanting Chilton to believe she could be married to someone so young and handsome.

"What's this?" Finbarr said, reaching the front stoop. The

burlap bag over his shoulder bulged with what she felt sure were apples. Only this morning she'd said how she loved apples, and now here they were. Orange Pippin she supposed from the time of year. How she looked forward to biting into the crisp fruit.

"Darling." It wasn't the first time she'd called him that. He had nightmares. When she was wakened by his cries, she would go to him and calm him. *There, there, darling,* she would say. *You're perfectly safe.* Finbarr started a little, to hear her use the endearment in daylight, and in front of a stranger.

"This is Inspector Chilton. He seems to have mistaken me for a lady who's gone missing. What did you say her name was? This poor lost lady?"

"Mrs. Agatha Christie."

"Oh, dear. Poor thing. I do hope she'll be all right. And I do wish you luck in finding her." Good manners may have forced her to open the door, but they also made it frightfully easy to manage prying strangers. Follow the script, that was all she had to do.

"So that'll be all then," Finbarr said with a brusque nod at the inspector. Finbarr slipped by the man, nodding to Agatha in a polite, deferential manner that no man on earth would use with his wife. He started to close the door, but Chilton raised his hand and stopped it.

Finbarr draped an arm around Agatha's shoulder. She smiled again. In a few days they'd discovered a surprising amount in common. Their love of dogs, for instance. *I much prefer them to people, don't you?* And he had agreed before adding, *Most people, anyway.* Last night when she woke him from one of his terrible dreams, to comfort him, she'd thought about kissing him. That would serve Nan right, wouldn't it?

Now looking at Chilton, she was shocked to find herself thinking about kissing him as well. Despite what threat he posed to her continued hideout, he had such a nice kind way about him. He reminded her of Tommy, the fiancé she'd thrown over for Archie's sake. She refused to blush. Perhaps that was what women did when they found themselves abandoned by their husbands. Perhaps they thought about kissing new men. She wondered how this impulse jibed with her assurances to Finbarr that they had the same mission, convincing Nan to release Archie from her clutches. Part of Agatha felt nothing would assuage the pain of Archie being with another woman as effectively as being with another man.

"I beg your pardon," Chilton said, "but considering the resemblance, I'm afraid I have to insist you tell me your name."

"Her name's Nan Mahoney."

How annoying, and predictable, for Finbarr to supply that name. Agatha's smile disappeared.

"So if I go to the town registry," Chilton said, "I'll see this house belongs to the Mahoneys."

"Of course you will," Agatha said, at the same time Finbarr said, "We're letting it."

They looked at each other. Caught. But what did it matter? She hadn't committed any crime, other than squatting in someone else's house, which didn't seem so grave.

"Listen, Mrs. Christie. I know it's you. But I can give you another day to think things over and prepare yourself. I'll come back in the morning and we can decide together what you'd like to tell your husband. He's very worried, you know."

Agatha laughed, so harshly she worried she'd erased any doubt he might still have as to her identity.

Finbarr said, "Good day, Inspector." And closed the door. Before he took his arm off her shoulders he gave her a little squeeze of comfort. Her protector.

"Not to worry," he said.

Chilton walked back to the car, his head fairly swimming, trying to sort out what he'd just witnessed. If all of England were a haystack, with hundreds of police officers combing through the stalks, how extraordinary that he should be the one to find the needle. He picked up the photograph and studied it again. It was her, the same lady, he was certain of it. She was alive and would not be discovered at the bottom of any lake. What a happy thing, despite the myriad questions her discovery created, principal among them the identity of the young Irishman, whom so far today Chilton had witnessed with his hands on two unlikely but unprotesting women.

And what should Chilton have done? Marched her at gunpoint back to his car? And should he now go directly to Leeds and inform his friend Sam Lippincott that he'd found her?

No. Better to keep his promise. Give her another day to collect herself. Give himself another day to return to the Bellefort Hotel and soak in the hot pools. Eat Yorkshire pudding and sleep in the bed that was twice as wide and soft as any he'd ever owned. If Mrs. Christie were in danger, that would be one thing. But it seemed she was only in a rugged love nest with a handsome Irish bloke.

No. He would not expose Agatha Christie today. He wasn't sure exactly why he'd come to this decision. Perhaps he would change his mind tomorrow. But not today.

The Disappearance

Marriage has a hold not often acknowledged in the popular imagination. I never understood it fully until I was married myself. Whether a marriage begins in duty or convenience, or whether it begins in secret, whispered words and irresistible passion. Even when it begins in resentment or drizzles into nothing over the years, a bond is formed that's not easily broken. With his wife missing, Archie buckled under the strain of a yoke he'd believed he'd escaped. Over the last two years, since I'd come along, he'd thought of his wife mostly as Agatha. Now with her missing, possibly in danger, he began thinking of her, rather fervently, as "my wife."

Deputy Chief Constable Thompson stood firmly unmoved by Colonel Christie's professions of anguish. "We know about the girl," Thompson had announced the day before, arriving at Styles first thing in the morning.

Surely Archie had been tempted to say, *What girl?* But he

was smart enough to know when he was caught. "I know how this looks," he'd admitted, mistakenly taking on a tone of authority rather than contrition. "But I love my wife and would never harm her." Archie knew he had done no physical harm to Agatha, but the constable's furious gaze made him feel as though he had. Remembering the emotional pain to which his wife had been subjected, Archie felt simultaneously indignant with innocence and abject with guilt.

"We'll see about that," Thompson had said, regarding Archie with a scarcely contained rage. If Agatha Christie was found dead, it would be a tragedy, of which the only resulting pleasure could be marching her husband off to jail. Thompson ordered the search intensified.

Now Archie sat at his desk, the copy of the story Agatha had written—typed out but for the title, "The Edge," written across the top in a madwoman's print, as if the pen had nearly punctured the paper. He read it again. The husband came across all right. And the woman, vanquishing her rival, sending her rolling down the cliff to her death. Archie thought of his wife with a frightened kind of respect: *I don't know her*, he said to himself. *I don't know her at all.*

They might be searching for Agatha in every corner of England, but the main hub was Berkshire and Surrey. By Wednesday the counties abounded with hounds and police officers. Even airplanes, the first time they'd ever been used to look for a single missing person. The staff from the Coworth House, the largest estate in Sunningdale, took a day off to employ their knowledge of the region, which was naturally far superior to that of any police force. Professionally tight-lipped, they did not repeat any gossip relayed by the paltry staff at Styles (unaware that Anna had already seen to the matter, just what one could expect from a second-rate housemaid). They were all sure Mrs. Christie was now a corpse and took great umbrage at the idea of anyone other than themselves discovering it.

How disappointing when two first footmen *did* find poor Miss Annabel Oliver, frozen in a shallow stream, caught up in a snarl of brambles. A great cry went up at the sight of her, followed by disappointment. She was too old and too small to be Agatha Christie. One body would have been valuable. This body, belonging to someone nobody had reported missing, was not.

Archie walked down the road with Peter on a leash. He could hear the airplanes overhead, rotors slicing the air. Hounds bayed in the distance, a sound that had become ubiquitous since his wife disappeared.

If Agatha had done this to drive him mad, hats off to her. Peter pulled disobediently on his leash, and Archie yanked him back to his side. The dog had never liked him. But Deputy Chief Constable Thompson had asked Archie to bring Peter to the site where the Morris Cowley had been found. He could have driven but hoped the air—wind, really, cold enough to chap a man's skin—would do something to ease the unrest swirling inside his chest. *What have I done, what have I done?* Blown his life to bits, that's what. Caused this swirling mass, this appalling and unceasing to-do, all about him. The search was like Agatha's anguish come to life. And he had caused it, for the sake of a girl who was good at golf. The newspapers were blaring the news of

Agatha's disappearance all the way to the continents. The police knew about his affair, though they hadn't been able to track down Nan for an interview (he felt grateful to me, for lying low as promised). Still, how much longer before everything else came out, everything he'd done? Once Agatha saw the story of Archie and Nan made public, would she change her mind about wanting him back? When the whole world knew? Or had he ruined his marriage, his whole life, for what he'd begun to think of as nothing, a madness, a dalliance.

Police waited by his wife's car, still at Newlands Corner, where they'd pulled it back from the chalk pit. The officers regarded Archie sternly, many of them certain he'd done some foul play. As if that were possible. As if he had it in him. Couldn't they tell how desperate he was to see his wife found?

"Here you go, Peter," Archie said. The dog pulled on the leash again, in the direction of home. Agatha had spoiled him, allowing him on furniture, feeding him from her plate, walking him with no leash at all. Frustrated, Archie bent over to pick him up. Peter wriggled in his arms, whining. Two of the younger policemen exchanged glances. Amused or disgusted? The dashing colonel could no more control this little dog than he could his wife.

"Come on now, Peter." Archie placed the dog by the car, but Peter didn't sniff, he didn't do anything but turn round and round in whimpering circles.

"Well," said the more disapproving of the two officers. "I suppose that's enough of that."

"I suppose it is," Archie said. He unclipped Peter's leash and the dog immediately bolted down the road toward home.

"Hold up there," a voice called, as Archie set to trudge after the dog. It was Thompson, looking even sterner than usual.

At moments Archie felt sure the man was just on the brink of throttling him.

Archie opened his mouth to speak but found no voice came out at all. Instead it was Thompson's voice, obscuring whatever Archie had meant to say, with the calamitous words "There's been a development, I'm afraid. The search has turned up a body."

A body. Agatha? Surely not. To his horror Archie's knees buckled. His own body, which had always been such a faithful servant to him, committing so humiliating a betrayal. He had to reach out and grab Thompson's collar to keep himself from crumbling to the ground.

Thompson bent at the knees himself, leveraging his weight to keep the colonel upright. He wore an undecided and consternated expression. Was this grief he witnessed, or was it guilt?

My wife, thought Archie. *A body.* It wouldn't do. He couldn't bear it. The world rearranged itself into an inhospitable and unforgiving place. He would have let go of the officer, fallen to the road and wept, if only he'd been a different sort of man.

Early that same morning in Yorkshire, Chilton opened the door of his room to see the American woman Lizzie Clarke walk down the hall dressed for traveling. He pulled the door closed before she could notice him and saw her rap on a door, a delicate knock, careful to rouse only the occupant and nobody in neighboring rooms. Once the door had opened then shut, Mrs. Clarke disappearing into the room, Chilton removed his shoes and padded down the hall to listen.

"Donny's had a telegram," the American voice said. "We have to cut things short. Go back to the States."

To Chilton's ears, the voice that responded—female, British—sounded as though she knew someone was listening. A little too loud and not quite genuine. "I do hope everything is all right."

"Yes. Everything is perfect. *Perfect.*"

Chilton imagined the two women, sitting together on the un-made bed, hands clasped. Even with the note of falsehood in the other woman's tone, he sensed a kind of intimacy. He returned to his room and sat on the bench at the foot of his bed to lace his shoes, which he noticed were going about the seams. He would have to tell Lippincott this morning. *I've found Agatha Christie,* he would say. *Right as rain. No distress. All she wants is her privacy.*

Perhaps he and Lippincott could be kind about it and hatch a plan that would suit the authoress. They could tell the husband and no one else, call off the search, let her reappear when she was good and ready.

But even if the law could be convinced to let it rest, the press never would. Newspapers around the world were making a mint off this story. It was Mrs. Christie's good luck that some-one from the police had found her, instead of someone from the press. Mrs. Christie seemed to have chosen the one place in England nobody expected her to be.

And still she'd been found. Such was the world. There was never any hiding for long. He finished dressing and headed down to breakfast. The Clarkes were at the front desk settling up with Mrs. Leech.

"How do you do?" he said to the three of them. He pulled out a cigarette and brought it to his lips but did not light it. Mrs. Clarke looked uneasy for a scant second, then adjusted herself to a stark inscrutability.

"Good morning," she said, sharp American *r*. The husband said nothing, just shuffled bills into Mrs. Leech's hand.

"Thank you, Mr. Clarke," said Mrs. Leech. "So good of you to pay in full." More than one guest had fled since the two deaths, and not all had been so generous. "Prayers for your safe voyage."

Mr. Clarke turned to Chilton, drawing a match from his pocket and lighting the other man's cigarette. His wife said, "I'm looking forward to it, actually. Getting back on a ship. I think these hot pools are overrated. No offense." She glanced at Mrs. Leech with apology. "I just like cold water. Give me the open sea any day over a hot steamy cave."

The young husband returned the matchbox to his inside pocket and placed a hand between his wife's shoulder blades, maneuvering her toward the front door as if their exit were a dance.

"Bon voyage," Chilton said quietly, watching them go. The bellboy pushed a trolley holding their modest collection of luggage. Then Chilton said to Mrs. Leech, "How curious of them to come all this way, only to stay a few days. You'd think they'd at least go see the continent."

She asked him if he needed the telephone. In fact he had not only a need but an obligation. But he found himself saying no thank you. "Not just now. But I wonder if you know: Are there many abandoned houses in Harrogate?"

"Abandoned, certainly not. Unoccupied, yes, there's a few. Country homes for city folk, they come so rarely I wonder why they don't just stay in a hotel. I never did care for the city myself, Mr. Chilton."

"Nor I." He pulled at the hem of his tweed jacket, which felt loose, as though he'd lost still more weight. *It's important to eat*, he reminded himself. *It's important to work. To go through the motions.*

He proceeded to the sparsely populated dining room. Among the few guests, a young woman sat alone, staring intently out the window, a cup of tea cooling untouched on the table in front of her. Chilton walked over directly.

"May I?" He pulled out a chair for himself.

What choice did I have but to answer, "Yes."

Inspector Chilton had an advantage over me, the kind a police officer enjoys. He didn't know how I was connected to Agatha Christie, but he knew I *was* connected. I had no idea he was possessed of such information. I was still fairly reeling from the news Finbarr had given me: that *us* meant him and Agatha, that she was in hiding with him here in Harrogate. How much more would I have reeled if I'd known Chilton shared this knowledge? As it was, he hardly worried me at all.

What did worry me was Finbarr, and the effect his reappearance would have on my future. How could I return to Archie's arms after being in Finbarr's? *One must respect the psychology.* It had taken a good deal of work on the part of my own psychology, working through warring emotions to carry out my plan and become Archie's wife. Finbarr's appearance threatened to upend every bit of that.

Three years ago, when I set my sights on Archie, I knew it would never do to approach him. Instead I placed myself in his line of vision. I found out what he liked and became that, looking away instead of allowing our eyes to meet. The perfect golf swing, the shyest smile. Like following a recipe that results in a beautiful cake, each step worked out just as it was meant.

Chilton didn't seem the sort of man who'd require that sort

of game. He was approachable. Humble but not in a lowly way. In a likable one. He smiled almost sheepishly as he unfolded his napkin. Everything about him seemed frayed—his clothes, his face, and his hair, which needed combing rather badly. He took tea instead of coffee.

"Jitters," he explained, holding out his one good, slightly trembling hand, "since the War."

"I'm sorry."

Finbarr had no tremors. Each man carried the War differently. I liked that Chilton announced his weakness rather than attempting to hide it.

He said, "I see your friend has left."

"My friend?"

"The American lady, Miss Clarke."

"Yes, she did say she was leaving. But we're not particular friends. I only just met her the other day."

"Did you?"

"Yes. I've never been to America."

"And her first trip to England?"

"I don't believe we discussed it."

Chilton looked at me in a way I found unsettling. It was a full, unabashed examination. Not a leer, not at all, but searching, and then assessing what he found. I did not love his questions about Lizzie Clarke, but at the same time I found him endearing, and faced with his gaze, I couldn't help but bestow a small smile, as if I needed to comfort him.

The waitress approached our table but he waved her away.

"How do you know I don't want to order something?" I asked. Something I would never say to Archie. Or Finbarr, only because he would never dismiss a waitress without first finding out if I was hungry.

"Do you?"

I shook my head.

"It's an astonishing business," Chilton said.

"You mean the disappearance? That lady novelist?"

"Why no. That's not what I meant. Though surely that's astonishing as well."

"Have they found her?"

"No indeed. Her whereabouts are still very much a mystery."

"I think it's wonderful. For a lady to become an author."

He looked surprised by this slant change in subject. "Why yes. I think so, too."

"I used to dream of becoming one myself. But life got in the way."

Chilton nodded. He wasn't surprised at my confiding. It's the sort of thing that happened, at these hotels, away from the usual world. People told each other things. It's why my fast friendship with Lizzie Clarke was not suspicious.

"But you're still young. Surely you've time to write a hundred books, if you like."

"Surely." I clattered my coffee cup back to its saucer.

"What's astonishing to me," he said, returning to his purpose, "is the Marstons."

"Yes. Astonishing. Would you excuse me, Mr. Chilton? I've finished here. I do wish you a good day." I put my napkin on the table and stood. "If you don't mind, Mr. Chilton, I must say, you don't seem at all the type to holiday at a spa."

"Have I said I'm on holiday?" He tilted his head and for

just a moment he did not look unassuming. He looked rather shrewd.

"No, of course. You're searching for Agatha Christie. I wish you good fortune in that endeavor, Mr. Chilton. Good day."

I left the dining room, unsure of what to do with myself next. The conversation with Mr. Chilton left me exhausted. How difficult it is to walk through the world with your insides intact.

Looking back on this stretch of time, not just my days in Harrogate but all the years between the two Great Wars, I often think how fine it should have been. We allowed ourselves to believe evil had been defeated, as if evil never did rise twice. We had so many of the modern conveniences—telephones, automobiles, electric lights—but not *too* many of them, and not too readily available. Later there would be an overabundance of noise and glare. We could all be too easily reached. The very stars dimmed from the lights reflected on earth, and you could never do what I'd just done, escape from your ordinary life and fade away, undetectable.

I went up to my room and sat on my bed, picking up *The Great Gatsby* to read its final chapters. My eyes scanned the text, but it was my own story that filled my mind. The Clarkes had packed up and gone away. What if I did the same? I could never go back to Ireland. But what if I said to Finbarr, *Forget Ballycotton. Let's go away somewhere else. Anywhere but Ireland. Anywhere but England.* I could leave Agatha and Archie Christie in the past and take hold, finally, of my own future. Begin anew. As if such a thing were possible.

A distinct sound reached me through the window I didn't remember opening. Perhaps my imagination. Certainly it couldn't have come from the hotel. It might have come from a pram

ambling down the road. But I felt for certain I heard a baby crying. That sharp, insistent mewl of need and hunger. A pain stuck
my breasts, stinging, as if they wanted to let down milk. I threw
my book aside, stood, and pulled the window closed. I could
never leave England. Not even with Finbarr.

Chilton knew it would not do to let Mrs. Christie go undiscovered for long. Resources were being lost. People were worried.
He thought it might be less embarrassing to her—that she
could rectify everything more quietly—if she allowed him to
deliver her home. He decided to go to her straightaway and
make this offer. The two of them, driving through the countryside. He found himself thinking less about the moment he
appeared with her in Sunningdale—a hero—and more about
the journey itself. What would they find to talk about, as they
drove the country roads?

But when he arrived at the house where he'd discovered Agatha, intent on convincing her of his plan, no smoke was spiraling from the chimney. Where the car had been hidden there
were only the tire marks it left behind, the branches that had
covered it neatly stacked on the grass. Chilton pushed the front
door gently, not even touching the knob. It swung open without
resistance or complaint. The rooms he walked through were
empty of occupants. The ash sat cold in the fireplace. In one
bedroom a light scent of lavender lingered. Atop the dresser
was a crisp five-pound note.

Chilton sat on the bed and pressed a pillow to his face. Inhaled. By the time the home's rightful occupants returned, there'd
be no discernible trace of the perfume, but the next person to

sleep on this pillow would inexplicably dream of fields filled with purple flowers.

He might not care for his career anymore, but he still had a modicum of pride, plus Lippincott to consider. Unless he managed to find Agatha a second time, he couldn't possibly reveal, to anyone, the first.

Here Lies Sister Mary

We slept in a dormitory on the second floor of the convent, narrow beds in a row, close together. During the day, the room was locked so nobody could steal upstairs to rest. At night, once we were in bed, the doors were locked again, the nuns the only ones who had the keys. Sometimes I still dream about the convent catching fire, all of us locked inside that room with no escape.

It was a restless place to sleep, even in our exhaustion. The nursery was just below us, and we could hear babies wake and cry. When Susanna last stayed here, there had been a different Mother Superior. At night the nuns would pin the babies' gowns to their cots and leave them till they could be nursed in the morning. "It was the worst agony I ever felt," Susanna said, "hearing my baby cry with no way to get to her. Of course it's no accident they have us sleeping where we can hear them."

Punishment, wherever it could be found. The new Mother Superior was kinder, at least when it came to the babies. I'd only ever glimpsed the woman at Mass, so far across the chapel that I had no sense of her coloring, age, or features. During her reign, two girls were chosen to work as night attendants. When inconsolable wails reached us, at least we knew the children weren't all alone, but held and rocked. Every morning, the most recently delivered mothers' gowns would be soaked with milk, letting down for their out-of-reach babies.

The girls cried, too, at night. Not just the nursing mothers but girls who'd just arrived, mourning their austere fate. Girls whose babies had been adopted or fostered out or moved to the adjoining orphanage even though they were not orphans, their mothers mere yards away, longing and toiling and hoping against all expectations. We were a desperate lot, and the desperate seldom sleep well.

Bess's bed was next to mine. I woke one night to hear her sobbing and sat up to squint through the darkness, making sure it was her. My hands went immediately to my burgeoning belly, the little child kicking and rolling, dancing and thumping. I didn't yet think of my baby as "her." But that's how it is in memory. Her, my baby, my little girl. I see her, smiling at me, and waving. I wave back. I blow kisses.

"Bess," I whispered. "Is that you?" I put my thin blanket aside and went over to her. She startled like a war veteran when I put my hand on her shoulder. "Hush now, Bess, it's only me. Nan."

She put her hand over her mouth, shaking, trying to pull herself together.

I sat on the edge of her bed. "You don't have to stop crying on my account." I stroked the strands of her cropped hair off her forehead. She had a sweet face, fresh and pretty. It was easy to imagine a young soldier falling in love with her. She should have been out in the world, wearing long hair and fetching clothes. Laughing.

"I can't bear it. I thought once I got bigger, he'd leave me alone. Move on to someone else. But he won't. He won't." Bess pushed herself up on her elbows. Eight months pregnant, at least, but one of those women who carries small. Her whole figure was slight and spare except for the globe of her belly.

I gathered up Bess's hand and kissed it, searching my mind for something helpful or comforting. "We could tell Sister Mary Clare."

Bess didn't have the heart to tell me. Sister Mary Clare already knew. *Come now, it's nothing you haven't done before,* she'd say in a singsong voice. Other times she'd change her tune as if Bess wouldn't remember anything Sister Mary Clare had said before. *Of course Father Joseph would never do such a thing. He's a man of God.*

How I wish Bess had told me, but it was kindness that prevented her. She wanted me to hold on to whatever comforts I'd managed to find. Instead she said, "And what can Sister Mary Clare do? She's only another woman. None of them can do anything. I should've been brave enough to throw my body off a cliff before they could ever bring me here."

"Don't say that." I told her, in a few quiet sentences, about Colleen.

"She was a smart girl, your sister."

"Please. I mean it. Don't say that."

"I'm sorry, Nan. I am. I have five brothers and a sister back in Doolin. Every day I think about my little sister, Kitty. For all she knows I did throw myself off a cliff. Whatever Da told her, it wasn't that he brought me here." Bess lay back down on her side. She placed her hands in a *V* and laid them between her pillow and cheek. "Kitty wants to be in pictures. She's pretty enough, too. Only twelve years old. I hate not being there with her. I wish I could write to her and say, 'If you ever get in trouble, don't tell the priest, don't tell Da. Don't tell anyone. Just get yourself away.'"

Away to where? I thought, but didn't say. If there was a place in this world that welcomed pregnant unmarried girls I hadn't heard of it.

"I hate to think of Father Joseph touching Kitty," Bess said fiercely. "I'd have to kill him. I would."

She started to cry again. I hated myself for feeling terrified that Father Joseph's attentions would turn toward me if he ever lost interest in Bess. A few days earlier I had hid from him, ducking into the kitchens when I saw him walking down the hall with Sister Mary Clare. "All girls are the same," I heard him say to her. He sounded as if it made him angry.

"Father, you can't say that," the young nun replied, with her light and cheerful trill. I would have thought it flirtatious if I hadn't known that's how she always spoke. "Why, we nuns are nothing like these girls, are we?"

Father Joseph stopped and touched her arm. "Surely no. You're the purest angels, tending to the most wretched devils. Snow-white lilies alongside ragwort. It a wondrous thing to behold."

We girls, identical devils. And the nuns, identical angels, each with the same grave awaiting: HERE LIES SISTER MARY. I had seen Sister Mary Frances strap the palms of girls not much older than Bess's little sister, Kitty. In the months I'd been here, nobody had touched my palms. I hadn't received a single lash. I kept my head down and did what I was told. Obedience seemed

the safest plan. I hadn't learned yet. In this world it's the obedient girls who are most in danger.

Bess moved a hand from under her cheek and I held it. If we
were all the same, and if Father Joseph could choose Bess, when
she did indeed grow too large, he might choose me. I persisted in
that way of thinking, even though it amounted, in my mind, to
turning her over to him for the sake of myself. One of the worst
aspects of this prison life was the way it could make us ruthless
mercenaries, fighting in an army of one.

"I'm sorry," I told Bess. "I wish I could help."

"It's all right." She moved over and I lay down beside her facing the opposite direction, both of us squeezed onto the narrow
cot, close enough that through her belly, pressed into my back,
I could feel a great bold kick. We drew in our breaths, hearts
lifting at least for a moment.

"Oh, this baby's a strong one," Bess whispered.

"Could be it's a boy. Could be when he's grown, he'll take
care of Father Joseph for you."

"No. I'd never let him. It's my job to protect him. He'll never
know a priest and he'll never go to war. I swear it."

"Have you chosen a name?" Any name we chose wouldn't
last. We could see them, the couples who arrived to adopt our
babies. In those days women seldom delivered their babies in
hospital, but at home. They stayed in confinement, their last
months, rather than roam about visibly pregnant. So it was easy
to not only steal our children but pass them off as their own.

"If it's a girl," Bess said, "I'll name her Genevieve. If it's a boy,
Ronan. That means 'little seal.' Do you have seals where you
come from, Nan?"

"No." There were seals on the rocks at Ballywilling Beach,

but I didn't want to come from there anymore. I had abandoned the idea that Ireland belonged to me or me to it. I came from London. My mother's daughter. Not my father's.

"Whenever trouble comes to land, Ronan will swim away. Whenever trouble comes to water, Ronan will return to shore."

"Why Genevieve?" I asked.

"The patron saint of young girls. So she can look out for herself."

I hugged my own belly, liking the sound of that.

"No harm can reach this baby ever," Bess said. "I'll make sure of it."

It sounded like what we wanted to be true. Never mind where we were. All the good things would happen. Our young men would return for us. Our babies would stay close to us always and we'd watch them grow. I pictured myself at a kitchen table, my baby playing with Alby at my feet, Finbarr making tea while I filled a notebook with stories. They hadn't taken the wishes out of us, not yet.

All girls are the same. Father Joseph's proclamation dogged us until we could almost believe it was true. There was the occasional rebellion—such as the girl who escaped through the open gate when the milk truck arrived. The bells sounded, nuns scurrying everywhere, demanding one door be locked, another opened. We cheered, risking their wrath, then were disappointed when the escapee returned the same evening, face streaked with dust and tears. A pointless day of walking had led to the full realization there was nowhere for her to go.

"Be glad for a roof over your head," the nuns told us. "It's more than most would give you."

One morning Bess and I worked scrubbing the entry hall. Often the floors they made us clean were already spotless, but summer had begun with plenty of rain, and the girls who'd been working outdoors had tracked a good deal of dirt over the tiles. I left Bess on her hands and knees to fetch more hot water for our buckets and on my way back found Sister Mary Clare humming through the corridor.

"Sister, I wonder if I could ask you a favor."

"My English rose." She smiled. "You can ask me anything at all. I hope you know that."

"If you could send a letter to Ballycotton, to Finbarr Mahoney. Just a few lines to tell him where I am."

A look of sad hesitation crossed her face.

"You don't have to tell him to come for me. You don't have to say anything except 'Nan's at the convent in Sunday's Corner.' He'd come for me if he knew, Sister, he'd marry me, I know he would."

"Sure and I know it, too." She pressed her hand into my shoulder. Despite the pregnancy there was no flesh for her to grab onto. The diet they gave us was spare at best. Bread in the morning and evening and a thin stew for our midday dinner. "I'll write to your Finbarr, Nan. I do believe you could be one of the lucky ones after all."

The nun walked me back to the front entryway. She did not offer to carry one of my buckets, the scalding water sloshing onto my shins and clogs.

"Sister," Bess said. She struggled to her feet. The stone

floor glistened with moisture and so did Bess. Sweat formed in beads on her brow.

Sister Mary Clare stepped toward her solicitously, the same plump hand rising to touch her cheek.

"I'm feeling poorly. Cramped and clammy."

Sister Mary Clare moved her hand from Bess's cheek to her forehead. "You don't feel feverish."

"Please. I feel like I'm close to my time. I have pains coursing through my belly like I'm on my monthlies. You need to transfer me to hospital."

"Oh, is that what I need to do?" Sister Mary Clare's voice was amused but also warning. Even she would not brook impudence from the likes of us.

"I need to go to hospital," Bess rephrased, the sound of her voice already hopeless.

"Look how tiny you are. Why, I can barely tell you're with child. You're nowhere near close, dear, trust me to know what that looks like. We can't have you lying in for weeks like a queen, can we?"

The nun looked from Bess's face to mine and must have been struck by the dismay. "I'll tell you what. I'll sneak you upstairs for a little rest. Our secret. What do you say to that?"

"Thank you, Sister." Bess's shoulders sagged.

I took the scrub brush from her damp hands. It was unheard of for any girl to be allowed to rest during the day. Not only did I feel glad for Bess but encouraged for myself. Perhaps Sister Mary Clare really would write to Finbarr. I could already see him, striding through the front gates, past the pregnant lawn crew on their knees, straight to the Mother Superior to demand my release.

Bess and Sister Mary Clare walked off together. No other nun would have agreed to it. How lucky we were that at least one of them was so kind.

Bess knew having a nun beside her wouldn't work as protection. Her heart sank when she saw Father Joseph emerge from the office he used when he visited the convent. Bess didn't believe in prayer anymore, but old habits were hard to break. She found herself praying every day for her stomach to bloom into an obstruction. She prayed for a belly a hundred miles wide, the most pregnant woman to ever walk the earth.

"There you are, Bess." The priest's voice was booming and unashamed.

Despair can be as real as any other trap. Like a fishing net—thrown into the air, widening, then falling to make its catch. In the hallways and in church Father Joseph had a great smiling face.

Sister Mary Clare said, "Bess is feeling poorly, Father. I was just taking her upstairs to lie down."

"She can lie down in here."

Bess turned to Sister Mary Clare and grabbed her arm. The nun looked down at the grip, then at the priest, who stood with his arms crossed, the picture of fatherly reproach.

"Please," Bess said. "He won't listen to me. But he might listen to you."

Sister Mary Clare laughed, determined to prove she was the jolliest person on earth. "My goodness. You'd think you were going to your execution, rather than private prayer with the most revered man in County Cork."

Bess couldn't look at Father Joseph, who no doubt beamed at hearing this praise. As if the most revered man in any county would be assigned to ragwort such as us. Bess was certain this scene only made him more eager to be alone with her. Instead she looked at Sister Mary Clare, the enforced cheer on her face, the willful refusal to see what was right in front of her. Or worse, the refusal to admit what she knew full well.

"Sister, can you really believe you'll get to heaven when all this is done?"

The nun wrenched her arm out of Bess's grasp, darkness finally crossing her face. "Come now, Bess," she all but hissed. "The Father knows what's best for all of us. You know he does." She put her hand to the small of Bess's back and propelled her over the threshold.

The office door shut. The priest's face changed. Furious. As if Bess were at fault, forcing him to defile an already defiled girl.

"You said you wanted to lie down. Lie down. There." He pointed to the floor behind his desk and removed his collar, slapping it down to the floor like something to be conquered and discarded.

"Father." Her voice cracked. She hated calling him that. "I really do feel poorly."

"I've heard that before, haven't I?"

It was no use. The fastest way to get upstairs was to do as she was told. Bess lay down. She closed her eyes.

"None of that, now. Eyes open. Wide open."

She opened her eyes. When Bess first arrived at the convent, when Father Joseph first began forcing his way into her, she would wait for it to be over. Now, even as she wished for a deliverance that left her and her baby intact, Bess knew it would never be over. Not after the priest's final grunts and pushes. His righting of his costume and her escape back into the halls. If she ever left this place, if she lived to be a hundred years old. The priest's face would hover over hers, darkening all the moments to come that should have been happiest, even intruding upon her past. When she thought of her brothers, she imagined them delivering her to Father Joseph's door. When she thought of her little sister, Kitty, only twelve years old, she thought of Father Joseph, ordering her to lie down and keep her eyes open. Until Bess had to push the beloved face out of her mind, to save her from this horror, even if it only existed in her imagination.

"I hate you," Bess whispered, before she realized the words had left her mouth. She braced, thinking he might hit her, but instead her words seemed to do the trick and bring today's ordeal to one final, thrusting end.

All the while, Sister Mary Clare stood outside in the hall. Waiting. Smiling as if nothing had happened when Bess emerged, shaking, to be led upstairs.

"You see," Sister Mary Clare sang, musical voice caroming from one stone wall to the next. "Now your rest will be all the better. Father Joseph always knows just what to do, doesn't he, to restore a girl's soul."

In our dormitory, Bess lay down on her cot. She heard the door lock with a click, and Sister Mary Clare's humming off into the convent. Downstairs in the nursery a baby cried, then another. One of the girls assigned to night duty had been released from the convent only last week, leaving a lone harried attendant tending the babies. But during the day there were plenty of hands, including the nuns', so most wails quieted before too long.

When was the last time Bess had been in a room alone? Truly not many times in her life, coming from a family as large as hers. Her body ached in pulsing, insistent waves. Next time she'd refuse. Whether or not he was done with her, she was done acquiescing. He might be able to do whatever he wanted to any of us, but he didn't want a scene. He didn't want to hear the things he did spoken out loud. He wanted to move among us as a ruddy, fatherly figure. Pious and jolly. He wasn't so jolly when she flinched away from his meaty hands. He wasn't so jolly when he groaned himself into her. Sometimes she would lie beneath him, her eyes wandering to things she might grab and plunge into his neck. She had her teeth. If she sank them into his jugular—so close and exposed—and pulled hard enough, would a flood of blood open, rushing over her, him unable to make a noise, falling off her to the side, clutching? Enough time for her to grab something—the thick glass paperweight from his desk perhaps, or a lamp, or the letter opener—and finish him off?

Downstairs I raked the scrub brush back and forth over the tarnished grout, my lower back aching, and thought of Bess. I imagined Sister Mary Clare, accidentally on purpose leaving the door to the dormitory unlocked. And Bess, swift footed despite her advanced pregnancy, stealing away. An open gate somewhere. Her American soldier waiting outside the convent. She held details about him close, so I didn't know his name, or what he looked like. But he'd arrive still in uniform. Once she was delivered, I'd never see her again, but would not permit myself to miss her. Because her escape would prove as evidence. Any of us might be rescued at any moment. And one day I'd be back home in London, and a letter would arrive, across the envelope the address she'd memorized so faithfully. And we could write each other to say how everything had worked out fine in the end.

Upstairs, Bess had not escaped but fallen into a sleep she couldn't battle her way out of. She imagined her little sister, Kitty, standing in the corner of the room. *You must wake, Bess,* Kitty called, and Bess tried like mad to wrest her eyelids open, tried to find the voice in her throat to call back, *You must run, Kitty, you must run away from here.* From far away she heard Sister Mary Declan's footsteps, pounding into the dormitory, furious to hear Bess had been allowed a lie down. For Bess it was like being at the bottom of a pool, fathoms deep. Far off above her she could see the faint suggestion of light and echoes. But there was no swimming to the top. None at all. She imagined Sister Mary Declan's footsteps belonged to Kitty, not running toward but away from her, fast as she could on coltish twelve-year-old legs, fast and sure and so far away. Now that Kitty was safe, it felt fine for Bess to stay deep under the water. Everything up top was vile and brutal. *Let me stay under,* she thought. *Don't ever make me come back up.*

She didn't know, finally her American soldier had made his way to her father's door. "I'll marry her the very hour they let her go," he promised, when he learned where Bess had landed.

"Bess!" Sister Mary Declan cried. She slapped one cheek, then another, not in anger but genuine fear. Sister Mary Clare looked on, clutching her crucifix. It was important to all the nuns, to believe anyone who called them angels. By evening they would already be offering each other forgiveness, running down the rosary. Naming their sins and flinging them aside, ready to commit more tomorrow.

There was no time for hospital, or even to bring her downstairs to the mattress by the laundry. Susanna and Sister Mary Declan helped Bess deliver as best they could, right there in the dormitory. By the following morning Bess had finally clawed her way to the surface of the water, alive and whole. A miracle.

Another miracle: that same morning her young man appeared on the doorstep of the convent, demanding to see the Mother Superior. In time to walk Bess out of the convent, but too late for their baby boy. Little Ronan was one of the few babies who left the convent at Sunday's Corner in his mother's arms, swaddled in a yellow blanket: perfect and round faced and stone-cold dead.

The Disappearance

The Berkshire bloodhounds weren't doing the job any better than Agatha's dog had done. Deputy Chief Constable Thompson called in a woman from Belgium whose dogs were said to be the best in Europe. These expert hounds followed Agatha's scent in circles, concentrating on the spot Finbarr had flagged her down, where she'd stepped out of the car, lavender beads of sweat plopping to the earth. The scent ended where it began, as she'd hopped into poor Miss Oliver's car and sped away. The dogs sniffed and bayed uselessly, finally catching a whiff of a rabbit and leading the searchers on another fruitless chase. Even expert dogs are, in the end, dogs.

"Agatha, Agatha," Archie moaned, taking turns about Styles, the house and its grounds. He found Teddy's hoop, abandoned under a bush at the edge of the property, and gave it a spin. It rolled a few feet, teetered, and fell sideways on the grass. He didn't join the searches, not only to avoid his neighbors' suspicious glances, but because searching seemed to be an admission there was something to be found—another body, this time Agatha's—and he refused to consider that possibility. She was alive. It would be one of the policemen from an unlikely county to notify them and deliver the happy news: she'd been found, whole and well and ready to come home.

Noel Owen came round to keep him company. They drank late into the evening and took dinner in the sitting room.

"Back when it first began with Nan," Archie confided, "it was all so new and exciting. A kind of newness and excitement I believed gone from my life. And I won't lie, the forbidden nature of it, it was all so ... so ..."

"Irresistible?" Noel was not above prurient interest, though as far as I know he was always true to Ursula, to the extent any man can be.

Oh! The cynicism of that remark. *To the extent any man can be.* It doesn't bear out the way I feel, and what I believe, deep down in my heart. Some men can be true to the greatest extent. Finbarr, for example. He was always true to me and would always have been, if ever we'd been given our natural chance to be together. If the world had unfolded on its own, without wars and churches. What laughter there would have been. What joy. Dogs and books and children of our own, starting with our eldest, our own darling Genevieve, whom I'd secretly hold in my heart as my favorite, though I'd never let the other children know.

"Irresistible," Archie agreed with Noel Owen, tasting the word as if it were a kind of poison. "The things I told myself. About Nan. About my marriage. If I'd been able to look ahead and see this moment, I believe I would have acted differently. I do believe that, Noel."

Noel had been Archie's friend a long while and never seen him so full of doubts. "You can't have known Agatha would react this way." Noel stood up to pour Archie some more whiskey. "Men leave their wives every day, don't they, without all this wretchedness. Agatha always seemed to have such a good head on her shoulders."

Archie filled his pipe and stared out the window, everything outside still and quiet as if the chill had frozen the wind. No branches moved. If Agatha broke through that stillness, if she appeared at the top of the road. A figure coming toward him, calm and resolute, like something of his own invention. He knew he would spring from the house and run to her, but would it be to collect her in an embrace, or to strangle her for what she'd put him through? He reminded himself, uncharacteristically, that he'd put her through plenty.

Now that she was gone, and he had no way to locate her—powerless, impotent, for the first time in his life—she occupied his thoughts as the beautiful face he'd carried through the War. Peach silk. Slim as a reed. Eyes wide with adoration. The stories she scribbled just a pleasing eccentricity, nothing to eclipse anything and everything he'd ever accomplish.

The things they'd come through together, Archie and Agatha. Even his relationship with Nan they had gone through together, in their way. Agatha had been a part of it, unwitting, but still a dynamic and important part. Her presence driving the secrecy, the delicious illicitness. Then the way she'd clearly known but held her tongue, waiting for it to end. And then he *had* ended it, but not in the way she'd so patiently awaited, instead in a way that crushed her, and she'd stepped out of his life, out of the world. And all he wanted was for her to come back.

"Oh, AC," Archie said out loud, when Noel left the room. Archie pressed his hand against the windowpane. "My dear wife. I'll do anything. I'll atone. I won't hold a grudge, for all this worry you've caused, all this uproar and shame. I'll give up the girl. If only you come back whole and well."

Archie had no talent for magic. The road lay empty, the room sat quiet. The conjuring accomplished nothing.

Meanwhile in Harrogate, in his autopsy of Mr. Marston, the coroner discovered potassium cyanide.

"There was a mark," the coroner explained in Lippincott's office, the door for once closed. Both Lippincott and Chilton had elected not to see the body again. "A tiny mark on the man's hip. It was injected, is my thought, right through his trousers. This was not a natural death."

"What about the wife?" asked Chilton.

"Strychnine. A lethal dose. Ingested, not injected."

"Both poisons easy enough to obtain," said Lippincott. "Any housewife with a wasp or rat problem knows their uses."

"Indeed." Chilton pictured the couple, perfectly ordinary in every way. Who on earth would want those two dead? "It had to have been someone in the dining room, then."

The coroner nodded in agreement.

"I'd say this points to the wife." Lippincott was naturally protective of his cousin's livelihood, and nothing would empty out the hotel for years to come like a double murder. "She offed her husband by injecting him with potassium cyanide, then killed herself with the strychnine. Did she seem particularly troubled to you?" he asked Chilton. "Before her husband's death, of course."

"Quite the contrary. She seemed like someone who'd never known a moment's trouble. Rather jolly. Oblivious. Annoying, really."

"There, there," said Lippincott. "Don't make yourself a suspect."

The three of them laughed, forgetting themselves and the somber nature of their discussion.

"But why would she want to kill her husband?" Chilton said.

"Clearly," said the coroner, whose wife greeted him nightly with a burnt dinner and a new list of grievances, "you've never been married."

"Do the murderous feelings generally begin on a honeymoon? The woman can't have been more vocal in her adoration."

"All the more suspicious," said Lippincott. "Protesting too much and all that. It's rather clear to me, but long as you're already there, you may as well poke around a bit to confirm my theory. Discreetly. Don't make a fuss about it. See if Mrs. Marston confided anything useful to the other ladies. It's a good way for us to get our money's worth out of you."

Chilton nodded, but instead of driving directly to the hotel to start conducting interviews, he drove down a back road or two, eyes on the winter landscape. The deciduous trees provided a view into the wood. No signs of the young Irishman or Mrs. O'Dea or Agatha. When his search yielded nothing, he gave up and went to the hotel. He would have a massage, he decided, so long as he was there, and send his mother a postcard telling her he had done so. It would please her to think of him relaxed and happy.

Mrs. Leech presided over the front desk, her cheerfulness seeming an effort. Chilton gathered more guests had precipitously checked out following Mrs. Marston's death. Any of those departed guests could be the killer, but now that he thought on it,

Chilton tended to agree with Lippincott: the death of the couple was almost certain to have been a family affair.

"I thought I'd book a massage," he told Mrs. Leech.

She smiled warmly, taking up her pen. "I'm sure you know that won't be included in your gratis accommodations."

Suddenly the idea of a stranger kneading his naked skin seemed less appealing. Chilton went instead to the baths. He had the place to himself, but despite the solitude and the restorative waters, he did not relax a bit. His mind stayed on the roads he'd driven, frozen and empty, no sign of the black automobile, all the houses with smoke rising from their chimneys inhabited by their rightful owners. It panicked Chilton the way a miscalculation can. He'd had her right before his eyes and allowed her to slip away. Lippincott had tasked him with finding Agatha Christie as a lark. But what would he say if he knew that Chilton *had* found her, yet managed to daydream the quarry away? Could he do nothing right with the days he had left on earth?

After dinner Chilton took his pipe into the hotel's small library so he could turn to the matter of confirming Lippincott's theory regarding the Marstons. Ladies often complained about cigarettes, but seldom about pipes—a man with a pipe reminded them of their fathers—and it satisfied his craving while also making him look as if he had something to do. The books on the shelves were mostly from the previous century. He perused the spines and landed on *Bleak House*, then settled onto the couch, where anyone who came in would have to sit beside him or across from him in one of the generous and well-worn armchairs. He'd seen Mrs. O'Dea carrying a book, and a reader on holiday is soon in need of a new one. If she should venture in, he might also begin to discover her connection to Agatha Christie, killing two birds with one stone.

Before long a young, dark-haired woman entered the library, with a cozy pink shawl over her shoulders. Miss Armstrong, Chilton reminded himself, the girl he'd dined with the other evening. She smiled at him perfunctorily and went straight to the bookshelves.

"Not much contemporary fodder," he said as she examined the spines. "You won't find the new Dorothy Sayers, I'm afraid."

"Oh, I'm not much for detective novels. I like a love story." She pulled out a dusty copy of *Jane Eyre*, brushed off the cover, and sat down, as he'd hoped, in the seat opposite him.

Mrs. Leech poked her head into the library. "Do you two have everything you need?" she asked brightly, anxious to retain the guests she had left. "Would you like some tea?"

"Tea would be lovely," Miss Armstrong said. After the inn-keeper's retreat she said to Chilton, "I love seeing that. Mr. and Mrs. Leech, I mean. Together, and nobody seeming to mind."

Chilton nodded, not wanting to tell her there were plenty who minded. Instead he said, "People can certainly be beastly about the things that affect them least, can't they?"

"They certainly can. But Mr. and Mrs. Leech never let that stop them. It's just too romantic, isn't it?"

Mrs. Leech returned with the tea tray, all business, not a hint of romance about her. Once she had gone, and their cups were full and steaming, Chilton said, "Terrible business about the Marstons."

"Oh." Miss Armstrong closed her book with a snap, as if she'd been dying to talk about it. "Isn't it awful? And beautiful, in its way? They were star-crossed, Mrs. Marston told me. Longing to be together for ever so long. And then just when they finally were . . ." Tears welled up in Miss Armstrong's dark eyes.

It wasn't that Chilton had lost his powers of observation. He could see things and even assess them. The loveliness of this girl before him, her impeccable manners, the way her eyes were so dark one could barely make out the pupils. He could also note the particular sweetness of a young woman very much wishing for love to enter her life, even as she bravely asserted her independence. Chilton knew he himself was not the sort of man occupying her daydreams; he also knew he should at least be moved to some sort of emotion. There should be desire lurching forward, to be suppressed, with perhaps a sigh of sadness at what could never be. But regarding Miss Armstrong felt no more personal or emotional than reading a newspaper. He saw everything but felt nothing.

"Did you meet Mrs. Marston? She was chatty and friendly, wasn't she? Oh, I liked her, Mr. Chilton. And I feel sure she died of a broken heart." At this she set down her teacup and brought her hands to cover her face.

Mrs. Marston had certainly gone out of her way to make her love story known. Might there have been a method to her garrulousness? Chilton fished the handkerchief out of his pocket and handed it to Miss Armstrong.

This is how I found them when I entered the library. Chilton had appraised me correctly. Having finished *Gatsby*, I longed for something, anything, to distract me from the maelstrom of circumstances at the Bellefort Hotel. If I'd been smart, I would have gone home as the Clarkes had done. Instead I'd extended my stay, telling Mrs. Leech I'd be keeping the room indefinitely. How could I do anything different with Finbarr haunting the vicinity?

Miss Armstrong turned to look at me, her eyes widening in embarrassment, then correcting with that lift of her chin, daring me to judge her. I might almost have thought I'd walked in on a moment of romance if Chilton hadn't appeared so detached. He looked more interested in my sudden appearance than the lovely weeping girl before him. This put me immediately on my guard.

"Mrs. O'Dea." He gestured toward his tearful companion.

I sat down next to her and placed my hand on her shoulder. "Are you all right, Miss Armstrong?"

"You're very kind." She dabbed at her eyes with a shabby handkerchief that couldn't have been her own. "It's silly. I didn't know them until a few days ago. But talking to Mrs. Marston, hearing her story. She was already a friend. And they were destined to be together, those two. There's a Chinese legend called Yuè Lǎo, have you heard it? When we're born, the gods tie an invisible thread around our little finger, which connects us to our one true love. No matter what forces try to keep us apart."

"That's lovely." To my own ears I sounded insincere. I wasn't immune to that sort of romance. I could believe in a thousand red threads connecting Finbarr and me. I just had a hard time applying this legend to the Marstons.

"It's so sad and awful"—Miss Armstrong wept—"that they would die like that, right under our noses, right when their threads finally found each other. Just when they were on the brink of happiness."

"Not on the brink." I eased the handkerchief out of her

grasp and handed it back to Mr. Chilton, then gave her my own, which was silk, and monogrammed, and far better suited to her delicate skin. A gift from Archie, special ordered from Harrods. "They had some days of happiness. Perhaps more than they deserved."

Miss Armstrong stopped crying abruptly and stared at me, eyes full of rebuke. "Whatever do you mean by that?"

"You said yourself you hardly knew them. They might have been wretched people."

Chilton let out a caustic little laugh.

"Why, Mrs. Marston seemed the nicest lady in the world," said Miss Armstrong reproachfully.

"Seeming is different than being. Best not to mourn people whose sins we don't know."

Miss Armstrong looked at me as if I were the coldest, hardest woman in the world. Which I may well be. But I should have known better than to reveal it. Nothing is more suspicious than an unfeeling woman.

I stood and went to examine the selection of books. Miss Armstrong held her handkerchief out to return to me but I waved it away. "Keep it, I have loads."

Chilton and Miss Armstrong busied themselves reading, though the air felt as if they absorbed nothing, just stared at the words on the page, waiting for me to leave so they could discuss my outburst. I should have been more careful, but I had no idea Chilton had seen me with Finbarr, let alone that he knew Agatha was hiding in the vicinity. Chilton was keen to keep it that way.

Finally I settled on a Willy novel that had been all the rage when I was a girl, the first *Claudine*. The edition was in its original

French, and the effort of translating would make it all the more diverting. I said a curt goodbye to Chilton and Miss Armstrong.

When I emerged from the library, Mrs. Leech looked up from her station behind the front desk. "Mrs. O'Dea. A little boy just came by with a note."

I snatched it from her fingers, perhaps a little too eagerly. I worried it would be addressed using my first name, but the writing on the envelope—bold male handwriting—said *Miss O'Dea.* If Mrs. Leech registered the "Miss" instead of "Mrs." her face did not betray it. I felt a flush across my neck. It was worth whatever risk I'd taken, to use my real last name, so I could open this envelope and read what it said on the piece of coarse paper, butcher's wrapper.

Dearest Nan. Meet me at ten tonight just outside the front door. If I am not precisely on time, trust I'll be there and don't go any farther than just past the front door. It's not safe for ladies after dark.

I floated upstairs and waited obediently for night to fall.

Meanwhile, inside the library, Chilton asked Miss Armstrong if he could see my handkerchief. She handed it over as if eager to be rid of it.

"Rather a nice handkerchief," he mused aloud, "for anyone to have loads of."

"I don't see how she can be so cruel," Miss Armstrong said fiercely. "I don't know about you, Mr. Chilton, but I was raised not to speak ill of the dead."

Chilton nodded sadly, as if in agreement, though he had seen enough of the world to know some of the dead earned ill speaking. He didn't hold it against me. Much later he would tell me he did wonder why my handkerchief was mono-grammed with a large cursive *N* when my name was purported to be Genevieve O'Dea.

The brave or complacent guests remaining at the Bellefort Ho-tel were exhausted by the hot waters, the spa treatments, and the recent tragedy. By the time I came downstairs nobody was afoot. Even Mrs. Leech had left her post. The grandfather clock hav-ing finished its ten chimes, everything was quiet the way only a winter night can be, not even birds or bugs rustling. I had bun-dled into my lace-up boots and wool coat, mittens and a wool hat and scarf. I stepped outside, careful to open and close the door soundlessly. It was a well-kept hotel, and the door had re-cently been oiled. It would remain unlocked, I knew. There was so little crime in the English countryside, back then, between the Wars. No doubt that was part of the reason so many of us expected a perfectly reasonable explanation for what happened to the Marstons. Not to mention one thousand men to spare searching for a missing lady novelist.

Not that I knew this, yet, about how large the search had grown. The Leeches didn't keep newspapers at the hotel unless guests requested them. Time at the spa was meant to be time away from the troubles of the world, Mrs. Leech said.

My breath gusted out in front of me. The air felt wonderful. It reminded me that Christmas was approaching. When my sisters and I were little, we used to wait outside together, staring up at the sky for a glimpse of Father Christmas before our mother bus-tled us off to bed. "If you girls are awake, he'll pass our house right by." We'd eat chestnuts roasted over the fire and go to sleep with sticky fingers, smiles on our faces. It had been the time of year I most looked forward to, more than anything else in the world, before summers in Ireland began, and Finbarr.

Just as his name formed in my mind, he emerged from the shadows, hands in his pockets. I stepped forward and threw my arms around his neck. He hugged me back, three beats.

"Walk with me," he said in his hoarse, whispery voice.

I put my arm through his and we walked away from the hotel, down the road, into the kind of darkness that scarcely exists anymore. Electric lights weren't yet a matter of course out here in the country, and cars didn't often rattle down the road after dark. We had gone a little way when a dog ran out to menace us. Finbarr knelt, and within seconds the giant beast—half-collie, half something monstrous—was in his lap, getting his white mane ruffled, shaggy tail wagging joyfully. We continued walking and the dog followed us awhile, until Finbarr commanded, "Go home." The dog lowered his ears, dejected but obedient, and trotted off toward where he'd come.

"Have you got a dog of your own now?" I asked.

The question couldn't help but burgeon with memories of Alby, so that's how Finbarr answered it. He told me the man who'd bought Alby had joined the IRA. He used the dog to deliver explosives to an RIC barracks, and Alby had been blown to bits along with his target. "Remember how I taught him to crouch so still and not move for anything, no matter what? That was the death of him, Nan. I swear I'll never train another dog so well."

The pain that erupted in my chest was unbearable, so desperate was I to unknow what Finbarr had just told me. From that moment, for the rest of my life, I'd dream of Alby crouching, watching our tennis games in controlled stillness, only to burst into flames before we could call him back to life.

"It all feels like a long time ago," Finbarr said. "But it's not. Eight years since the War ended, twelve years since it started. It's only that the world's changed too much, in ways it shouldn't. And so it's changed how time passes. The trenches were yesterday, or an hour ago. They'll come back again tomorrow. You and me and Alby and Ireland, that was a hundred years ago, and also every day since."

"And Genevieve?"

"A thousand years ago and just this morning."

"But not tomorrow?"

"No, Nan. Not tomorrow."

The tears Miss Armstrong had wanted from me gathered in my eyes. We kept walking, far enough that I knew I wouldn't make it back to the Bellefort Hotel this night. Who would even notice? Inspector Chilton, with his sad, watchful eyes and one working arm? What did he think he knew about me? Nothing that could matter enough to change the magic of walking beside Finbarr. When I'd left the convent, all I'd wanted to do was walk. I would have walked the length of Ireland, and then England, I would have walked from Land's End to Thurso. Not knowing where to look but only that there was nothing in this world for me to do but search and search and search.

Finbarr did not walk with me the length of England, but to a long drive leading to a manor house, the trees on either side bare enough that I could see it up ahead in a patch of moonlight. Waiting for us. It was grand but not cavernously so. The country home of some wealthy Londoner, most likely.

"How did you find this place? Do you have permission to

stay here?" Even as I spoke, I knew he'd found it the same way he'd found our room in the midst of the Armistice celebration. Finbarr magic.

"The house gave me permission to stay. That's more important than permission from the owners."

Oak trees bent in a bald canopy overhead, sagging with the memory of their lost leaves, starlight making way through the branches creating a kind of mist with our exhaled breath.

"Shall we run to the front door?" Finbarr asked.

I laughed. But all at once before my voice could object, my body answered. I gave myself a head start by kicking off without warning, my muscles creaky but coming to life against the cold air. Finbarr overtook me quickly, but not so quickly that I didn't feel proud, almost at his heels, the good, lost feeling of blood and breath pumping through every ventricle to every cell.

Finbarr finished, slamming against the front door. We walked inside, breathing hard, past the smoldering fire in the front hall.

"Is Mrs. Christie here?"

"Yes. She's here."

I followed Finbarr up the staircase to what must have been the grandest bedroom, his spare possessions already settled into occupancy, a scarf over a chair, a battered satchel with his father's initials barely visible resting in a corner. Nice of Agatha, I thought, to let him have this room instead of taking it for herself. He knelt and rebuilt the fire while I stood, watching his face in the glow. My hands cupped their opposite elbows. I knew I should be shivering until the fire crackled in earnest, but instead I felt warm as I ever had.

Finbarr stood. He took off his coat and tossed it into a corner. He put his arms around me and pulled me close.

"Nan, I know you grieve. I grieve, too. We'll never forget her, but we can have another. We can be together."

"We can't be together," I said, even as I let him ease off my coat and felt his lips against my neck. "Because I have to be with her. I can't go off to live in a different hemisphere than my own child."

"Nan," he said more sharply. He gave my shoulders a little shake, as if trying to wake me. "I'm right here. But she's gone. There's no point in looking for something you'll never find, or holding on to something that's already lost."

Finbarr had never seen or touched our baby. He could love her but he couldn't understand. There was no point in saying so. I didn't want to argue. This night had arrived unexpectedly, a gift out of nowhere, and I just wanted it to continue, separate in time, a little bubble away from the world and everything it had done to us. I would have traded this moment with Finbarr in an instant if it would rearrange the past. But that wasn't possible. So I took it, never mind how it might affect the future. I hadn't packed my contraceptive sponge when I left London. Why would I? But I found myself not caring. Anything that happened this time would be very different from the last.

"Hush, Finbarr. Just hush."

I silenced him with a kiss that led us to the bed, finally a place and time carved out of all these years to be together in the way we were always meant to be.

Chilton learned to walk silently during the War. One of the benefits of not being a tall man, and slight in build, if he led with his heel, moving from the hip, he could walk with hardly any footfall, even with his longest strides.

And the truth was, even if he'd stomped, with no attention to keeping us from knowing he was there, we might not have known he was following us, so absorbed were we in each other. But follow us he did, undetected, even when Finbarr turned to point the dog toward home. Chilton froze then, arms by his side, as if he could make himself invisible even to an animal. When Finbarr turned, and we resumed our walk, Chilton didn't hesitate before resuming his stride. A sad pair, weren't we? Chilton could tell, he knew, we'd been separated by the War, only now coming back together. What he couldn't figure out was our connection to Agatha Christie. He just knew we'd lead him directly to her. And so we did.

Once we'd turned up the drive of the house, Chilton had secured our destination, so he began to take greater heed lest we discover him. He waited by the gate that Finbarr—country boy, mindful of fences—had closed and latched behind us. When we were far enough in the distance that he was sure we wouldn't hear it creak, Chilton opened the gate and walked down the road, noting, as I had, the bare-branch canopy, and thinking how lovely it must be in spring and summer, when everything was in bloom. He breathed in the night air to calm himself—anxiety taking him unawares as it so often did, the feeling that someone might be watching him, might be lurking, behind any shadow. Yorkshire was fine but Chilton had grown up by the sea. That was the thing, the only thing: to hear the waves upon the shore. To walk upon the rocks at Churston Cove and see the seals sunning there. To thrust your head into the salt water, even in the coldest months, and let its chilling shock clear your mind.

He stood before the house, a lovely old building, a great

stone box, shimmering with windows under the low light of stars. From behind one upstairs window a flicker of light grew; that would be the Irish fellow, stoking the fire for an evening with Mrs. O'Dea, if that was indeed her name. Whatever had separated us, Chilton hoped it could be sorted out, that we could be together. He had lost his own sweetheart because of the War. Katherine had waited for him patiently, praying for his return, but her prayers hadn't been complete enough, because a different man had come back from the one she loved. *I scarcely recognize you, Frank*, she'd said, weeping. Not long after she broke things off, she married the florist's son, who was set to inherit the business and hadn't been to war on account of blindness in one eye. It was one of the reasons Chilton had left Brixham for Leeds, years ago. One day he'd walked by the flower shop and seen Katherine arranging a vase full of peonies, round from expecting a child. He'd decided to take himself away, as if not seeing something spared you from its sorrow.

Torquay was close enough to Brixham that Agatha Christie might have bought flowers from that shop, even from Katherine herself. Or likely not. Likely it was a servant's job—to buy flowers.

Once over the threshold of the manor, he shut the door quietly behind him. Inside it was drafty and cold. There were so few furnishings—so little sign of life—Chilton thought it might be waiting for sale, or to let. It didn't have any air of waiting for its own family to return. He adjusted his scarf, then set about searching. It was a large house but not prohibitively so. He could make a quick turn downstairs to the kitchen, wine cellar (amply stocked for a house that seemed so deserted), and housekeeper's office. Then through the main floor into the parlor and library. He peered into every room except for the one the couple occupied, marked by the flicker from underneath the doorway. Light voices carried into the hall, including a soft laugh that gladdened him. It was difficult to imagine either of those two laughing, both so haunted and earnest.

In the attic there was a modest servants' quarters, with a row of closed doors. Beneath one of them, some movement, faint light, as though from a single candle. He knocked quietly, using only two of his knuckles.

"Yes, darling," came the voice, weary and slightly worried, like a mother addressing a child out of bed in the middle of the night. In his own family it had not been him but his youngest brother who woke their mother after dark. She was always sweet about it. How she loved all three of her boys.

Chilton knew Agatha's endearment, and its implied invitation to enter, wasn't for him. Still he pushed the door open. And there she sat, in a hard wooden chair—wearing a man's pajamas, hair loose and curling, lovely in the poorly lit room. There were two single beds, only one of them made up. On the dressing table, which she was using as a desk, sat a typewriter and two lit, dripping candles in tarnished silver holders. Stacks of paper were piled on a chest of drawers. More stacks of paper sat on the bare bed. Agatha stared at Chilton, fountain pen in hand, poised as if in midsentence.

"Oh, drat." She did not put down her pen.

He walked into the room and sat down at the foot of the bare bed, careful not to disturb her papers. He did not remove his coat. A small stove was in the corner, alight with coal, but he suspected it would be out by morning. He imagined her waking with a shiver, breath visible. Would she rekindle the fire herself or call for the Irishman, the geography of the house revised but not their roles?

"Mrs. Mahoney," Chilton said, with no faint measure of sarcasm. She had to strain backward in her chair to face him.

"Is this how the Yorkshire police conduct themselves?" A practiced tone of upper-crust umbrage was in her voice, but he could tell her heart wasn't in it. "Marching into a lady's bedroom in the middle of the night?"

"I did knock. You were expecting your husband?"

A sad look crossed her face. Chilton did not mean to make her cry. At least, as a man he did not. As an inspector he recognized emotional frailty might lead to an outpouring of information.

"I'm afraid your husband is downstairs in one of the bedrooms with another lady. I do hate to be the bearer of such unfortunate news."

Finally she released her pen, placing it on the bedside table with the exhalation of someone whose concentration has been truly and unwelcomely wrecked. "Let's not play games. You know very well he's not my husband."

"But wasn't it him you meant when you said *darling*? He's not . . ."

"Don't you dare say it. I'm not nearly old enough to be Finbarr's mother."

"I was going to say *your brother*."

"He has become very like a brother to me and is indeed darling. Though I don't see what business it is of yours."

"What business it is of mine, Mrs. Christie"—Chilton switched to her true name, though she had not yet confirmed her identity—"is that I am employed by the Yorkshire police. There are a good many officers searching for you."

"A good many? Searching for me? In Yorkshire?"

"Yorkshire and everywhere else in England."

Agatha frowned. She couldn't even curse her bad luck at landing in Yorkshire. If she'd run off to Derbyshire or Cumberland or Norfolk, there would be police to come knocking on the door of her hideout.

"Gracious," Agatha said, exhausted by the news. "What a fuss."

"So you admit you're Mrs. Agatha Christie?"

"I do no such thing." But she looked doubtful.

If Miss O'Dea (he had begun thinking of me as a *miss* almost without considering it) or any other woman had done what Agatha did next, Chilton would have been on guard, considering it an attempt at manipulation. But when she reached out her hand, touching his arm, closing her fingers around the thick wool cloth, he recognized the gesture as not woman to man, but human to human. A genuine and urgent entreaty.

"Mr. Chilton. Have you ever been in trouble? Real trouble, the kind that comes not only from without but someplace within? Some place you never even recognized?"

Her face looked open and painfully tender. Thirty-six is an age one looks back on as young. But at the time, living in thirty-six-year-old skin, it doesn't feel young. Women start believing themselves old so soon, don't they? Agatha didn't realize it was her youth that allowed her to sit for hours in that comfortless rock of a chair, staring at her pages without need of spectacles, nary a twinge from the small of her back. One day far into the future she would look back on this time in her life and understand she had not been old, or even middle-aged, but *young*, with the bulk of her life ahead of her, not to mention the best of it.

She trained her sharp eyes upon Mr. Chilton, assessing him frankly as she let go of his sleeve.

What a different life it had been for Agatha since she'd gone on the run with Finbarr. What a different person it had made her, already. Staying in an empty house without permission or even knowing the owner's identity. Like an outlaw. This time she wouldn't bother leaving money no matter how much of the household she helped herself to. She had chosen a servant's room for the sheer austerity of it, as well as the privacy. Sitting here now, with a stranger, a man, she felt no fear whatsoever, nor worry about impropriety. She had sidestepped right out of the world as she'd always known it and landed someplace where seemingly nothing mattered, not even great search parties, elsewhere, all for her benefit.

"Mr. Chilton."

He heard her and was struck again at the lack of ploy. A beautiful rawness exhibited either her character or what her character had been reduced—or elevated—to, thanks to whatever trauma it was that drove her.

One of the difficulties of having been to war: the impossibility of appreciating someone else's trauma at first glance. It all seems so insignificant. Now though, faced with her lovely furrowed brow, sympathy began to stir.

"Is there anyone else here. In Harrogate. Looking for me?"

"No. This area is my purview. And you might imagine the bulk of the search is closer to home. Your home. Dragging ponds and so forth."

"They haven't told Teddy, have they? My daughter. They haven't passed that worry onto her?" She stood up, the space where she sat no longer enough to contain the flood of concern.

"I wouldn't know about that." Then, because placation was useful under these circumstances (even if he hadn't precisely identified how to characterize these circumstances), he added, "I imagine not." He had never seen the child but could picture her, cosseted, protected from every bit of news or information that might cause distress, for the sake of the parents perhaps more than the child's. What's more inconvenient than another person's distress?

He wondered if Agatha Christie had ever in her life been as willing to wear her emotions so plainly on her face.

She made an effort to collect these emotions back to invisibility. "Let's not play games, Mr. Chilton." Her voice sounded as if she wanted to infuse it with accustomed authority, yet it shook. The candle on her desk fluttered. The stove needed more coal.

"That's the second time you've said that. You needn't say it again. I've no fondness for games. I only want to deliver you safely home." When she didn't reply, he added, "Mrs. Christie. Isn't that enough of all this? You've given your husband a fright. He's longing to see you. Surely it's time to put an end to it all and go home."

"Did you see that girl? The one you said came in with Mr. Mahoney?"

Now, they were getting somewhere. A mystery about to be solved.

"She happens to be my husband's mistress. My actual husband, Colonel Christie. She imagines she's shortly to be his wife."

The situation began to take a shape, albeit an unreasonable one. "She seems to have hit upon a hiccup, in that regard."

The house was still but also electric, with an awareness of

the floor beneath them and all it held. Those two young lovers, at last reunited (this much was clear). Not only what took place physically but the emotion swirling around them, oozing out from under the door, floating through the house like a new and intoxicating form of oxygen. He'd scarcely noticed that he had shifted to thinking of her as Agatha rather than Mrs. Christie. In that moment the mist surrounded them, intimate in its proximity.

(The Timeless Manor, Agatha and I named it later. I've never been back to Harrogate, or to this manor house. But sometimes I think if I did, if I tracked the coordinates precisely, I would find an empty stretch of moor and heather and bramble, the house having secreted itself into the mist for another hundred years.)

"Do you think she's beautiful?" Agatha asked. "That . . . girl."

She'd been on the brink of using a different word, Chilton could tell. He answered with a lack of propriety and a wealth of honesty, because both seemed to be what she needed: "Not as beautiful as you."

For a moment, based on the fervency that held every one of Agatha's features absolutely quiet, he thought she might lean over and kiss him.

But she didn't. She only said, "Please don't tell anybody you've found me. Not yet. Give me a day or two more."

He knew he should be objecting, cajoling, insisting. Rejecting the notion—to let her remain concealed—entirely. Instead Chilton got to his feet with an air of acquiescing. It wasn't as though a murder had been committed, after all. Why rouse people out of their beds with the shrill invasion of ringing telephones? She was a grown woman of means and station, free to make her own decisions. And he seemed to be rather enjoying himself. He seemed to be not wanting any of this to end. If he did his duty and reported her found, the odds of his ever seeing her again stood slim.

"I promise I won't tell anyone, for now. If you promise not to move again. Stay here, please, where I can find you if needs be."

"Done. I promise."

She held out her hand for him to shake. Soft, cool skin.

"Poor Finbarr. I do hope Nan's not toying with him."

"You're tenderhearted."

Agatha laughed. In agreement, he realized. "I expect that makes two of us."

Chilton had considered his heart so utterly undetectable for so long, it surprised him to believe her. "Do you know, I thought earlier, for a moment, when you were looking at me so intently, I almost believed you were about to kiss me."

"I haven't kissed a man other than my husband in years. Not since the day we met."

"You've been a good wife."

Agatha nodded vigorously. It made her furious to think what a good wife she'd been. To Chilton she looked breathlessly young and full of thoughts he couldn't read. It reminded him of his girl, Katherine, before the War. He felt his mind start to reach, by habit, for the next dark idea to follow, the bitter side of the world. And stopped himself.

"Mrs. Christie."

"Call me Agatha." She closed the distance between them and kissed him, a tentative but time-consuming kiss. Chilton didn't dare lift an arm to her waist. He was afraid if he moved at all, she'd realize what she was doing and it would end—her soft lips on his, her hands resting ever so lightly on his chest. Both their mouths open just enough to inhale each other's breath. She tasted like roses and spring grass.

"Agatha," Chilton said, when she finally stepped away.

"You better go now." It almost wounded him, how even and unfazed her voice sounded.

"Yes." He boasted no such calm. His voice cracked like a twelve-year-old boy's.

"But you'll keep your promise? And tell no one?"

"Yes."

Chilton closed the door behind him. He walked down the stairs and through the front door, feeling like a ghost, as if instead of stepping he were gliding, feet still and floating an inch or more above the ground.

The Disappearance

DAY SEVEN

Friday, December 10, 1926

S ir Arthur Conan Doyle loved a mystery too much to admit he'd never heard of Agatha Christie prior to her disappearance. There were whispers of a publicity stunt, and so what? If this was a publicity stunt, it was a damn good one.

People do like to be the ones to solve problems. The more people trying to crack a case, the more one wants to be the man to do it.

Donald Fraser, Agatha's new agent, cleared his schedule to take a meeting with Conan Doyle. The celebrated creator of Sherlock Holmes! Even if Fraser didn't see how Sir Arthur could help in discovering Agatha, perhaps the author could be persuaded to abandon his current agent and join Fraser's list?

Not that Fraser's feelings about Agatha were mercenary. He was worried. He felt horrible for Mr. Christie. Fraser's own wife had run off with one of his writers last spring. Fraser fully expected Agatha to have done something similar. She always conducted herself as an unassailable lady, but then so had his wife.

Fraser did not have confidence Conan Doyle could discover what every police officer in England had not. The man was an author, not a detective. What's easier than solving a puzzle of your own invention? Authors created problems, they didn't solve them. Another mystery writer of the day, Dorothy Sayers, had already invited herself to Sunningdale to search for clues and *test the energy.* Agatha Christie was not the sort to meddle in such nonsense. She wouldn't want charlatans involved, Fraser felt sure.

Conan Doyle at sixty-seven (a mere four years from joining the spiritual realm himself) cut a handsome and confident figure. It was almost endearing that someone so stalwart could believe in messages from the beyond. Once it became clear there would be no wooing him away from his current representation, Fraser resolved to get the meeting done with. The whole business made him sad. He wanted Agatha Christie found as much as anyone else and couldn't bear wasting time about it.

"Have you got anything of hers?" Conan Doyle's mustache sat wonderfully still on his face no matter how animated he became. "Personal possessions she might have left behind? Clothing is best. A handwritten note might do."

Fraser opened his desk drawer, where a lovely pair of leather gloves had lain going on nine months, waiting for their owner's return. He hesitated before handing them over.

"And may I inquire after your plans? The hounds have already got her scent, you know. There's a veritable army in Berkshire, searching for her." Fraser mentioned Dorothy Sayers's involvement.

Conan Doyle waved it away as ridiculous. "She has no idea what to look for." He snatched at the gloves as Fraser tentatively withdrew them. "A spiritual fingerprint is what's needed. I've been in touch with Horace Leaf."

Fraser blinked, indicating the name meant nothing to him.

"My good man, he's only the most powerful clairvoyant in Europe." How interesting that Doyle of all people employed spiritualism—mediums and divinations—rather than deductive reasoning. "And to our great good fortune he happens to reside in London. Have these gloves been worn recently?"

"Oh, very recently. Mrs. Christie was here just a day before she went missing. Sitting in that very chair."

Conan Doyle nodded, stroking the armrests as though collecting molecules Agatha had left behind. He held the gloves up as if he'd found them himself, a most important clue. "These will do nicely. Horace Leaf will solve this. We'll find Agatha Christie, alive or dead. By morning we'll know her whereabouts. You can be certain of that."

Fraser felt no guilt whatsoever. If Mr. Leaf had any powers at all, the first thing he ought to divine was that the gloves belonged to Mrs. Fraser, who'd belonged to Mr. Fraser, until she absconded to Devonshire and broke her devoted husband's heart.

The heavy door shut. Fraser stared at it, full of melancholy. Perhaps he'd go by Harrods and buy Mrs. Fraser a new pair, send them to her in Devonshire. As a present. Her hands might be cold.

It surprised Fraser that he hadn't felt starstruck meeting Sherlock Holmes's creator, only moved by the impermanence of life here on earth. Agatha Christie had a new novel, *The*

Big Four, coming out this January. Perhaps she'd be courteous enough to return to her husband by then. Or perhaps the more macabre imaginings would prove correct, and a corpse, rather than the woman, would turn up. Either way—whether or not anyone saw her again—by January she would be a household name in England, indeed if not the whole world. Which couldn't hurt book sales.

Fraser sighed, made melancholy by his avarice. Nothing in life unfolds the way you think it will. Does it?

In bed at the Timeless Manor, I propped myself up on my elbow, eyes trained on Finbarr's sleeping form, so I would see his face in the first light. The brick we'd heated in the fire to keep us warm had gone cold at our feet. The heavy curtains were drawn and the room stood black with the late-morning darkness of winter. By the time sunlight speckled into the room, his eyes were open, staring back at me. I thought of the night in Ireland I lay beside him, the only other time we'd slept all night in the same bed.

"Last time we slept together, you never opened your eyes in the morning."

He collected my hands and held them on top of his heart. "If I did, I would've married you that day."

Tears filled my eyes. "We'd be together now."

"We *are* together now."

"Not for long. And not all of us."

He sat up. I noticed for the first time something I'd missed the night before. His thick black hair was tamed and cropped. The back of his neck shaved. It gave him the unaccustomed and misleading look of order. It gave me proof of what seemed an impossibility: Agatha Christie was here, truly here. In this very house. With us. Living—as I'd never had the chance to do—with Finbarr Mahoney.

"Did she cut your hair?" I pictured Agatha's hands blowing the stubborn wisps off the back of his neck. Running her fingers through the thick silk strands to hold, snip, and release. Her hands, brushing the last of it off his shoulders.

"She did." He ran his hand over his scalp as if just remembering. "Do you like it?"

"I like it long." My head dropped back to the stale, bare pillow. The house was outfitted so meanly it was as if we were camping. Outlaws and borrowers. Finbarr got up to put another log on the fire. I stared at the ceiling, which had medallions carved into it, unnecessarily ornate. I had never once thought of Archie's hands on his wife with any kind of jealousy. But how I hated the thought of Agatha's hands on Finbarr. It gave me a clearer glimpse to how it must feel for her, Archie's hands on me, doing far more than cutting my hair.

"And she's here in this house, right now?"

"Of course. I've already said so. Where else would she be?"

"Her own fine house in Torquay. Or a fine hotel. She's got plenty of money, you know, she can well afford it."

"Like you're affording it?"

I didn't answer. Finbarr got back into bed. "She loves her husband, Nan. She wants him back. Give him back to her and come away with me. We can do what we should have done directly after the War."

"Oh, Finbarr."

"We can go back to Ballycotton."

"You're daft if you think I'm ever setting foot in Ireland."

"You can hate Ireland for what it did to you. But I'm Ireland, too. Do you hate me, Nan?"

"Never. You know that."

"And Ireland's not the only country where these things happen."

"But it's where it happened to me."

He closed his eyes. I stroked the cropped hair off his forehead, fingernails grazing his scalp, willing it to grow into its usual floppy disarray. And I felt what I always did. That he was my favorite person on earth, the one in whose presence I most belonged. At the same time, I loved Genevieve more.

"Finbarr," I whispered, to erase the hardness of what I'd just said, "you're my favorite. You're still my favorite."

He opened his eyes. Although his interior weather had gone cloudy, I could see it like a memory, the old insistence on sunlight. Perhaps I could bring it back to him. So we returned to lips and hands and furtive sentiments.

We couldn't hear Agatha, upstairs, clacking away on her typewriter. She knew it was mad to stay here, to not reveal her whereabouts. She ought to get in Miss Oliver's car and drive straight to the police station and turn herself in.

Turn herself in! She balked with indignation at her own interior words. What crime had she committed? None at all. She had every right to storm out of the world.

And still. With so many people searching and worrying, she knew she should return home immediately. For the same reason, she knew she could never return at all. Face all those people? Provide an explanation? Look again into Archie's face and see it entirely devoid of love? Impossible.

She hoped she could trust Chilton to keep his word. Last night his body had thrummed with respectful restraint. His lips were softer than Archie's. He didn't smell like any kind of soap or fancy emollients, just himself, a good grassy smell, a touch of salt water. She herself had traded her scent in these last few days, the last of the lavender fading in favor of woodsmoke, and good old-fashioned sweat.

No matter that Mr. Chilton was a police inspector. She could trust him to keep her secret. She knew she could.

Chilton was also awake at first light, not having changed his clothes or slept a wink. He could hardly remember the last time he'd kissed a woman. Ridiculous to feel happy. This was a conundrum. The whole world looking for a woman he'd found, and what had he done but kiss her and promise to keep her whereabouts a secret. However the years might have changed him, they certainly hadn't made him any smarter.

From overhead he heard an unexpected thump that put him on immediate alert. One doesn't wake to screaming one day without expecting more of the same. But after a few moments passed with only quiet, he allowed himself to breathe again. Today he would focus on the Marstons, so he could confirm Lippincott's theory and make sure there wasn't a murderer on the loose. Harm could be wrought by inaction as much as action. And since the War Chilton had made an oath to himself, to do no more harm in the world.

It's not something you imagine, as a boy, even as you pretend at swords or gunfire. The lives that will end at your hands. It was a German boy from a trench raid who stuck most consistently in Chilton's memory. The boy had been crawling out of the trenches on his hands and knees, and Chilton stooped to bayonet him through the heart. How surprised the boy looked, as if no one had told him going off to war might result in this outcome. Chilton felt so terrible, he'd knelt to give him a drink of water from his canteen, though for this boy there was no more wanting water, or wanting anything. *What are you doing, mate?* a corporal had said, tossing a bomb into the trenches. Chilton screwed the top back onto his canteen. The boy was so young he still had roses in his cheeks—translucent and girlish skin, as if he'd never shaved. Later, when Chilton heard his youngest brother had also been bayoneted, the two men swapped faces, and it was Malcolm, his baby brother, everybody's favorite, eyes glossing over with the shock of it. Young enough to be immortal amid the blaring cannons. Stupid bloody idiots we all were, Chilton thought. We walked over corpses and still believed death might not touch us.

From upstairs the silence was again interrupted. Chilton heard a shout, instantly muffled, followed by a door opening and closing. He hastened upstairs, quickly but not running, to avoid the pounding of footsteps that could wake the entire hotel. In the upstairs hall he found Mr. and Mrs. Race, such a beautiful pair, both faces flushed—the husband's with rage, the wife's with anguish. Mr. Race had his hand around Mrs. Race's wrist, a painful grasp that Chilton knew would leave a mark.

"There now, let her go." Chilton's voice was low and calm, as he might speak to a menacing dog while backing away. Except in this case he didn't back away, but took a step closer.

"This has nothing to with you, sir," Race said. "I suggest you return to your room."

"Good God, man. She's your wife. That's no way to behave toward her."

Mrs. Race wrenched her hand from her husband and held it to her chest. Her husband made a motion as if to grab her again, and Chilton took another step toward him.

"Before you wake the entire hotel," Chilton said, his voice still steady, "why don't I escort Mrs. Race to the kitchen for a cup of tea. While you go back to your room and cool off."

The couple focused on Chilton for the first time. He saw them registering that he was fully clothed, including his over-coat, while the two of them wore nightclothes, their attire, if not their behavior, far more appropriate for the time of day.

"Very well." Mrs. Race smoothed her hair back in one graceful motion. "I could do with a cup of tea. Thank you, Mr. Chilton."

Chilton had promised her tea, but the hotel staff had not yet convened. Instead of the kitchen he brought her to the drawing room just off the front hall. Chilton's nerves felt awfully frayed—too frayed, he thought, to calm someone else down. The young woman paced the small room, arms tight around her waist. He reached into his interior jacket pocket for a cigarette. When he lit it, she jerked her head toward him, as if she'd forgotten he was there. Chilton stood holding the open cigarette case toward her. She took one. He returned the case to his pocket and lit it for her. Always an intimate moment. He noted her wrist was not marked, as he feared it would be, but smooth and unharmed. Her bright blond hair was shoulder-length and silken. Uncurled and mussed from sleep. One of those women who probably don't know they're more beautiful without makeup, or done-up hair. Like Agatha Christie. A surprising, involuntary smile twitched his lip at the thought of her.

Mrs. Race inhaled her cigarette deeply, hungrily, then blew an expert stream of smoke to the side.

"It might be more useful to pour you a brandy. I've seen where Mrs. Leech keeps a bottle behind the reception desk, though I can't account to its quality."

"That sounds grand." Mrs. Race marched over to the couch and collapsed onto it. "Might as well become the sort of person who pours a scoop and lights a cigarette before the sun's properly risen. You see what I've let this marriage make me, Mr. Chilton?"

"I'm afraid you've married a brute."

"I'm afraid I have." She spoke through clenched teeth, staring at some point past him. "And now I'm stuck with him. My family would never abide a divorce. They're not much for scandal."

"Did you know what he was like? Before you married him?"

Mrs. Race took another deep inhale from her cigarette. "I had my suspicions."

"Then may I ask why you went through with it?"

"No. No, you may not, Mr. Chilton."

"Perhaps you can fill me in on another matter then. I'm curious about the other day. In the dining room. Poor Mr. Marston. You were quite heroic."

"Not at all."

"I wonder if you had the chance to talk to either of that couple. Before all the . . . unfortunateness."

"I did not. I've been rather preoccupied with my own unfortunateness." She stubbed out her cigarette, harder than was necessary, in the porcelain ashtray on the coffee table. Then she stood. "Thank you for your care, Mr. Chilton, but I'm off to face the music. Life's not a fairy tale. I thought that was something you old people learned during the War."

She glided out of the room, head held high, as if she had been a dancer rather than a nurse. Chilton inhaled his cigarette to find it already worn down to his fingertips. The small burn shook him awake, nearly taking the place of a good night's sleep, or any night's sleep.

Back at the Timeless Manor, as she had already begun thinking of it, Agatha sat downstairs at the long servants' dining table in the kitchen. She did not consider returning to Sunningdale. Unlike Styles, this house had a good energy. Or perhaps she had brought the good energy with her. Not just she, but Finbarr, brimming with the most unexpected good energy since they'd left Newlands Corner on the wind of excitement, leaving responsibilities behind. She could worry about Teddy but chose not to. The girl would diligently be cared for by Honoria. Agatha would *not* worry about Archie and had to admit it gave her pleasure, him worrying about her for a change.

Certain elements of the world had fallen away. She was writing as she always did, without thought of readers or agents or editors. Agatha wrote to entertain herself, the same way she'd made up stories in her head as a child, spinning her hoop round the monkey puzzle tree at Ashfield and inventing characters. Writing a book was a different world to live in. And she dearly needed a different world.

These past days, she dressed herself from the same collection of men's clothes she'd taken from the previous house, plus Miss Oliver's warm and well-worn coat. Vanity, gone. She still wore her pearl necklace; it had belonged to her mother, but her pearl ring she had pushed to the back of an empty drawer in the servant's room where she was bunking. This morning she had glanced at herself in the mirror, hair unwashed, man's clothing, and thought she could walk right by nearly any of her acquaintances and only those who knew her best would recognize her. And who were those people who knew her best? She couldn't come up with a single person, not even Honoria—a paid companion, if Agatha was honest—who understood her as well, or with whom she had such ease, as the Irishman who'd spirited her away.

Even in this house, large as it was, Agatha could hear Finbarr's nightmares. Every night since they'd run off together, until Nan showed up, Agatha had left her own bed to place her hands on his shoulders. *Finbarr, darling, wake up.* All at once his eyes would open, taking her in, and breathing in gratitude. Twice he'd put his arms around her and held her close. It was a shock to find herself clasped against him, and at the same time it wasn't. She didn't believe in reincarnation, but if she did, she would have thought they'd known each other, Finbarr and she, in a previous life. An unlikely pair in theory but in practice perfectly likely. It made her realize how large her husband had loomed. He had somehow become to her the face of all men, and the way he looked upon her reflected how she appeared to all men. Finbarr represented an entirely different species, and here she had fallen into this strange but perfectly natural step with him.

Which meant she could fall in step with another. Her mother wouldn't have liked the thought of her married to a police inspector. But her mother wasn't here to object, was she? Agatha found herself laughing—horrifying and such a relief, to laugh so quickly on the heels of remembering her mother's death.

"Something funny?"

It was me, standing there in the doorway. Flushed from love-making, my hair amiss, my chin raised in near defiance. The sight of me hardly moved her at all. She didn't envy me or want to hurt me. She didn't even find my presence a particular intrusion. Another fugitive. So long as I agreed to keep my silence, I might as well come aboard. She seemed to have forgotten already—the mission for which Finbarr had enjoined her.

"Hello, Nan."

"Hello, Mrs. Christie."

I didn't feel as sanguine about her, in this moment, as she did about me. It made me furious somehow. To see her at the servants' table. She who'd grown up in cavernous houses that had names. Whose idea of financial hardship was a hundred pounds a year for doing nothing. A five-room flat with a butler and a maid. A life of wanting things—a writing career, a husband, a child—and having them delivered to her, as if the wanting naturally equaled the having. For the sake of a woman such as her a hundred more always suffered.

"Come now," she said. I couldn't account for her cheery disposition. "Call me Agatha, would you? Surely at this point we can dispense with formality. Both of us on the lam."

"I'm not on the lam. I'm on holiday."

"It's rather an unusual holiday. I wonder what Archie would say about it?"

I didn't answer.

"There. I knew you didn't love him."

I sat down at the table.

Agatha stood to get another teacup. "I'm afraid there's no milk." She poured for me.

"I don't suppose Archie would have any right to say anything about it, would he. Not yet."

"True enough." She could have told me about her last night with Archie, but she didn't. It was the first time she and I had been together since the artifice had finally lifted for good. I suppose she liked having a bit of her own artifice. I expected her to start straight in on demands that I relinquish Archie, but she just sat there, sipping tea, watching me do the same. It softened me toward her somehow. Perhaps if I didn't begrudge her good fortune, I'd finally be due some of my own.

"What are the provisions like here? Would they last awhile?"

"There's tinned fruit. Tinned tongue, and kippers. Sardines. Loads of wine, if that's what you're about. Finbarr's been on some scavenges in town for fresh food. Apples and cheese. We have enough to last awhile. But not forever, of course. And we don't know when the proper owners will return."

"It doesn't look like they intend to anytime soon, does it."

"No. But there's no predicting what people will do."

"There's a part of me that could just go upstairs. Never eat or drink again. Wither away to a skeleton in his arms."

"Like Elvira Madigan and Sixten Sparre? Terrible story. If we could talk to their ghosts, I'm sure they'd tell us it hadn't been at all worth it. I never did go much in for romances. Especially not the tragic ones."

"Neither did I," I lied. If the idea of me dead in Finbarr's arms—dead anywhere—pleased her, paving the road back to her husband, her face did not betray it.

"Finbarr tells me you want to be a writer."

"Does he?" How humiliating. I wondered what else he'd told her. "That used to be true, I suppose."

Finbarr bustled in just then. Full of business and energy. "Good morning, Agatha," he said as if they were absolute equals, the best of friends.

"Good morning, dear Finbarr," she said with authentic warmth, and I remembered how everyone always loved him. I used to think it was because of his insistent happiness. But now that was gone and still the love he inspired remained.

Several minutes of domestic exchanges transpired. Finbarr produced a loaf of bread from the pantry, and Agatha found some marmalade and poured him some tea. It was a remarkable thing to witness. I sat, not helping, and eventually food was placed before me.

"Have you heard from our man then?" Agatha asked me, when all was settled again.

I glanced at Finbarr, whose face refused to darken or acknowledge anyone else as my man.

"I haven't. Not for days. He doesn't know where I am."

"That makes two of us."

"He's terribly worried about you," I said.

"How do you know if you haven't heard from him?"

"Well, he was, last time we spoke."

"I might have considered that good news a few days ago. Now I find myself not much caring, if I'm to be honest."

I had no way of knowing the smile on her face owed itself at least in part to last night's kiss with Chilton. I only thought, *Poor Archie. Last week with two women intent on his attentions, this week with none.*

"Finbarr has some things he'd like me to say to you," said Agatha.

"Does he?"

"Before I begin I'd like to remind you. In my whole life no one's hurt me as much as you have."

Partly because I couldn't bear Finbarr watching this interaction, I brought my hands up to cover my face. Agatha reached across the table and pulled them away. "We're not going to do that. We're not going to have me comforting you for all the wrongs you've done me."

I looked at Finbarr. He had his eyes focused on Agatha, counting on her to say what he wanted and set everything to right.

"There've been some wrongs done to me as well." I knew my voice sounded ominous, but I didn't care. "I lost something much more valuable than a husband."

"Finbarr's filled me in on some of your history. Things I didn't know. I daresay Archie doesn't even know. Does he?"

Was this a threat? I moved to shoot an accusing glare at Finbarr, for telling Agatha what so few people knew.

Then she said something that surprised me: "I'm sorry about what happened to you in Ireland." She still had her hands over mine. "Dreadfully sorry. A travesty. Abhorrent. An outrage."

It occurred to me this was the first apology I had ever received, from anyone, regarding my stay in Sunday's Corner. And I knew—and know still—it wasn't connected to what she said next:

"You won't tell anyone where I am?"

"No," I promised. "I won't."

In all the years since Agatha Christie disappeared, amid all the conjecture about her state of mind, and her activities, and her motives, not one single person has ever come to me for answers. People like to follow a very particular script. It never occurred to anyone that she and I might, after all, be friends. That the reason she stayed quiet, forever and always, was not to protect herself, but me.

Eventually she would move beyond all this. She would marry again (a significantly younger man) and become successful beyond anyone's wildest imaginings. Things would work out for her in ways they would never work out for me. In ways they seldom work out for anyone.

For now we sat, staring at each other across the narrow table, the fire in the stove crackling coziness. Refusing to say what the other most wanted to hear. While Finbarr sat with us, thinking his mission well on its way to accomplished, not knowing that one day soon, no matter what was said and done, my name would be Mrs. Christie, too.

Here Lies Sister Mary

Father Joseph loved England. In 1919 this made him an unusual Irishman. That June a small British patrol was attacked in Rathclaren, and during his sermon he interrupted his usual screed against lust to bellow his opposition. "Crown and country"—he pounded the podium—"it's what we went to war to defend, and now these ninnies are trying to upend it all."

"It's a relief, isn't it?" Sister Mary Clare said to me one afternoon. "That they don't hold being English against us. I've sometimes thought about going home, to an English order. But with Father Joseph in charge it hardly seems necessary." She smiled more to herself than at me. "In truth I believe it makes me his favorite. My being English."

She was walking beside me as all the girls filed through the corridor for Holy Hour, a ritual that took place the first Friday of every month. Sister Mary Declan looked back at me and frowned, but it was a nun talking to me, not another girl, so I went ahead and answered.

"Does it?" I tried to make my tone sound idle, but felt the blood leave my face, worried that being English might draw his attention to me.

"It's just a flash in the pan, all this IRA business," Sister Mary Clare went on, not noticing my discomfort. "I'll be shocked if it lasts another month. You'd think these boys might have had enough fighting, mightn't you, seen enough horror, to be causing more of it in their own country."

"Does Father Joseph know about me? Being English?"

"I've never heard him say a word about you one way or the other."

Her words should have given me relief. And I did seem to be invisible to Father Joseph—as if a magic cloak protected me from his notice—but I remained terrified this would change.

Sister Mary Clare squeezed my hand and walked away before we entered the chapel, humming her usual, eerie tune. She had a pretty voice, even though she never attached words to her songs. I could hear her as I stood with my fellow penitents, still as could be for fifteen minutes, our arms outstretched at our sides as if we were hanging on the cross. If anyone twitched, Sister Mary Declan made us start again. On this day we were in the chapel for a full hour. It was hard work not to tremble, thinking of the priest's love of England. I could feel my baby's little hands, pressing against the walls of my womb, and I was grateful she hadn't ever glimpsed the world outside.

A new girl arrived on a Tuesday, and on Friday she escaped, exactly how nobody could say. She simply vanished from our midst without a confiding word to anyone. The bells clanged and the nuns flurried. I took heart when she never returned. The next day, working in the nuns' graveyard, I looked through the bars to ascertain the route she'd taken. Through the fence that surrounded the graves I could see the entrance to the convent, the wrought iron gate that opened to let in visitors. And I noticed at the corner, where the gate met the cement wall, one bar had rotted away and fallen into the high grass. The space it left was still too small for my pregnant self to slip through. But I wouldn't be pregnant forever.

The two other girls worked in obedient silence, pulling weeds and cleaning lichen from the headstones. I knelt and pulled the bar into place, lodging it in so the cracks wouldn't be visible unless examined closely.

That afternoon Sister Mary Clare sat down beside me in the sewing room, where I worked alongside a group of girls, mending old uniforms. Other girls—who unlike me were handy with knitting needles—worked on the tiny matinée coats the babies would wear to keep warm. I prayed my baby would never have one of these. I'd get out of here too soon for the nuns to dress her. Whatever clothes my child wore, they would not be manufactured at this convent.

"Dear Nan," Sister Mary Clare said, perched on one of the same backless stools the rest of us used. "You don't seem yourself." She patted my arm.

Two nuns came in carrying babies, and the girls they belonged to put their knitting aside to nurse them.

"What would you have been," I asked Sister Mary Clare, as I executed a clumsy stitch, "if you hadn't been a nun?"

"Why, a mother, of course." She smiled over at the nursing

babies then quoted Coleridge, though at the time I believed they were her own words. "'A mother is a mother still, the holiest thing alive.'"

I let my work drop into my lap and covered my face with my hands, thinking of Bess. Was she still the holiest thing alive, now that her baby was dead? "Bess. Poor Bess."

"There, there. Don't you worry about Bess. Why, she's a wife now. She can have another baby, one that can be baptized properly. She can have ten babies all fat and happy, gathered round her feet."

I broke down sobbing, and Sister Mary Clare rubbed my back in gentle circles. She would have been a good mother. "Take heart. Bess's young man turned up for her. Could be yours will, too. He'll have read the letter I sent him by now." She handed me a handkerchief and I blew my nose.

"Here." She reached into her sleeve. "I've brought you a treat." She pressed a piece of soda bread into my hand, still warm, and slathered with fresh butter, a luxury I hadn't seen since I left home. I looked at the other girls apologetically.

"Go ahead and eat. Your friends don't begrudge you a treat, do you, girls?"

None of them looked up to meet her challenging gaze. *I should have seen it.* But I couldn't afford to. I bit into the soda bread, butter melting on my tongue. It tasted so good I had to stop myself from telling the nun I loved her.

That night I dreamed of Father Joseph's jowly face hovering over mine. His veiny hands pawing at me. His groans and snorts.

"No, no, no!"

I woke already sitting up. My hands, covering my face, smelled as if they belonged to someone else. This place was wholly foreign. Fiona sat next to me, patting my back, not asking. We all had identical dreams, good and bad. In this way and perhaps only this way, Father Joseph's theory of our sameness was correct.

"Tell me," I whispered. Fiona recited my parents' address in London, her voice light and cheerful as a fairy's.

There were so many more of us than there were of them. What if we'd banded together? An uprising? A hundred girls rising up against the handful of nuns and one lecherous priest? We had more to fight for than any soldier in the IRA. We could have taken our captors down and marched back into the world, our youth and our children reclaimed.

Bess and her American were married before traveling across the Atlantic, by an Anglican priest in London. They settled in Philadelphia. Did her parents back in Doolin weep when she never returned? Or did they rejoice at being done with her sin and shame?

She didn't care about that anymore. She missed her brothers and would always love her little sister, but the only sins she still believed in were the ones that had been committed against her. She'd never set foot in any church again as long as she lived.

At night she clung to her new husband. She never blamed him for arriving too late. They were a single unit in this, their loss, and the crimes that had been done to them both. But one crime done to Bess she bore entirely alone. She bore it daily, and nightly, unable to expel the memory of the priest's invasion.

And then there were her arms that ached the way only a mother's can, when they're empty of her child and always will be.

"Ronan," she said throughout the day, mostly when no one could hear her. In different tones. Fondly. Scolding. Laughing. Proud. As if his ghost accompanied her, the way he himself would have, had he been there, beside her, the reflection of all the emotions she should have experienced, rather than the ones she did.

The Disappearance

It rained in Sunningdale on Friday morning. The temperature had warmed. Teddy stood in the window of the nursery, holding a stuffed rabbit Agatha had named Touchstone. She'd given it to Teddy before she and Archie left to travel round the world. "Some of my love is stored inside him," she'd told Teddy, tying a blue ribbon round its neck. "As long as you hold him, my love is always with you. Whenever you hug him, I'm hugging you back."

"Touchstone is a girl, not a boy," Teddy insisted. She didn't much care for men. It was women who took care of her. Every toy with a face was a she. Sonny, the little whittled dog, was a she.

Despite the rain Sunningdale crawled with people. Teddy watched the pelting rain clutter her window. She saw scattered people in raincoats but didn't find them alarming; she was used to fusses on the property that had nothing to do with her. She put Touchstone down. Her mother's dog stood at her ankle, and she lifted him up so he could look out the window, too. Peter yapped twice at the sight of strangers, then settled, resigned, into a cuddle. Usually when Agatha traveled, she took the dog with her. Teddy was glad Agatha had left him behind this time; it was fun to have him all to herself, always right beside her. He barked, his funny little *arf*, as someone new trudged up the drive.

"There, there," Teddy said to Peter. "There's no need to bother about all that." She turned from the window and set to dressing for school. Likely she and Honoria would drive instead of walk, considering the weather.

The press had dubbed the search for Agatha "the Great Hunt." As if it were a novel or a film. A sporting event, a national pastime. Or a war. Police officers and civic-minded citizens spread out all over England, doing their part.

"Rather grand of you to dub this hunt *great*," Archie raged at Thompson, holding up a newspaper with the phrase emblazoned in a giant headline. "You haven't turned up so much as a thumbprint."

Thompson crossed his arms and regarded Archie, who had marched into his office at Berkshire Police Headquarters as if to scold an underling. Thompson certainly hoped Agatha Christie was found alive, but that seemed more unlikely with every passing day. Living people turned up quickly. Dead people took their time, especially if a murderer had taken pains to hide them.

"You're finding every dead woman in England," Archie went on unfairly. Only one dead woman had been found, poor Miss Annabel Oliver. "Except the one you're actually searching for."

Thompson attempted to raise an eyebrow and failed. A gesture Archie had in his repertoire, and it galled the officer to realize he'd tried to imitate it.

"Searching for a dead woman, are we?" Thompson's tone meant to remind Archie of who was in charge of whom, and who knew what.

"No," Archie insisted. "She's alive. I know she is."

"You're right to know we're not awfully good at finding women. You know who else we haven't managed to locate? A Miss Nan O'Dea. She seems to have gone missing from her place of employment as well as her flat." Thompson didn't tell Archie that he wasn't worried about my well-being. An officer had stopped in to the Imperial British Rubber Company and learned that I'd phoned to say my holiday would last a few days longer than expected. It would do just as well, Thompson thought, to wait on interviewing me until after a murder was confirmed.

"There's no need to trouble Nan," Archie said. "No need at all. She's the last person to know where Agatha's disappeared to."

"And who would you say is the first?"

A dark, sorrowful look crossed Archie's face, and he disappointed Thompson by breaking down in tears. Even if Archie Christie turned out not to be behind his wife's disappearance, the constable wished to waste no sympathy on him. Yesterday Archie had given a rather unfortunate interview to the *Daily Mail*, insisting his wife would never do harm to herself, but adding if she did, it would most certainly be with poison. Like so many men who believed themselves above reproach in deed and word, the manifest destiny of mattering in the world, Archie had no inkling as how to edit himself. Thompson, like so many men in positions of power who nonetheless found themselves tacitly subordinate to the Archies of the world, enjoyed imagining Archie's downfall. Thompson did not wish to feel a drop of kindness toward him, so it was most inconvenient that Archie Christie's tears appeared to spring from genuine, uncontrollable agony.

Archie drove to his mother's through the rain, shivering. He'd left Styles without his coat, most unlike him. He'd broken down in tears in front of another man and didn't feel shame or embarrassment or anything except the nagging, overriding, maddening question: *Where is she?*

He regretted the interview he'd given to the *Mail*. As if the police weren't looking at him sideways already. No more press, Archie vowed, thinking not of himself but his wife. She was shy. *Shy.* The idea some of the officers floated, that this might be a publicity stunt, was utterly preposterous. His wife would never do such a thing. If she was alive, how could she possibly avoid seeing the newspaper articles, splashed across England— the world!—screaming her name. She would be horrified. At first glance of a headline—blaring her age!—she would ring Archie or turn herself in to the police or simply board a train and come home. This was what worried him most. Where could she be that the publicity had not reached her? The only place he could think of was dead.

Dorothy Sayers, who fancied herself a medium as well as a novelist, had come to the Silent Pool and claimed to sense Agatha's absence from the region. Now *that* was a publicity stunt; atrocious woman, hopping on the coattails of the sort of infamy tailor-made to sell detective novels by the bushel. Sir Arthur Conan Doyle had phoned to deliver the sad news that he'd consulted a psychic who'd assured him Agatha no longer inhabited our mortal realm. "We're working on direct word from her," Conan Doyle had said, and Archie rang off without a word, Order of the British Empire be damned. Oh, it was all nonsense, this idea that spirits could communicate what hundreds of living men could not find with their own hands and eyes.

Still, when Archie reached his mother's house, he turned off the car and leaned his cheek against the glass of the driver's-side window. He closed his eyes and tried to sense whether Agatha was gone from this world. Can a man live with a woman for so many years, sleep beside her so many nights, without the molecules in his body palpably rearranging themselves after her death? He forgot they had ever separated, in body or affection. He forgot *divorce* was a word that existed in the English language.

She's alive, he thought. *I know she is.*

Agatha was shy and lovely and thoughtful and proper. Agatha was considerate. Agatha would be horrified by knowing what a fuss had risen, all in her name. She couldn't possibly be alive and avoid seeing a newspaper. And she couldn't possibly see a newspaper and not come rushing home.

Yet she *was* alive. She had to be.

"I *never* wanted you to marry that woman, did I?"

Peg Helmsley, as she made this grand understatement, held

out her silver-handled cane and thrust it in the air toward him, like a sword. Years ago, when Archie had first given his mother the news of his engagement, Peg had forbid it absolutely. He was nothing but a young subaltern and couldn't expect a penny from her. What's more, she'd disapproved of Agatha's Peter Pan collars. Showing off her neck! Peg was from a strict Irish Catholic family, one of twelve children. The bare-necked Agatha, who'd already been engaged once before, might as well have been a chorus girl. When the two had gone ahead and married despite Peg's objections, she had burst into tears and taken to her bed for days.

"You can hardly blame this on Agatha," Archie said. Part of him did blame Agatha. If only she'd handled his affair with a stiff upper lip, as she was raised to do. Then all he'd be contending with, as far as his mother, was the unavoidably violent reaction she'd have upon discovering Nan.

Peg lowered her cane. Her second husband, William, was off on a walk. It was just the two of them, Archie and her, the perfect time for a confession. She stepped close to her son and closed her hand onto his lapel.

"You haven't done something dreadful, have you, Archie?"

"Good God, Mother. Of course I haven't." He stepped back so sharply the old woman lurched forward unsteadily. Archie took his mother by the elbows and helped her into a chair.

"I've had to stop William bringing in the papers," Peg said with an indignant thump of her cane. "A person could have a stroke, couldn't she, reading about her own family in the papers. It's a humiliation, is what it is. Oh, if Agatha isn't dead, I will be so cross with her."

Archie sank onto the settee across from her. He would have nodded in agreement if it hadn't hit him so hard, his own mother believing he could kill his wife. But then his answer, *Of course I haven't*, wasn't precisely true. He *had* done something dreadful to Agatha, and that had spurred her going missing. He remembered the marks on her wrists and his callousness toward them. The one and only thing he hadn't done to his wife, at this point, was murder.

Home in the evening, Archie smoked his pipe and poured whiskey after whiskey until sentimentality overtook him. He climbed the stairs to Teddy's room, where she lay sleeping with deep, untroubled breath. It was the first he'd seen of her all day—perhaps several days—the two of them rattling in different corners of the house, her caretaking not Archie's duty. He sat down on the bed. Peter lay beside her. Archie would have stroked Teddy's brow but he didn't want to wake her, so instead he picked up the stuffed rabbit Agatha had given her and sobbed into the velvety fur.

Teddy lay there, eyes closed shut so he wouldn't know she was awake. It made her uncomfortable, having Archie there. Hearing him cry for goodness' sake; fathers weren't meant to cry.

Not that she felt afraid of him. She didn't feel afraid of anyone. Thanks to the life Agatha and Archie gave her, Teddy never did find out what men can be.

Back to morning:

It rained in Harrogate, too, pelting the windows of the Timeless Manor. After breakfast, Finbarr, Agatha, and I walked upstairs, Agatha continuing on to the top floor to write. I wanted to return to the bedroom, but Finbarr shook his head. "They'll worry about you at the hotel. Best not to draw too much attention. Unless you'd rather leave England with me today?"

"Of course that's what I'd rather do." In a tone that indicated clearly it wasn't what I *would* do.

He drove me back to the hotel in Miss Oliver's Bentley. When I walked into the lobby, Mrs. Leech proved him right by saying, "There you are, Mrs. O'Dea. We were almost ready to set the hounds out after you."

"So sorry. I do love walking in your beautiful countryside."

"In this weather? That'll be the death of you. Why don't you book a treatment, Mrs. O'Dea?"

I promised I might later and she sent me into the dining room. Breakfast had passed but tea and scones were on the sideboard. I wasn't particularly hungry but sat myself down, staring out the long windows. My whole body thrummed with Finbarr. I sipped my tea, gone a little cold.

"Mrs. O'Dea. May I join you?"

It was Chilton, rumpled and handsome and blurred about the edges. I hadn't heard him come in—more like a ghost than a man.

"You're something of a prowler, aren't you?"

"Not at all." He sat down, though I hadn't said yes. "Mrs. Leech tells me you extended your stay."

"Did she? How indiscreet of her."

"She was worried about you. And apparently I'm the expert on missing women."

Chilton had this way about him that made everything he

said sound like a musing rather than a pronouncement. An interior loveliness, a willingness to question himself, apparent on his exterior. I expected I would feel fond of him right up to the moment he clapped my wrists in handcuffs. Perhaps even afterward. Mr. Chilton was not the sort of man one blamed. He was swept up by the world like the rest of us, doing his best to muddle through it. He was so entirely unthreatening to me that I couldn't have been taken more off guard when he said, "I've been to the coroner."

"Have you?"

"Yes. Poor Mr. and Mrs. Marston. I never got the chance to properly meet them. Did you?"

"No. Frightful business. You hear of it often, don't you. One-half of a married couple dies, and the other follows for grief. Would you excuse me, Mr. Chilton? I think I'd like to lie down awhile."

I stood and pushed back my chair too abruptly. It scraped horribly. Behind my throbbing temple, the beginnings of a headache. One couldn't function on so little sleep.

"Good night, Mr. Chilton." Then I amended, "Good morning."

Chilton watched me leave, thoughtful. He lit a cigarette. He picked up the uneaten scone I'd abandoned and took a bite. Disappointed, somehow, that I didn't seem to know he'd been at the manor last night. Did he imagine Agatha and me gossiping about their kiss like schoolgirls?

The rain let up. He touched his lips and stood to leave the dining room. He thought to get some sleep but changed his mind and walked to the Harrogate Library. The small and cozy building was overseen by a white-haired librarian, who greeted Chilton as he entered. He asked her if she knew off-hand whether they had any books by Agatha Christie.

"All checked out," the librarian, Miss Barnard, said. She held up the daily paper and showed him a picture of Agatha, with a wide-eyed little girl sitting in her lap. "Quite an interest in that lady these days. What with her tragic disappearance."

Miss Barnard pointed him toward a table stacked with an array of new novels. Chilton looked through them, thinking he'd try to find something more to my liking than the Willy novel he'd seen me take from the shelves at the Bellefort. He could tell I'd chosen the book without enthusiasm and believed it would behoove him to make friends with me despite my resistance. After some perusal he landed upon *The Silver Spoon*, John Galsworthy's latest installment of the Forsyte Saga. As he tucked the novel under his good arm, his eyes landed upon a woman, sitting at a table in the next room, a stack of books in front of her, studying the open one intently: Mrs. Agatha Christie. For the outing she had changed into her own clothes, skirt and stockings. They were much the worse for wear, wrinkled and muddied about the hem, making her appearance almost as conspicuous as if she'd been wearing her man's clothes.

Chilton crossed into the alcove on swift feet. She was engrossed enough that it took her a moment to look up at him.

"Why, Mr. Chilton." She turned wonderfully, beautifully red. As if surprised by the way her face warmed, she touched her cheek, then removed her hand quickly, further embarrassed at being so transparent.

"Please, call me Frank."

With no spoken agreement the two stood. Agatha put on a long wool coat, rather the wrong size for her, too wide and too short. Chilton helped her to gather up her stack of books and they went together to the desk. Chilton started with surprise to hear Agatha give her name as Mrs. O'Dea.

Miss Barnard looked up with a smile. Then something in her face changed. "My goodness. You look just like the missing authoress. The one he was asking after." She pointed to Chilton, then turned the newspaper toward them, again showing the picture.

This was Chilton's fault. He should have warned her, kept her from showing herself to the librarian. He watched as Agatha brought her hands to her pearl necklace, paling almost as dramatically as she had colored earlier. By way of coming to her rescue, he put his arm around her shoulders. "Darling, there is a bit of a resemblance, isn't there?" To the librarian he said, "My wife hates being told she looks like anyone else. Wants to be an original."

Dubious, Miss Barnard returned her eyes to the picture, then back to Agatha. "Well," she said, half-convinced, "I do hope they find the poor lady alive. Seems unlikely at this point, doesn't it?"

"Yes, indeed," Chilton said.

Agatha, absent her stack of books, had already turned and headed for the door. Chilton gathered everything—including my Galsworthy—and bade goodbye to the librarian.

"You're certainly not cut out for this," he scolded when he caught up to Agatha outside. "Not much of a poker player either, I would suppose."

"Did you see that headline? My photograph? 'The Great

Hunt'? How can I ever go back? How can I ever face the world again?" She covered her face with gloved hands, then stepped forward and pressed the crown of her head against Chilton's chest. He wasn't much taller than she so she had to stoop to do so. Chilton lifted his arm to hold her, and the books clattered to the ground. From where they stood, he could see the librarian, standing in the window, watching them.

"Agatha."

She stepped back and they knelt together to pick up the books.

"Will you drive me back to the manor? I don't feel fit to do it myself."

Chilton cranked up the Bentley while Agatha settled in the passenger seat. Miss Oliver's coat smelled like rose water. The Bentley was too large for Agatha's taste. How she missed her own little car. She thought of it left in so precarious a spot and hoped it was all right. That some good soul—Archie, even— had pushed it back onto the road and driven it home where it belonged. When she was a girl, in the tidal wave of financial wreckage following her father's death—and the other times in her life, early in her marriage, for example, when the specter of money troubles loomed, her mother-in-law's warnings bearing out, numbers not properly arranging themselves in the ledger. What if someone had told her then that one day she herself would make enough money, by her own hands, to purchase such a thing, her dear Morris Cowley? Would she ever see it again? Was it worth leaving it behind, along with everything else— Teddy—to never have to face the questions the whole world would ask if she reappeared?

When Chilton got behind the wheel, she said, "I can't bear

going home and facing the world. But how can I do anything else? The more time they spend looking for me, the worse it will be. You should drive me to police headquarters straightaway. Just end this whole thing here and now."

"I don't find myself able to do that. Not yet."

So many police, so many people, discharged in the search for her. What luck that such a lovely one had been successful. She reached over and grabbed Chilton's hand. "I don't like romances. They ring false to me. Especially when people meet and fall in love at a glance."

"What about several glances?"

She laughed and let go of his hand. They both sat and stared through the windscreen for several minutes. Then she said, "She's still watching. The librarian. You'd better drive."

Back at the Bellefort I had not gone upstairs to lie down, as I'd told Chilton, but only to change my clothes. Having made an appearance at the hotel, assuring the general public of my remaining presence in the world, I escaped from it again almost at once. The day had warmed. The rain had lifted. *Solvitur ambulando.* When I reached the Timeless Manor's drive, I ran the length of it.

"Look what I found," Finbarr said, meeting me on the lawn outside, as if he'd known I would come straight back. It was a tennis net, rackets, and balls. He set it up and we played two sets, me winning them both handily.

A big black car came sputtering up the drive. I lifted my hand to shade my eyes. There in the driver's seat sat Mr. Chilton. All the workings of my body halted. No breath to my lungs or blood from my heart. Agatha had been found. Was Chilton here to arrest Finbarr? All of us, for trespassing? Worst of all, regardless of what happened next, would this time come to an abrupt end, all of us returning to life as it had been unspooling?

Instead, Finbarr called out, as the two of them emerged from the automobile. Cheerful as you please, as if he'd known the man for ages, he said, "Do you play, Mr. Chilton?"

And Chilton said, absolutely casual, "I did once or twice before the War. Afraid I'm a bit of a liability now." He indicated his bad arm.

"It's just for fun," Finbarr said.

Chilton nodded. He looked at me as though he'd fully expected to find me here. "Hello, Miss O'Dea." He pronounced the *miss* pointedly.

"I haven't got an eye for balls," Agatha said. "I never have." Still she went upstairs to change back into her men's clothes. Finbarr, Chilton, and I stood on the grass. I wanted to ask Chilton when he'd discovered Agatha, but something silenced me. I didn't want to say anything, lest I break whatever spell allowed this to happen—all of us discovered and yet not ruined. I felt a burst of love for Chilton, that he had found her, yet apparently had no intention of alerting the world.

"It's rather magical here," I said, instead of posing any questions.

"Indeed it is," Chilton agreed.

Agatha returned. Since I was the best player I took Chilton as my partner. For once I held back on my need to win, letting Chilton swing at balls I could easily have reached. Despite her disclaimer Agatha played quite nicely. All the upper-crust girls were passable at tennis. The four of us played while our hands reddened and chapped along with our cheeks. But the same magic that had brought us all here together without spelling disaster seemed to keep us warm enough, half-dead tennis balls tossed in the air, scores called out, the pop and whack of slicing rackets.

How long did we play? How does one measure time in a place where time has vanished? At some point the shaggy dog from down the road leaped out from the bushes. He stole our ball in midplay, running off with it, and though we could easily have given it up for lost, Finbarr and I reenacted our youth by chasing after him, calling to him, running in mad circles until the dog tired and dropped the ball at Finbarr's feet. The two of us collapsed in a laughing heap, ruffling the dog's fur and letting him lick our chins. Finbarr scooped up the ball and stood.

"Make a wish."

He could see from my face. I knew how this game worked. You can declare a wish granted but that doesn't make it so. He dropped the ball, the laughter gone. Finbarr's magic powers had their limits, and they were fatal ones. I looked off, into the trees, not ready to face the broken spell.

By the time we thought to look around us, Agatha and Chilton were gone.

In silent agreement they had walked up to the top floor, where Agatha lay down on the bed she hadn't bothered to make that morning, used as she was to someone else performing that task. Chilton rekindled the fire, then lay down beside her. She did not object. Nothing real existed. It was a span out of time. No consequences. She acknowledged what she ought to be feeling—the rekindled romance between Finbarr and me could represent her road back to Archie. Instead she felt something different and altogether more liberating.

What she felt was, she could allow herself to kiss Chilton. She could allow him to remove her clothes, and she could even assist him with the garments that required more than one hand. She could take him inside her and enjoy it immensely. If she became pregnant and went back to Archie, she could pass the child off as his, and that would serve him right. If she became pregnant and Chilton disappeared from her life, and she and Archie divorced, her marriage would still protect her, as would her money, the living she was quite capable of making on her own. Among Agatha's enviable qualities, perhaps the most significant was her ability to thrive in this man's world. Following the rules but managing also to rise above them.

Her new novel was coming out in one month. As aghast as the headlines made her, in the new flat calm of throwing aside all social mores, she allowed herself to think, *How many more people will recognize my name, now, when they see* The Big Four *in a bookshop's window?* Curiosity so often amounted to money spent.

But that was a secondary point of thought. The main point was this bubble, away from every ordinary concern.

A while later, when Chilton lay staring at the ceiling and Agatha lay naked in his arms, several thick blankets piled on top of them, he said, "I have to ask. You've told me Miss O'Dea is your husband's mistress."

"Yes." A small sigh. Nobody wanted the past or the world at large to intrude on such a moment.

"But that's not the only point of connection, is it?"

"No," Agatha said frankly. "Miss O'Dea is my husband's mistress because she believes my daughter belongs to her."

And so she told Chilton everything Finbarr had told her, about my time in Ireland, and how it all ended.

Here Lies Sister Mary

My little girl was born on August 5, 1919, at the county hospital in City of Cork. They say first children come slow and hard, but not mine. A few hours, that's all. Susanna had warned me I wouldn't get stitched afterward—punishment wherever it could be found was encouraged for the girls from the convent at Sunday's Corner, even at hospital—but the midwife who attended me was kind. She had green eyes and freckles that reminded me of my mother and Colleen. Nothing in the way she treated me indicated she knew where I'd come from, though certainly she did know, from my short hair and gray uniform, not to mention the desperation with which I reached for my child, as if I'd never be allowed to hold her again.

"What will you name her then?" the midwife asked, so gently I could believe whatever name I chose would stand forever.

"Genevieve," I whispered, running my fingers down her tiny nose, flattened from her battle into the world. We memorized each other's face as she nursed for the first time. *A mother is a mother still, the holiest thing alive.*

"Will you send a letter for me?" I whispered to the midwife. At the same time sifting through my options since Sister Mary Clare's letter to Finbarr hadn't worked. My mother. Megs or Louisa. Aunt Rosie.

The midwife's face darkened with sadness. "Hold your baby, sweetness," she said, by way of saying no. "Give her all the love you can."

And so I did, all the ten glorious days I lay in at hospital. A cot was beside my bed, but Genevieve didn't occupy it a single time. Instead we slept cradled together, the scent of colostrum and then milk wafting from her lips as she exhaled her tiny, contented breath across my chin.

You might be thinking, those ten days were my chance. There was no iron gate. At night I wasn't locked in. I did think about an escape. But these thoughts led to images of myself out on the road in the dark, clutching a helpless newborn. Not a penny to my name. My hair and clothes announcing my identity to the world, begging me to be returned to the convent, or someplace even worse.

So I bided my time obediently. I returned to the convent, lying on my bed in the dormitory that first night while Genevieve lay unreachable in the room below. I thought I'd known what the other girls experienced, hearing their babies cry while unable to go to them. I thought I'd been sharing in their grief. But I hadn't known the half of it. If I could have made my way out a window and scaled down the wall to the nursery, I would have. Instead I held my rock-hard breasts, determined that not a drop be released until I could get to her. But then a cry would come through the floorboards, and I'd know it was Genevieve, and the milk would let down without my baby to catch it.

"Such a good nurser," Sister Mary Clare cooed in the morning, as Genevieve gulped with desperate relief, her little cheeks hollowing out with the effort, her face flushed red and sorrowful from her first night away from her mother.

"Please," I begged the nun. "You've only one night attendant. Don't you need another? Couldn't that be me?"

"It's not usually new mothers who get that job," Sister Mary Clare said, dubious.

"Please. I'll work so hard. I'll be so good. I promise you."

"I'll see what I can do." She chucked my chin, eyes alight with fondness.

That night I lay in bed, desperately needing to sleep but only able to listen to my baby cry. I got out of bed and went to the door, rattling the knob despite having heard the key turn hours earlier. It stood firmly locked against me.

"It's no use," Susanna whispered from her cot. She was due any day now. Years later when I was pregnant the second time, married to Archie, I would sleep with no less than five pillows, propped all around me. Susanna lay on her side, the thin pillow meant for her head clutched against her belly.

I perched on her bed and gently rubbed the small of her back, thinking she'd shoo me away, but instead she sighed with relief. Closing my eyes, I saw the difficult but preferable future I'd scuttled by coming to Ireland in search of Finbarr. The one where I'd taken my grandmother's wedding ring and run away with its shining virtue on my finger. Boarded a ship to America, given birth in New York City, or San Francisco, as a war widow. I could have been anybody except the girl who'd put her own and her child's fate into the hands of foreign strangers.

In the morning Sister Mary Declan escorted me and the other nursing mothers to our babies to feed them before prayers. As I settled on a stool with Genevieve, Sister Mary Clare marched in, a triumphant smile on her face.

"I've done it, Nan. The Mother Superior has given her permission. You can be a night attendant, starting this very evening."

I clutched Genevieve tightly enough to unlatch her. Her eyes blinked open in frustration, and I saw they had changed from the steel gray of a newborn to the shocking, layered blue of her father's.

"There, there." I wiped the dribble from her chin and brought her back to drink her fill. "Did you hear that? We're going to be all right. We're going to be together."

I refused to sign the papers Sister Mary Declan thrust before me, agreeing to let the church put Genevieve up for adoption.

"Is that what you want, then?" Sister Mary Declan scolded. "That she should grow up in an orphanage? If you truly loved her, you'd let her have proper parents."

"She *has* proper parents."

Sister Mary Declan gave me a lash with her strop for that, but it was half-hearted. She still had enough humanity to feel sorry for me. Looking back on any kindness the nuns showed me, I feel a fury. It was those small kindnesses—as if refraining from beating me were a kindness—that kept me there too long.

I was so grateful for small favors. Such as Father Joseph

walking by me without a second glance. Such as being allowed to stay up all night long, tending Genevieve and the other babies in the nursery. Any time a baby cried I would think of its mother, listening upstairs, and cuddle and rock the poor thing until there was quiet. After my night duty I would nurse and bathe Genevieve, go to prayers and Mass, then up to the dormitories to sleep until our midday meal, then return to work scrubbing floors or washing clothes until evening

Sister Mary Clare continued to sneak extra food to me. "Don't worry," she would say, placing a biscuit or boiled egg into my hand. "I'll keep Genevieve hidden for you. Nobody will adopt her, I promise you that. Your young man will arrive any day. Pretty as ever, I told him you were. You'll be one of the lucky ones. I know you will."

Susanna went off to the county hospital to give birth, returned to us for three weeks, then was sent to a Magdalene Laundry in Limerick. Her baby boy stayed on at the convent.

"We can't have a second offender staying on too long, contaminating the rest of you girls," said Sister Mary Declan, when they sent Susanna away. Sunday's Corner and Pelletstown were twentieth-century inventions, specifically for mothers and babies. The Magdalene laundries had originally been established to incarcerate prostitutes, but as the Irish State closed in on its independence, they increasingly became a repository for any girl suspected of sexual impropriety. This could include girls who were considered flirtatious or too pretty. Girls who made the mistake of telling a priest or family member they'd been molested. Girls with nowhere to go after their debt was worked off. Girls such as Susanna, who'd proven themselves beyond redemption by landing at Sunday's Corner twice. *Fallen away.*

For all I know, Susanna spent her whole life at the Magdalene Laundry. She wouldn't have been the first woman to do so, nor the last.

Meanwhile Fiona's little son was adopted, and the nuns refused to tell her where he'd gone. Her cheerful words persisted. When she said, "The nuns know best. He'll have a better life than I could ever give him," her hands shook, and her fair skin looked whiter still. Sometimes she'd step forward to bring the laundry to the rooftop, then freeze, remembering her little boy was no longer there for her to see and worry over.

"Tell me," I'd say, in the moments she looked about to crumble. And she'd recite my parents' London address, a soothing mantra, representing a time that might come after the convent.

Once a week in the nuns' graveyard, autumn chill creeping into the air—I would check to make sure the rotted bar hadn't been repaired. The winter before, I'd arrived with a young woman's hands. Soon I'd leave with an old one's, dried and cracked. But I was strong, and it was better to go in the cooling weeks of autumn before bitter cold set in. My hands were old but I was not. Beneath my shapeless dress the bulk of my pregnancy had diminished with hard work, nursing, and scant meals.

Tomorrow, I said to myself, day after day. *Tomorrow I'll steal from the nursery, out into the graveyard. I'll pass Genevieve through the bars of the gate, lay her on the grass, then squeeze myself through. Scoop her up and find my way to the boat that will carry us home to England. If*

I had to steal, or sell my body, I'd do it. Anything to get us away free and clear.

Susanna's son and Genevieve were the only babies under four months old. At night the older babies could be soothed if we rocked them or let them suck our fingers. During the day, the nuns fed Susanna's boy milk-soaked bread, though he was barely six weeks old. At night when he cried, I would scoop him from his cot and nurse him myself.

One morning after Mass, Sister Mary Clare looked over my shoulder as I bathed Genevieve. "How fat and rosy she is!" the nun exclaimed.

So many of the other babies were thin and pale from feedings spaced too far apart. But Genevieve looked healthy as any babe under her own mother's care. Her bright blue eyes blinked away water as I dabbed gently at her face. I lifted her from the soapy basin up into the air, then back down so I could nibble her cheek, and she giggled for the first time.

"Oh," said the nun. "Is there a more glorious sound in the world than a baby's first laugh?"

I did it again, lifted Genevieve, then rushed her down to nibble her cheek, and she laughed, a belly-shaking, chortling sound. My own laughter scratched my throat, the muscles shaky. I had a flash of remembrance, how much I had loved my mother when I was a small child. The overwhelming joy and safety of her presence. I longed for Mum's green eyes and freckly face, and for her to see me now, with my own baby, loving me in just the same way.

Over and over, I lifted Genevieve up, then down, the baby laughing, the nun laughing, me laughing, breathing in my baby's spicy scent with each nibble, until the front of my apron was splashed through with water. I cast a look of smiling camaraderie at Sister Mary Clare. She was no substitute for my mother, but it was nice to have someone laughing along with us, a witness.

Finally Sister Mary Clare took Genevieve from me, wrapping her in a towel. "You go off to rest. I'll find a special treat to bring you later."

Sister Mary Declan arrived to escort the other night attendant and me upstairs to be locked in the dormitory for our few hours of sleep. I cast one last glance over my shoulder to see Sister Mary Clare, cooing sweetly at Genevieve as she carried her away.

That afternoon I pushed a cart of wet linens to the flat roof above the conservatory, hanging out the sheets to dry in the sun. From up there I saw a man step out of an automobile, with a regal bearing and slicked-back hair. From three stories above, the details I noted were ones of outline, the sheen of wealth that radiated even to where I watched from a distance. A certain kind of girl would have thought him dashing. But dashing didn't interest me. It never would.

Still there was something about the man, and he stayed in my mind, though I barely caught a glimpse of his upturned face. When I brought the next load of wet sheets up to the roof to dry, I saw his car had gone. On my way back to the laundry room I slipped into the nursery. Ordinarily I never went where I wasn't meant to during the day, for fear of running into Father Joseph, or losing my nights with Genevieve. But something urgent drove me, and I hurried under the high archways and over the multi-colored tiles, stepping carefully so my wood-soled shoes wouldn't clomp. It would be trouble if another nun was in the nursery, but if it was Sister Mary Clare, she wouldn't mind my breaking rules. She was in on the joy of it, Genevieve's laughter.

When I got there, my baby's cot lay bare and empty. No sheets, just a tiny stained mattress where countless other babies had lain. Sister Mary Clare walked toward me with her arms outstretched, a look of consternated sympathy puckering her jolly young face. And something else. A twinkle in her eye. I saw it. Whatever she was about to tell me would account for the day's excitement. A bolt of understanding landed in my heart with the first murderous twinge.

"Where is my baby?" I demanded.

In another cot a little boy old enough to stand pulled himself to his feet, bright copper hair in disarray. He held out his arms to be picked up, and Sister Mary Clare swerved away from me as if to accommodate him. I grabbed her billowy sleeve.

"Where's Genevieve? Bring me to her right now, please."

The nun was the barest bit shorter than me but considerably broader. "Oh, Nan. Poor, dear Nan. Don't you worry about that baby."

The other nuns always did that. Called our children "the baby" or "that baby," as if they were still in utero and would only be born when delivered to their counterfeit parents or transferred next door to the orphanage. But at least in my presence, until this moment, Sister Mary Clare had always called my baby Genevieve.

"Your baby is gone. To the nicest family, Nan. They'll give her a wonderful life."

"You can't adopt her to anyone else. She's mine."

"There, dear. Of course she'll always carry you in her heart."

"Where is she right at this moment?"

"Now, Nan. I'm not supposed to tell you. I could get into great trouble for doing so, but I believe this will please you. It's an English family who's adopted her. A lovely English family, she'll be raised right and proper."

"Where in England?" It came out as a bellow. A scarcely contained roar. To my own ears I sounded like an animal. How must I have sounded to Sister Mary Clare? Fierce enough that she took a step backward, looking less confident in her ability to soothe me.

How could I ever have believed her? I felt seduced. My hand still clutched the fabric of her sleeve. I closed the distance between us, my nose almost touching hers.

"You bring me to my baby right now." Not a bellow this time but a growl. I finished the sentence in my thoughts: *Or I swear to God I will kill you where you stand.*

Now she saw it. Now she was afraid. As if the threat hadn't just been in my head, but I'd said it aloud. The jolliness disappeared from her face along with the sympathy. I stepped closer. She stepped away. Now she was near enough to the wall to feel its cold stone through her habit.

Genevieve's molecules still inhabited this room. Her laughter still echoed from its stones.

It was the man I'd seen earlier. I knew it. Had they brought her directly to him? Or had they let him shop, as if for a puppy?

Perhaps he had walked up and down the rows of cots, peering into every one, until my Genevieve's bright blue eyes stared back at him. So alert. So beautiful. So plump and rosy on mother's milk. Worth any price the nuns asked. Perhaps she'd performed her new trick for him and laughed. Enchanting. *I'll take this one.*

And Sister Mary Clare handed my baby right over to him. Genevieve, bundled into a stranger's arms and carried away. And all the while I was working in the very same building.

The nun stared straight at me. You'd think the shape of my face would be something she'd remember her whole life, but her eyes never took me in. Not really. All she saw was her counterfeit kindness, reflected back at her as something real. Her gaze was no more authentic than the studied furrow in her brow now, as if she cared about me. As if she hadn't presided, jolly and smiling, over the kidnapping of my child.

A criminal. In this story thus far I have described to you a variety of crimes. But none—*none*—is more heinous, more violent, more unconscionable, than this one. The theft of my baby. Nothing I could unleash upon Sister Mary Clare could ever equal what she'd just done to me.

My fingers twitched. They rose, almost without me. I placed both hands around her neck. How satisfying her gasps—first of shock, then of pain. She tried to gasp but couldn't. No oxygen for her, my hands saw to that. Her eyes bulged. Her hands came up to claw at my arms, but I worked with the strength of a mother protecting her child—too late but none the weaker. She tried to bat me away but her blows were like air, as if she knew she had no right to defend herself.

It felt good. It felt like the beginning. I would kill her and then I would leave the convent and find the rich, slick-haired man and retrieve my baby. But first this sweet task, choking Sister Mary Clare until her face turned blue. Once she was dead, I would smash her head against the stone wall, one sharp blow. When she fell to the floor, I'd smash her head a final time, breaking it open on the hard tile floor, that cruel pink and blue. Sister Mary Clare made a gurgled sound of fear, which only fueled the pleasure I took in harming her. *Soon you will be dead.*

I could feel her pulse beneath my hands, steady and stoppable. Slowing down. Against my palms, her throat tried to gurgle but couldn't. I pressed harder. Her eyes bulged. Good. Excellent. Good. I'd scarcely known my own strength. It was the first religious moment I'd encountered between these hallowed walls.

Then, a baby cried. Perhaps it was Susanna's baby. That distinct hungry mewl, sharp and desperate. My milk let down with a searing sting, soaking through my shirt and apron. I let go of the nun. Sister Mary Clare raised her hands to her throat, stroking away what damage I'd done, reclaiming the room's oxygen with great honking inhalations. I could see welts, red now; by evening they would be black-and-blue. She stared at my chest, milk spilling through my dress and apron, its sweet smell filling the room.

How far away was Genevieve at that moment? Every second took her farther and farther from my arms. If I raised my hands again, if I killed Sister Mary Clare—I'd be incarcerated for good. There would be a trial. My parents would discover my whereabouts through newspapers. The harlot who strangled a bride of Christ. I would spend the rest of my life in prison, if I was lucky enough not to be executed.

So I kicked off the clogs and ran from the nursery with my soiled apron, in my stockinged feet. Out of the convent. Into the nuns' graveyard. The children from the orphanage played in the yard, I could hear their voices rising up into the air. When I got to the iron gate, I only had to kick the bar, turn sideways, and squeeze myself through, just as I'd practiced. I ran away from the road, across the fields. After a while, in the distance I heard the convent's bells, then a constable's siren.

The bells were for me. I knew the nuns would be scurrying and exclaiming and running in useless circles. But the sirens sounded for a different reason. Luckily for me the police were engaged elsewhere. An RIC patrol had been ambushed in Cobh, and every available officer was rushing in that direction. Every girl in the convent could have escaped without capture, if only I'd known to tell them.

First I ran, faster than ever, joyless. I flung off my cap and my apron, in motion, never missing a stride. I ran off the road, through fields. Not the barest slip or side sprain of an ankle. Clean, fast strides, as if I'd been in training. I passed a farmhouse where laundry dried on the line, swaying in the cool crisp afternoon. I should have stopped and stolen clothes, disguised myself. The front of my dress was soaked through with milk, drying from my flight and the sun. But I didn't stop. I ran and I ran.

"Whoa, there darling," a woman said.

I hadn't seen her, leaning against a barn. Wearing trousers and a thick jacket, a cigarette in one hand, the other raised up in the air as she stepped out in front of me, stopping me short. She had wild gray curls and a wind-burnt face, standing close enough that I could smell last night's whiskey on her breath.

"Please. Please let me go."

Her eyes landed on my chest, the milk stains dried by now, then traveled to my shredded stockings and feet. She blew out a stream of smoke, then dropped her cigarette dangerously into the hay. Took a moment to stomp it out.

"And where is it you're going, then?"

"I don't suppose I need to tell you." I sounded more weepy than defiant. Nothing had ever felt more incorrect than standing still. I had to run, away and also toward.

The woman took off her coat and placed it over my shoulders. "I know where you'll be going," she said, raspy voice wanting to be kind, forcing itself to be stern. "Straight to the boy who got you here in the first place. But you mustn't go to him, dear. Listen to you. Sounding like England. That's where you belong, then, isn't it?"

Her name was Vera and she brought me inside, gave me a change of clothes, and fed me. I think she told me about her life, the friend she lived with, and her feelings about the nuns and what they called charity. I didn't hear any of it. For the longest time I didn't hear a word anyone said to me. I was a shoeless girl on foot, desperate to win a race against cars and boats. From the moment I discovered I was pregnant I had only ever been a girl on foot.

Another woman arrived, also wearing a man's work clothes,

and smelling of smoke and whiskey. "Good gracious," she said at the sight of me.

"That's Martha," Vera told me.

Martha looked directly at my breasts, swollen to lopsided rocks with breast milk. "Come with me, love. I can help you with that."

She brought me into the small bedroom and unwound a cloth bandage for me to wrap around my breasts. "You want to let the milk out a little bit, every now and then. Enough to relieve the pressure but not so much to keep you producing."

Thinking about it now, I wonder what babies were in her past, whose milk she'd had to stop. But I didn't wonder at the time. Vera and Martha emptied a biscuit jar of pound notes and shillings. They bundled me up in what may have been one of their best coats. Vera's shoes fit me better; she gave me a pair of soft leather boots. Then they loaded me into the back of their wagon.

"Lie low and still," Vera instructed.

So I left Sunday's Corner the same way I arrived, in a horse-drawn carriage. Martha sang as she drove the horses, the tune Sister Mary Clare used to hum, echoing like bagpipes through the stairwells and hallways of the convent. Finally I learned the words:

Come, all you fair and tender girls
That flourish in your prime
Beware, beware, keep your garden fair
Let no man steal your thyme

The song and the women carried me to the train station, where they bought my ticket to Dublin and gave me the rest of the money for the boat back to England.

"How will I ever repay you?" I asked.

"Be well," Vera said, "and be happy."

Martha's dress was far too big. I kept the good coat buttoned to my chin. When the boat docked in Liverpool, a group of English soldiers were waiting to be dispatched to Ireland. I wondered, in the history of the world, had one soldier ever been sent to win back a mother's stolen child? In the coming months I'd search for Genevieve in the most illogical ways. I walked from London all the way to Croxley Green, straight through the night, the soles of my shoes worn down, speckled with holes. I peered into every pram, wary mothers or nannies rolling them back, pulling up the hood.

Once you've lost a baby, its cries will reach you anywhere. Across miles of parkland. From an open window two streets away. You wake in the middle of the night and find yourself in the wrong place; you're supposed to be elsewhere, *with* someone. Wherever she is, you know she's waking, too, blue eyes opening in the dark, searching for the one person in the world who answers to the name Mother. Not a pretender. Her own real, true mother. The body knows, even when the mind does not.

When I finally made it home, gray faced and ruined, I found a stack of letters from Finbarr waiting for me, some of them with money enclosed—for the journey to Ireland he didn't know I'd already taken.

"Why won't you answer, Nan?" he wrote again and again.

His parents never told him how I'd landed on their doorstep.

He knew nothing about the night I'd lain beside him, holding myself against his feverish body. Sister Mary Clare had never written to him, I was sure, and even if she had, the Mahoneys would have thrown the letter away.

"If you don't love me anymore," he finally wrote, in a letter that landed in England before I did, "I want to hear you say it to my face. I'll come to London to hear you say it."

I picked up pencil and paper to write him back. But there was too much to say. Too much sorrow to deliver.

When my mother wrote to Aunt Rosie to tell her what had happened, Rosie traveled from Dublin to Sunday's Corner and insisted on speaking to the Mother Superior, who sat her down and showed her a death certificate.

Mother: *Nan O'Dea.*

Baby girl: *Deceased.* And there written beside the word was the same day in November they'd sent her off with the man I'd seen from the rooftop.

It was Sister Mary Clare's handiwork. I knew it.

"I'm so sorry, Nan," my mother sobbed, when she told me. Never having seen Genevieve that day, the laughing picture of health.

"She's not dead," I promised.

My mother looked at me, sorrowful for my loss, and possibly my delusion.

What could I do then but walk, all over London and beyond, refusing to rejoice in my freedom, wanting to search for Genevieve but not knowing where to begin. I clutched my body, cruelly bounced back to what it had been before, my stomach flat and smooth, my milk dried up.

If I'd been right enough in the head to track time, I could tell you the date I returned home to find Finbarr, sitting on the curb in front of our building, a satchel at his feet. It was the only time in my life where my heart didn't leap at the sight of him. There was nothing I could do but break *his* heart once by telling him about Genevieve, and twice by sending him away.

If only he'd come for me just a little later, when I was at least able to pretend to be my old self. By the following spring I was working a few afternoons at Buttons and Bits. Megs was already training as a nurse. Louisa, still home but already engaged, was taking a secretarial course. At our kitchen table she taught me the shorthand and typing that would one day lead to my job at the Imperial British Rubber Company. By that summer I could walk through the world and present a face that didn't look entirely broken, or constantly searching.

I was, though. Constantly searching. Did I ever stop? No. Did I ever plan to stop—did I ever think there would come a time, or a moment, when I'd admit defeat and the impossibility of my quest? Of course not.

Four years after my return to England, quite by chance, I found her. Unmistakable. I was visiting my sister Megs at her new home in Torquay, where she worked as a nurse.

Megs took a day off and we went for a walk on the beach. A little girl ran toward us with the peripatetic zigzag of small children. At first I thought the child was on her own, but as my eyes searched through the sunlight, I saw two women a long ways behind her, distant enough that I could barely make out their forms. When the little girl found Megs and me in her way, instead of running around us she threw her arms around my legs.

"Oh," I said, looking down into a pair of bright blue eyes. She had a high forehead, and shiny dark hair cascading backward as she looked up at me. Sweet, pointed little chin. I knew her in an instant. And she knew me, too. I know she did.

"Nan," Megs said sharply as I stooped to gather the little girl in my arms. "You can't just pick up other people's children."

The little girl didn't agree. She returned my embrace as if she remembered the last time her mother had held her. Her real mother.

"Teddy," one of the women called out. "Look here, Teddy, we must head back to Ashfield."

The child's consciousness returned to her present-day life. She squirmed out of my arms and ran back to the two women, who turned and walked off in the other direction. I grabbed Megs's arm to steady myself.

"There, there," Megs said. "You'll have one of your own one day, Nan, you will."

"I already have one of my own," I said out loud. Inwardly I said, *Ashfield*, again and again in my mind, memorizing it without a doubt, and vowing to discover all there was to know about the people who lived there.

Was she beautiful?

Yes. More beautiful than you can imagine.

The day Finbarr finally came to fetch me, I sent him away, returning, against his protestations, the money he'd sent me. We had barely talked an hour before he trudged off, out of sight, heavy with the added sorrow I'd given him.

"You'll always know where I am," Finbarr said before he left, tears streaming down his face. "I'll never live anywhere without sending you word. You'll change your mind one day. I know you will."

A mother bat can find her pup in a cave full of thousands, even without eyes that see. When your child has been stolen, you measure her age by the days that pass. You look into the faces of other children, to make sure. You do this so many times you know with your whole being, you haven't made a mistake when at last you find her.

Sometimes I wonder if Agatha learned it from me. About the worst violence you can do to a person. What you might be driven to in its aftermath. The wars that can be started, the justice that must be served. All for the sake of avenging a child.

Part Three

"Evil never goes unpunished, Monsieur.
But the punishment is sometimes secret."

—Hercule Poirot

September 16, 1926

Dearest Finbarr:

I hope this letter finds you well after all these years. My goodness, I hope it finds you at all, and that you will be happy to hear from me. I must admit that even after all that's happened, even though I haven't answered your letters, whenever I see your name on an envelope (whenever I see the words *Love, Finbarr* written across the bottom of a page), my heart somersaults backward up to the sky.

And so I must tell you what I'd promised myself I wouldn't, which I take a risk in doing. I have found our baby, our girl, our darling Genevieve. I have seen her and even held her in my arms. She is happy and healthy and living with "parents" at a house called Styles in Sunningdale, Berkshire. If you could only see her! She has your eyes, Finbarr. She's smart and brave and beautiful. She loves dogs and books. In that way at least one of our wishes has come true.

The people who have her are named Archibald and Agatha Christie. And here is the difficult part. Archie Christie plans to leave his wife and marry me. Did I engineer this? Did I plan it? Yes. To you alone I confess that

I did. For the only reason that could excuse me. To be a part of my own child's life.

If I received such a letter from you, if you told me you were about to marry, it would cause me great sorrow, but I would thank you for telling me yourself. I hope you understand this is all I can do. It's too late to take her away from the only family she's known. At least this way I can be her stepmother. At least I can land my eyes upon her, and embrace her, and call her by her real name when she's asleep.

I don't love Archie. But I can't afford to hate him despite his role in all that happened. He's my only road back to Genevieve. So I do what must be done. And, Finbarr, nothing could be like us, could it. My heart belongs, as ever, to you.

Love,
Nan

The Disappearance

Saturday, December 11, 1926

Finbarr caught Agatha at the top of the stairs on the second floor, his hand on her elbow, urgent but gentle. The house was dark, just after midnight. She and Chilton had missed their dinner. She'd only wanted to gather some tins of food to sustain them.

"Agatha," Finbarr said, his hoarse voice full of urgency. "Please don't say you've decided not to help me after all?"

She looked at him, his face barely visible in the flicker of the candle she held, but strikingly earnest. She thought, *What a fool Nan is. Any woman with her wits about her would run away with him the moment he asked.* The conviction with which she thought this, while Chilton sat waiting for her upstairs, could almost make her sympathize with Archie, the twin desires, the divided loyalty.

"All it would take is one word from you. Tell her. That your daughter is your daughter. That she's not Genevieve."

"One word! I could offer ten thousand words and she'd never

believe me. I could show her a birth certificate and she'd say it was forged. Don't you see she's been convinced of this for years now? To accept any evidence to the contrary would be to lose her child all over again."

Did Finbarr stop in that moment, or any moment, and consider whether *he* believed Agatha's denials that Teddy and Genevieve were the same person? That when Agatha said *her* child, she also meant *his* child? I doubt he did. It would have been too contrary to his primary goal. I had already told him Teddy's birthday was the same as Genevieve's. That Archie's mother came from County Cork, so he'd have known the perfect place to collect a baby to pass off as his own.

The nuns wouldn't give a baby to Protestants, Finbarr had said.

Archie's mother is a Catholic. And please don't ever think to tell me what nuns wouldn't do.

That face. Finbarr had knelt in front of Teddy when he'd given her the whittled dog. His own eyes, looking back at him. How could he not have seen it?

A person does adhere to the mission at hand. We believe what furthers our own cause. I don't blame Finbarr for this. What was stolen from me was stolen from him, too, even more completely, so that he never understood what he had to fight for. He thought he only had to fight for me.

"That's why you've got to convince her," he said to Agatha. "You haven't even tried."

Agatha looked away, off into the dark distance. Frustratingly silent.

"Tell her then, how it's hurting you. To lose your husband." I never heard Finbarr say Archie's name, not once. "Nan's not cruel. Tell her you can't live without him."

"But I think perhaps I can live without him. You can live without her, too."

"I know I can. I've done it all this while, haven't I. But I don't want to. Agatha, don't you want your husband anymore?"

"I can't say that I do. Not entirely." And then, she wasn't sure if it was to assuage him or if it was true: "I don't know, Finbarr. I'm sorry, I just don't know."

He let go of her elbow and touched her cheek with the coarse, lovely flat of his palm. Then he turned and walked away. She hated the sag of his shoulders. She wanted to give him hope, she did. But not enough to relinquish her own.

When daylight arrived, the first thing Agatha felt was a rush of happiness. How wonderfully foreign it all was, and what a release. Casting all propriety aside could almost eliminate the question *What would she do now?* Having left the world so publicly, how could she return privately?

"Can one woman cause such a fuss," she said to Chilton, that morning, lying in his arms under a mountain of scratchy wool blankets, "and then just return without any explanation?"

"Absolutely not." Chilton had a complicated way of wrapping both arms around her, using the good to hoist the bad. In this way he managed to clasp too tightly for her to sit up and look at his face. "It's quite clear you can never go back. You'll have to stay with me."

She touched her fingers to his lips, eyes fixed on the ceiling.

"I've had a murder to solve, you know," Chilton told her.

She broke free from his grasp and sat up so she could face

him. This was the first she'd heard of it. Chilton told her about
the Marstons.

"How sad." Tears did come to Agatha's eyes. She'd forgotten
the wider world and its inhabitants in the midst of her various
conundrums.

"What do you think? You write detective novels. Should I
agree with Lippincott's theory and call it a day?"

"Oh, I couldn't possibly solve a crime I hadn't invented. The
point of a good detective story is to make it all obvious. You
throw in enough variables so the reader doubts his own solution, then at the end he can be pleased with himself for figuring it out. In life I imagine Occam's razor applies. The simplest
solution is usually correct."

Chilton smiled. It pleased him enormously to listen to her.

"What do you think?" she asked. "Do you suppose your man
Lippincott is right about the wife? There's no reason to suspect
anyone else, is there?"

"To be perfectly honest I find myself not caring as I should."
She kissed him.

"I'd like to read your books. I'd like to read every word you've
ever written."

Agatha smiled and pressed her forehead to his. "I'm not at
all ready to go home." Their kissing recommenced in earnest.

Who would have known it was possible to make love so rap-
turously and still entertain so many thoughts? Agatha kept her
eyes open. Taking in the spartan room, and the man who'd been
a stranger mere days before. She thought she would always be
grateful for this span of time, and then she thought she might
make it last forever. She could start calling herself Mrs. Chilton
today, and the two of them could go off somewhere together

where nobody knew either of them. She would never have to associate herself with that terrible word *divorce* or face the music from running away and causing such a brouhaha. Back in Berkshire, Teddy would bear a scar, but we all acquire those along the way, don't we, despite anyone's best efforts. Nan would take up the mother mantle with a fervor few daughters had ever seen.

Eventually, if Agatha remained hidden, the world would forget she'd ever gone missing or existed in the first place. She imagined herself shedding everything. Her old life scattered to the wind, melting into the air as mist off the sea. Nan could claim it all— the house, the husband, the child. This would prove terrible for Finbarr. But sometimes a person had to think of herself.

She could sidestep into a new existence, taking nothing but the writing with her. She could start fresh under a new name. She could change her hair, starve or stuff herself till she was unrecognizable, the woman she'd been before nothing but an unsolved mystery. While Mrs. Chilton clattered away on the typewriter and took long walks on the beach and rolled under the covers with her gentle husband, who adored—who *worshipped*—her.

"Darling Agatha," Chilton said, lips against her ear.

It felt so good to be darling, being lost didn't matter.

A little while later, Chilton drove back to the Bellefort through the damp, late morning, his frayed wool coat on the seat beside him, one chapped hand on the steering wheel. The rain from Sunningdale had made its way north, falling gently. A smile contoured his face, twitching at his lips. He didn't know the turn Agatha's fantasies had taken—running away with him and becoming Mrs. Chilton. But he would have agreed to it in a heartbeat.

For the first time since the War he felt as though he might have recovered something of himself. Not his innocence, never his brothers, but something wonderfully important. A will to live beyond the need to spare his mother further pain. Only a few days prior, if he'd heard word of his mother's death, he might have boarded a train home, kissed her corpse's forehead, then turned his father's old Purdey shotgun on himself and drawn the trigger with relief. At last.

Now though. Now he felt as if he might stick around another few days, just to see what happened. When he held Agatha in both his arms, good and bad, Chilton believed, the way a person does in that first miracle of reciprocated ardor, that one night of passion could translate to forever. And why not run off with her now? As far as the whole world was concerned, she was already gone.

When Chilton parked his car at the hotel, he saw Mr. Race, smoking and pacing out front, thin curls of smoke followed by thicker exhalations of breath. The sight made Chilton realize he'd forgotten to smoke himself, for hours, even for an entire day. He reached into his inner coat pocket for his cigarette case and then stopped himself. He wanted nothing in common with Mr. Race, whom he imagined to be the same breed as Archie Christie. The kind of man for whom Chilton felt nothing but disdain. Not that such men would care or notice. They considered disdain their own particular province. Belligerent and concerned only with themselves, even at their most generous. *Men who served in the trenches, and men who served in the air.* Race may have been too young to belong to either group, but Chilton placed him firmly in the latter.

I must say Chilton's opinion of Archie was unfair, Chilton

having never so much as laid eyes on him, let alone having spent the better part of the night and morning making love to his wife. Chilton knew that. But clinging to his bad idea of the man was part and parcel of clinging to the woman.

As Chilton stepped out of the car, he saw Race do something that surprised him. Race dropped his cigarette to the dirt, ground it up with his foot, then scooped up the remains, tucking it into his palm as if he meant to throw it away later. Chilton hadn't pegged him as the sort to clear away his own mess. Mrs. Race emerged from the hotel a moment later, bundled up in a hat and coat. Upon seeing her husband, she broke into the happiest smile and stepped immediately into his arms, looking up at him with profound delight.

Chilton knew enough of the world not to be surprised by a woman returning to a beastly husband. But something about this did not look right. The woman might have been two entirely different people. Mr. Race, who had seen Chilton, seemed aware of the discrepancy. He placed his hands on his wife's shoulders, and she looked over to see Chilton. Whereupon she stepped back rather abruptly.

"Good day, Mrs. Race," Chilton called out, trying his best to be jaunty. "Mr. Race."

They murmured hello, newly subdued.

Inside the hotel, Chilton waited a moment. Then he stepped back outside. The Races were gone. He walked quietly round back, where they stood together, quite close, holding onto each other's elbows. They appeared not only loving, but trusting and intimate.

He didn't dare creep close enough to hear what they were saying, or they would surely have seen him. But from where he stood, observing in secret, he tried to listen. And although no words became distinct, he could have sworn they both spoke with Irish brogues.

Earlier, Finbarr and I had driven back to the hotel in the gray winter dawn.

"I've been thinking," I said. "Can't a person train dogs in England as well as Ireland?"

He pulled the car over to the side of the road and turned toward me. "What are you saying, Nan?"

I saw I'd given him false hope. I couldn't offer him precisely what he wanted. But I could offer him a version of it. "I'm saying . . ." I stopped, trying to think how to word it. "My plan could stay in place. And you could be a part of it. Think, Finbarr. Archie travels. He works all day. Why, just two years ago he left England for an entire year. We could be together often as not. I could even bring Genevieve to you sometimes."

"Good lord, Nan, what have you become?"

The pilot light of shame, always ready to be struck into full flame, flickered inside me. I doused it with anger. "I've become what I've been since August 1919. A mother who loves her child. And a woman who's ready to do what's necessary. That's what I've become."

He didn't move for a long moment. "We could take her, then," he finally said. "The two of us. Out of England, to anywhere you like, and raise her as our own."

"How can I do that to her, Finbarr? Kidnap her? If she were still a baby, fine, but now? What would that do to her? And if there's an army searching for Agatha Christie, what will there be to search for her child? I've no way to prove she's mine. It's too late for that kind of justice. I wish it weren't, but it is."

"And what if you discover a month from now you're carrying my child again? What will you do then?"

(Oh, Finbarr. Oh, reader. Must I know and provide an answer for everything?)

I closed my eyes against tears, and he gathered me up in his arms. Holding me tight, he spoke into my ear. "How can you stand that man touching you if you truly believe he stole our child?"

I was silent awhile, as if reasoning it out in that moment, though in truth I'd thought it through a long time ago. I didn't blame Archie, not fully. He'd availed himself of something readily on offer, without considering how it came to be so. The way all men like him do. He might inhabit the world unthinkingly, in the manner men of his station were allowed. But Archie hadn't invented the world, only been born into it like the rest of us.

"It's the same way a diplomat makes peace after war," I said. "And having me as his wife will be punishment enough. Especially if you live nearby."

"I'm not meant for that. To be on the sly. I'm meant to be your husband. You know that, Nan. What's more, I'm not sure I could lay eyes on that man without killing him."

This might have been hyperbole, but I knew that urge well enough to take him at his word. I couldn't risk it, Finbarr losing his freedom over killing Archie. Or Archie being killed, for that matter. Whatever he was guilty of, nothing he'd done was terrible enough to merit death as punishment.

"The only answer," Finbarr said, still holding on, "is for us to leave this place together."

I didn't agree out loud. Neither did I disagree. Somewhere in our embrace, in the tightening of his grip on me, I could feel Finbarr take heart in my silence.

By the time Chilton arrived at the Bellefort I was already back in my room. He knocked on my door, and when I opened it, he pressed the Galsworthy novel into my hands.

"Thank you. How very kind. Though I don't imagine I'll have time to read it before it needs to be returned. I do need to get back to London before long."

"Do you? I thought perhaps you'd be returning to Ireland with Mr. Mahoney."

"I will never return to Ireland."

Chilton must have noticed, I didn't say I'd never go away with Finbarr. "Speaking of Ireland, I must tell you the strangest thing. I heard Mr. and Mrs. Race talking just now, and it was as if they were two entirely different people. Not only kind to each other, but sounding like they just got off the boat from Dublin."

My face went hot and my eyes flooded. I didn't want him in my room. "You know, Mr. Chilton, if you've opted not to reveal Mrs. Christie's whereabouts, shouldn't *you* be going back home?"

"I imagine my reasons for staying are similar to yours." He said it kindly. He said everything kindly. But that didn't necessarily bode kindness, did it.

"Won't you be in terrible trouble," I said pointedly, "when they find out she was here all along?"

"It's not trouble if you're never caught. Is it?"

I remembered my hands around Sister Mary Clare's throat. I imagined a gravestone behind the convent, marked like all the rest: HERE LIES SISTER MARY. But this one was just for her.

Down the hall a door opened. Young Miss Armstrong emerged, her black hair loose, her face bright and clean of any troubling past. If only I could have willed my soul out of my own body and into hers and lived my whole live differently.

"Oh, Mr. Chilton," I said, and the floorboards rushed to meet my face.

Chilton hadn't meant to upset me, at least not to this degree. It was part of his job to disarm people, make them vulnerable and get them talking. He did it almost by force of habit. What was less practiced was disarming himself. Before I hit the floor, he reached out his good arm—sufficient only in protecting my head from a more severe blow.

"My goodness," said Miss Armstrong, bustling to my side. "Shall we get her into bed?"

"No." I sat up and pulled at the collar of my dress. "I'm fine." I shrugged away from both pairs of hands. "I just need some air. Some room and some air."

"Let me at least walk you downstairs for luncheon," Miss Armstrong said. "The combination of cold air and hot water is said to be so healthful. But I've been feeling rather light-headed since we arrived. Perhaps that's what killed the Marstons. Some kind of shock to their system. It must be all the worse, for old people." She glanced at Chilton as if in concerned warning.

Chilton remained focused on me. "You're sure you're all right?"

"Perfectly fine. Just feeling a bit ridiculous."

"Is that nurse afoot?" asked Miss Armstrong. "Mrs. Race?"

"I don't believe she is," Chilton said. "Perhaps you can consult with her later."

"That won't be necessary," I said.

Accepting Miss Armstrong's hand, I got to my feet. I would eat to oblige them. Then steal away to see Finbarr. I should have returned to London already. One more day, I kept telling myself. Just give me one more day.

Chilton watched as Miss Armstrong and I walked off, her arm wrapped around me with genuine concern. *People can be so kind,* he thought. *Women especially. The way one woman naturally allows another to lean on her in times of trouble.*

The Disappearance

Would it surprise you to know that most women, if they saw Finbarr and Archie side by side, would choose Archie as the handsomer? Especially after the War, once Finbarr had lost his joyful gleam.

Whereas the years had made me more attractive than I'd been as a girl. Something about the way I learned to conceal my shattered self. It made me fascinating to men.

"Oh, Nan," Archie said, taking me into his arms that night at the Owens', before we knew what tomorrow held. If you can see your way to never minding that he'd taken his own wife in much the same way not twenty-four hours earlier, then try to understand: he loved me, he did.

Do you think, as Finbarr did, I should have hated Archie? Perhaps I did. When it all started, I did, I'm sure of it. As I look back now, it's hard to say. I married the man, after all. I bore him a child, whom I love as dearly and deeply as the one I lost.

Thousands of days and hundreds of thousands of hours have been spent alongside him, both waking and sleeping. From this particular hour the only answer I can give, as to whether I hated him, is sometimes. And in some ways. If that's what you'd like to call hate.

The way a certain man can walk through the world. If in that day and country Archie had been allowed more than one wife, he might have had ten and loved us all, with waxing and waning preferences. Which is not to say he loved Agatha or me as possessions. He did *see* us in his way. On the golf course he would stand back, arms crossed, assessing my swing, my form, the arc of the ball I propelled. "Ripping," he would say, for all to hear. And when we were alone: "Ripping, gorgeous girl."

I could have won at golf with Archie, but I never let myself. He wanted me to be good but not better than him. He liked to watch me play tennis at the club, against other women. And it pleased me that this aspect of myself pleased him. My plan to land Archie was born of urgency, but that didn't mean I never found pleasure in it. Running again, swinging a racket, winning.

Funktionslust. It's a German word for the joy of doing what one does best. Seducing Archie, stealing him away from his wife, had a specific purpose. But as it turned out, I was good at it. Better than good. It might have been a tennis match. No other woman at the club, no other woman anywhere, could touch me.

"Oh, Nan," Archie said. Smooth hands down my smoother side. He had good lips, Archie did, tasting like Scotch in the evening. By now I'd learned how to arch and whisper, how to climb and conquer. The night before Archie's wife disappeared, I could sense enough to understand the imperative of reclaiming him. Now that he'd decided to move forward, there could be no more lapses or wavering. My claim on him as a shark, swim or die.

I clamped my hand over Archie's mouth, hard enough that it may have hurt him. "Hush," I commanded.

"Nan," he answered, a tight gurgle.

Then, when all had come to rest: "I love you."

The covers had been thrown to the floor and my head rested on his slick chest, his breath still coming out hard and forced.

"Dear Nan. How I love you."

In nine days' time it would finally occur to Archie to wonder in earnest, Where had I gone?

He would have an afternoon to escape the confines of Styles and the chaos of the fruitless search. He would travel to London.

Turning his collar up against the cold, he would march down city streets to my flat. Walk up the steps and rap on my door. Hold his ear against it when there was no answer. The silence inside sounding as if it had taken time to build. An un-inhabited place.

Nothing in the world removes the ills a wife causes like the balm of a mistress. Even as Archie listened for me, he thought if I were to swing the door open and welcome him inside with a seductive smile, I'd be nothing but a poor substitute, the satisfaction I offered him temporary, fleeting. Only enough to carry him through this terrible grief until his wife was found.

My door sat sealed, the room on the other side of it sound-less. My neighbor, old Mrs. Kettering, opened her door. It wasn't the first time she'd seen Archie, and she frowned at him as she always did. He responded with a placating smile. People such as her, who'd witnessed us together, might be trouble down the road.

Still the question bubbled up inside him, impossible not to ask. "Good afternoon, Mrs. Kettering. I wonder, have you seen Miss O'Dea?"

"Not for days. More than a week, I'd say. Not a glimpse of her nor a peep from her. Here's hoping she's run off with some bloke her own age." Mrs. Kettering bestowed one last, hawklike glare before slamming the door behind her and stomping down the stairs. There are too many women in the world helping men with their dirty work. But so many more taking one another's side in unexpected moments.

Equally unexpected, Archie would find the moment of reprieve he'd wanted. For the first time in days, his mind went blank with sheer perplexity. The question eclipsed emotion, for just one moment. *Where has Nan gone?*

He hurried down the stairs to the street. Walked quickly, his breath coming out in gusts. Willing his hands not to rise and cover his face. Any tears in his eyes could be explained away by the cold. Miles away in Harrogate I wasn't thinking of Archie. Hardly a bit. Hardly at all.

While he was thinking, *How peculiar, and what has precipitated this? The Age of Disappearing Women.*

The age of disappearing women did not begin with Agatha Christie. It had begun long before Agatha hopped into a car and motored away from Newlands Corner with Finbarr. And it would continue for quite a bit longer. We disappeared from schools. From our hometowns. From our families and our jobs. One day we would be going about our business, sitting in class, or laughing with friends, or walking hand in hand with a beau. Then, poof.

Whatever happened to that girl? Don't you remember her? Where did she go?

In America we went to Florence Crittenton homes. In England to Clark's House, or any of the various homes run mostly by the Anglican Church. In Australian hospitals, babies were taken from mothers who were drugged, incapacitated, unwilling. And some of us didn't go anywhere at all. We bled to death on butcher's tables. We jumped off bridges.

The age of disappearing women. It had been going on forever. Thousands of us vanished, with not a single police officer searching. Not a word from the newspapers. Only our long absences and quiet returns. If we ever returned at all.

Before Agatha disappeared. Before I knew Finbarr had returned to Britain. The plan I'd authored was well under way. In the Owens' house, in the borrowed bed, my arms wrapped tight around Archie. The overriding element was mercenary, true. But there were other elements.

"I love you, Nan," Archie said, as if he couldn't say it enough, as if the words needed to be repeated ad infinitum until the world conspired to let this moment last, the delicious, breathless secret of it.

I loved him, too. If that's what you'd like to call love.

The Disappearance

In the midst of all the maelstroms, Agatha's work was another place for her to go. A world to visit apart from her own. She could lose herself there no matter what occurred. In the Timeless Manor the typewriter keys clicked and clacked. Let them search. Let Archie worry. When her fingers flew over the typewriter keys, it was the whole world that vanished. Not her.

I was not so lucky. In Harrogate, in the moments without Finbarr, my mind assaulted me with fear, worry, and misgivings. I tried to concentrate on reading the novel Chilton had given me. I'd barely fought my way to the second chapter when a rap came on my door. I opened it to find Mrs. Leech.

"There's a man downstairs to see you." I knew from the way her brow cocked, not sure of the propriety, that it was Finbarr, and my face changed so suddenly—lighting up—that Mrs. Leech smiled.

"You're not really married, are you. *Miss* O'Dea."

"No," I admitted. "I'm not."

"There, there." She patted my shoulder to comfort me. Anyone who's been in love knows it's a state that requires comforting. "You go on downstairs. Tell him to cheer up, that's all. And you mustn't bring him to your room. We're not that kind of hotel."

"Of course. Thank you, Mrs. Leech."

In the lobby Finbarr sat on the settee, his peacoat open, rubbing his hands across his knees. He stood, and we walked outside together into the cold, where I stepped to him, sliding my hands into his coat pocket. I felt a square of paper, glossy against my fingertips, and pulled out the photograph I'd sent him years ago. It was bent and battered, tearing around the edges. Tiny holes at its corners gathered upon themselves, indicating it had been pinned to more than one wall.

Have you ever looked at a picture of someone—from when the person was very young—and thought, *How sad. All that promise, all that hope.* The girl looking back at me from that photograph may have known sadness (her broken mother, stiff upper lip, bringing her to have the picture made), but she didn't know where her own road led. She grieved for her sister but felt sure no such fate would ever befall her. She knew the War was on but didn't quite believe it. How could any war reach English shores? Impossible. If I had presented that girl with any of the obstacles approaching her—as predictions—she would have offered intractable solutions to each one. The face staring back at me believed better things lay ahead. Making a picture for a soldier, who'd return from the War exactly as he had been to marry her, escorting her off to Ireland and perpetual happiness.

"I wish I had a picture of you from that time," I said. "Why is it girls send pictures to soldiers but not the other way round?"

"Listen to me, Nan." Finbarr took the picture back from me carefully, a precious relic, and returned it to his pocket. "Come away with me now and I won't carry this with me anymore. We'll have a new one taken. We'll put this one in a book to show our children."

"But then I'll never be able to show myself again. To our child."

"We've both become things we never saw for ourselves. I never wanted to go to war. I never wanted to fall sick. I never wanted to leave my own country, or even Ballycotton. What I never wanted most of all is the things that happened to you."

I grabbed his hands and kissed them.

"I'll tell you something terrible," he went on. "If I had a choice to make every man that died in war, from 1914 till now—Irishmen, Englishmen, Australians, Germans, Turks, all of them—if I had the choice to go back in time and let them live, or put our baby back in your arms, they'd all remain dead, every last one of them."

"If you can see that, Finbarr, can't you see I need to continue?"

"There's only one road back to you, the real you. The road back to yourself, Nan. And that's with me."

"But I don't want the road back to me. I want the road to Genevieve."

For the first time in a long while I pictured my daughter's face not as the little girl purported to belong to the Christies, but as the baby I'd last seen, seven years ago, carried away by Sister Mary Clare. I breathed in, unexpectedly harsh, as if my own lungs had received a dose of mustard gas. Perhaps the kindest thing Agatha Christie could do—not only for Finbarr, but for me—was convince me the child was indeed hers.

By the time Chilton reached the Timeless Manor's second floor, the sound of Agatha's typewriter was audible. A cheerful and industrious click-clack, click-clack. He could imagine the way it would fill a house of his own. Every evening he would come home and put on a kettle, the sound of the typewriter from the other room, she so absorbed that she wouldn't know he'd arrived, until he came into the room with a steaming mug of tea. *Oh, darling,* she would say. *The day was lost to me.* That would be fine with Chilton. He was used to doing for himself and would be glad to do for her, too. *You keep writing,* he'd say. *I'll take care of dinner.*

Now she answered his knock, industry ceasing, her face alight with the joy of seeing him. Once he was no longer a novelty, disturbing her work would be something they'd quarrel about. It pleased Chilton to think of it, how he'd have to learn to tiptoe. He'd become adept at removing the teakettle just before it whistled, slipping a mug quietly on the table beside her, and still she'd scold him for breaking her concentration. *Must you always interrupt me?* He'd kiss the crown of her head and steal away, leaving her to her work.

But for now she stepped aside and let him in. He flopped onto the narrow bed—their bed, he thought of it now—and reached for a piece of typewritten paper on top of a neat stack on the second bare bed. Agatha snapped it out of his hand, put it back where it belonged, and returned to her seat.

"But when can I read it?"

"When it's printed, bound, and sewn, and not a moment sooner."

She went back to typing, a twitching smile betraying how his interest pleased her.

While she clicked and clacked, he told her about what he'd witnessed between Mr. and Mrs. Race.

"Are you listening?" he asked after a while. "Or are you writing?"

"I'm doing both." But she stood and collected the missing pieces of him by falling onto the bed. It had been years since he'd felt he had two arms, but Agatha wrapped them both around herself. "I never knew kissing could be such fun," she said, after much agreeable time had passed.

But she had known, hadn't she? Agatha had learned how much fun kissing could be years ago, in her early days with Archie, when he was a different man, when his invincibility had the power to protect rather than harm her. What she hadn't known, really, is how bereavement can shift. How it can open up the world to a place where there's nothing to lose and you can make a grab for joy in the form of a rumpled but really rather lovely police inspector.

Chilton went down to the larder and returned with two tins of tongue. She had already made a vow never to eat tinned tongue again, but she found herself starving, so much so that even this poor, repetitive food tasted wonderful.

"Do you know what I'd like to do?" Agatha said. "Go to the baths."

"A long walk in the cold followed by grotesquely hot water?"

"What could be better?"

They walked briskly, arm in arm. Few cars were on the road. A young farrier driving a horse-drawn carriage stopped and offered a ride. They said no at first but changed their minds, running after him, calling to him, and climbing in the back when he drew his team of two bay mares to a halt. Agatha sat on a bale of hay amid clanking tools, petting a panting Labrador, who cuddled up beside her. She laughed when the dog licked her chin, and kissed him back for good measure. The cold made color rise in her cheeks. Her laughter sounded like wind chimes.

"Tell me, Mr. Chilton," she said, raising her voice above the clatter of hooves and jingling metal. "How do you feel about dogs?"

"I think they're just fine." As Agatha put her arms around the beast and pressed her face into its dirty fur, he decided to be more emphatic. "I love them." He added, "You look wonderful. You look like a young girl."

It was the wrong thing to say. Her smile vanished and her color waned. "But I'm not a young girl." Soon as she spoke the words, it became so. Lines on her brow, a shadow across her jaw.

The farrier let them off at the Karnak Baths and Spa, and they parted quietly, Chilton to the dressing room and Agatha to the gift shop to buy a bathing dress. This would mean showing herself to more people, but who was observant enough to connect the proper woman in the photographs to the one before them, with her wind-mussed hair, and men's clothing? She buttoned Miss Oliver's plain wool coat to her chin in the hopes of not looking quite so odd. In the shop she bought the most modest bathing dress she could find, a green-and-blue V-neck that just skimmed her knees. She bought a matching cap, too.

Unlike the segregated caves at the Bellefort, the Karnak's baths were open to men and women in an airy atrium, humid and dripping with ferns, the fog from hot water and human breath obscuring what should have been visible through the glass ceiling. Chilton was already soaking when Agatha returned from the dressing room, wearing a thick dressing gown issued by the establishment. Steam rose around them as she removed the dressing gown and stepped gingerly into the hot water, flinching in pain and pleasure as she lowered herself in, smiling at him once again.

Chilton felt a restriction in his throat. A catch. He regretted leaving the manor. Outside in the world time revealed itself as fleeting in a way no amount of wishing could reverse.

"Agatha," he said.

She glanced with concern at the other bathers, worried they'd hear her name and connect it to the morning's headlines. But the only person who seemed to have noticed was a young woman with kindly eyes, not bothering with a cap but with her black hair piled high on her head: Miss Cornelia Armstrong.

"Oh, hello," Miss Armstrong said, ever sweet natured. "You must be Mrs. Chilton. Come to join your husband?"

Agatha smiled. It pleased Chilton no end that she might like the sound of that: Mrs. Chilton.

"Yes," Agatha said. "He claimed this was a trip for work, but to me it sounded like a holiday. So I thought I'd join in."

Chilton said to Miss Armstrong, "I thought you'd gone off these hot waters."

"Oh, not at all, Mr. Chilton. One must keep trying new things and soldier through. And when I thought how my mother would object to this particular bath, I couldn't resist. Men and women bathing together. Quite scandalous." Miss Armstrong spoke the last as if it were the most delightful word in the English language. "I'm determined to enjoy myself despite the bad business with the Marstons." She turned back to Agatha. "Has your husband told you? About all that's been going on at our little hotel?"

"Yes. How awfully sad."

"You've no idea. That is, I'm sure a man wouldn't tell it right. Their love story was something special. All those years of longing to be together. And then when they finally were, when the moment they'd longed for arrived, all the years ahead of them were taken away. Just like that. There's a lesson in that, don't you think, Mrs. Chilton? A person can't waste time being unhappy."

"Quite right," Agatha said. "I far prefer to waste my time being happy."

Chilton thought, *If I can talk her into boarding a train, first thing in the morning, we could waste the rest of our lives being happy.*

For the moment what seemed to make Cornelia Armstrong happy was waxing sorrowful about the Marstons' untimely end. She moved over to sit directly beside Agatha. Chilton felt thankful none of the hotel guests were privy to the information about the poison that had been discovered in both Marstons.

"Do you know," Miss Armstrong said to Agatha, "that before marrying Mr. Marston, Mrs. Marston had been a nun?"

"You don't say?" Agatha looked to Mr. Chilton, interest changing from polite to sincere.

"She told me so herself. She asked me not to tell anyone. But I suppose that doesn't matter now."

"I suppose not." Chilton poised himself, the way he did when someone was about to reveal something important, hoping the acceleration of his heartbeat wasn't detectable.

"She had been a nun," Miss Armstrong said, her voice giddy with the romance of it. "And Mr. Marston, he had been a priest. Oh, it sounds like a novel, doesn't it? The two of them torn and in love, all those years working side by side until they couldn't bear it a moment longer. They'd only just renounced their vows and run off, so they could be together." Miss Armstrong lowered her voice to a whisper. "You know I'm not even sure they'd even married yet, really. But that could just be me wanting more scandal." She laughed, a gentle twitter that might have been delightful, this show of happiness from the lovely young woman, if only it didn't spell possible doom for another.

"Do you happen to know," Chilton said carefully, "what sort of order they'd come from?"

"An orphanage." Miss Armstrong spoke warmly, as if this were the most philanthropic venture she could imagine. "She was such a loving person, Mrs. Marston, you could see it plain as day. I'm sure she took wonderful care of all those children."

"I'm sure she did," said Mr. Chilton. "Did she say where this orphanage was located?"

"County Cork, in Ireland. And I remember the name of the town. So poetic."

Before Miss Armstrong could speak the words *Sunday's Cor-*

ner, Chilton looked over at Agatha. He could see from her face that, in her mind as well as his, everything had just come clear.

Perhaps you surmised in that moment, along with Chilton and Agatha: Mrs. Marston and Sister Mary Clare were one and the same. Or perhaps you figured it out pages and pages ago. I wasn't finished, that day in Sunday's Corner, when my fingers circled around Sister Mary Clare's throat.

In the baths, the world dripped with warm moisture. The ceiling was good and high, no need for claustrophobia as Chilton made the connection he'd felt certain was there, between his two cases and the element that connected them both. Me.

"Funny," Agatha murmured. "My mother-in-law comes not far from Sunday's Corner."

"Oh." Miss Armstrong turned to Chilton. "Is your mother Irish?" At his vague nod she said to Agatha, "Mrs. Marston was such a jolly person. Wasn't she, Mr. Chilton?"

He nodded again, just as dishonestly. Mrs. Marston had the precise sort of jolliness he'd never believed in. The sort that masked something, or else the lack of something. He wished there were a way to convey this to young Miss Armstrong. It seemed an important lesson for a young person. It wasn't only the angry people that should make one wary. The jolly ones could be even more dangerous.

"And where do you return to, Miss Armstrong," Agatha asked, "when you go home?"

"Mundesley."

"Lovely," said Agatha. "How I prefer the sea, Miss Armstrong, to this countryside. Even in the winter. I don't care what sort of natural springs a place has to offer, or how they try to lure me. This is all well and good, but there's no place so refreshing as the seaside. Do you know my mother believed salt water cured everything, from spots to heart disease?"

"My father says the same," said Miss Armstrong.

"Give me a plunge in the cold brine." Agatha actually looked cozy, even refreshed, by the hot water. She sank low so that it covered her ears for a moment, as if someone might contradict her and she didn't want to hear it.

From outside a cold wind blew, strong enough that a little chill crept in, the glass ceiling rattling as if flimsier than promised. Agatha's love song to the seaside was a welcome sound to Chilton. Very welcome indeed.

Chilton and Agatha bundled back into their clothes and headed outside with their hair still damp. Strands froze; Agatha scrunched a handful to hear them crackle.

"You know what I like to imagine?" she said as they walked toward the road.

Neither had discussed what they'd learned, not yet, only come to a silent agreement. *That's love*, thought Chilton, *when your mind works in concert*.

Agatha seemed to know better than him that at the moment there were more important things to think of than their romance. "I like to imagine it wasn't just Nan. That every single woman staying at the Bellefort had a hand in it. When you think of all the girls who passed through that place, and others like it. Seems a pity for just one to have revenge when so many deserve it."

This was the last thing Chilton expected. "I suppose I'll have to get a confession out of Nan."

"You'll do no such thing."

"But, Agatha. This is murder we're talking about, not a game."

"What some call murder, others might call justice."

Chilton stopped walking but Agatha continued, with firm and determined footsteps. He put his hands in his pockets—first hoisting the useless one—and thought of the killing he'd done in the War. The bodies beneath his feet as he ran through no-man's-land. All of it sanctioned, in fact demanded, by the world. Perhaps a woman has a different kind of measuring stick. For when it might be acceptable, or even necessary, to commit a murder.

Here Lies Sister Mary

Not long after my escape, Fiona was released from the convent to work as a housemaid for a family in Sunday's Corner. She dutifully attended Father Joseph's services at the parish church. Her misspelled letters to me swelled with her old false cheer, claiming she couldn't be happier or safer, and that she prayed every day for her little boy. "I hope he's never told where he came from," she wrote. "The nuns always knew what was best for us, didn't they?"

Upon reading that line I ripped Fiona's letter into a hundred pieces, the fiercely torn shreds turning up for weeks when I swept my room.

"Don't be angry at Fiona," Bess wrote. "She was raised by the nuns. If believing in them keeps her from going mad, who are we to take that away from her?"

I couldn't stop myself sitting down and writing to tell Fiona how her little boy would always have a memory of her, deep in his bones and blood. That's how it works with humans. "A baby never entirely leaves a mother's womb," I wrote. "Traces of your boy—the very cells that comprise his living form—are still contained inside of you."

She wrote back to tell me the roses that year were the most beautiful she'd ever seen. And she'd gone to the convent to buy milk and radishes for her household, and all the nuns seemed wonderfully well.

In Philadelphia, Bess tried to be happy. It shouldn't have been so difficult. Her husband was a kind man who adored her, and he found good work as the manager of a shipyard. They lived in a white clapboard house in a pleasant neighborhood. Two bedrooms waited to be filled with children: her husband wanted two boys, two girls. But when Bess walked into these rooms, she didn't see them as empty of future children, the family she couldn't convince herself to start. She saw them empty of Ronan, who'd kicked and swam inside her, promising his arrival, and then emerged as a cold, unbreathing bundle.

"Do you remember how beautiful he was?" she would ask her husband late at night. He held her close in his arms and kissed her hair and hoped one day she could find a way to move past it all.

"But I can't move past it," she confessed to her doctor. He was bald, with shockingly dark eyebrows and a compassionate bearing. "It's left me so afraid."

"You're perfectly healthy," Dr. Levine promised her. "There's no need to be afraid. You're young."

"Do you think that is was the priest who caused it? The stillbirth?" On previous visits she had told Dr. Levine what she'd endured, to explain scarring he'd found when he first examined her and worried her husband was the perpetrator.

He raised his eyes to the ceiling before answering. Thinking. Wanting to give her an honest answer.

"I can't say for certain one way or the other," he finally said. "But I do know it can't have helped."

She wept, and he patted her shoulder. Bess hadn't left Ireland unable to accept human touch from a man. She could take comfort from Dr. Levine's kind thumping. She could enjoy making love with her husband. Father Joseph hadn't taken that away from her.

But she couldn't recover what she believed with all her heart he *had* taken from her. She would walk outside her cozy house, a mug of coffee in her hand (a full-fledged American now, no more tea), to wave goodbye to her husband as he walked off to catch the train to work. Once he was out of sight, the mothers began emerging, to play in the pretty yards with their children. Bess would see, so clearly, her Ronan. Whatever age he would have been. Riding in a pram. Toddling after a cat in the garden. Rolling a toy truck along the drive. Chalking the sidewalk.

He should be here. He should be here, he should be here, he should be here.

"I want to leave my old life behind," she wrote to me. "I send letters to you and Fiona and my sister Kitty. Apart from that, I'm only interested in what's here for me, here and now."

Even as she wrote the words, she knew they weren't entirely true. Bess wanted children. She would have happily, joyfully filled those rooms upstairs. But not while Father Joseph drew breath and Ronan didn't. The hatred in her heart had nothing to do with being a mother. And only one thing in the world would vanquish it.

Such a thing never seemed possible. Until a letter from Fiona arrived with the gossip from Sunday's Corner. Sister Mary Clare and Father Joseph had fallen in love and renounced their vows.

"She was in the village, chatty as ever," Fiona wrote. "She told me they'd be married next month and then leave for Yorkshire to honeymoon at a place called the Bellefort Hotel. She told me I might as well start calling her Mrs. Marston as that would be her name soon enough."

Bess could easily imagine the cheery laugh that followed. A plan had to be hatched quickly. But she knew it would be easier to complete, now that Sister Mary Clare and Father Joseph would be together, in England. And she'd have such a willing accomplice in me.

The Disappearance

DAY FIVE

Wednesday, December 8, 1926

B ess and I knew perfectly well Chilton was listening at the door. Not because we'd heard him—he was quieter than a mouse—but because we expected him to be watching us. We'd known we'd be facing perils enough, with our plans to murder two seemingly innocent people. Little did we know we'd also have to contend with my lover's wife and the inspector who was searching for her. Not to mention Finbarr, come to reclaim me.

"Donny's had a telegram," Bess said, so loudly I nearly laughed at the contrivance of it. "We have to cut things short. Go back to the States."

She sat down on the bed beside me and clasped my hand. We stared at each other, eyes full. No matter what happened next, it had been worth it.

The poisons had been easy enough to obtain, though potassium cyanide was an odd purchase for winter, with no wasps afoot. I went to two different shops in London, one for the potassium cyanide and another for the strychnine, the beauty of a populous city, where nobody would remember me or think to connect the substances with any death in Yorkshire. Archie might not have read Agatha's books, but I had. I knew poison was the best way to accomplish a quick and easy murder—easy to perpetrate but not to solve.

Sister Mary Clare, now Mrs. Marston, was so untrue and unthinking in her every word and deed. At the Bellefort Hotel she stared directly at me. Never into my face. Only glancing at the surface. Bess, too; Mrs. Marston trained her eyes on both of us and spoke about herself. Just like at the convent, she smiled, she chatted, she landed her plump hands on our shoulders as if she believed herself fond of us. But when we appeared again in her life, she recognized nothing about either of us. To her all girls were the same.

It was Hamlet, wasn't it, who said, "One may smile, and smile, and be a villain."

To the man who'd never bothered to smile, at least at us—the ragwort—some girls stood out. Father Joseph knew Bess the moment he laid eyes on her. In the hotel dining room, doing what needed to be done, Bess had felt no fear. None at all. Only a gladness at witnessing his discomfort. Knowing he'd be dead before he could alert his wife to our identity.

Bess's sister, Kitty, and her husband, Carmichael, posing as an unhappy English couple, had caused the necessary diversion—a great row that commanded the attention of everyone present. Bess had been able to step forward and plunge the syringe into Father Joseph's flank, then secret it back into the pocket of her dress almost before he felt the prick. Kitty—pretending to be a nurse—had flown to his side not to help him, but to make sure he was dead. She had a secondary needle waiting in her own pocket just in case, but that proved unnecessary.

Bess couldn't call it gladness, exactly, watching the man die. She wasn't cruel. It was a distasteful but necessary task. The world had offered no justice, so we made our own.

Kitty, the little girl Bess had told me about in Ireland—the pretty twelve-year-old who'd wanted to be in pictures—had grown up to marry a young man not only blessed with a family fortune, but theatrical aspirations of his own. With his help Kitty pulled off the greatest performance of her career before it even began. She and Carmichael stayed on at the hotel afterward, continuing the ruse, so no one would suspect their row was connected to Mr. Marston's collapse.

In my room at the Bellefort, with Chilton's ear pressed against the door, I said, also loudly, "I do hope everything is all right."

"Yes," Bess said. "Everything is perfect. *Perfect*." Then, in a whisper that wouldn't be heard no matter how closely Chilton hovered: "Kitty and Carmichael will stay on, and they've paid for your room through the end of next week. But we're leaving. Back to America. You should come with us."

I shook my head, vehement.

"Stay in England if you must. But go back to London. Get out of here, fast as you can."

"That would only make me look guilty, wouldn't it?" But I wasn't thinking about looking guilty. I was thinking about Finbarr's arms, a brisk walk away. Soon enough I'd have to face my whole life without him. But I couldn't do it just yet. I needed just a little while longer. Even if it did increase my risk of being caught.

Bess and I embraced, our hands clutching at the other's clothes, faces buried in each other's neck. We had done what we'd come to do. Now the world would unfold however it needed. Having removed Father Joseph from the world, Bess could go on with her life. We didn't know she was leaving England already pregnant with a little girl who'd be born—the squalling picture of health—that September.

And I had taken care of Sister Mary Clare. By bringing a steaming cup of tea to her door and gently rapping.

"Oh, my dear," the former nun said, when I peeked into the room. "How good of you to come to me. I'm afraid I shan't sleep a wink tonight. Not one wink." Her face was swollen and blotchy. She covered it with her hands and wept some more.

I walked to her bed and sat down, pressing the cup into her hands. "Drink this," I said in my most soothing voice. "There's a bit of brandy in it." I wore a dressing gown, my hair loose. Hers was gathered up under a nightcap. I could see the gleam of cream upon her face, still tending to the usual ministrations, imagining a tomorrow despite her bereavement.

"Oh, you're a darling. That doctor gave me a sleeping draft but my nerves are overcoming it." She took the cup and sipped.

The English love of tea as solution to life's ills does make us easy to poison.

"I can't say where I'll go tomorrow. We had a plan, Mr. Marston and I, for where we'd go next. Manchester, where I lived as a girl, before I was sent off to Ireland." She was speaking to herself, not realizing I'd heard this story before. "But my family's not there anymore. How can I do it without Mr. Marston? I've never lived alone, you see. I used to be a nun, if you can believe that."

"Oh, I believe it, Mrs. Marston. I do."

She cried and sipped, cried and sipped. I sat beside her and patted her knee. It had only been seven years, and not years that particularly age a person. At twenty-seven I looked passably as I had at twenty. She'd seen me every day for months. She'd been with me when Genevieve first laughed. She was the last person I ever saw holding my baby. I stared and stared, willing her to stare back. The ghosts that ought to have haunted her fluttered away, unthinking.

"You're a dear." She handed me the empty cup.

I put it on the bedside table. Later I would be sure to wipe it clean of fingerprints and residue. Sister Mary Clare lay back. She reached out and clasped my hand. "You'll stay with me, won't you? Until I fall asleep."

"Of course I will."

Her eyes fluttered closed. If I waited, the poison would kill her. But unlike Bess I wanted hands on my quarry. The coroner would find the strychnine. But I'd have her dead before it did its work. I hummed a few bars of the same haunting tune she was always so fond of, but even that didn't make her realize. She smiled a bit and said—very quiet, eyes still closed—"Oh, I do love that song."

A few more moments passed. The clock downstairs chimed but I didn't count the hour. I picked up a pillow; no doubt it had lain beneath Father Joseph's head the night before. Then I tapped her to make sure she hadn't fallen asleep. Her eyes fluttered open. I smiled, dearly wanting her to see love and kindness in my face. She managed a wan, thankful smile in return. Then down came the pillow.

I took one risk, in the middle, taking the pillow away for the barest second. Sister Mary Clare rewarded me with the second honest expression of her life: fear and shock and anguish. I could have told her who I was, in that moment. But I liked adding confusion to the terrible emotions overcoming her. So I pressed the pillow back down. I held the woman down. Until she stopped struggling. Until she stopped causing harm. Until her body came to rest, and her breath ceased to flow. When I pulled the pillow away, her face held no false cheer, no false kindness. Her lips spoke no empty promises. All she had were eyes newly made of glass, open but not seeing. Her mouth open, frozen in its useless attempt to find oxygen.

For years I'd been swept in directions I never meant to go. I'd made mistakes, acting by accident or imperative. Finally in this moment I was the author of my story. The universe must not have held it against me because I was rewarded almost at once with my days in the Timeless Manor.

When Sister Mary Clare lay dead before me, how the air metamorphosed. Particles that had been charged became inert. The rage inside me quieted. A violent storm had ended.

The urge to murder. It never left me until the job was done.

The Disappearance

Finbarr was downstairs stoking the kitchen fire when Chilton and Agatha returned to the Timeless Manor. On the table were bottles of wine—he had helped himself to the collection in the cellar—along with a tray that held three loaves of fresh bread, various kinds of sausage, a wheel of Swaledale cheese, and tins of peaches.

"You said you were tired of tongue," he told Agatha. "So I went on a little scouting mission."

"Aren't you a darling," she said.

Chilton frowned the slightest bit, looking from one to the other. Agatha sat, weary, the force of these days away, this time away, still not seeing the future take any shape she could recognize. Chilton pulled out a chair and sat beside her. In a calm voice he told Finbarr what they'd pieced together. The Marstons' true identity, and my hand in their murder.

Finbarr listened, his face unmoving and inscrutable. When Chilton had finished, he said, "Good."

"Good?" said Chilton. "Come now, man. You can't mean that."

"But I do mean it."

Agatha poured wine into a teacup. This seemed the right night to make an exception to her abstinence. It occurred to her she ought to be glad of the thought, me headed to jail, which would not only get me out of the way but punish me for the pain I'd caused her. But even before our escape, accidentally mutual, such a thing wouldn't have made her glad. She wasn't that sort of person and never would be. She might be capable of imagining other people's plots of revenge and the bitterness that drove them. She could even sympathize with mine. But she could never carry them out herself. She was better than me in that way. Or else just luckier.

"What happens next, then?" Finbarr asked.

"I'm afraid I'll have to tell the Yorkshire police what I know," Chilton said. "About who the Marstons are. And what Nan and her friend are guilty of. I'm afraid the inquest will take it from there."

"Not today," Finbarr said. Agatha heard the rasp of mustard gas strangling his voice, worse than usual.

"Yes," she agreed. "Not today."

"But, Agatha." Chilton turned to her as if Finbarr couldn't hear. "That will give him the time he needs to escape with her."

"Would that be so bad?" Agatha said. "Sometimes an escape is precisely what's needed."

Chilton looked dubious. How many of his duties would he let float away before all this was over? What if Agatha wanted

Nan to escape to form a road back to her husband? Though surely my arrest would net the same result. Archie would not have stood by me through a murder trial. He might not have stood by me if he heard me speak with the working-class accent I'd so carefully expunged.

"One more day," Agatha said softly, delightfully aware of the romantic power she had over Chilton. "Perhaps two."

One more day undiscovered. Perhaps two. One more day exempt from time and repercussion. One more day dispensing with propriety and responsibilities. One more day as if her mother had never died, and her husband never left her—indeed as if both of them had never existed at all, to cause her joy or pain. Why not two more days? Why not a thousand?

"One more day," Agatha said again. "Just one. We'll decide tomorrow. We'll make a plan?" The question mark was a brilliant stroke. Implying he was in a position to argue.

"Come with me," Finbarr said, as if they'd all reached an agreement. He picked up the tray and left the kitchen, moving his head ever so slightly, indicating that Chilton should collect the wine.

Upstairs, the great room was nearly empty of furniture except for a settee covered by a dustcover, and a cluster of large pillows thrown to the floor (as if we had not been the first squatters the Timeless Manor had seen, and someone else had sojourned here and made do with what could be found). On the floor beside the settee sat a Victrola—of the gramophone variety, old-fashioned even for the time, with a great mahogany horn.

"I found it in the butler's pantry," Finbarr said. He wound it up and placed the needle on its record, and scratchy big band music filled the cavernous room.

To join the party, I had but to follow the music. Finbarr lounged on the floor against one of the big pillows, a goblet filled with wine in one hand. Chilton and Agatha were dancing, her face aglow from the firelight and the day in the baths, looking as lovely in her trousers and cardigan as she ever had wearing any gown in any ballroom.

Three faces turned toward me, fondly, withholding the devastating information. Tomorrow. It could all be saved until tomorrow. For now we would let our disappearance extend a little longer. It would continue into the night and small hours of the morning. One thing we'd learned since discovering this place: there was nothing in the world that couldn't wait.

"Oh, Nan," Agatha said, as Chilton dipped her, her head thrown back, her tone joyful, as if I were her best friend in all the world. "Come have some wine and cheese, come have a dance. For who knows what tomorrow will bring?"

Remarkably, my ears did not hear this as ominous. It sounded like an invitation. If I had been a different sort of person, raised in a different time and country, I might have told her I loved her. And she might have said it back. Instead the two of us smiled at each other. Not rivals but landsmen. A shared sorrow can create unexpected warmth, even as it illuminates all the ways our world is ruined.

The Disappearance

The machinery of the world had already started grinding against our remaining undiscovered. The Harrogate librarian, Miss Barnard, picked up newspapers with increasing fervor, looking at every new photograph, and thinking that she knew—she absolutely knew—the woman she'd seen was the missing mystery writer. Finally she telephoned the police department in Leeds. The officer who answered, hearing the emotional certainty in her voice, utterly dismissed her concerns. But still. A seed had been planted.

Inside the Timeless Manor, though, everything was beautiful.

That night we stayed up past dawn, the records singing, the wine flowing, the four of us twirling and laughing and dancing. Agatha felt young again. Truly young—once again the girl who had slid off her horse when her hair flew off into the wind, to collect it with gales of laughter. All the house parties she'd attended as a girl, jumping from one to the next—sometimes out of necessity, because the money had run out, and Ashfield was let. Without society Agatha would have had nowhere to go. But when she was a guest, everything was taken care of, everything was bright and gay and fun. But never so much fun as this. Nobody, ever, like Finbarr. Nobody like Chilton, certainly, with his hand at her waist, traveling at will. A strange, gorgeous echo of her old life but with the oddest, most unlikely people, and no rules at all.

What would her mother say? Liberating to have that question melt into the air, unanswered, unimportant. How it used to hover over her every move. How she had watched herself, even in her youth. Never too much to drink if anything at all. Don't say this. Don't say that. Don't wander upstairs, into a bedroom, with a man not your husband, and do whatever the two of you please. Now her mother was gone but life did go on in new ways. Humane ways. That was the thing. To be sensible and to be humane. Even if it seemed at the moment she wasn't particularly sensible anymore. For what seemed the first time in her life—and only for this short window—Agatha owned her own virtue, and thereby her own fate.

When she and Chilton had disappeared upstairs, Finbarr and I stayed behind, dancing awhile longer. So I forgot to return to the Bellefort Hotel, my room there empty yet again. Kitty and Carmichael would have left by now. The ruse of their misery had gone on long enough to fool everyone; nobody would ever think back and recognize it as a diversion. They didn't return to Ireland, but headed to America, to stop in Philadelphia with Lizzie and Donny, then on to New York, both of them destined for the stage. Before they left, they made sure my room was paid through a few more days. Mrs. Leech would never give them up as my benefactors. And she wouldn't send anyone hunting for me, at least not yet. She knew about Finbarr. Young lovers. She'd shake her head with a secret smile, remembering a time when her romance had seemed impossible, too.

Morning light had long since arrived by the time we went to sleep. All our heads fuzzy with wine and giddy with love. Nobody got around, that day, to accusing me of murder.

On Monday morning in Sunningdale, Teddy woke, horrified to find her father sleeping beside her, on top of the covers, still wearing his suit and even his shoes, his mouth open, spittle winding its way from his mouth to the pillow. She jumped out of bed quick as she could, collected Touchstone, and held her close to her chest.

"Colonel Christie!" she exclaimed, deciding only the most formal address would do.

Archie started awake and swung his feet to the floor. "Dear me. I must have fallen asleep."

"Indeed." The little girl's face looked dark with rebuke.

Archie lifted a hand to his brow. Unruly curls loose on his forehead. Reflected in Teddy's glare, he had no way of knowing he'd never been handsomer, in all his undone vulnerability. He had no interest in being vulnerable. Over the past ten days he'd become everything he most detested—melancholic, sickly, in-effectual.

"I only want to be happy," he told Teddy, hanging his head, hating the pathetic sound of his voice.

Because she was a kind child, Teddy patted the top of his head. "And so you shall be," she promised.

Like Miss Barnard, the woman who worked at the Karnak gift shop had been thinking about Agatha Christie. But she waited until Monday to say anything, Sunday not being a proper time to cause any kind of upheaval.

"I've seen that missing lady novelist with my own eyes," Miss Harley announced, when she walked into the Leeds Police Headquarters. She was middle-aged, unlucky in love, always rheumy with remembering the man who should have proposed before he left for the Boer War, never to be heard from again.

The young fellow at the front desk called Lippincott over.

"Are you quite sure?" Lippincott demanded, assessing Miss Harley to no particular advantage. "I've got a man reporting daily on that case." In fact, he realized, he had not heard from Chilton in several days. "He says he's not seen head nor tail of her."

"Well, I've seen the head and the tail." The wattle on Miss Harley's neck became tremulous with indignation. "She was in the hotel gift shop, staring right at me, looking just like her picture. She bought a bathing dress and picture postcard. I thought I might be imagining things but I saw another photograph of her in the papers today, and it was her. I just know it was."

That's what you get when you don't take matters in your own hands, thought Lippincott. He headed over to the library to question Miss Barnard.

"Oh, I'm quite sure it was her," Miss Barnard said, thankful to finally be heard. "She went awfully pale when I pointed out the resemblance. Can you say someone has a resemblance to herself?" Miss Barnard laughed, then stopped abruptly when she saw Lippincott was unamused. "Took some books out, too. Detective novels, mostly."

"What name did she give?"

"Mrs. O'Dea. Said she was staying at the Bellefort Hotel and Spa."

"The Bellefort!"

The thought of Agatha Christie right under Chilton's nose this whole time—not to mention Lippincott's own family—was more than any man could bear. Fond of Chilton though he was, Lippincott marched out of the library with his fingers twitching, ready himself to do everything that needed to be done.

That evening the phone rang at Styles. The maid Anna found Archie at the dining table, his food before him uneaten, a tumbler of Scotch in one hand. His eyes, persistently, on the window. Dark now, only returning his own sad reflection.

"Colonel Christie. There's a police officer on the telephone. Says he's calling from Leeds."

The Disappearance

Over the years, since our time in Yorkshire, Agatha and I have managed to steal a private moment or two, when our paths crossed—accidentally, in London, or at a family function. The funeral of Archie's mother, for example. Teddy's wedding. Times the blending of families past and present could not be avoided.

She and I agreed that although we'd spent not even a week in the Timeless Manor, in the dead of winter—bare branches and foggy windows—we remembered the house in every season. We could see the glorious canopy, dripping with moss and green, arching over the drive. The lawn where we played tennis soft with recent rain, so our feet left divots in the earth as we played. Birds making a racket when we woke, sun arriving too early and pouring through the curtains. The fields that rolled behind the house carpeted with dahlias, lilies of the valley, and primulas. We remember Teddy running through the flowers, picking the brightest ones, hem of her skirt stained with mud and grass, though truly she was never there at all.

"To call it amnesia never quite feels like a lie," she once told me. "Because it all seems still a marvelous dream. The kind you create to take the place of something terrible."

"We should steal away together," I suggested at least once. "We should go back."

Agatha admitted she'd thought of finding the owner and buying the house. But she never did, and neither of us returned there, not together or apart. The house lived on only as a place we visited in conversation and memory, no more visible to the outside world than we had been, inhabiting it, undetected.

Sometimes at night I have a marvelous dream of my own, a party. The manor's not dusty or spare of furnishings, but bright and fully appointed. Genevieve, and my little Rosie, and my sister Louisa's children, and even Colleen's: they sit in the upstairs hallway peering down through the banister long after they were sent to bed. Finbarr is there, and Chilton, and my parents. Fiona and her son, the raspberry birthmark faded. Bess and Donny and Ronan—plus the three girls they'd go on to have. All three of my sisters. The Mahoneys and Uncle Jack and Aunt Rosie. Seamus, grown to a man, laughing as though he never knew a moment's sickness. Alby, black-and-white fur gleaming, a perfect gentleman, exactly at Finbarr's side. Sparkling lights, and trays of brimming champagne flutes, and the most cheerful music—not scratchy from an old Victrola, but a live orchestra. It's the happiest moment in the world. It's everything I've ever wished for, finally bestowed.

The four of us slept most of the day before adjourning again to the great room, settling with food and wine before a crackling fire. We'd exhausted the supply of fresh food, and Finbarr hadn't ventured out, so it was back to tins of tongue and kippers, laid out on a large linen tablecloth going yellow at the edges.

Once wine had been poured, Finbarr said to me, "It's time to come out with it, Nan. They think you've done murder."

People can seem especially beautiful by firelight. Agatha sat cross-legged, looking like a lady explorer in her man's clothes, hair vivid and tumbled, cheeks rosy. Chilton looked younger than I supposed he had in years, lying on his side, downright insouciant. Finbarr reached out and clasped my hand. I kissed his cheek.

"Do they" is all I said.

Agatha held out a plate to me, but I waved it away, not a bit hungry. "Would you like to hear a story," I said, "about a time I could have done murder?"

It was a good night for ghost stories. Some wind outside. Nothing but the firelight. The four of us, close and safe and strangely delighted. I told them about my escape from the convent, and my hands around Sister Mary Clare's throat.

"And that was Mrs. Marston," Chilton said.

I didn't agree, but told them another ghost story, about a priest, and a pregnant girl. Iron bars, plus laws of God and man, imprisoned us all inside a rambling stone convent. The priest had license to do what he would. Inside the convent there was forgiveness for his sins, but not those of the girls he abused.

I didn't provide every piece of the story. Not Kitty and Carmichael (Chilton, as it turned out, was no Hercule Poirot—he had forgotten all about hearing their Irish accents), or Bess's real name, or where she lived.

"I've never done murder," I said. "I've only made my own justice."

From upstairs a door creaked on its hinges, the wind rattling it open. Agatha's eyes moved to the ceiling, alert to anything that could indicate her discovery. I didn't want her thinking about that. I wanted her to realize and admit. When she had taken that baby into her home, she'd accepted something stolen.

"Tell the truth," I said to her.

"Yes," Finbarr urged. "Tell her. Put an end to it once and for all."

The joy had snapped out of the room.

Agatha said, "I thought you knew without a doubt. Both of you."

"I do know," I said. "But I want to hear you say it. I've confessed. Now it's your turn."

"Very well then. It's all true."

Finbarr got to his feet. He rolled up his sleeves, almost as if he would hit her. Chilton tensed and sat up, ready to stand between them.

"Which?" Finbarr said. "Which part is true?"

"Nan's part."

"That's not right," Finbarr said. "You know it's not."

"I'm sorry, Finbarr. But that's what I've got to say. Nan's right. I couldn't have a baby of my own, so Archie got one for me. And I didn't know, I didn't think. The cruelty of it was lost on me. I'm sorry."

"Nan," Finbarr said. "Don't listen to that. She's said just the opposite to me all along. I don't know why she's changing her story now." He fell to his knees and gathered up Agatha's hands. Looked at her with his melting, convincing eyes. Convincing for just the right reason. Not because he was scheming or had any ulterior motive. But because he was true to his core in every word he ever spoke.

"I'm sorry, Finbarr," Agatha said. "I truly am."

He let go of her hands and stood. "I don't know why you're doing this. I'll never know."

But I knew. Everybody stared at me. Perhaps I was beautiful in the firelight, too.

It could be Agatha admitted Teddy was mine because she didn't want Archie anymore and knew her pronouncement would make me go back to him. Or else she knew it was inevitable, that her marriage was over, and now she'd ensured that no matter what happened next, I'd always look out for her daughter as if she were my own. Perhaps she felt terrible for all I'd been through and wanted to let me believe Teddy was mine because my real child was lost to me forever, and with this kind lie she could return her to me, if only in deception.

Or perhaps the solution was simpler. Occam's razor. Perhaps she told me Teddy was Genevieve for one reason and one reason only:

Because it was the truth.

Upstairs, Finbarr sat on the bed. I stood in front of him, his knees bracing either side of me. He tucked a strand of hair behind my ear. "Remember when you used to wear it long?"

He'd never seen it cropped far shorter than this, up above my ears. "I remember everything."

"Will you remember this?"

"Always."

If not for the fire, the room would have stood completely dark. As it was, our faces were obscured enough to look like they had our first summer—open to and untouched by the future. I could almost pretend I didn't know: we'd never be together like this again.

The room glowed with the fire's warmth. Smoke from the manor's chimneys should have given us away—four love-struck outlaws. The flames made the windows glow. This night in particular: when I picture the Timeless Manor, I picture the view from outside, every last window thrumming and glowing like a place possessed.

The Disappearance

I woke long before dawn and put more wood on the fire. At any moment the owners of the house could return, from wherever their primary residence was, or else the new owners, if this was a time of transition. Or, more likely, servants sent ahead to prepare. Whoever walked through the door next would find clues we'd been here. Ashes left in the fireplaces. Tins of food gone missing. Empty bottles slid back into place on the cellar's wine rack. And perhaps the remnants of happiness infusing the rooms, swirling like dust mites.

I kissed Finbarr's sleeping head and stole out of the room to walk the country roads in the low mist, not afraid of a thing: not of dogs barking from their fields, or the frigid air, or even the form of a man, who walked by me as a shadow and tipped his hat. If I'd walked right off the road into another world, it wouldn't have surprised me. But no matter how lovely the other world turned out to be, I'd do anything I could to claw my way back into this one, because my child still lived here, and I must never be far from her, not in this lifetime.

I crept up the stairs at the Bellefort and crawled into bed, where I slept for hours, until I woke to the sound of a familiar voice, loud enough to reach me from the lobby, searching— but not for me.

Chilton woke early, too. He sat up in bed beside a sleeping Agatha. Last night they'd decided to move to one of the grander bedrooms on the second floor. He hadn't questioned Agatha's assertion about her daughter (did it contradict what she'd told him previously?), nor the assumption all three of them made, that he would protect me. Two people dead. And Chilton expected to just let it go.

He stroked Agatha's hair, softly, so as not to wake her. Somewhere in what passed between them a tacit agreement had been made, never to say the words. But now that she was safely, deeply asleep—her lips parted, her face flushed with that childlike fever dreams can induce—he let himself whisper it: "I love you, Agatha." Beneath their lids her eyes moved. A slight smile curled across her lips. Why shouldn't they expect him to do the wrong thing where Nan was concerned? He'd done the wrong thing for Agatha.

For want of a nail the kingdom was lost. How many crimes were being neglected, throughout England, because of the manpower devoted to the discovery of the woman who lay beside him now, safe and sound and intoxicating, her warm breath across his face all he wanted of life from this day forward. He crept out of bed and walked to the window. He always did his best thinking while contemplating a landscape. From behind him he heard the rustle of Agatha waking. She rose and glided to him. Still he didn't turn toward her. She pressed herself against his back, wrapped her arms around his waist, rested her pointed chin on his shoulder to share the view with him, the farther-reaching hills obscured by a stand of fir trees.

"I suppose you're thinking about Nan," she said.

"I am."

"Do you know the artist Claude Monet?"

"Lilies and blurs?"

"That's the one. He died earlier this month. I read in a notice about his death that he once said, 'To see we must forget the name of the thing we are looking at.'"

"And that means what, precisely?"

"This is your case. You're the one looking at it. By grand good luck, you're the one who's been charged to solve it. So can't the solution, the name, be anything you like?"

"I suppose it can be."

"Good." She stepped away from him as though the matter was settled.

"And then what? We can't stay here forever."

She sat on the edge of the bed.

"There can be no more days." Chilton knelt in front of her and took up her hands. "Or there can be all the days. If we leave, you and I. Together. Today. Let the disappearance last a lifetime. Why not?"

"Why not."

He didn't want to interrupt the joy bursting forth within him by muddying her agreement with details. They could work that out later. A car, a train, a destination.

"I'll go back to the Bellefort and collect my things. Then we can work out a plan."

"I'll go with you. I could do with some air."

"But, darling. You can't be seen with me."

"That will make our life together rather difficult, won't it?" She laughed and put on his hat, pulled it down over her forehead. "Nobody will recognize me. They might even take me for your brother."

Perhaps Chilton was unnerved by the word *brother* and that's why he didn't protest. Perhaps Agatha—in her heart, more than she was able to admit—wanted to be found after all. Or perhaps, as far as they knew, all the chances they'd taken so far had netted no danger. So why not take one more? Plain sight had proved as good a place to hide as anywhere.

While Agatha was upstairs in Chilton's hotel room, helping him gather his things, Archie and Lippincott arrived at the Bellefort. Mrs. Leech ushered them into the library. She brought out the guest ledger for the two of them to look over.

Archie's eyes immediately landed on my last name, O'Dea. "This"—he pointed—"this is my wife's handwriting." As if he'd forgotten me entirely, my name as well as my hand. A sleight of mind, confusing the two of us. One of his women's penmanship, what did it matter which? To give him credit, the mistake was likely born of hope. He wanted his wife before his eyes, whole and alive. If he erased my existence by assigning my name and handwriting to her, he could make everything right. He could conjure her finally, safe and well.

Never knowing that I hadn't been erased. I was just upstairs.

My feet directly above his head, gliding over the floorboards, my heart dropped into my bowels, as I pressed my face against the door.

Mrs. Leech was adamant: the lady in room 206, Mrs. Genevieve O'Dea, was not the missing novelist.

"Why, Sam," she said to Lippincott, "Mrs. O'Dea has been with us more than a week. I know her face perfectly well. She's a smaller lady. Younger. Dark hair."

"Hard to determine hair color by a photograph," Lippincott told Mrs. Leech. "I've seen photographs of my own mother I'd swear weren't her. Devilish art form if you ask me."

"Well, I know my own mother in photographs. And I know Mrs. O'Dea and this isn't her."

Mr. Leech bustled into the room. He greeted his cousin with a heartily fond handshake, then squinted at the picture obligingly. "I think this Mrs. O'Dea could very well be this woman."

"Good gracious, Simon. You've scarcely glanced at her," said Mrs. Leech. He wasn't even wearing his spectacles. She huffed off without a goodbye or backward glance.

"I say." Mr. Leech smiled at Lippincott. "It'll be marvelous publicity, won't it, Sam? The Bellefort Hotel splashed over every newspaper in the country. Good enough for Agatha Christie." He'd never heard of Agatha Christie until this moment, but if her name was in the papers over a few days unaccounted for, she had to be enormously famous.

Lippincott, Leech, and Archie formulated a plan. They agreed Archie should not confront his wife by going to her room or standing at the bottom of the stairs waiting for her to come down to breakfast. Instead they situated him in the drawing room, an open newspaper obfuscating his identity, while Lippincott waited in the lobby to intercept.

"Isabelle assures me Mrs. O'Dea is in her room," Mr. Leech told his cousin. "And while she's been in and out a good bit, she usually does take a meal upon rising."

His words had barely left his mouth when Chilton and Agatha came down the stairs. They were engrossed in each other, heads close together. She had forgotten to wear his hat, as if she believed herself no longer visible to the outside world, but could move through it undetected, in any situation. Chilton did not have his arm around her waist, luckily, but his hand fluttered as he talked, cupping the air by her elbow in a manner that appeared intimate. Lippincott's jaw dropped. Partly at the audacity of it. Partly at the change that had come over Chilton in the mere days since last Lippincott saw him. Chilton looked taller. His hair was neatly in place. And he seemed terribly lighthearted, not only for himself, but someone who'd been investigating a missing person and possible double murder.

But it was the woman who surprised him most. Looking younger than her photographs, and also light, happy, incandescent even. Dressed as if she'd just walked in from plowing a field, wholly inappropriate. He'd expected, if it was indeed her, to find a ghostly shell. The woman who stood before him—blind to surroundings apart from her companion—was quite the opposite.

"Mrs. Christie," said Lippincott. And just like that, the bubble burst.

Agatha and Chilton snapped their gazes to the foot of the stairs. Their hands came down to their sides. Lippincott was a kindly man on the whole, but his tone in this moment—the four abrupt and indignant syllables, distinctly chastising with additional phrases implied: *Mrs. Christie. How dare you. Mrs. Christie. What on earth do you think you're doing?* A tone used freely by all kinds of men, meant to return a person to reality, meaning proper behavior, befitting whoever it was they'd proclaimed her to be. Her imperviousness vanished. The shame whose absence she had marveled at descended, a bucket of water, a shroud.

"Well, Mr. Chilton," Lippincott said, his voice changing entirely, aghast but with a whiff of admiration. "I see you've found her."

Archie, listening from behind his newspaper in the drawing room just off the main hall, could bear it no longer. He had to see if it was really her. He imagined two scenarios. One, feasting his eyes upon his wife, upon Agatha, seeing her alive and whole and well, knowing this entire nightmare had finally ended. And two, seeing a stranger, someone wholly irrelevant, this trip another dead end, a needless waste of time like dredging the Silent Pool or engaging spirit mediums, his life forevermore this circus of public scrutiny and unanswered questions.

Stepping into the front hall, he drew in his breath. There Agatha stood. Wearing trousers and a man's cardigan. Hair grips holding back the wisps off her forehead like a girl. If he had registered Chilton and his proximity to her, he might have sprung at him. But Chilton was not the sort of man Archie registered unless he needed something. If he had walked into a room and seen Chilton close by, Archie might wordlessly have handed him his coat and hat.

Relief flooded Archie's body as if it had been administered

by syringe. He had pictured his wife's lifeless body in so many places—at the bottom of a lake, in a ditch, in the bonnet of some maniac's car. All the ways Agatha herself had imagined bodies ending up dead, Archie had imagined hers. And he was not an imaginative man. Now he felt too overcome to recognize the dismay on her face. It didn't occur to him she hadn't wanted to be found. He should have realized. At one glance he should have known he'd lost her.

"Agatha."

"Archie." Unnaturally loud, in case I was in the hotel. To warn me. There was no need for both of us to be caught.

Archie pointed to the door of the library. His hand trembled before him as if it belonged to a hundred-year-old man. That's what these eleven days had done to him, how much they'd aged him. But there were things to be said in private that might restore him yet.

Agatha stood frozen, like a misbehaved schoolgirl summoned by the headmaster. The newspaper headlines and all their readers. The manpower wasted on the search for her, and all the worry. Her child left at home without so much as a goodbye. Everything she'd been miraculously able to turn a blind eye to came rushing in with the force of a river when the dam is lifted.

She dared not look at Chilton. She stepped away from him, bowing her head, and descended the stairs. She walked into the library obediently and sat on the very edge of the worn sofa, as if worried she'd dirty it, suddenly aware of how she was presenting herself to the world, in these outrageously inappropriate clothes, no jewelry. As if she were an urchin caught playing in the streets.

But Archie. He did something wholly unexpected. Alone

in a room with her, seeing her mortified face—dear, pinched, pretty, familiar face—he dropped to his knees. He laid his face in her lap, immune to any foreign smells, wrapping his arms around her.

"AC," he said, his voice as close to weeping as she'd ever heard it. "You're alive. Are you all right?"

"I am." Her voice sounded frightfully weak. She knew she was supposed to say it back, *AC*, but she couldn't bring herself to do so.

He grasped at her hand and kissed the bare spot where her wedding ring should have been, then pulled the sacred jewelry out of his pocket and slid it back on her finger. Forgiving her for running off and creating all this worry (forgiveness from her for everything he'd done apparently a foregone conclusion).

"Where were you?" Archie said, as if the question had been plaguing him so it needed to be asked, despite her just being found in the place she'd presumably been. "Where did you go? What did you do?"

The first thing she thought to say was *Here. I came here.*

But that didn't feel true. So she said the next thing she could think, that somehow felt less like a lie, because everything had become so strange and confusing. And after all, she was not the only party with a story at stake. She had already decided to protect me, and from that she would never waver for an instant.

"I can't remember."

And so it would stand for the rest of her life.

The Disappearance

DAY OF DISCOVERY

Tuesday, December 14, 1926

Upstairs I packed quickly as I could and dragged my suitcase across the hall to Cornelia Armstrong's room. You'd think with two unexplained deaths she might have locked her door, but the same determined, trusting spirit that made her remain at the hotel and travel alone let her leave it open. When I walked in, she was sitting at her vanity brushing out her hair and turned toward me with a start. I hadn't knocked. I held my finger to my lips.

"Please. May I leave this suitcase with you? And will you promise not to tell anyone that it's here. Or that I was here?"

Miss Armstrong paused for a moment, then stood, took my suitcase, and slid it under her bed. "I'll never say a word."

"Dear brave girl." I crossed my hands over my heart. "If I never come back for it, everything inside is yours."

"Don't be silly. Of course you'll come back." At the same time she nodded. Not long afterward I would catch news of her quite by chance, in an item in the *Daily Mirror*. Mere months after our time in Harrogate, Miss Armstrong took a trip to explore the ruins of the Memorial Theatre in Stratford-upon-Avon, which had recently burned to the ground. While marching directly into the rubble, she caught the eye of a fellow adventurer, a disobedient and exceptionally handsome young earl. They married within a fortnight, and she moved with him to his estate in Derbyshire, the star-crossed romance and happy ending for which she'd longed. As I never was able to return for my belongings, I like to think she was wearing my cashmere cardigan and faux pearls when they met.

For now I clasped her hand to bid her goodbye, then crept to the top of the stairs in my stockinged feet, carrying my shoes. When I peered down, I saw Archie follow his wife into the library. Once inside, Agatha might tell Archie how I'd targeted him, seduced him, for the sole reason that I believed their daughter to be mine. That I had, during this time apart, been locked in a romantic and carnal embrace the likes of which he and I had never approached. That I'd known nearly all along where his wife was and hadn't told him. That I'd committed one murder and abetted another. Which of these actions, I wondered, would he find most egregious?

And why should I ever worry for a moment about what *he* would forgive? When Archie left Sunday's Corner, driving away with that bundled baby he'd bought and paid for, taking her home like a diamond to bestow upon his wife, did he ever for one second give a single thought to that child's mother?

I had to take this chance. I flew past poor, stunned Chilton, and the gaping Leeches, and the consternated Mr. Lippincott, through the hotel door. Once outside I put on my shoes and

slid behind the wheel of Chilton's borrowed police car. Whatever his next destination, he would have to go on foot. I drove
clumsily, determined to arrive back at the manor before time
returned with its brutal roar.

Luckily, Simon Leech pulled Lippincott into the drawing room
before the police chief could give Chilton the lambasting that
was clearly brewing.

Chilton seized upon the opportunity. "Mrs. Leech," he said,
as the proprietress marched from the dining room to the front
desk. "May I have a word?"

The mind is a remarkable thing, its exterior and interior
layers. The way Chilton was able to conduct himself, speaking
words he hardly heard, while his mind could only concentrate
on the horror of it—that this husband, who oozed arrogance
like a honeycomb oozed honey, would abscond with Agatha.

"You must help me," he said to Mrs. Leech. "At least by withholding contradiction. Listen. Agatha Christie has been here
at the Bellefort all this while, registered under the name Mrs.
Genevieve O'Dea. She has been taking curing baths and massages and keeping to herself."

"Absolutely not. As a point of honor, Mr. Chilton, I never
lie." Mrs. Leech folded her arms, her voice sounding all the
more musical. The words comforted Chilton. Anyone who says
I never lie has by that very statement told at least one.

"Have I had a chance to tell you? I've concluded my inves-
tigation. Of the Marston incident. And I've determined there's
no murderer at large."

Leech and Lippincott emerged from the drawing room in

time to hear this pronouncement. Mrs. Leech blinked slowly, absorbing whether a bargain was being offered.

"No need for word to get out," Chilton went on, confirming her suspicions, "as there's no danger to the public and never has been. Mrs. Marston killed her husband and then herself."

"There." Mr. Leech clapped, with an expression that couldn't have been jollier. "Just as Sam thought all along, eh? We'll keep that unpleasantness nice and quiet. And the Christie woman stopping here, we'll keep nice and loud. Business will be booming, Isabelle, just you wait."

Mrs. Leech let out a stream of breath. As her husband turned to say something to his cousin, Chilton whispered, "It will help Miss O'Dea and her young man a great deal."

Finally Mrs. Leech nodded, acquiescing. She preferred the idea of lying to help Nan to lying to save her hotel's reputation. "I knew she was a miss and not a Mrs.," Mrs. Leech whispered back. "I have a sixth sense for that sort of thing. I do hope she'll marry that sad, handsome fellow. I love a happy ending, Mr. Chilton."

"So do we all," Chilton said. "So do we all."

The library door opened, and Archie and Agatha emerged. Chilton had never wanted anything so badly as to catch her eye in that moment; but she kept her gaze steadily to the floor, like a child who'd been properly chastised.

"Mrs. Christie," Chilton said, trying to regulate his voice into an official capacity. "Perhaps you'd better return to your room, so we can conduct an interview."

"She'll do no such thing," Archie said. "This case is solved. There's been no crime. Only a misunderstanding. There's no need for any more police, we've had quite enough of that to last our lifetime."

Chilton wondered if he himself had ever spoken with such certainty. It pained him to note that when Archie turned to his wife, he spoke much more softly.

"Agatha, darling. Go collect your things. We need to be on our way before the newspapers get wind of your discovery. I'm afraid you'll have rather a to-doing with them in the next weeks."

Still without a look at Chilton, Agatha climbed the stairs to my room. Chilton took a step, as if to follow her, but Lippincott caught him by the sleeve.

Upstairs in my hotel room Agatha looked around, as if the place where our identities overlapped could betray anything about me, or herself, that she didn't already know. Her eyes landed on a flash of lilac, a shawl thrown across the chair by the table. She picked it up and sat down. The paper and pen I'd bought sat on the desk, unused. Agatha took up both, printing words so that her hand would not be recognizable, then folded the piece of paper in half and wrote "Inspector Chilton" in large block letters. She didn't worry someone else might find and read it. She knew he'd be here searching for clues the moment she left the hotel.

Agatha wrapped my shawl around her shoulders, as if it could transform her mannish outfit into something more respectable. She glided out of the room and down the stairs to her husband, who stood waiting for her, his face open and relieved all over again, every bit of love and hope she'd longed to see when once it had gone missing.

"Where are your things?" Archie asked, a tremor of fear in his voice, as if worried she'd decided to stay.

"There's nothing I need here."

She walked past him, out of the hotel, into the waiting car, my new shawl pulled tightly around her. On the drive back to Sunningdale, Archie plied her with all the questions that had befuddled him to the point of madness.

"Why did you abandon your car so precipitously?"

"How did you manage to get to Yorkshire?"

"Why are you dressed like that?"

"Didn't you see the papers? Didn't you know how many people were looking for you? I can't believe you would stay away if you knew about all that fuss."

She didn't answer, but rolled down the window a touch, needing the cold air to revive her. Archie shivered. Two weeks prior she would hastily have closed the window. Now she decided he'd have to endure it. She remembered her pearl ring and necklace, left behind at the manor house. They would do nicely to pay for her time there, and all the provisions they'd stolen. Already she was returning to lawful ways of thinking.

"Did you know, AC?" Archie pressed. "How many people were looking for you?"

"I don't remember." She watched the landscape roll by through the window. Again and again, when pressed for an explanation, that's what she said: "I don't remember." Because to say anything remotely resembling the truth would not only damn me, but possibly land her where, until recently, she'd wanted so badly to be: with Archie, forever.

When they arrived home in Sunningdale to face the press, Archie—whose job it was to shield his wife, and who had so little imagination of his own—told them the answer she'd given him.

She doesn't remember.

"The next year in my life is one I hate recalling," she wrote in her autobiography.

Years later, reading that sentence, I found myself smiling, as I often did when I saw little bits of our time out of time in her books. She scattered pieces of it, little remembrances, I never knew where or when they'd show up.

"Must you read every one?" Archie would ask when I brought her newest novel to bed.

"I'm sorry," I always answered. "They're just so diverting."

Agatha may have hated recalling some of that year. But not all of it. Certainly, not all of it.

Chilton watched Archie drive away with Agatha, then went back inside the hotel. He was aware of eyes upon him. The Leeches and Lippincott. He knew it should be an effort to remain composed. But it wasn't. He didn't feel numb. He only felt the absence of feeling. Which, strangely, gave him hope.

"Chilton," Lippincott said, sterner than he cared to be with his dear friend. "I believe you have some explaining to do."

"I was tasked with finding Agatha Christie. And so I have."

Before Lippincott could answer, Chilton turned and walked up the steps, taking them two at a time. Miss O'Dea's door had been left ajar. He pushed and it swung inward with a sad creak. No doubt Leech would oil the hinge before the next guest arrived. He might already have been envisioning a plaque for the door, commemorating the author's stay.

There on the desk, a folded piece of notepaper, Chilton's

name written across it in plain letters. He walked over and touched it. Brought it to his nose. If she had been living, these past ten days, in her own world it would have smelled of Yardley Old English Lavender. But instead, from the brief interaction she'd had with the paper, the side of her wrist resting as she wrote, it smelled of woodsmoke and pine. The barest bit of sweat. Even a little like himself. He opened the paper carefully. He thought it might say *I'm sorry* or *I love you*. He most hoped it would contain instructions as to where they should meet, what their next course of action should be, how they would manage. To be together.

"Please see to my typewriter and most importantly my papers," her note read. "I must have my work returned discreetly and as soon as possible."

He turned it over once, then twice. But that was all she'd written.

As for me:

When I was a girl, I fell in love with the sea. I fell in love with impossible green, and the long, cheeping syllables of skylarks, and kind, gentle people. "It's like a country full of Father Christmases," I told Da, the first summer I returned from Ireland, and he laughed and said, "You make me wonder why I ever left." Neither of us could know what the future held for us, back when I loved him without reservation, so we hugged in solidarity.

When I was a girl, I fell in love with sheep roaming emerald hillsides, and the dogs that chased them. Swooping gulls and plovers. The clattering of hooves and the dampness in the air, salty sea-foam spraying the land. Seals lolling on rocks. The lilting sound of the brogue, which my mother teased me for acquiring whenever I returned to London.

And I fell in love with a boy. The years took away my love for all but the last. Never an accomplice but my fellow victim, the only one on earth who could comprehend the barest thread of what I'd lost. And I knew if I saw him even one more time, my resolve would waver. Finbarr had never seen Genevieve or held her. He'd never learned she existed until after she was already gone. And so he might persist in his attempts to lure me away, and if I saw him even one more time, I might well succumb.

I thought of Cornelia Armstrong's Yuè Lǎo. The invisible thread. But not the one between Finbarr and me. The one that connected me, still and always, to Genevieve. I could feel it like a living, tactile object, stretching out from my heart to hers. Taking me not to the Timeless Manor, but the train station. Chilton had agreed not to prosecute me for murder. I felt safe in assuming he'd overlook auto theft as well. After all, anything I could do to win Archie back was to his benefit.

If Agatha and Archie reunited, I'd never again have access to Teddy. I needed to see her at least one more time. I needed to tell her if she ever found herself in trouble, she could find me, and I would take care of her. Whatever it took. I don't know why I believed that would help. My mother had made me the same offer.

I love you. I sent the message telepathically, which was not something I believed was possible. But still I hoped and prayed Finbarr—however abandoned—would hear it and understand. Perhaps a part of me hoped I'd return to London to find myself shut out of the Christies' world. The failure of the plan I'd worked on single-mindedly for three years was the only chance for Finbarr and me to be together. If I had to accept its failure, then so be it. But I would never be the one to let it go.

Meanwhile Chilton had to go on foot to the manor house—no longer timeless—to collect what Agatha had asked of him. Her typewriter, and everything she'd written in the midst of this adventure. She would never think much, in later years, of the work she did while she was away. A short story or two, and the beginnings of her novel *The Mystery of the Blue Train*. She always said it was the least favorite of all her books. But she published it just the same. She published everything she wrote—even the short story "The Edge," which ended with my doppelgänger dead at the bottom of a mountain. It appeared the following year in *Pearson's Magazine*, with the ending changed so that my character was not pushed, but leaped.

Chilton had no plans to transport Agatha's typewriter and work to Sunningdale. He would take it with him back to Brixham, so that she'd have to find him there.

"But where's Nan?" Finbarr asked, when Chilton told him Agatha had been discovered.

Chilton placed a sympathetic hand on Finbarr's shoulder. Chilton had already given me the gift of freedom. He did not have the remaining generosity to wish for Finbarr's romance resolved in favor of his own.

"I'm sorry. If Nan's not back by nightfall, I don't expect she ever will be."

"She'll be back," Finbarr said, but he didn't sound sure. As if to confirm this, he said, "If you see her, tell her I'll be waiting in Ballycotton, ready to go anywhere in the world she likes. She can find me there when she comes to her senses."

But, alas. I never did.

A New Year

1928

You don't need to guess. You already know. Agatha and Archie's reunion did not last. The urgency to continue her marriage had left Agatha. Instead she mooned about Styles mourning the loss of the Timeless Manor. All I had to do was reappear before Archie—smiling and smiling. Agatha left, this time for good, taking Teddy with her.

But eventually she sent Teddy back to Styles. By then Archie and I were married—a diamond ring and wedding band replacing Finbarr's claddagh. Teddy would stay with us a full year while Agatha went off on her own, adventuring, the first of many journeys she'd take aboard the Orient Express.

Honoria brought the child to us from London. I had planned to be downstairs with Archie to greet Teddy on her arrival. But when the car pulled into the drive, I found myself overcome with emotion I didn't want my husband to witness. I'd seen Teddy several times since returning to Archie, but this would be our first extended stretch, together in a home we shared, with me her official stepmother.

"Are you quite all right?" Archie asked, placing a hand at my waist. He had learned a bit about being solicitous since his first marriage.

"Yes, I'm fine. Just the tiniest bit light-headed. I believe I'll go upstairs and rest."

As I crested the stairs, I heard them—Honoria and Teddy, one dark and stern voice, one small and light. I walked through the hall of what was now my own home and went into the nursery, nobody here anymore to scold me for intruding. Honoria would be heading back to London. "I'm happy to take care of her myself," I'd said to Archie, when he asked me how we'd manage. "In fact I'd like to."

And I would take care of her myself, many times, in the years that followed. I would rush to her when she woke up crying from a terrible dream. I would hold her hand, my arm round her shoulders, when the doctor put stitches in her wounded knee. When she married during the Second World War, a small and hasty ceremony without even Archie in attendance, Agatha made sure to send a telegram so that I could be there, too.

There on the windowsill stood the dog Finbarr had carved for her. Sonny. I picked it up. I could hear Teddy walking quickly and purposefully down the hall. Whoever coined the phrase *the patter of little feet* might be the most brilliant person in history. How the sound filled the house, the music of a child living inside it. I drew in a breath, determined my eyes not be full of tears when I turned toward her.

"Nan," Teddy said, coming through the door of the nursery to find me with the whittled dog still in my hands. "I was looking for you."

I returned Sonny to the windowsill and knelt, putting one hand on either side of Teddy's face, bright blue eyes staring back at me. Then I gathered her up in my arms, almost believing her hair—grown darker since I'd seen her last—smelled of the Irish Sea.

"I was looking for you, too."

Finbarr returned to Ballycotton, where he received word of my marriage to Archie. I sent him a letter with the news, along with a lock of Teddy's hair. In a few years he would marry an Irish girl. It pained me to think of it, and at the same time, how I did wish him happiness. How I loved him enough to wish him all the dogs, all the books, all the everything, we had planned for ourselves. He fathered three sons, and I can imagine how much he loved and enjoyed them before he died young, from a slow-burning cancer in his lungs, one last gift from the mustard gas.

The rage that lingers, when one thinks of war.

But forget all that. As readers our minds do reach toward the longed-for conclusions, despite what we know to be true. Pretend there is no Second World War come to bombard England again, what no one should have to endure once in a lifetime, let alone twice. This story belongs to me. I hold no allegiance to history, which has never done me a single favor. Still I can't end my own story with Finbarr, even in my imagination, because any ending with him is an ending away from our child.

But Agatha's story, I can end that however I like.

Let's pause another moment and go back in time. One month after leaving the Bellefort Hotel with her husband and returning to Styles, Agatha charged Honoria with packing a bag for Teddy. After placing a letter to Archie on the table in the front hall, she went through the morning's post and found a small package sent by, of all people, Sir Arthur Conan Doyle. She opened it to find a pair of lovely leather gloves that she'd never before seen in her life, which made his note ("So glad to hear you are safely at home. Allow me to return these to their rightful owner") all the more perplexing. Still she couldn't refuse a gift from him of all people, and it was chilly out, so she pulled them on to her hands.

Before she left, she made sure to gather the small staff at Styles and announced to them clearly, "I'm going to Ashfield. I'm taking Teddy with me. If anybody doubts my whereabouts, please send them round to Torquay. If I'm not at the house, I'll be walking by the shore."

Agatha loaded her dog and Teddy into her dear old Morris Cowley, and off she drove, passing all chalk pits and bodies of water without incident. The Silent Pool shimmered, reflecting the cold blue sky as if nobody had ever been pulled, lifeless, from its silty depths. She drove past the length of stream where

Annabel Oliver had been found and pressed a hand to her chest, a kind of salute, a sad but grateful thanks.

Chilton had a place of his own by then, in Brixham, close enough to his mother's house that he could check in on her daily. A cottage by the sea, one could be let for a song in those days. Although he'd quite given up on seeing Agatha again, he knew the moment he heard it, the knock on the door was hers. He opened the door to find her standing there in the chilly dusk, wearing a skirt and blouse under a fur coat, her hair a beautiful mess, her smile wide and liberated. Holding on to Teddy, who had fallen asleep in the car, the little girl's cheek flattened against Agatha's shoulder.

"I saved your work," Chilton said. "It's all here."

"Thank you."

He stepped aside so she could enter, then closed the door quietly behind her. The little dog by her feet wagged its tail, regarding Chilton as if wanting to be properly introduced.

"Here." Chilton gestured with his good hand. Agatha followed him to the spare bedroom and stood quietly while he hurried to put sheets on the narrow bed. Then she laid Teddy down—deaf to the world as only sleeping children can be— and pulled the quilt up to her chin. Kissed her forehead.

"She's a lovely little bloke, isn't she," Chilton said.

"Yes, she certainly is."

The dog hopped onto the bed and curled up beside the child. Chilton and Agatha watched Teddy sleep awhile, the simple rise and fall of her chest. A child's breath has a different quality from an adult's. Deeper and more precious. They shut her door tightly and went together into the kitchen. The cottage was small and cozy, ceilings nestling close above their heads.

"Cup of tea?"

"No. No thank you."

And here came the embrace. It lasted a long while, Chilton feeling so happy, so grateful to be alive, he scarcely recognized himself. Oh, while we're at it, let's give him back the use of his left arm. It rose as if by magic, wrapping around her strongly enough to communicate he had no interest in ever letting her go.

"It's a sweet cottage," Agatha said, somewhere past midnight, the two of them tangled companionably in his bed. "Wonderfully close to Ashfield. Teddy and I will settle there in the morning."

"Yes. You want to be sure and be there when they come looking for you."

The two of them laughed and laughed. The happiness swirled through the small house. Teddy, in the other room, smiled in her sleep.

"You don't like love stories," Chilton reminded her.

"Not as a rule. But I like this one."

A mystery should end with a killer revealed, and so it has. A quest should end with a treasure restored. And so it has. A tragic love story must end with its lovers dead or parted. But a romance. That should end with lovers reunited.

Beyond the confines of these pages life will go tumbling forward. But this is my story. I can make anything happen, unbeholden to a future that has by now become the past. I can leave you with a single image, and we can pretend it lasts forever.

So for this part of our story, at least, let's stop here. With Chilton and Agatha, walking together on the beach at Torquay. Her little dog hopping from one rock to another. Agatha's arm through Chilton's. Both of them smiling under a bright blue sky. Dwelling in the realms of day. Only for a time, like everything. No need to question or go forward, past this moment.

Indulge yourself instead, and close this book on a happy ending.

Acknowledgments

In February of 2015, my agent, Peter Steinberg, sent me an email whose subject line read, "What about writing a novel about this?" Attached was an article from *The Lineup* written by Matthew Thompson: "Lady Vanishes: The Mysterious Agatha Christie Disappearance." Five years and much gentle encouragement followed as I worked on this book. I'm grateful every day for Peter's championship, and his friendship.

Nan's theories of lucid living couldn't have conjured a more perfect editor for this project than Jennifer Enderlin, who knows how to ask all the right questions. I am immeasurably grateful for her brilliant insights, her unfailing catches, her warmth, her support, and her kindness.

I'm thankful to everyone at St. Martin's, including but not limited to Lisa Senz (author of the best email I've ever read), Sallie Lotz, and Steven Boldt.

Thanks also to Yona Levin, Maria Rejt, and Sabine Schultz. And to everyone at Gotham Group, especially Rich Green, who is such a bright light I wish I could bring him with me everywhere I go. My dear old pal Scott Rittinger knows everything about antique cars and is quick to answer out-of-the-blue texts. Celia Brooks shared her knowledge of London geography. Thanks to my friends, colleagues, and students in the creative writing department at the University of North Carolina Wilmington, especially Philip Gerard, who advocated for time I needed away from the classroom, and Rebecca Lee, who's the most fun to share books with. My brother, Alex, helped with proofreading galleys. My parents have forever provided unfailing love and support. Melody Moezzi dreamed a crucial, prophetic dream; telling her and Matthew Lenard that it came true was one of my all-time favorite nights.

Danae Woodward is always my first and best reader.

This story is an imaginative history of sorts; I'm indebted to many books, documentaries, articles, and papers for grounding it in actual events. Even if *The Christie Affair* had never come to fruition, I would be enormously glad to have read *The Adoption Machine* by Paul Jude Redmond. It's a beautifully researched, gorgeously written, hauntingly personal book, and I encourage anyone moved by Nan's story to read it. Other books that were invaluable to me include *The Light in the Window* by June Goulding, *Ireland's Magdalen Laundries and the Nation's Architecture of Containment* by James M. Smith (Dr. Smith was generous with responses to my questions; he recommended June Goulding's memoir and put me in touch with his equally generous colleague Claire McGettrick), *The Great Influenza* by John M. Barry, *Agatha Christie and the Eleven Missing Days* by Jared Cade, *An Autobiography* by Dame Agatha Christie herself (if you've never read it, you have a great treat awaiting you), and of course, my stack of Christie's detective novels, in particular *Death on the Nile*, *Murder on the Orient Express*, *And Then There Were None*, *The ABC Murders*, *Death in the Clouds*, *Peril at End House*, *Crooked House*, and *Endless Night*, as well as her short story "The Edge." For various period details and anecdotes, I was helped by too many articles and academic papers to list, chief among them "When the World's Most Famous Mystery Writer Vanished" by Tina Jordan (*The New York Times*), "The Mysterious Disappearance of Agatha Christie" by Giles Milton (HistoryExtra), *Unmarried Mothers in Ireland, 1880–1973* by Maria Luddy, "Unmarried Mothers and Their Children: Gathering the Data" by Dr. Maeve O'Rourke, Claire McGettrick, Rod Baker, and Raymond Hill, and the aforementioned "Lady Vanishes" by Matthew Thompson.

The stories from Peter Jackson's documentary *They Shall Not Grow Old* helped me imagine Finbarr and Chilton. And I will forever stand in awe of the brave women in Steve Humphries's arresting documentary *Sex in a Cold Climate*. My thanks, love, and admiration to Brigid Young, Phyllis Valentine, Martha Cooney, and especially Christina Mulcahy.

And thanks most of all to David and Hadley. I would spend a hundred years looking, and go everywhere in the world, to find you.

THE CHRISTIE AFFAIR
by Nina de Gramont

About the Author

• A Conversation with Nina de Gramont

Behind the Novel

Keep On Reading

• Discussion Questions

Also available as an audiobook
from Macmillan Audio

For more reading group suggestions
visit www.readinggroupgold.com.

ST. MARTIN'S GRIFFIN

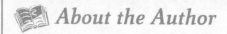 *About the Author*

Could you tell us a little bit about your background, and when you decided that you wanted to lead a literary life?

"A writer is a reader driven to emulation." I've seen that quote attributed to both Saul Bellow and F. Scott Fitzgerald, but whatever its origin, the quote certainly applies to me. Reading was my earliest passion and it remains my best escape. I was lucky to grow up in a house where the walls were lined with books, and novels were discussed at the dinner table, so it's hard to pinpoint an exact moment I decided to lead a literary life. I did recently unearth a scrapbook from seventh grade that included a note from a teacher that read, "I hope to see your writing published!" That may have been what made the possibility become real to me. I wish I could remember the teacher's name but she only signed the note "Ms. H."

Is there a book that most influenced your life? Or inspired you to become a writer?

To this day, the book that springs to my mind most often is Madeleine L'Engle's *A Wrinkle in Time*. I read it so many times that it served as a bridge from when I was young enough to believe in its magic to when I was old enough to see the metaphors for how our world is bruised and ruined. Particularly its stance against conformity has given me something to aspire to in my career and life. I love knowing a novel has embedded itself in my psyche so deeply that it can pop out of my memory when I need comfort or perspective.

Reading Group Gold

About the Author

How did you become a writer? Would you care to share any writing tips?

I teach creative writing at the University of North Carolina Wilmington. The writing advice I always come back to for my students is, "Read like a maniac." Read broadly, read constantly, read all different kinds of books. Pay attention to what you most enjoy reading, and pay attention to the kind of writing you most admire. That confluence is the secret to your best work.

My road to becoming a writer was pretty traditional. The year after I graduated from college I lived in a ski town and wrote an unpublishable novel. A couple of years later I went to grad school for creative writing. I didn't finish my degree but I did write a collection of short stories that was published in 2001. Until my first book was published I worked as a nanny and a bookseller.

That's the long answer. The short answer is I became a writer by writing and writing and writing until I finally produced something that someone wanted to read.

What was the inspiration for this novel?

Easiest question ever! *The Christie Affair* was inspired by the eleven days Agatha Christie went missing in 1926. When she was discovered at a spa hotel in Harrogate, she'd registered using the last name of her husband's mistress. I loved this detail—the pain, the pathos, the uninvited intimacy with an interloper. To me it begged to be turned into a novel that explored all possible aspects of that complicated and fraught connection.

Can you tell us about what research, if any, you did before writing this novel? Do you have firsthand experience with its subject? Base any of the characters on people from your own life? What is the most interesting or surprising thing you learned as you set out to tell your story?

The most fun—and most challenging—aspect of writing about a specific time period is the gifts it gives you. When I began writing *The Christie Affair*, I knew certain pieces of history would have to play a role, like World War I and the Spanish influenza epidemic. I read books and academic papers about unmarried pregnant women in Ireland in the early twentieth century.

Lots of research led to more research on subjects I hadn't originally thought of, like the Irish War of Independence. All proved quite fascinating.

Of course I read lots of Agatha Christie novels, as well as her autobiography and her memoir, *Come, Tell Me How You Live.*

Are you currently working on another book? And if so, can you tell us what it's about?

I am, but it's too soon to talk about!

How does one go about creating a fictional version of Agatha Christie, arguably the most beloved author in the history of the English language? With terror and respect. And, luckily, with lots and lots of source material. When I set to writing *The Christie Affair*, a fictional account of the eleven days the author went missing in 1926, I looked to the Queen of Crime's own work for evidence of the characteristics that most clearly defined her.

First and foremost? A sense of humor. Christie's wit is wonderfully apparent even in her darkest stories, and it's no doubt one of the reasons her work has been so enduring. Her novels abound with irony, one-liners, and straight-up jokes. One need only read the mah-jongg scene in *The Murder of Roger Ackroyd* to know she was a woman who enjoyed a good laugh. Even though *The Christie Affair* imagines one of the most difficult stretches in the author's life, I knew my version of Agatha Christie would be able to see the ridiculous in even the most heartbreaking moments.

And I couldn't write about Agatha Christie without including a dog or two. Christie adored dogs, especially terriers. At the time of her disappearance, she had a short-haired terrier named Peter. The dedication of her novel *Dumb Witness* reads: "Dear Peter, Most Faithful of Friends and Dearest of Companions, A Dog in a Thousand." I would wager if any of the enormous search parties had actually found Christie, she would have knelt to pet the hounds before thanking her human rescuers.

A frivolous point, but it felt important that the Agatha in my novel be pretty. Christie was only thirty-six when she disappeared. "I was good-looking," Christie writes of her younger self in her autobiography, and pictures from the time prove that statement true. She was also humble to the point of self-deprecating. This humility, combined with her sense of humor, are illustrated in the line that follows her uncharacteristic boast about her good looks: "My family, of course, laugh uproariously whenever I say that I was a lovely girl."

Humble, pretty, full of good humor, usually with a dog at her heels. And one can tell from Christie's travel writing that she treated people well. In *Come, Tell Me How You Live*, she writes about feeling intimidated by a young architect who worked for her second husband. By this time Christie was a world-famous author, not to mention married to the architect's boss. But Agatha Christie would not be someone who pulled rank or put on airs. She looked at people and really *saw* them. She remembered the stories they told her, which is another reason for her lasting legacy. Even the most peripheral characters in her novels get a reference to their past, a witty remark, or meaningful worry to make them more than fleeting faces in the crowd.

Adventurous! Christie was devastated by her husband Archie's defection to a younger woman. Little did she know his abandonment would pave her way to a much bigger life. She would journey to the Middle East as a single lady aboard the Orient Express. She would one-up Archie by marrying a much younger man, an archaeologist, and join him on digs in Syria, Turkey, and Iraq. "How much I have loved that part of the world," she writes in her autobiography. "I love it still and always shall."

For all her adventurous good humor, Christie understood the world's sorrow, and was keenly aware of its disparities. Many of the murders in her books are driven by social ills and class divides. One of her most compelling later novels, *Endless Night*, takes its title from William Blake: "Some are Born to sweet delight / Some are Born to endless night."

Which brings us to the most important aspect of any protagonist: vulnerability. How to make Agatha Christie—embedded in our imaginations not only as stalwart and formidable, but successful beyond anyone's wildest dreams—vulnerable? For that we have only to look at the history, the bare facts of her disappearance. "I realized," she wrote later, "that the only person who can really hurt you in life is a husband."

In 1926, a husband hurt the world's greatest mystery writer deeply enough that she vanished. I knew that telling a story inspired by this vanishment would need to portray Christie as very much in possession of all the traits that made her singular. At the same time, she would be heartbroken and lost. Just as we have all been—or will be—at some point in our lives.

Behind the Novel

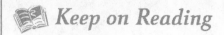 *Keep on Reading*

A Room with a View by E. M. Forster

Nan loves Forster's writing, and this is what she's reading when she and Finbarr first connect as friends. Throughout *The Christie Affair* there are nods to this novel as well as Forster's *Howards End*.

I Capture the Castle by Dodie Smith

One of the most delightful and charming books you'll ever read, this novel also provides a lot of reflection about its own construction. I wanted to give Nan that same ability as a narrator to talk to her reader about the book as its story unfolds.

The Adoption Machine by Paul Jude Redmond

Redmond was born in a mother and baby home in Castlepollard, Ireland. This beautiful and informative book is part memoir, part history, and part survival story. It's a truly deep and gripping read.

The Light in the Window by June Goulding

In 1950, June Goulding worked as a midwife at a mother and baby home in County Cork, Ireland. It's such a brave and heartbreaking book, and she's so modest about what a hero she was to these girls, it wasn't until I read Paul Jude Redmond's book that I learned how many lives she saved.

An Autobiography by Agatha Christie

Oh, I just love this book. It's so warm, witty, and frank—full of wisdom and fascinating detail about twentieth-century England.

Any novel at all by Agatha Christie! Especially *Murder on the Orient Express, Death on the Nile, Endless Night, And Then There Were None, The ABC Murders, The Murder of Roger Ackroyd,* and/ or *The Mysterious Affair at Styles.*

1. Consider the three lines attributed to Hercule Poirot, which open up each of the three parts of the novel. What did you think of the author's choice of those particular lines? How do they connect to the narrative of *The Christie Affair*?

2. Discuss the narrative structure of the novel: the narration from Nan O'Dea's perspective, and the alternating time lines. How did it affect your reading experience, if at all?

3. On page 43, there is a line that reads, "Sometimes you fall in love with a place, dramatic and urgent as falling in love with any person." How is this proven to be true in the novel? What are the places that are most meaningful to the characters, and why?

Discussion Questions

4. Lucid dreaming and lucid living are mentioned several times in the novel by Nan. Why do you think she spends time thinking about these concepts? In what ways has she tried to incorporate them into her life?

5. Consider when Nan says, on page 263, that, "Among Agatha's enviable qualities, perhaps the most significant was her ability to thrive in this man's world. Following the rules but managing also to rise above them." Do you agree with this statement? Throughout the novel, in what ways is this proven to be true?

6. On page 292, Agatha says, "The point of a good detective story is to make it all obvious. You throw in enough variables so the reader doubts his own solution, then at the end he can be pleased with himself for figuring it out." In what ways does *The Christie Affair* align with this? In what ways does the structure of the novel echo Agatha Christie's work?

7. Consider the lines on page 327, "For years I'd been swept in directions I never meant to go. I'd made mistakes, acting by accident or imperative. Finally in this moment I was the author of my story." From the beginning of the novel, what did you believe Nan O'Dea's motivations were? What did you think when they were ultimately revealed? Did it change your opinion about her character? Why or why not?

8. Discuss marriage and relationships in the novel. What are some of the different depictions throughout it? Which relationships stood out to you as the most meaningful, and why?

9. Examine motherhood and its representation throughout the novel. What are some things that are revealed about the complexities of motherhood through the narrative?

10. On page 317, Agatha says, "What some call murder, others might call justice." Do you agree with this statement, particularly in the context of the novel?

11. Consider the last line of the novel, "Indulge yourself instead, and close this book on a happy ending." How did the ending make you feel? If you choose to consider what the future holds for the characters beyond the ending of *The Christie Affair*, what do you imagine?

Tasha Thomas

NINA DE GRAMONT is a professor of creative writing at the University of North Carolina Wilmington. She is the author of *The Last September* (Algonquin 2015), as well as several young adult novels.

Also by MAURENE GOO

Since You Asked
I Believe in a Thing Called Love
Somewhere Only We Know

THE WAY

YOU

MAKE

ME FEEL

THE WAY

YOU

MAKE

ME FEEL

Maurene Goo

SQUARE
FISH

FARRAR STRAUS GIROUX
New York

SQUARE
FISH

An imprint of Macmillan Publishing Group, LLC
175 Fifth Avenue, New York, NY 10010
fiercereads.com

Square Fish and the Square Fish logo are trademarks of Macmillan and are
used by Farrar Straus Giroux under license from Macmillan.

Our books may be purchased in bulk for promotional, educational, or business use. Please
contact your local bookseller or the Macmillan Corporate and Premium Sales Department
at (800) 221-7945 ext. 5442 or by email at MacmillanSpecialMarkets@macmillan.com.

Library of Congress Control Number: 2017956980

ISBN 978-1-250-30880-1 (paperback)   ISBN 978-0-374-30409-6 (ebook)

Originally published in the United States by Farrar Straus Giroux
First Square Fish edition, 2019
Book designed by Elizabeth H. Clark
Square Fish logo designed by Filomena Tuosto

1   3   5   7   9   10   8   6   4   2

AR: 4.8 / LEXILE: HL670L

In memory of Jonathan Gold,
the heart and stomach of our fair city

But when the palm trees bow their heads,
No matter how cruel I've been,
LA, you always let me back in.

—RILO KILEY,

"Let Me Back In"

THE WAY

YOU

MAKE

ME FEEL

CHAPTER 1

THIS PAPER PLANE WAS NEAR PERFECT.

Crisp edges, a pointy nose, and just the right weight. I held it up, closing my left eye to aim it toward the stage. Rose Carver and her short-brimmed black hat were in fine form today, a perfect target, her face lit up beatifically by the stage lights. As she went on about junior prom announcements, I grew more focused.

"Clara, aim it at her face."

My eyes swept over to Patrick Keen sitting next to me. He was slouched so far down in his seat that his chin was touching his chest, his long, pale limbs folded into an impossible position.

"That's not how I roll, jerk," I said.

"Yeah, we're here for the giggles, not tears," Felix Benavides whispered from my other side. He looked at me for approval when he said it, eyebrow arched.

Sometimes these two really knew how to kill a joke. Glancing around the auditorium to make sure no teachers were watching, I lifted the plane into my line of vision . . .

"Clara Shin!"

I startled, the paper plane dropping by my feet with a clatter. The voice had come over the speakers. Why was Rose saying my name up there?

I cupped my hands around my mouth and bellowed, "WHAT?" It reverberated off the wood-paneled walls and high ceilings.

Rose rolled her eyes and exhaled into the microphone, making it squawk. "I just said you're nominated for junior prom queen." She held up a piece of paper and stared at it, in disbelief at the words she was seeing.

Patrick and Felix burst out laughing and then reached over me to high-five each other. *Oh my GOD.* "I'm going to *kill* you guys," I hissed. As people swiveled their heads to look over at me, I started to form an idea.

Rose cleared her throat into the microphone. "*Anyway*, the other nominees are—"

I stood up, making the folded upholstered seat bounce loudly as it closed. "Thanks, Rose!" I hollered. She frowned, then squinted into the audience to see what I was doing. I remained standing, then held up my arms dramatically. "And thank *you*, student body, for this honor." I projected my voice as I looked around. I saw a few teachers get up. *Need to make this quick.*

"Thank you for letting me into your hearts. And now, my promise to you: if I get voted prom queen, there will be some much-needed changes made to Elysian High . . ."

Rose's voice interrupted me from the speakers. "You don't get to *do* anything if you win prom queen. It's not like being class president!" she scoffed into the microphone. She would know; she *was* junior class president.

"Regardless!" My voice boomed. "I will promise you all one thing . . . as Queen Clara." I racked my brain for what, the improvisation making me buzz. Then, an idea struck. I motioned for Patrick to hand me my backpack. He tossed it to me, and I reached into the front zippered pocket. "I promise that us girls will not be prisoners to our bodies! We will have equal rights!" Some girls cheered in the audience.

Rose spoke again. "We *do* have equal—"

"So, in the spirit of feminism and equality—THERE WILL BE FREE TAMPONS FOR ALL!" I yelled, releasing fistfuls of my tampons into the crowd. Good thing I had just bought a new box that morning. Yellow-patterned, regular-flow—they flew into the air and landed on the heads and laps of the people in the rows around me. The laughter came in waves, and girls sprang out of their seats to pick up tampons off the floor, some chasing them as they rolled down the aisles. Boys threw them at one another. More teachers stood up to calm everyone down. Rose Carver stomped offstage in a huff.

The disruption and mayhem fed my soul, and I looked around the auditorium triumphantly.

"Aren't you glad we nominated you?" Felix asked, popping a toothpick into his mouth and grinning. Felix thought chewing on toothpicks made him look like James Dean or something.

I shrugged. "It made things interesting."

"Clara."

I looked down the row of seats toward the voice of my young, white homeroom teacher, Mr. Sinclair. I threw him a wide smile. "Hey, Mr. S."

"Hey, yourself. I'm reporting you to the principal, let's go." Because these assemblies were always held during homeroom, Mr. Sinclair was left in charge of me. Lucky him.

Patrick let out a low whistle. "I'll go with you, Mr. S." He winked at him.

Young, handsome Mr. Sinclair, with the chiseled jaw and thick blond hair, rolled his eyes. "Not this time. Clara. Now." He adjusted his tortoiseshell glasses, a nerdy little signature gesture that made everyone in his classes swoon.

I grabbed my backpack and took my sweet time walking by everyone in my row to get to him. The audience was already starting to disperse when I followed Mr. Sinclair down the aisle toward the double doors.

"Nice stunt," Mr. Sinclair said as we wove through the streams of students headed out of the auditorium.

"I live to please."

He shook his head. "Aren't you sick of detention by now?"

"Nope, can't get enough."

"Why can't you channel that smart-mouth into your school-work?"

The May Los Angeles sunshine blinded me the second we stepped outside, and I pulled on my mirrored aviators. "Are you saying I'm *smart*?"

Before he could answer, someone called out my name from behind us. I turned around and made a face. It was Rose Carver.

Tall, graceful, and precise in her movements, Rose walked briskly over to me. Her skinny jeans fit her dancer's legs like a glove, her floral-print blouse was tucked in, and the pixie cut under her hat showed off her delicate features. Rose looked like a long-lost Obama daughter.

When she reached me, I was annoyed that I had to look up at her. "What?" I asked.

Her expression was focused and determined. I could feel the bossiness rolling off her in waves.

I *hated* Rose Carver.

She jabbed a finger into my shoulder. "You need to shut this down."

"Shut *what* down?"

"This whole prom-queen thing. You had your fun. Tampons, *hardy har har*," she said, throwing her head back. Then she focused her laserlike eyes on me again. "Now, drop out of the running and let someone who *actually* cares have a chance to win."

Her condescension was like manna from the gods. I squinted up at her. "You mean, someone like *you*?"

She rolled her eyes. "Yeah, or anyone else, really."

"You're so selfless, always thinking about the greater good," I said with a smile.

Her eyes closed briefly, as if she was harnessing all that impeccable self-control exercised by high-achieving ballerinas everywhere. "I didn't spend *months* as the head of the prom committee only to have you make a joke out of the whole thing." The thought of spending months caring about prom was suffocating.

I stood on my tippy-toes to try to be at eye level with her. "I'm not going to apologize for you wasting your social life on *prom*." Her eyes flashed and I continued, "You know, I was considering dropping out. But you just made me change my mind."

"Clara, Rose. That's enough," Mr. Sinclair said. "Let's go."

I patted Rose's arm before walking away. "See you at prom, Rose."

From behind me, I heard her shout, "You're *such* a child!"

I continued down the familiar path toward the principal's office.

CHAPTER 2

THERE WEREN'T ENOUGH HOT DOGS AND FLAMIN' HOT Cheetos in the world to satiate Patrick and Felix. After my inevitable detention that afternoon, I met up with them at one of the thousands of 7-Elevens in Los Angeles, this one on Echo Park's main drag—Sunset Boulevard, a few blocks away from Elysian High.

Despite what it means to popular culture, Sunset Boulevard isn't a glamorous street littered with movie stars driving around in convertibles or something. For one thing, Sunset runs here all the way from the beach. It's like twenty-two miles long. It starts at the Pacific Coast Highway, passes by mansions near UCLA, gross clubs and comedy bars in West Hollywood, tourist traps in Hollywood, strip malls with Thai food and laundromats in East Hollywood, juice shops and overpriced boho boutiques in Silver Lake, and then lands here in Echo Park, another quickly gentrifying eastside neighborhood full of coffee shops and taquerias.

When I got to the 7-Eleven, the AC hit me with an icy blast as I stepped inside, the electronic bell chiming. Patrick and Felix were picking out change from their wallets to pay for their hot dogs, and Felix's girlfriend, Cynthia Vartanyan, was there, too. She sat in front of the magazine rack, her skinny, crossed legs encased in sheer black tights, her long, thick black hair tucked into a knit beanie, her fingers flipping through the latest issue of *Rolling Stone*. Of course. She was one of those insufferable snobs who pieced together a personality with obscure music facts.

We didn't get along. One, because Felix was my ex-boyfriend from freshman year, and she couldn't hang with that no matter how many years it had been. Two, my favorite thing to do around her was ask if she'd ever heard of *X* band—a band that was always on the radio. The self-control needed on her end not to go off on some pretentious rant about mainstream music was amazing.

"Hey, kids." I dropped my backpack down next to Cynthia, and she looked up at me with a small, tight smile.

"Please keep your belongings on your person!" barked Warren, the gawky and perpetually greasy-haired clerk.

I opened a bag of Cool Ranch Doritos and popped one in my mouth. "Only if you ask nicely, babe." He flushed but let it go. Warren secretly loved having us hang out here. Once, we ran off a potential robber by throwing candy bars at him and screaming until the guy dropped his switchblade and bolted. There was an unspoken rule from that day on that we were allowed to loiter for as long as we wanted. And that's literally all we did. Hang out at 7-Eleven. My adolescence would end up being represented by a variety of Frito-Lay products.

"What's up, future prom queen?" Patrick asked before taking a huge bite out of his hot dog. Patrick probably ate more calories in a day than Michael Phelps, but he still looked like a Goth scarecrow.

I tossed a chip at his head. "Thanks for *that*."

Felix grinned, his teeth straight, white, and slightly vampiric. "It was a last-minute stroke of genius." Like me, Felix lived for pranks and disruption. Compact and graceful, he was basically a male, Mexican American me, but with much better personal grooming habits. And that's what ultimately killed our relationship—turns out when both people in a couple are stubborn and easily bored, things get tiresome, fast.

And if there was one thing that bonded the three of us, it was the ease of our friendship. There was never any drama or conflict. We existed in a carefully balanced ecosystem of chill—while making sure we kept things interesting, always.

And normally something like running for prom queen would be considered too much work. I looked at Patrick and Felix, who had gotten me into this mess. "You know, this backfired on you guys. I was going to drop out, but then freaking Rose Carver confronted me after the assembly," I said, swinging myself up on the counter by the coffee machine.

"Clara!"

I blew Warren a kiss. "Just keepin' it warm." He harrumphed but continued to organize cigarettes.

Patrick frowned. "What did Overlord Carver have to say?"

"I should drop out since I don't *really* care about winning."

Felix plopped down next to Cynthia and tossed an arm across her shoulders. "Who *does*?"

Cynthia snorted as she snuggled into Felix. "Dorks."

Felix and Patrick laughed, and I let out a brief guffaw. Something about Cynthia's jokes never flew with me, but I knew if I didn't laugh I'd hear it from Felix later. He was always asking me to be *nicer* to her, as if we should naturally be friends by our gender alone. Or by the fact that we've both had his tongue down our throats.

"So, are we gonna do this? Really?" Felix asked.

I nodded. "Yup, good job, bozos. We're in this now."

"All right. I guess we've gotta up our campaign game," Patrick said, tossing the foil hot dog wrapper into the trash. "Signs, slogan, the whole eight yards."

My eyelid twitched. "Nine yards."

He shrugged. Precision was not Patrick's strong suit. He was funny, though—quick to abuse his slim body to make us laugh, and a pitch-perfect impersonator who once made me pee my pants during a school play by imitating the lead's nasal voice, which had vibrated with phlegm on every vowel. I was never bored with Patrick.

I leaned back against the wall. "Can I just be the pretty face of the campaign?"

"Consider us your campaign managers," Felix said, feeding Cynthia some Sour Patch Kids. *Ugh.* While Patrick and Felix brainstormed ways to win me the junior prom crown, I flipped through a celebrity tabloid magazine, making Warren rate all the outfits.

The smell of frying fish hit me the second I stepped into my apartment. Although I had eaten an entire bag of Doritos (topped off with Red Vines) mere minutes ago, my stomach grumbled with hunger.

Nineties hip-hop was blasting, and my dad was in the kitchen, fanning the smoke detector with a dish towel. Our cat, Flo, hid under the sofa, her striped tail poofed like a raccoon's and sticking out in plain view.

"Pai, it smells like all the grease in the world came here to die," I said, flinging some windows open to air the apartment out.

"You're such a poet, Shorty," he said as he tucked the towel into his back pocket and checked the pans on the stove before facing me to ruffle my hair—long, unruly, and growing out of its lavender dye job on the bottom.

"What's for dinner?" I asked. I peered over his shoulder.

"Fried catfish. I found a cool recipe that uses a batter inspired by KFC's secret recipe," he said, adjusting the splatter guard on one of the pans.

I swiped a bottle of some fancy root beer on the counter and took a sip. "Uh, like Kentucky Fried *Chicken* KFC?"

"No, the other one, Kentucky Fried Corn."

Root beer bubbled into my nose as I laughed. My dad hit my back, hard, when I started to choke.

My dad, Adrian, was always experimenting with recipes. As the owner and chef of a food truck, that was pretty much his job. Since before I was born, he'd always worked at various restaurants, starting off as a busboy when he first immigrated here from Brazil ("Adrian" was the Americanized "Adriano"). My clearest childhood memories were the nights when, after his late shift, my dad would pick me up from my babysitter's and carry me home on his shoulders as I dozed off. Finally, two years ago, he had saved up enough money to open his own food truck, the KoBra—a literal and metaphorical merging of Korea and Brazil. My grandparents had made the trek from Seoul to São Paulo, a city with an established Korean immigrant population, where my dad was born. Months before *I* was born, my parents packed up for LA.

The food was symbolic of my dad's upbringing. People were always confused by my dad's Korean face and Portuguese-accented English. It helped with the ladies, though, which was gross.

While it hadn't been a wild overnight success, the KoBra had a pretty loyal following. My dad's dream, though, was to open a restaurant. He was hoping the KoBra could springboard that.

I pulled myself up onto the counter and swung my legs back and forth as I watched him cook. "Guess what?"

"What?" He drizzled some olive oil on a neat row of green beans laid in a cast-iron pan.

"I got nominated for junior prom queen."

He looked at me quizzically, a half smile on his face. "Are you serious?"

"Yeah, Patrick and Felix nominated me, and somehow I'm on the prom court. Which means people get to vote on whether or not I become prom *queen*."

My dad cackled as he opened the oven and slid the pan of beans onto a rack. "You? Prom queen? I would pay good money to see that."

"I know, right? Anyway, I wasn't going to take it seriously until this uptight B literally ordered me to drop out. So I'm going to stay in the game."

He closed the oven and grinned at me as he straightened up and wiped his hands on the dish towel. "Ah, my Clara, always shaking things up." My dad pronounced my name differently from everyone else, *Clahhra* instead of *Clerra*.

"You know it," I said.

"When's prom?"

I shrugged. "I dunno. Probably soon since school's almost over."

"Time flies, Shorty. I can't believe you'll be graduating high school next year. Makes me feel old."

I snorted. "You're like two decades younger than everyone

else's dads." My dad was only thirty-four; he had me when he was eighteen, just a couple of years older than I was right now. Patrick called us the Gilmore Girls.

"You age me, every day," he said, smacking my leg with the dish towel. "Go set the table."

I grabbed some plates and headed over to the round dining table tucked into a small nook in the apartment. Flo finally came out of hiding and rubbed against my legs.

"Anything as epic as my prom-queen nomination happen for you today?" I asked him.

"No." He paused. "Well, actually, kind of."

I pushed piles of bills and mail aside. "Oh yeah, what?"

"Vivian can't work the KoBra this summer—she got an internship at a production company or something."

"Bummer," I said, moving another pile of mail out of the way.

"Yeah, have to find a replacement. *I wonder who?*" His voice took on a singsong quality.

"Please."

My dad sighed. "Worth a shot." Ever since he first started running the KoBra, my dad had been trying to get me to work on it. But the idea of being stuck in a hot, cramped truck for hours on end literally made me want to die. Although my dad had turned his life around from former-punk-kid to man-with-a-dream, I was happy to be kept out of it.

"Good luck, though," I said as consolation. Then a colorful postcard caught my eye.

I picked it up, already knowing who it was from. The front

of the card had a photo of a bustling outdoor market filled with beautiful baskets and textiles. When I flipped it around, the familiar handwriting made me smile. Large, loopy, and scrawled:

M'dearest Clarrrrrrra,

You MUST come with me on my next trip to Marrakech. It was INSANE. The hotel we stayed at—oof! Like, fountains IN MY ROOM. Tiles were bananas. I got you a few trinkets that will look GORGEOUS on you. Also, hello, the men there are no joke.
   I miss you, filha. But see you SOOOOON! Tulum awaits!

XxxXxxxxX
Mãe

The contrast between my mom's life and my own was never more sharply in focus than when I got a postcard from her travels while the smell of frying fish wafted over me. She was a social media "influencer," paid to traipse around cool destinations.

"Why is August so far awaaay?" I whined as I tucked the card into my back pocket. My mom had invited me to Tulum this summer, and ever since I got the invite I had been counting the days, minutes, seconds. Because my mom traveled so much, it was really hard to pin her down. The last time we saw each other, she was in town for *twelve hours* at some launch party for a purse at the Chateau Marmont. I'm not kidding.

My dad made a noncommittal noise, not looking up from cooking. While most people thought my mom's globe-trotting life as an Instagram influencer was glam, my dad had little patience for her. Probably had something to do with the fact that she had left him to follow her dreams. First it was fashion school, which she dropped out of. Then modeling, which my dad persuaded her to quit when she started struggling with an eating disorder. And now it was having four million followers while she traveled the world looking like a babe.

Sometimes I wondered if my dad was so cautious with everything because, if you thought about it, his relationship with my mom was a big failure. And that failure had repercussions that were wide and deep for our family. My dad had been a mess for a while, overwhelmed by raising me when he was almost a kid himself. In my opinion, the level of investment needed to share your life with someone was insane, and knowing the aftermath of how it came crashing down on my young parents? I always viewed it as a cautionary tale.

"Move your butt," he barked, walking by me with the sizzling pan of fish. Placing it on the worn-out blue trivet, my dad glanced over at me. "Did you make sure your passport's not expired?"

"No, but I will tonight!" I said as I sat down at my seat.

I couldn't wait. It was going to be the best two weeks of my life.

CHAPTER 3

I PINNED ONE OF PATRICK'S HANDMADE BUTTONS onto my prom dress. It was huge, round, and filled with rainbow glitter, and featured a drawing of a tampon with the words VOTE WITH YOUR OVARIES, VOTE CLARA.

We were milking the tampon moment for all it was worth.

It was the night of the junior prom, and the past couple of weeks had been spent hard-core campaigning. There were about one billion other things I should have been focused on as my junior year came to an end, but . . .

Weren't there *always* more important things you could be doing instead? I chose to live *in the moment*.

And at *this* moment, music was blasting in my cluttered bedroom, pink twinkle lights casting the room in a warm glow. I stepped onto the pukey purple-and-brown woven rug that my dad had bought for me when I was ten years old. The reflection in the full-length mirror bolted to my bedroom door startled me, and I covered my mouth. Oh *my*.

I was wearing a floor-length peach satin gown with thin spaghetti straps and a cinched-in waist that I had found at Goodwill. Given that I was a whole five feet two inches tall, I looked like a little girl playing dress-up in her mother's clothes. The dress pooled around my feet, so I stepped into my white platform boots. There, *much* better. My hair was twisted into a bizarre-looking updo with curled tendrils grazing my cheeks. I reached over to my desk—littered with makeup, books, and Sanrio pens—for a tube of drugstore lipstick in an old-lady coral shade. I applied it in two big sweeps.

Perfect.

I grabbed my faux-leather jacket with faux-fur trim and tossed it on before heading downstairs. My dad was sprawled across the sofa watching a baseball game in his lucky black Dodgers cap. He looked up at the sound of my clomping footsteps.

"Meu Deus," my dad blurted, nearly falling off the sofa laughing.

"O-M-Deus is the effect I was going for," I said with a twirl. My phone vibrated with a text. Patrick, Felix, and Cynthia were here.

"Enjoy your evening, Father. Wish me luck!" I called out as I grabbed my skateboard by the door.

My dad waved from the sofa. "Good luck, Shorty. Don't stir up too much trouble."

I opened the front door. "I will!"

The first person I saw when we got to the dance was Rose Carver.

She was greeting everyone at the cafeteria door and handing out little slips of paper. Rose looked every part the prom queen—wearing an airy dress in dark blue with fluttery sleeves and a deep V-neck, showing off her sculpted dancer's shoulders. The length was short and her legs were endless in her strappy gold heels.

When I reached her, she held up a piece of paper. Her lips pursed. "*You're* definitely going to need this."

I tilted my head, looking at it for a second before taking it from her. "What bribery are you attempting at the eleventh hour?" When I glanced down, I saw that it was a coupon code for a ride share.

"So people don't drive home drunk," she said flatly, giving me and the rest of my group a meaningful glance.

Cynthia let out a snort of laughter. I smiled. "What a helpful citizen. It shall be a privilege to be your prom queen."

Patrick reached over and took another flyer from Rose. "Just in case," he drawled.

Her deep fuchsia lips turned down. "People *do* drive drunk, you know. It's, like, an actual problem."

"Thanks!" I said cheerfully, lifting up my skateboard before hiding it under my dress to head into the cafeteria.

The rest of prom was mind-numbingly boring, as expected. If I saw another guy dancing along to Bruno Mars in a sexy fashion in front of his date, I would torch him. And for some reason, the theme of our dance was *1001 Arabian Nights*, which I found offensive. It just manifested in colorful scarves draped around the cafeteria and rugs tossed on the floor.

We passed the time by taking Snapchats of people making out or groping one another on the dance floor.

Then it was time for prom queen and king announcements, and the lights dimmed before Rose stepped on the stage. Everything was dark except for a spotlight on her and the flickering LED candles hanging in decorative Moroccan-style lamps. "Good evening, junior class of Elysian High!"

Everyone cheered. Except for Cynthia, who booed. Always the subtle subversive, that one.

"It's the time you've all been waiting for! The prom king and queen announcements!" More cheers. Someone yelled, "CLARA!" I waved from my slouched position.

Rose opened up an envelope dramatically. You'd think this was the Oscars. "Drumroll, please!" she commanded. We thumped the tables with our hands, Felix and Patrick doing it with gusto— making the table bounce.

"Elysian High's junior prom king is Daniel Gonzales! And the prom queen is . . . oh. Clara Shin."

There were some audible gasps and then roaring cheers. I

stood up, pumping my arms in the air before giving Patrick, Felix, and Cynthia high fives. Patrick handed me my skateboard from its hiding spot under the table, and I stood on it with Patrick and Felix on either side of me, pushing me toward the stage. Slowly making my way, I waved my right hand like a beauty-pageant contestant, smiling widely. Daniel Gonzales and Rose were waiting for me, him awkwardly wearing a crown and her glaring at me.

Before I got up onstage, Patrick leaned over and whispered, "It's all ready."

I nodded. "Wait until I say *honor* before dropping it."

Rather than take the stairs to the stage, I hoisted myself up, hiking up my dress enough to get a few catcalls. I flipped my middle finger in their general direction, then walked over to Rose. She placed a tiara on my head, every part of her resisting— like a ghost was trying to wrestle the crown away from her.

She also handed me a pink satin sash, her fingers extended toward me with distaste. Instead of taking it, I bowed my head forward, waiting for her to place it on me. She muttered something unintelligible as she tossed it over my head.

Everyone cheered as I faced the crowd, and I soaked it all in, closing my eyes like a complete weirdo. Then I glanced at Daniel. "Do you have a speech?"

He made a face. "A speech? *No.*"

"Okay, good." I faced the crowd again and stepped up to the microphone. "Dear wonderful classmates. I can't believe I've finally become the queen of your hearts. I've dreamed, nay, *prayed* for this moment since I was a little girl." Several people laughed. Rose cleared her throat loudly behind me. I kept going. "I promise you, that in my reign as queen for the next two hours, I will keep things interesting. Things will *not* be boring." I looked over at Felix by the side of the stage, nodding slightly. "It will truly be an *honor*."

As soon as the word was out of my mouth, something cold and wet doused the top of my head, knocking my crown off into my hands. Within seconds, I was covered head to toe in blood.

Some people screamed, a few laughed. I blinked, the fake blood dripping off my eyelashes. When I glanced to my right, I saw Felix immediately dart off. Excellent. I smiled, and I could feel the red liquid slip over my bared teeth. My head turned toward everyone slowly, and I raised my arms. The laughter turned nervous.

And now for the finale. Dramatically holding up my crown, I opened my mouth to let out a scream, but before I could, someone shoved me so hard from the left that I toppled over, slipping in the blood.

I wiped off my face and saw Rose Carver towering over me, her gold heels planted on the bloody stage somewhat precariously. *What in the WORLD?* Before I could react, she bent over and snatched the crown from my hand.

She pointed it at me, as if brandishing a sword. "You. Little. *Freak.*" The word was picked up by the microphone, and it reverberated throughout the cafeteria. You could hear a pin drop.

Laughter bubbled out of me, uncontrollable. This was going

*so much bette*r than planned! I knew Rose was uptight, but this was new levels of cray. I pushed myself off the floor, my hands slipping a little. I could see a few teachers headed for the stage. "You're *totally* going to get suspended for that," I said gleefully.

The fireballs in her eyes were growing huge. "You think this is *funny*? Is *everything* a joke to you? You *ruined prom!*"

I rolled my eyes, reached over, and snatched the crown from her. "Get a *life*." I was about to place it back on my head when Rose's hands grasped for mine.

I held on to the tiara, enjoying watching her struggle to stay balanced. But then one of those beautiful heels slipped, and she knocked into me. We crashed onto the floor, me backward, and a sharp pain shot up my back as she fell on top of me with a surprised *oof.*

"Get *off,*" I screeched, feeling panicky—being smashed by a five-foot-nine ballerina made of pure muscle was on my top ten list of nightmares. I struggled to push her off.

"I'm *trying!*" she screamed. But she punctuated that by kneeing me in the stomach.

"OW!" I yelled.

"Sorry, I didn't—"

But it was too late. I grabbed a fistful of her short hair. "I'm sick of this!" I yelled. She screamed again, grabbing my wrists. We were both covered in blood, so it was hard for her to hold on to me.

"*Clara! Rose!* Stop this immediately!" Mr. Sinclair yelled, his voice sounding far away.

Someone grabbed hold of Rose's shoulders, but she shook them off, still holding on to me fiercely. My breathing quickened, and my heart pounded so hard that I felt its vibrations in my jaw. "I can't breathe!" I cried out.

"I don't care!" Rose growled as she let go of one of my wrists to take another swipe at my crown. The crown was smushed behind my head at this point, poking my scalp. Everything was starting to hurt, and my panic was rising.

"Stop it! Stop it! *Stop it!*" I screamed. There were a few people onstage now, dragging us apart. Just as I was freed from Rose's death grip, my right foot got tangled up in some cables on the floor. Rose took that moment of vulnerability to lunge toward me again, pulling herself away from a couple of teachers who were holding on to her. Her arms were stretched out, and one of them got caught in the dangling chain on a lantern.

The lantern crashed onto the floor. We both looked at it momentarily before a stage light also came crashing down between us. I froze and Rose hopped back from it. The glass lens shattered and sparks flew—into the fake blood surrounding us. Then the blood caught on fire. *No way.*

People started to scream, and Mr. Sinclair ran over to the flames, taking his blazer off in one swoop and batting at the fire.

An English teacher named Ms. Leung ran up to the mic and cried, "Everyone remain calm but slowly start making your way to the exits in an orderly and—"

The stampede of feet and people screaming drowned out the rest of her words.

I was headed down the steps when the dark blue curtain hanging to my left burst into flames. I jumped back and yelled, *"Good God!"*

Someone pushed me toward the stairs. "Hurry, you idiot!" Rose screamed from behind me.

We both scrambled off the stage with the teachers behind us, including Mr. Sinclair, who had left his blazer up onstage, now a little ball of fire surrounded by burning fake blood.

I took one last glance before being rushed out of the cafeteria, the cool night air hitting my face at the same time I heard the sirens.

CHAPTER 4

THE PRINCIPAL'S OFFICE WAS FAR ENOUGH AWAY FROM the cafeteria that it didn't smell like smoke. Instead it smelled like stale coffee and a barfy cinnamon pumpkin Yankee Candle.

I sank deeper into the green fiberglass chair facing Principal Sepulveda. She frowned from behind her desk. "Clara, you're getting blood all over my chair."

The chair squeaked when I sat up straighter, another smear of blood appearing as the sleeve of my jacket rubbed the armrest. I looked at her with a shrug. "I think it's a lost cause. You can hose them down later, right?"

"Or you can just sit like a human being," Rose muttered next to me. She was perched on the very edge of her seat, her back straight, chin held up high, and her ankles crossed like royalty.

A very bloody royal. There was a smear of blood on her cheek, bloody handprints on her neck, and her dress was an abstract study in blues and reds.

"Shut it, you two," Principal Sepulveda snapped. "I don't want to hear anything out of your mouths until your parents get here." The stern tone was at odds with her appearance—she was wearing a fleece vest over a thin floral-print nightgown. When the fire department had called her an hour ago, she had been home in bed watching true-crime shows.

The fire was out now; luckily the firefighters got to it before it spread beyond the cafeteria. Everyone had gone home, but Principal Sepulveda had shown up with guns blazing and had trapped Rose and me in her office. Mr. Sinclair sat in the corner, trying hard to stay awake. She wanted him there as backup, I guess.

"Principal Sepulveda," Rose started with that bossy tone of hers, "wouldn't it make more sense to discuss this on Monday? We've had quite the scare." What the heck, who *talked* like that. Did grown-ups really fall for this act?

"No." The word sliced through the air like a knife.

I smirked. "Nice try."

Rose ignored me, looking down at her cuticles. Oh, so *now* she was above it? Where was all this poise when she was losing her mind attacking me onstage? When I looked at her, resentment oozed out of my pores—she was the reason for me being stuck in the principal's office at midnight. I couldn't believe Rose had gotten me into this crap again.

Because in ninth grade, Rose Carver got me my first suspension.

It was the first time I had smoked. As I nervously lit up the cigarette in the bathroom stall, I heard someone come in and froze mid-puff. A second later, the door I'd forgotten to lock slammed open—and there was Rose. She ran out to tell on me before I could stop her. First cigarette, first suspension.

After that I had a reputation for being someone who got into trouble. At first it worried me—did I want to start high school with this label? But it stuck before I could really do anything about it. My teachers had low expectations, and I, well, I went with it.

It was easy and almost always more fun than actually trying. I saw old friends from middle school get sucked into that rigid college track. The more we drifted apart, the closer I got to Patrick and Felix, who were way more on the same wavelength as me.

And Rose? She was the epitome of all this high school drudgery. Everything about her rubbed me the wrong way: her inability to chill; her uptight, follow-the-rules compulsion; her stupid narc tendencies; and her need to get ahead in life. So, whenever I could, I made life very untidy and chaotic for her. Where I saw an opportunity to poke and irritate, I did. Like the time I coordinated a flash mob during her first dance competition. Or the time I added sugar to all the lettuce in the salad bar where she got her lunch every day. Any punishment handed to me was always worth it.

An eternity went by. I was dozing off with my neck bent at an impossible angle, my knees tucked under my long dress, when the office door flew open.

"Rose!" An elegant black woman ran over to her. She looked exactly like Rose except shorter, with long, wavy hair that was perfectly styled even in her harried state. Rose clearly got her height from her dad, a tall and ruggedly handsome black man with a little bit of dignified gray in his black hair.

"Are you okay?" Her mother grasped her by the shoulders, then widened her eyes. "Oh my *God*, why are you covered in blood?" She looked over at me. "Why are *both* of you covered in blood?"

"It's fake, Mom. I'm fine, it's not a big deal," Rose said, with that arrogant self-confidence that usually drove me mad. Right now, however, I actually appreciated it. I hoped that it would get us out of this.

But her mother wasn't fooled. She raised a thin, arched eyebrow, and her words came out measured and careful. "Not. A. Big. Deal?" For the first time ever, Rose was visibly uncomfortable and squirmed in her seat. Her hands stayed clenched.

Before anyone could react, the door opened again, and my dad's cap-covered head popped in. *Yessss, time to bust out of this joint.*

"Come in, Mr. Shin," Principal Sepulveda said, waving at him.

"Call me Adrian," he said before stepping in reluctantly. My dad had gotten into so much trouble as a kid that he hadn't graduated high school. So he never felt comfortable having to set foot on a high school campus.

He did a double take when he saw me. "What happened to *you*? Are you okay?"

"It's fake blood," Mrs. Carver said before I could answer. Bossy genes in full effect.

The adults stood around us awkwardly.

"So . . ." Rose's dad started, clearing his throat.

Principal Sepulveda stepped around her desk and leaned against the edge of it, arms crossed and facing all of us. She was a tall woman who used to be an athlete—even in a nightgown she was an imposing presence. "Your daughters caused quite a scene at the prom tonight."

"Is the cafeteria okay? How bad is the fire damage? Did anyone get injured?" Rose's mom asked, her voice in professional lawyer mode. Joanne Carver was kind of a big deal around LA because she had been the prosecuting lawyer in a big police-beating case a few years back. She'd also been featured on the cover of *Ebony* magazine and was named one of *People*'s Most Beautiful People. So there was that.

"Well, Mrs. Carver, the fire was contained, and it was only the stage that was damaged. And, thank God, there were no injuries. No thanks to these two."

My dad glanced over at me. "So what happened, exactly?"

Principal Sepulveda wagged a finger at both of us. "Why don't *you two* let us know what happened? From Mr. Sinclair's account, it was very confusing."

From his corner, Mr. Sinclair began to stand, kind of crouching there and holding up a hand, like he was a student asking for permission. "Uh, I think it was because Clara won prom queen."

"You *won*?" My dad whipped around to look at me.

I shrugged.

"Yes, she *won*," Rose interrupted. "And it was a joke. She went up there on a skateboard and gave a *speech*. I mean, who *does* that? And *then*! The best part: one of her lackeys dropped a bucket of blood on her head."

My dad let out a snort of laughter. Principal Sepulveda shot him a reproachful look, and he turned the laugh into a cough.

Rose's mom threw her hands into the air. "So what, Rose?" At the same time, Rose's dad looked over at me. "Oh, like *Carrie*?"

Betrayal flashed across Rose's face for a second as she looked at her mom. "So *what*? Mom, she made the entire thing a *joke*."

"Well, Rosie, it's not exactly the most important thing in the world," her dad said with exasperation.

Rose's voice shook with emotion. "It's important to *me*!"

The room grew silent, and I shifted in my seat. Rose's *feelings* about prom were seriously cramping my prank style. In the many years I'd known Rose, I'd never seen her so rattled before.

"Okay, so then what happened?" her mom asked more gently. Rose stubbornly set her jaw.

Pivoting slowly on his sneakered heel, my dad looked at me. Pointedly.

I sighed, clomping my boots down onto the linoleum floor with a loud thud. "This nutjob attacked me."

My dad rolled his eyes. "Clara, give me a break."

"It's true! Tell them, Mr. Sinclair!" I twisted around to look at him in the corner.

He cleared his throat. "Well, it does seem like Rose started the fight."

Mrs. Carver stared at Rose. "Is this true?"

Rose looked straight ahead at a spot on the wall and nodded without saying anything.

"Yeah, you *know* it's true," I said. "She literally tried to take this stupid crown off my head and then we ended up . . . I dunno, fighting and stuff."

Mrs. Carver looked at me. "Can you clarify that?" Dang, no wonder Rose was always so precise in her language. And even though I tried to remain cool, being the object of Mrs. Carver's attention was like having the Eye of Freaking Sauron on you.

"We fought."

"Physically?" she asked, her voice a little more high-pitched this time.

"Yup. Your daughter sure knows how to fight dirty."

My dad poked me. "Watch it." He looked over at Rose's parents, his face a mask of deep shame for having me as a child. "Listen, I'm sure it was all Clara's fault. She pulled that *Carrie* stunt to provoke people, which is exactly what happened. She can take full responsibility."

"What!" I exclaimed.

But Mrs. Carver was already shaking her head. "No, Rose is to blame, too, for losing her cool." She turned to Rose again. "We're having a little *discussion* later."

Principal Sepulveda raised her hands. "*Both* of the girls are at fault here. Clara, you pulled another crazy stunt that was not only . . . disturbing, but dangerous, with the fake blood. Which happened to be *flammable.*" My dad dropped his head and shook it. Principal Sepulveda looked over at Rose. "Rose, you started a fight. And all those things added up to almost *burning down the cafeteria.* You are both suspended for a week."

"Suspended?" Rose cried, jumping out of her seat. "I can*not* be suspended! This is ridiculous!"

"YOU. STARTED. A. FIRE!"

Principal Sepulveda's booming voice startled us, and I let out an involuntary nervous laugh. Everyone's heads swiveled toward me.

My dad stared at me with an unrecognizable stony expression. Something had transformed since he walked in—his typical loose, relaxed demeanor had solidified into something tougher, more stern. "This one isn't going to learn anything from another suspension," he said calmly.

Pardon? *This one?!* I opened my mouth to respond, but he held up a hand. "Quiet. Not another word. You're going to pay back the damages for the cafeteria. And you're going to do it by working the KoBra. *All summer.*"

"WHAT!" This time it was *my* turn to jump out of my seat. "There's no freaking *way.* What about Tulum?" I sputtered to my dad, standing directly in front of him.

But Pai shook his head, resolute. "This is what a *punishment* is. All your wages from this summer will go toward paying back the school."

Before I could respond, Mr. Carver snapped his fingers together, the sound reverberating through the room like a firecracker. "Wait! The KoBra? You mean the Brazilian Korean food truck?"

My dad blinked. "Yeah. That's the one."

"Are you the owner?" Mr. Carver asked, excitement propelling him as he stepped across the room toward us.

"Yeah, hi. Adrian Shin," my dad said, holding out a hand. Mr. Carver shook it firmly. He was so tall that my dad looked twelve next to him.

Mr. Carver couldn't stop grinning. "Jonathan Carver. Call me Jon. Amazing! Man, I love your food. I used to work downtown, at the bank building on Sixth, where you'd come by."

My dad's face lit up. "Oh wait! Yes, I recognize you. Kimchi pastel?"

"You got it!" The two laughed like old golf buddies.

I made a face. "Can we bromance later?"

Mr. Carver looked at me, and then a shrewd expression came over his features. "Adrian. Do you think Clara will need an extra hand this summer?"

My dad's lopsided grin, which usually charmed everyone around him, sent a legit chill down my spine. "Yeah . . . she could *definitely* use a hand." They both looked over at Rose, who was fanning her face.

She stopped and stared at them. "What?"

Her dad pointed at her. "If Adrian is cool with it, you're also working for the KoBra this summer."

Rose froze. "Huh?!" she screeched, arms outstretched.

"You heard me. You've been busy with summer school and internships since sixth grade—it's time you learned how to work a good old-fashioned summer job. Minimum wage." He looked for confirmation at my dad, who nodded.

Rose's mom looked like she was going to protest, but Mr. Carver sent her some spousal-telepathy signal. She nodded her head slowly and said, "That's a great idea. *All* the money you two earn will go to paying back the school. How does that sound to you, Principal Sepulveda?"

I was too stunned to speak. *What* was happening? Principal Sepulveda and our parents talked in a huddle, and Rose and I just stood there, helpless to our fates.

"Am I still suspended?" Rose asked, hands on her hips. "Hello?"

But they were absorbed in their conversation. I kicked the chair I had been sitting in, making it wobble but not fall over. Everyone ignored me.

The grown-up pack finally broke up, everyone looking satisfied. Principal Sepulveda pulled on her jacket. "All right, girls. Your parents have convinced me to hold off your suspensions since there are only two weeks left of school. *If* you work all summer to help us pay for the damages, we can revisit this in the fall when school starts."

Rose looked relieved, but I wasn't. "Just give me the suspension! Leave me out of this UN deal!" I cried.

Principal Sepulveda chuckled. "It's going to be an interesting summer, Clara."

I looked helplessly at my dad, whose grim expression wasn't changing. He turned his back to me and headed toward the door. When I looked over at Rose, our eyes met. I scowled, and a spark of hate ignited in her eyes before she swept out of the room with a flourish, her skirt twirling around her.

This is some *nonsense* you've started, Rose Carver. Ready your body for the worst summer of your life.

CHAPTER 5

MY DAD GROUNDED ME FOR THE LAST TWO WEEKS OF school. I was *forbidden* to see Patrick and Felix outside of Elysian. They found that hilarious. I'd go to school then head straight home.

"What about Tulum?" Patrick had asked when I told them about my summer sentence. I swear he was more invested in my Tulum trip than I was. Patrick and Felix were kind of enamored of my mom. My mom's life was, in general, #goals. Sometimes the only thing that got me through high school was knowing that a life like my mom's was possible. Although she technically lived in São Paulo, she was barely home—never staying in one place long enough to get bored or bogged down by complicated relationships. If someone's *life* could be a role model for us, it was hers.

I had assured Patrick there was no way my dad would hold me to this for the entire summer. He would cave, because that's what he always did. Especially this year, when I wouldn't get to see my mom as much as I usually did. Despite her schedule, my mom always made sure to show up for my birthday and the holidays. And I always got to visit her twice a year, usually in New York or some other big city. But last Christmas she was sick and stuck in Thailand, and I hadn't been able to make it out to visit her during spring break because of a visit from my grandparents. So there was no way my dad could make me skip yet another visit with her.

With this in mind, I played along with the punishment. While grounded, I didn't sneak out, especially since my next-door neighbor Mr. Ramirez would have snitched on me in a second. Mr. Ramirez basically lived by his front window. He was the first person to catch me drinking, with a boy over, and sneaking out of my bedroom window. I thought people like him only existed in 1950s suburbs.

So the last two weeks of school was Netflix and chill. Literally.

And every single day that passed was filled with more dread than the day before because I knew it brought me closer to my KoBra prison sentence with Rose. Even though I was sure this entire punishment would end prematurely, the thought of spending *any* time with her made me want to puke.

* * *

The first Monday of summer break, I woke up to the blinds snapping open and sunlight flooding my room. "Bom dia, daughter!" my dad announced cheerfully, sipping from a giant thermos of coffee.

"No!" I yelled, throwing my pillow at him.

He knocked it out of the way with a soft punch. "Yes."

When my eyes adjusted to the ungodly amount of light, I saw my dad holding up a KoBra T-shirt and a matching cap. I groaned. "I'm not wearing that."

"I'm sorry, do you think you have a *choice* in the matter?"

In this light, my dad looked like a merch-wielding devil-angel—the sunlight haloed around him majestically.

"What time is it?" I grumbled, grasping for my phone on my nightstand.

He took another sip. "Six a.m. We have to replenish our ingredients today, so it's an early one."

Ugh.

After dragging out my morning routine for as long as humanly possible, I met my dad downstairs in the kitchen, where he was making fried-egg sandwiches.

"So, I can't believe you're actually making me do this." I set my elbows onto the kitchen counter, my feet kicking at the stool rung.

He cracked an egg over a cast-iron skillet, and it sizzled loudly. "Believe it."

"You're being so weird. Since when do you punish me?"

Pai looked up from the stove and leveled his gaze at me. The seriousness of his expression unsettled me. "You know, Shorty. That question itself is kind of a problem, don't you think?"

"No," I muttered while taking a sip of the milky Masala chai that my dad made. It was usually the only breakfast I had—Indian tea made with spices in a stained and chipped Dodgers mug as big as my head.

"It's a problem because *I am your dad*." He leaned against the counter. "Something happened while I was in that principal's office. Rose's parents? They acted like parents. And I was . . . embarrassed."

The tea burned my tongue, and I put it down. "That's nuts."

"No, actually, it's not. I know I was a little punk in school, but I had my reasons. My parents and I—the gap between us was, like, catastrophic. You and I, Clara? We don't have that problem. There's no good reason why you should get into so much trouble. The only reason is that I've been slacking, trying not to be overbearing like my parents were. But it's clearly backfired. I've been getting my act together for the KoBra, but not with you."

My dad talking like this made me feel itchy, and I looked beyond him, at a spot on the kitchen wall.

He plopped an egg sandwich in front of me. "I'm not slacking anymore. And it's starting with breakfast. Eat up." I wrinkled my nose and lifted the corner of the whole wheat bread. Sriracha mayo.

I sniffed. "Fine." With every gulp, unease filled me in

incremental doses. My dad's moment of enlightenment didn't bode well for my plan to get out of this punishment. Pai had told me he would e-mail my mom, but I hadn't heard from her, so it was most likely an empty threat. Or she didn't believe him. They didn't get along, and I knew my mom thought my dad was kind of a nag.

Once I finished the dishes, we headed out. My dad was locking the door when Mr. Ramirez's curtain flicked open and his face peeked through. "Good morning!" I said loudly. He cringed and closed the curtain.

"Remind me to bring him some food tonight as a thank-you," my dad said with a sly grin as he shut the screen door.

"Yeah, I'll be sure to poison it."

We headed down the steps and said hello to the occasional neighbor on the way out of our complex. It was small, holding only twelve units arranged around a courtyard.

"Good morning, Adrian!" Mrs. Mishra called out as she watered her roses in a lavender Juicy Couture sweats combo. She glared at me. *"Clara."*

I glared back at the little old Indian lady. "Mrs. *Mishra.*" The hose got an extra glare. A couple of years ago she had seen me making out with my boyfriend and drawn that same exact hose on us.

My entire apartment complex was basically a bunch of old-people narcs. Good thing there were only a few things that would actually piss my dad off: boyfriends in the apartment, drugs, and being a jerk to elders. Being a jerk to jerks was sanctioned, but old people were off-limits. My dad asked for very little, and I was pretty good at avoiding any of his major no-no's. So this sudden, very strict grounding and his forcing me to have a summer job was something new. I hoped it wasn't an alarming trend.

It was still early enough in the morning that there was a chill in the air. Our summers were brutal scorchers that lasted until Thanksgiving, but the evenings and mornings were almost always cool no matter how hot the day. I hugged my sweatshirt tighter around me as I kept in step with my dad. The parking lot where the KoBra lived, called the commissary, was a few blocks away from our apartment, and Rose was going to meet us there.

We walked down our hilly street filled with duplexes, old Craftsman homes, and small apartment complexes like ours. Just a block down, we hit Echo Park Avenue, one of the main drags in our neighborhood. Palms and mature jacaranda trees lined the street where the beginning of commuter traffic passed by. A coffee shop was already bustling with hipster moms pushing strollers. Right across the street was a little liquor store in a strip mall where two workers were changing shifts for the day—the one off duty getting into his ancient Toyota Corolla, the car protesting with a groan when it started.

While we were waiting on the corner for the light to turn green, a homeless white man sporting a full head of snowy hair and wearing a soccer jersey walked up to us.

My dad held up a hand. "Jerry, I don't have cash today."

Jerry cackled, his blue eyes flashing with good humor before he spat onto the sidewalk. "Maybe not you, but Clara here?"

I shook my head. "I wish. I'm about to spend my entire summer working on this guy's food truck."

"Bummer," he said. Jerry used to be a bike messenger in the 1960s. One too many concussions brought him to our neighborhood streets, but he claimed he loved the "yokeless life."

My dad promised him some food when we were done at the end of the day, and we crossed the street. A couple of blocks later, we passed by my favorite fruit stand, a rainbow-umbrella-adorned cart run by a middle-aged Latina woman named Kara who sliced fruit, then tossed it with lime juice and chili powder. Fruit crack, basically.

"Bom dia, Adrian," she said with a wink.

He winked back at her. "Buenos días, Kara."

I rolled my eyes as we walked past. "You're like freaking Mr. Rogers of Echo Park."

"That reminds me, been thinking of getting a cardigan."

I stopped in my tracks. "WHAT?"

My dad kept walking, pulling on his mirrored Wayfarers. "No, Shorty, they're cool now."

I kicked a purple jacaranda blossom. "Cool for grandpas like you."

"When are you gonna learn that I'm just innately cool?" He had the nerve to do a little spin. My dad used to be a break-dancer back in the day; it's how he got my mom's attention. With his sweet moves.

My feet flew as I walked ahead of him. "New rule: you must always walk five feet away from me."

But that only got me to the commissary quicker—and waiting for us, standing in the middle of the parking lot holding a giant Starbucks cup, was Rose Carver.

CHAPTER 6

"RIGHT ON TIME, ATTA GIRL!" MY DAD BELLOWED, raising his hand for a high five.

Rose awkwardly held up her hand, and he slapped it with gusto. Then she swept her eyes down to her feet, looking away shyly. God. Everyone crushed on my dad. It was so offensive.

We didn't greet each other. I looked at her outfit, though—sweat shorts over a black bodysuit. She caught me looking at her and said, "What?" Then she adjusted her hair. "Because of this *punishment*, I have to squeeze in a barre in the morning."

"Whatever that means," I said with a yawn.

My dad interrupted us. "Okay right, shorties, here's the deal. Today's going to be KoBra 101. We're gonna go over all the basics, and you'll also shadow me to get a feel for what a normal day is like. Understood?"

I nodded at the same time Rose replied, "Yes," in a nice, clear voice. Teacher's pet until the end.

My dad spread his arms wide. "This mild-mannered parking lot is actually what we food truck people call a commissary. It's where we park our trucks, plug in for the night, dump out our oil, clean up the trucks, refill our ice, and even keep some of our food in the industrial kitchen back there." He pointed to a small concrete building in the corner of the lot. The rest of the lot was closed in on three sides by tall pine trees. Although I had never formally worked the KoBra, I'd visited the truck and the commissary plenty of times. With all the truck stuff dumped out here, it was kind of gross, but I always liked it anyway—it felt tucked away from the rest of the city.

"Rose, can you find the KoBra?" Pai asked, arms crossed.

Setting this up like a pop quiz was wise. Rose's eyes lit up as she inspected the four trucks parked neatly against one of the walls of trees.

She instantly zeroed in on the black one. My dad nodded. "You got it. Let's go over and introduce you to her."

I *hated* when my dad gendered the stupid truck. To retaliate, I called my boobs Brock and Chad, which my dad hated with equal fervor.

We walked over, and Rose's mouth dropped open slightly.

The truck was painted a glossy black, and an illustration of a coiled snake sat beneath pink neon letters that spelled out THE

KoBra. The headlights were painted to look like menacing eyes, and the grille was a mouth. Gleaming gold. The first time I'd seen it, I felt an intense wave of secondhand embarrassment very specific to kids with parents who tried to be cool.

"Wow," Rose managed to utter.

My dad beamed. "Isn't she just completely rad?"

No, Pai, you are not *innately cool.*

"Very . . . eye-catching!" She was good, that one.

"If you want your eye to catch gonorrhea," I muttered. The truck only seated two people, so we got into Rose's car to trek to a few different markets to pick up produce: onions, parsley, garlic, green onions, red pepper, tomato, and pear. The KoBra did supply pickups Mondays and Fridays and kept most of the ingredients in the commissary kitchen before we prepped on the truck. Thank God that on most non-supply days we started prepping around nine a.m.

"Couldn't we get this stuff from like, Vons?" I asked as we stopped at one of the markets in East Hollywood's Thai town. It was a tiny one, owned by a woman listening to a loud Thai talk show on the radio while ignoring us.

My dad pressed a bunch of green onions to his chest in mock horror. "It's all about keeping it local and *authentic LA.* Vons . . . whose daughter *are* you?" He was always saying stuff like "local" and "sustainable" and a plethora of other foodie words that I liked to parrot back at him while munching on Flamin' Hot Cheetos.

Then we hit up Korean and Salvadoran butcher shops for cuts

of beef rump and various pork parts. We even went to an Indian market in Atwater Village to pick up spices. It was tedious and never-ending.

Rose, on the other hand, couldn't get enough. She was fascinated by every store, every stop. Taking notes in a little notepad.

"Have you ever been to Los Angeles, California?" I asked her as she marveled at the row upon row of teas at India Sweets & Spices.

She threw me a withering glance. "God, Clara, will I *ever* be as cool as you?"

My dad called us back to the car before I could respond, letting Rose have the last word.

After we'd gone to every single grocery store in the county, we went back to the commissary. We had about an hour and a half before our first stop of the day—a bustling coffee shop in Silver Lake. "Okay, shorties. We're going to actually *make* food now. You ready?" my dad asked us. He was wielding a large butcher knife and wearing a KoBra apron.

Rose pulled out her notebook again. "Yes." But she started taking these weird shallow breaths. Probably some, like, control exercise that Sheryl Sandberg or someone recommended in order to be bossier. Before I could make fun of her for it, my dad looked at me pointedly. I made a face. "I don't need *notes* for this."

I waited for Rose's snippy retort, but she was staring down at her notebook, her mouth moving silently as she read. Well, well, well, Queen Carver actually felt unsure about this. I, however, felt fully confident. The quicker I figured all this out, the quicker I could get it over with and prove to my dad that I had learned my lesson and blah blah. Tulum was still very much a possibility.

The KoBra had two main dishes:

- Picanha (beef rump) grilled on skewers (in the Brazilian style of churrasco) in traditional Korean galbi marinade
- Lombo (pork loin) grilled churrasco-style with a spicy vinaigrette sauce (similar to pico de gallo)

There were also various pickled veggies (very Korean) that you could add as a side, homemade beverages like lime caldo de cana (sugarcane juice with lime added), and a kimchi-and-cheese-stuffed pastel—a traditional Brazilian pastry. That was my personal favorite.

It was all delicious, actually.

"Okay, so we already have the meat on for lunch," my dad said, pointing at the skewered pieces of beef roasting over the small grill. In addition to the grill, the truck had a griddle top, two burners, and an oven. There was no AC in here, so the truck's roof had windows for ventilation, and my dad had installed a fan in the corner. And, as expected, the truck was already turning into a mini greenhouse. I felt a drop of sweat roll down my forehead, and I glared at Rose, because everything was her fault.

The picanha would be sliced off as it was cooked so that the pieces served were never stale. My dad continued, "But we're going to prep the meats for tonight."

He had us prepare the galbi marinade for the beef: mixing

together soy sauce, sesame oil, sugar, loads of garlic, sesame seeds, Korean chili powder, onion, ginger, and thin slices of pear. "You get me the ingredients and I'll mix," I ordered Rose.

She put a hand on her hip. "Excuse me?"

"This is my dad's truck; I have seniority."

A throat cleared right behind me. "Excuse *me*?" my dad asked.

I closed my eyes. This was going to be a pain in the butt every step of the way.

"You two are *equals*. There's no *seniority*, you kidding me?" My dad tapped the rim of my hat so that it fell over my eyes.

Rose grabbed a metal bowl and whisk. "You probably know where everything is, so doesn't it make sense for *you* to get the ingredients?"

"She has a point there," my dad said, not able to hide his glee.

Once Rose finished blending everything together, my dad placed the beef rump in a giant metal bowl, then poured the marinade over it. "This is for later. We already have some marinated meat for the next stop. I'll leave this here until after this stop, and we'll come back for it and start roasting. It needs at least three hours to marinate." He sealed the bowl shut with plastic wrap, then took it to the giant commissary fridge.

He believed in making the marinades fresh, the day of. "It would probably be more flavorful if we made a large batch and kept it for a long time, but I like the freshness of the marinade in contrast to the roasted meats. It's different," he said as he handed me the ingredients for the vinaigrette: onions, tomatoes, parsley, vinegar, olive oil, and bell peppers. Rose was jotting all this down, her cap and apron impeccably placed. She looked like she was attending the Harvard of food truck schools.

"May I please make the sauce?" I asked her, waving a wooden spoon in front of her.

She shrugged. "Sure, I'm fair."

Gritting my teeth, I mixed the ingredients in yet another large metal bowl. From what I could tell, everything in the KoBra was made in a giant metal bowl—the kind that older Korean ladies, ahjummas, use to make vats of kimchi. My dad's Korean-ness always came out in these stealth ways that I don't think even he noticed.

Last were the pasteis. These had been my favorite, ever since I was a kid. They were deep-fried hand pies—half-moon shapes with crinkled edges for the KoBra's version. Traditionally, in Brazil, they were stuffed with various meats like ground beef and chicken, or cheese and veggies, and sold on the street. My dad put a twist on tradition by stuffing them with kimchi and cheese. When my dad had first made them a few years ago, I was seriously grossed out. *Kimchi* and *cheese*? In a pastel? But once I had taken a bite of the melty, crispy goodness, I was a convert. And now, it was what the KoBra was known for.

The pastry dough had been premade by my dad. He put his hands on his hips. "Are you guys going to fight about who rolls out the dough?"

Rose and I looked at each other.

"You can do it," I said magnanimously.

Rose smiled, tight-lipped with dead eyes. "No, after you."

"No, you."

My dad sighed and took off his cap. "You're trying my patience here. Rose, your turn."

Ha! I hated rolling out dough—whenever my dad made pies I skipped that step. It was always so hard to make it a nice circle shape without the delicate edges falling apart on you.

Rose drew a deep breath and took the rolling pin from my dad. He guided her a bit as she rolled out the dough on the metal countertop, then cut out circle shapes with a metal ring the size of a dessert plate. She messed up at first—the dough breaking off when she rolled it out. I could sense that she was keeping her immense frustration under wraps, but her teeth practically bit holes into her bottom lip. She eventually got it right, but you could tell it kept bothering her. Jeez.

My dad let me have the honor of tossing handfuls of shredded mozzarella into each circle. After that, I laid thin strips of kimchi on top of the cheese, adding a small cube of butter at the end before folding the dough over. My dad popped the pasteis into the oven, where they would bake for a bit before being deep-fried.

In an hour everything would be ready, fresh and piping hot for the customers.

"Not so bad, huh?" my dad asked with a grin, tossing a dish towel at me.

I shrugged, deliberately missing the towel and letting it fall to the floor by my feet. Rose picked it up with the end of her fingertips and tossed it into the sink.

"Butt-kisser," I muttered. My dad shook his head and settled into the driver's seat.

CHAPTER 7

USUALLY, THE KOBRA HAD TWO TO THREE STOPS A DAY, and it was in business every day of the week. During the school year, when my dad had Vivian and other part-time workers, he would have days off. But this summer, it was just the three of us, and we'd each have to work at least five days out of every week.

On weekdays, the first stop was always from ten a.m. to two p.m. and, depending on the day, we'd either go to a coffee shop or some workplace, like an office park or movie studio. Our evening shift began at five p.m., and we usually stopped at various bars or events in the city, like farmers markets or festivals. Fridays and Saturdays were always coffee shops in the day and events at night. Sunday evening was the only time the KoBra took a break.

Although it was Monday, my dad decided to keep it to one stop because so much of today would be taken up by our training.

I rode with Pai in the truck and Rose met us at the location, a coffee shop called Wildfox, which was completely packed in the middle of a weekday. Everyone was on their laptops, and no one looked like they were over the age of thirty. "Does anyone in this town work anymore?" I grumbled as I pulled on my cap.

Rose almost elbowed me putting on her KoBra shirt over her body suit. "It's called *freelancing*."

"And it's called *sarcasm*, you humorless bag," I snapped.

"What?!" Rose yelped.

My dad stepped between us. "Are you two going to get your act together, or do I have to kick you guys to the curb?"

Rose immediately straightened, properly chastised. I snapped my gum. "Fine."

Before we opened the order window, Pai pulled out his phone and took a photo of Rose and me for the truck's Instagram account. He tried to make us smile, but we refused.

"You two," he said, shaking his head. "By the way, we document every stop, so I'll give you guys the passwords to our social media accounts." The wheels started turning for all the weird stuff I could do with this power.

My dad pointed his phone at me. "Don't even think about it. I'll be reviewing every post and have the ability to delete at any given moment."

"Do you have guidelines?" Rose said, pulling out her little notepad again.

I scoffed. "How complicated could it be to take a photo?"

He jabbed a finger into my temple. Very Korean. "Rose, I'll e-mail you everything you need to know, no worries."

She beamed and my dad rubbed his hands together. "All right, this is the real thing, you guys. Girls. Ladies. Whatever. Clara, we're going to handle the food. Rose, you'll handle the orders."

"By myself?" Rose asked, her voice abnormally fearful.

He smiled at her, and her expression changed to adoration. Barf. "Don't worry, I'll come over and help," he said, chucking her playfully under the chin. She floated off to the order window.

Before I could gloat about getting kitchen duty, my dad said, "After thirty minutes, you'll switch." Then he popped open the windows. Just like that, without any warning. Rose's eyes grew wide, and I knew she was equally surprised.

There was already a line. Rose nervously smoothed down the front of her shirt then glanced at my dad—waiting for permission, it seemed. "Go ahead and ask what they'd like," he said, nodding encouragingly.

She leaned over the counter and spoke loud and clear. "Hello, what would you like to order today?"

I laughed. "You sound like a robot."

Another poke in my temple from Pai. "Knock it off, Clara. Get ready to prep." He pushed me toward the food prep counter, which was on the opposite side from the windows.

A nebbishy white guy in round tortoiseshell glasses ordered one lombo and one pastel, which my dad repeated loudly to me. Rose fumbled with the cashbox, dropping wads of cash onto the floor. "Oh God!"

My dad swept it up and handed it to her before she could even reach down. "You're fine, Rose," he said with a wink. She smiled but still looked rattled taking the next order. Dang, she really was nervous.

The nervousness seeped into me, too, suddenly. Why was I in this stupid predicament? Sweating over a stove, worrying about people's dumb lunch orders when I should have been floating on an inflatable unicorn in a swimming pool. I took a breath, then started to prep the ingredients—my dad would put everything together later.

Things were going smoothly until the orders started coming in quickly. Really quickly. And a harried Latina girl with thick black bangs and a nose piercing put in an order for five different plates and ten pasteis.

Sweat pooled under my cap, and one thick lock of hair kept tickling my nose as I rushed to get all the ingredients together. "What the heck, is she catering an *event* in that dumb coffee shop?" I cried, opening the jar of pickled daikon radishes.

"You guys made an extra lombo order instead of picanha!" Rose hollered, her voice panicky and on edge. The three of us were so smashed into that small space that I felt her breath on the back of my neck as she yelled.

Pai was plating another batch of pasteis. "That's okay, you can—"

"Just *deal* with it!" I yelled back, at my wit's end. I lifted up a hand as I said it, and the latex glove that I had been pulling off flew into the air. I swiveled around to see where it had landed, and when I did, I was standing face-to-face (or to be more accurate, face-to-neck) with Rose.

The kimchi-coated glove was plastered to her cheek.

I burst out laughing at the same time that someone outside yelled, "Yo, where my pasteis at?"

"Coming right up!" Rose called out as she peeled the glove away from her face.

"Coming right up!" I mimicked in a high-pitched voice. I couldn't help it; my stress levels were off the charts and my resentment had failed to die down over the course of the day. In fact, it was increasingly fueled.

My dad was handing out food through the pickup window. "Clara!" he barked in warning.

"Can't you just do your *job*?" Rose snapped. "You're such an incompetent clown."

Without thinking, I whipped off my other glove and threw it so hard at her face that it made a satisfying *smack*.

She gasped and clutched her cheek.

My dad stepped between us again. "I swear to God I am going to kick you both out of here unless you calm down. Can you manage to grow up for three seconds and do that?"

Rose nodded, taking a deep breath, smoothing down her shirt

again. It was like rubbing the shirt gave her magical calming powers. "Sorry, Adrian," she said with a little smile.

He looked at me, arms crossed, his forearm tattoo of my birthday written in Gothic font obnoxiously displayed.

I tilted my head back and rolled my eyes as deeply as humanly possible. *"Okaaaay."*

Rose went back to taking orders and me to cooking and assembling them. I had just finished wrapping the pasteis up in foil when Rose bumped into me as she reached for the cashbox.

We glared at each other but didn't say a word, feeling my dad's eyes on us. But when I turned to hand the pasteis to my dad, Rose stepped back again and her shoulder knocked my head, shooting a jolt of pain straight through my skull.

I grabbed my head. *"Watch* it, clumso!"

"You watch it!" As she said it, Rose swept her arm and knocked over a bowl full of vinaigrette onto the floor.

We both froze. My dad turned at the sound and cursed. "Are you kidding me right now?" His voice did this funny squeaking thing.

"Sorry!" Rose said as she reached over to grab a towel.

I picked up the bowl. "Has anyone ever told you it's annoying when girls say sorry all the time?"

She threw the towel on the floor where it landed with a wet splat. "That's *it*. I've tried to be the bigger person here and let you act like a little jerk to me. But you need to be put in your *place*!"

Something about Rose's anger really gave me life. I let out a brittle laugh. "This isn't Elysian. You have *no power* here."

Her face was inches away from mine. "We'll see."

The guy who was ordering at the window clapped his hands over his head. "Fight, fight!"

"PARE!"

We all stared at my dad. He shook his head. "I mean, *stop.* That's it. You guys are not only acting like kids, you're affecting business!"

And within seconds, we were both pushed out onto the sidewalk and the KoBra's door was locked against us. I pounded on it, but my dad refused to open it.

"PAI!" I yelled. "You're being a total fascist!" I kicked the door and stalked off, throwing my cap onto the ground as I walked away.

Rose followed behind. I was steaming but didn't know where to go, and I was annoyed that Rose was following me. "Can't you go to your *car*?" I seethed as I walked rapidly down the sidewalk. She didn't respond, but I could still feel her on my heels. Where had she parked? God!

"Too good to talk to me now?" I asked while glancing behind me.

She looked at me, then huffed with frustration. "Will you, like, turn into a toad or something if you stop talking for more than one minute?"

I glared at her. "Don't be jealous of my charisma."

She just made a repulsed face.

I continued walking and clenched my jaw. "You do realize that this entire thing is your fault? That if you hadn't lost your mind at the dance we wouldn't be in this mess?" We passed by a group of hipster dudes who laughed at my raised voice. I flipped them off.

I could almost hear Rose's eyes roll. "If you hadn't felt the narcissistic need to pull a prank at junior prom and make it all about yourself, then we wouldn't be in this mess."

I stopped walking and turned around to face her. "Narcissistic? I was *entertaining*. It was a selfless act—someone needed to spice up that dance."

She scoffed and walked right up to me, her posture challenging. "I've known you since middle school. You are a classic narcissist. Inflated sense of self-importance? Check. Need for attention based on some issue with your absent mother, clearly? Check."

I felt an uncontrollable anger rising up—something that I usually had a grip on.

"And, here's the kicker, you have absolutely no empathy for others. Never wondering if the stuff you're always pulling might *actually* hurt other people. Like, did you know Kathy Tamayo really wanted to win prom queen? That her little sister recently got into a car accident and was badly injured and maybe this would have been a nice thing for her to win?" Her voice was louder now.

I felt a brief flash of guilt before anger took over again. "How was I supposed to know that? And it's not *my* fault her sister's hurt or that she didn't get enough votes! It was supposed to be a *joke*!" I was yelling at this point.

A sharp whistle interrupted me. "Girls, can you move along?" I looked over and saw a man leaning out of his shoe repair shop. He had an annoyed expression on his face.

"*You* move along, sir!" I snapped back but then stomped off, leaving Rose standing on the sidewalk behind me.

A bus ride later, I was home, and I headed straight to the bathroom, my heart pounding and my hands clammy. I splashed my face with cold water, trying to wash myself of Rose's self-righteousness. Who the heck did she think she was? Like she was just *so* kind and never self-serving! What a load of utter crap. And how was I supposed to know about Kathy freaking Tamayo and her sister?!

Guilt pooled inside me—insidious, unfamiliar, and very unwelcome. I holed myself up in my room and started reading an old John Grisham novel that I had read so many times the cover was creased beyond recognition. Then I blasted girlie Motown and settled deep into my pillows, Flo curling up into a ball comfortably on top of my head.

But when I found myself reading the same paragraph for the fifth time, I tossed the book aside, making Flo growl deeply and jump off my head.

"Excuse me for living, Queen Licker of Butts," I muttered as I pulled out my phone. I went to Facebook and took a deep breath. In the search bar, I typed "Kathy Tamayo." When I got to her profile page, I saw photos of her in a sparkly silver dress at junior prom. I scrolled down farther and saw a link for a crowd-funding page for her sister, Jill. The photo accompanying the link was of a little Filipino girl, maybe ten or so. Shiny black hair, big smile with dimples. I bit down on my lip. For Pete's sake.

I clicked on the link and read about the car accident that had injured Jill a few weeks ago. And then I read about the medical bills.

Good thing I had memorized my dad's credit card number a long time ago. I donated thirty dollars on the site. Then I scribbled a note on a piece of notepad paper and slipped it under my dad's door.

Pai, I owe you $30, you'll see a random charge on your credit card.

CHAPTER 8

MY DAD HAD US TAKE THE NEXT TWO DAYS OFF. I WAS excited about it until I realized he wasn't going to talk to me. He didn't make Mr. Ramirez check in on me, and he didn't make me breakfast.

I went out with Patrick and Felix, but I couldn't enjoy it. I'd never gotten the silent treatment from my dad before.

I tried to butter him up with pizza and ESPN Classic, but he ignored me and went straight to bed. *Without eating dinner.* The only time my dad skipped meals was when he had mad diarrhea. And even *that* didn't stop him sometimes.

On day two of silent treatment, I wore clown makeup and an orange wig, then waited for him to come home, sitting on the sofa in the dark. I knew things were serious when he didn't react and instead walked straight up to his room. My dad did not kid around with clowns.

I called my mom the second night of the deep freeze, needing sympathy from someone who would understand.

I had to FaceTime because my mom refused to do anything else. When she picked up, raucous laughter rang out before she could say hi to me. The video on the phone was wobbly and I winced. "Mãe!"

"Clara, one sec!" I heard her laughing, the camera on her face but also moving wildly. I turned my head away to avoid feeling nauseated.

Finally, she steadied the camera on herself—all tousled hair and perfect brows. "Hey, filha, sorry. We're in the middle of this shoot for Whimsy."

"What's Whimsy, and where are you?" I was already annoyed at not having her full attention.

A flash of sunshine from the window behind her blinded me for a second. "Whimsy's a new online styling service, and I'm in Brooklyn!"

"You are?" I felt myself cheer up, just knowing she was in the same country as me. "For how long?"

"Leaving in a couple of days, actually. Have this trade show in Italy."

I flopped down onto my bed and stared at the dusty yellow light streaming through my threadbare curtains. "Oh, this little ol' thing in Italy."

She laughed, her teeth white and recently veneered by some

fancy dentist who sponsored it when she live-Storied the proce-
dure. "We'll go together one day and stuff ourselves with pasta."

My eyes closed, imagining a day when I wasn't stuck in LA
all summer, desiccated as the plants.

"So what's going on?" she asked, interrupting my brief daydream of eating gelato in a cobblestoned alley.

"Pai's pissed at me."

"Uh-oh. What did you do?"

"Why would you assume it was *me*?"

Her sharp bark of laughter made me cringe. "Give me a break,
Clara."

I couldn't help but smile. "Well, my first day on the truck with
Rose didn't go so great."

"I can't help but think that might be an understatement."

It was hard to fool my mom because we were so similar. Every
time I tried to gloss over something or play it cool, she called me
out instantly. "We just got into a fight. What else is new? Rose
and I have never gotten along."

"You're going to have to, though. You're working with her all
summer, right?"

Flo decided this was the perfect time to hop onto my chest, her
sturdy paw digging into my boob painfully. I winced but let
her stay there because I was always at her mercy. "Yeah. But don't
worry! I'm going to try and make it to Tulum, no matter what."

A low voice on the other end interrupted before my mom
could respond, her gaze drifting somewhere to the left of her
phone. Suddenly, Brooklyn seemed light-years away.

"Clara, I have to run. But don't worry about Adrian; you know he always gives in. Wear him down!" With that, she gave me, or the phone rather, an air-kiss and was gone.

I went to bed that night still feeling unsettled and craving a giant bowl of spaghetti.

Thursday morning I was woken up by blinding sunshine again. I squinted and saw my dad taking a sip of coffee next to the window.

"You have fifteen minutes to meet me downstairs, Shorty."

Relief pulled me out of bed at record speed. My dad was waiting for me with an avocado toast and tea in a thermos. Not my favorite breakfast, but I didn't complain. I was just happy that he was talking to me again.

He pulled on his shoes, a pair of pristine black Nikes with neon green stripes running down the sides. "Okay, today we're doing two of our regular stops. Rose is meeting us at the first stop. And I swear to God, Clara, if you two don't figure out a way to work together, I'll have a bigger punishment in store."

I bit into my toast. "Yeah, yeah." I hid my excitement at being back on speaking terms with my dad, the bread covering my smile.

After prepping the food, my dad and I headed to Pasadena, which was just northeast of us. But to get there, you had to take the Western United States' first freeway, the 110. Pretty cool, except the lanes were about as narrow as a bicycle and the on- and off-ramps were two feet long and often set at ninety-degree angles to the freeway.

And this time, I was driving.

"This is, like, terrifying," I said, my sweaty hands clutching the steering wheel.

My dad patted my shoulder. "You're good. I taught you how to drive this freeway last year."

"Yeah, in a normal car, not the KoBra!"

"Nah, you got this." If only his confidence in my driving skills was at all warranted.

We finally got off Murder Freeway and arrived at our destination in one piece: an office park filled with grass, big shady trees, and depressing 1980s architecture. "Oh, so this is where your youth goes to kill itself," I announced as we pulled in.

As we parked the truck alongside the curb by the lawn, I caught some movement out of the corner of my eye: an Asian guy my age or so standing on the corner, holding one of those arrow-shaped signs that advertise a business. It said JAVA TIME and had a hand-painted illustration of a mug of steaming-hot coffee.

I wanted to look away from the secondhand embarrassment of it, except I couldn't. This guy was *good*. He was tossing the thing up in the air and catching it behind his back. Then when he got sick of *that*, he did a backflip and held the sign up with his *feet* while doing a handstand.

"What in the world is *that* guy putting in his 'java'?" I asked with a snort of laughter.

My dad followed my gaze, then grinned. He jumped out of the truck and hollered, "Yo!"

The guy caught the sign in the middle of spinning it around the top of his head like a helicopter propeller. "Hey, Adrian!" he called out. He trotted over to us—his step light, his body agile and bouncy. Like a Labrador. He and Pai exchanged an elaborate fist bump involving fingers wiggling, slapping, and some weird elbow tapping. Okay, bros, we get it.

Then he glanced over at the truck, and I almost choked.

Upon closer inspection, the Labrador was *very* good-looking. Not my type at all—I usually fell for guys who looked a little malnourished and tortured. This guy was the picture of health and vigor: broad-shouldered with the lean yet muscular build of a runner, thick hair cut short with a few wavy locks flopping into his eyes, high cheekbones, and the nicest skin you ever saw on a male—he was practically *glowing*. He was like the photo you would find when looking for a stock image of "happy handsome Asian teenager."

"Hey, you must be Clara!" he exclaimed, walking over to the truck with a giant, toothy grin. His very sharp canines seemed to glint against the sunshine. I blinked.

Smile still firmly in place, the Labrador deftly placed the sign against his hip and held his hand out. "I'm Hamlet Wong."

I stared at his hand then looked up at him. Who in the world our age *shook hands*? I held up my hand in greeting instead. "Hi. Your name's Hamlet?"

"Yeah," he answered, unfazed.

"Why would your parents do that to you?"

My dad, who was standing behind Hamlet, shook his head. "Clara."

I feigned innocence. "What! It's an honest question!"

Hamlet shrugged. "Oh yeah, I understand. My parents, uh, liked the idea of naming me after a prince." He laughed loudly, startling me.

My incredulity was genuine. "A Danish prince who no one else in the entire world is named after?"

Before he could reply, Rose popped up next to me, magically. She must have gotten here before us. "Hi, I'm Rose Carver," she said as she held out her hand. Her smile was dazzling. Why was I not surprised when they shook hands.

Hamlet's eyes lit up even more than the lit-upness they already were. "Oh wow! I didn't know there was a new employee!"

My dad leaned in the doorway to the truck. "Well, these two are working the KoBra this summer as punishment."

"Really?" Hamlet's eyebrows practically rose into that amazing hair of his. "What'd you guys do?"

I looked at Rose. "Let her tell the story. She's really unbiased, like Fox News."

She did this little head flip—if her hair had been longer, it would have whipped my face. "We got into an argument and almost . . . well . . ."

"You attacked me. And we almost burned the school down," I said flatly.

Hamlet did a little surprised hop, raising a fist up to his mouth. "No *way*!"

Rose made a face at me. "Don't *exaggerate*." Then her eyes flitted over to Hamlet—a split second of self-consciousness. "We didn't burn it down! And anyway, we only fought because she pulled this prank at junior prom—"

"What kind of prank?" Hamlet's head swiveled toward me and his eyes sparkled. "I really love prank stories."

I frowned. It was like the time a lady pointed at my bloody-bunny T-shirt and said, "I *love* creative shirts." The truly earnest made me so uncomfortable. I muttered, "I reenacted the end of *Carrie*."

Confusion clouded his features. This guy's emotions were closed-captioned on his face. "What's that?"

"What's what?" I asked, almost just as confused.

"What's *Carrie*?"

My jaw dropped. "What! You don't know what *Carrie* is? Jesus, do you live under a rock?"

He shrugged. "I grew up in Beijing."

Rose shoved me, getting closer to him. "Wow! When did you move here? Your English is flawless."

I tsked. "That's so racist."

She bit her lip, mortified. "Oh! No, I didn't mean . . ."

Hamlet laughed and held up his hands. Two nice, strong-looking hands, with elegant fingers. "No, no, it's fine! I moved here in sixth grade. I've had time to get pretty good."

Rose tilted her head and smiled. "Cool! I'd love to talk to you about that experience one day!"

For Pete's sake.

"Oh, for sure! But I actually have to run—starting my second shift," he said regretfully, picking up his sign. "It was great meeting you guys. I'm sure I'll see you around this summer then?" Was it my imagination or did he hold my gaze a bit longer than necessary?

He ran off, leaving us with a clear view of my dad. Pai was grinning. "Oh, you girls."

"What!" Rose blurted, spending an inordinate amount of time tucking her hair into her cap. She glanced at me. "Do you think he was offended when I made that comment about his English?"

But I wasn't paying attention. Instead I watched Hamlet run toward a coffee kiosk under a big shady tree. He whipped off his shirt, tugging it from the back of his collar. My mouth went dry. He was bare chested and glorious for a full two seconds before pulling on a white polo shirt, a navy apron, and a matching cap. Then he served someone coffee.

"What in the world?" I asked out loud, pointing at Hamlet.

Both my dad and Rose looked to where I was pointing. Noticing us, Hamlet waved and yelled, "Jack-of-all-trades!"

Before I could stop myself, I laughed. My dad smirked at me, and I threw a towel at him.

CHAPTER 9

THE MORNING AND LUNCH CROWD AT THE OFFICE plaza was pretty mellow, and we managed okay. That is, when Rose and I didn't have to talk to each other. She handled the customers, and I was in charge of the food again. Then we swapped. My dad helped, and other than a few little missteps (oops, leaving oil smoking on a pan for too long and giving someone a twenty-dollar bill instead of a five), the first stop went smoothly.

Every once in a while, Hamlet would holler jokes, and he even came over with iced drinks for us. At every contact, I felt his gaze linger on me for a half second longer than necessary. Hm. Was this dweeb crushing on me? But I pushed the thought aside; I had *no* desire for a food truck summer romance. I just wanted to get this over with, no strings attached.

We wrapped up the Pasadena stop and headed back to the commissary for a break before our next stop, a bar in Echo Park where we'd catch the happy hour and evening crowd.

After cleaning up the truck, Rose sat down in the passenger seat and pulled out a thick AP biology book.

"A total beach read," I said as I locked up the cabinets holding our supplies.

She responded without looking at me. "Since I'm not going to summer school, I'm taking night classes at the community college for credit. Is that okay with you, nosy?"

"Your boring life, not mine."

She put her earbuds in and propped the book on her knees.

My dad was handling some bookkeeping and social media updates, so I had time to grab an ice cream from the liquor store across the street.

Much too freaking soon it was time for us to get back to work, and we arrived at the bar just as the sky turned a pale peach. There were a ton of people there already. It seemed like once you became an adult, your life revolved around the next glass of rosé.

Parking the truck, I pulled on my cap and apron, then turned on the griddle. Rose parked next to us and hopped into the truck, pulling out the cashbox and the iPad Square.

My dad opened the order window, then turned to us. "Ready to roll?" he asked, looking at both of us sternly.

"Yup," Rose answered, with her patented future president smile.

I held up my plastic-glove-covered thumbs.

Things went smoothly for a while—I realized that working in the KoBra was almost like a finely choreographed dance. Because the space was so small, the three of us had figured out a way to stay in our little spheres. It helped that I was so short; both my dad and Rose were able to reach for things above my head, and I was able to duck easily under various limbs to get what I needed.

Just as I was in the zone, concentrating on skewering some beef onto a stick for the picanha, I heard a familiar peal of laughter. My skin prickled in recognition.

"Felix, get me a pastel, yeah?"

Cynthia and Felix.

"Yo, isn't this Clara's dad's truck?"

And Patrick.

I shuffled over to the dark corner farthest away from the truck's windows. Of all the people to run into! My dad walked over to me to reach for the picanha plate. "Clara, what are you doing? Get the two pasteis orders plated."

"Shh, Pai. My bozo friends are out there. I don't wanna deal with them right now," I whispered loudly.

But the truck was small, and Rose had the hearing of a bat. She popped her head out the window, practically on tippy-toes, so half her torso was hanging out. "Hey! Are you guys *Clara's friends?*" she shouted out.

77

"Shh!" I hissed, shrinking farther into my corner.

I heard Patrick's voice again. "Rose?" Confusion and disbelief.

Rose waved. "Hi, guys. Didn't you hear? Clara and I are working the KoBra this summer."

In fact, they hadn't heard. They knew I had to work, but I had left out the part about Rose. I didn't even know why. Sometimes I simply didn't want to deal with the Patrick and Felix peanut gallery. It could be a lot.

"She's right here," Rose said with a smile, looking back at me. Like an obvious cartoon villain.

Handing my dad the two pasteis, I reluctantly walked over to the window, mouthing *You're dead* to Rose.

When I looked out, my heart sank. It wasn't just Patrick, Felix, and Cynthia. They were with a few other people we partied with. No doubt they were using their fake IDs to get into the bar tonight. Pangs of jealousy and resentment flared again.

"What's up?" I asked, not a care in the world.

Patrick and Felix were grinning, and Cynthia looked pleased to see me in a compromising position for once. She held on to Felix's arm with less possessiveness than usual, her denim jacket tied around her waist.

Felix tapped the top of his head. "*Sweet* hat, Clara."

"You look *adorable*," said Cynthia with a giggle.

"Better than your ratty Cubs one," I said easily to Felix. "Which I still have, by the way." I didn't even look at Cynthia, but I felt her glare. You simply couldn't out-jerk a jerk like me.

78

"Save the socializing for after-hours, children," my dad said, handing an order out the window. "Clara, back to the kitchen."

Heat crept up my neck. Patrick widened his eyes at me and cocked his head to the side, telepathically signaling, "Come out here."

Every part of me wanted to toss my cap on the floor and join them—preferably by jumping out the window in a swan dive into the line of people.

But I couldn't. I ignored him. "Have fun at happy hour, kids," I said before stepping back to my station.

A crappy mood settled over me. Every single thing Rose did made me want to scream. I tried to zone her out, concentrating on cooking. When we got an order for a vegetarian option—a grilled eggplant in place of lombo—I tossed some thinly sliced Chinese eggplant into a skillet.

Suddenly, Rose was all up in my space. "Did you cook pork in this pan beforehand?"

"Yep."

"Clara! You can't do that! Some vegetarians are really picky about that! And pork is actually *forbidden* by some religions and cultures."

I watched the eggplant sizzle in the oil, bubbles popping. "What they don't know won't hurt them. They'll just have to wonder why their food is suddenly more delicious. Hint: pork."

Rose gasped. "Clara, I'm serious!"

"I know you are, and I don't *care*." I grabbed a bunch of scallions and chopped them. Aggressively. "If I had to use a new pan for every freaking vegetarian order, I'd be behind and washing pans constantly."

"But it's *the rule!*" Rose said. "Adrian went over this our first day. Right, Adrian?"

My dad turned from the pickup window. "What?"

I threw the knife onto the cutting board with a clatter. "Are you *kidding* me right now? You just *narced* on me to my *dad*?"

Rose blinked. "What? I wasn't—"

"Yes, you were! It's not enough you got me suspended freshman year, you have to hover over me in *my dad's truck* after you got us into this mess?"

A flash of anger passed over Rose's face. "I didn't *know* you would get suspended! And also? YOU WERE SMOKING! You do something wrong and then you freaking blame it on *me*? You have some real issues with misplacing blame. Hint: LOOK IN THE MIRROR."

Rage that had been building inside me since prom reached its freaking boiling point. I thought of ninth grade, of how that suspension had put me on a specific trajectory before I even had a chance to figure myself out. "Screw you, Rose. You don't know me. *At all.*"

My dad stepped between us. "Hey! Both of you, cool it. Now."

Rose's shoulders slumped for a second before she took off her cap. "Hey, Adrian, I'm sorry, but I don't think I can do this. Thanks for giving me the opportunity."

Before my dad could say anything, she placed the cap on the

counter and left the truck, walking down the street, away from the bar crowd.

"What a drama queen."

My dad looked at me, hard. "You have so much to learn, Shorty."

Behind us, the eggplant burned.

CHAPTER 10

THE NEXT DAY, I WOKE UP TO MY ALARM. NOT MY DAD.

Hm. Still in my pajamas with toxic morning breath and cuckoo hair, I crept over to his room and knocked on his door. Nothing. "Pai? Are you still asleep?"

Still nothing. I was about to knock again when someone tapped my shoulder. I jumped about a mile.

"Morning, Shorty." My dad held out a mug of tea.

I took it and smiled. "To what do I owe this princess treatment?"

He ran his hand through his hair and yawned. That's when I noticed he was still in his pajamas, too. A worn-out Clippers T-shirt and flannel pants. "Well, there's a change of plans. You and Rose are running the truck without me today."

The tea scalded my tongue. "Huh? Are you sick?"

"Nope."

"Uh, do you have a meeting?"

"Nah."

"Then what?"

There was a mischievous gleam in his eye that chilled me. A gleam that I've inherited. It never means anything good.

"It's a test."

I stopped drinking my tea. "No."

"Yes."

"FATHER!" I yelled.

He pointed at me, at once stern and ridiculous with his spiky hair and giant threadbare T-shirt. "You and Rose need to figure out how to get along. Not just put up with each other and work, but to *actually get along*. Rose is cool, and I want you to see that."

I exhaled loudly. "Okay, Dr. Phil. But Rose quit, remember?"

"I talked to her parents and they convinced her to give it one last try. Actually . . . a one-week one-last try."

I shook my head like I had water in my ears. "Pardon me?"

My dad already had one foot in his bedroom. "Yeah, the test is for one week. Good luck today, see you later!" He rushed inside and locked the door.

I banged on it. "No way!"

His voice was muffled. "Rose is waiting for you at the commissary. You guys know the drill by now. I'm not concerned about mistakes, I just want you to make it work, or a fall suspension, and you'll be grounded for the *entire* summer!" He paused. "Text me *only for emergencies*."

"The only texts you'll get from me will be barnacle photos!" My dad had severe reactions to images of things with a lot of holes or bumps clustered together, like barnacles and seedpods. This revulsion/fear, called trypophobia, was always my Hail Mary when my dad was being a jerk. Like today.

"So what are *you* going to do all day?" I hollered through the door.

"Today, I take the day off. The others? Work on the restaurant hustle, handle business to get things started," he responded, his voice sounding far away and much too relaxed.

"Well enjoy your day off with *barnacles*."

By the time I reached the commissary, seven photos and gifs of barnacles had already been sent to my dad. He didn't respond—but I kept them going. I wanted him to live in abject terror. I was *not* into Strict Adrian.

Rose was already there, of course. Leaning against the KoBra, in a white cotton tank and powder blue shorts, her feet in dainty brown sandals. She looked at me through her tortoiseshell sunglasses, arms crossed. "I actually thought I liked your dad," she said in greeting, voice dry.

"Well, even cool dads are actually just *dads* in the end. Lameness guaranteed at some point."

Rose straightened up. "My parents were going to make me quit the dance team if I didn't finish this job." Given that she'd been captain since freshman year, I knew that was a big deal.

We were quiet for a second, neither of us sure where to start. And then we both started talking at once.

"So your dad e-mailed me the social media info—"

"My dad wants us to stick to—"

We both stopped talking. I would have laughed except Rose Carver was like the antidote to mirth. I walked toward the commissary kitchen. "Well, let's start by looking at the food supplies. Today's a grocery-run day."

After a quick survey, we realized we were short on meat, so we needed to head to Koreatown before our usual stop at the office park.

"Should I drive, then?" I asked as we both stood in the truck. Politeness clipped my words.

She shrugged. "Sure, seems to make the most sense," she said as she buckled herself into the passenger seat. Because I couldn't stand to make the fifteen-minute drive to K-Town in silence, I turned on the radio. It had been so long since I listened to the actual radio that I had to fiddle around a bit to find a station that wasn't offensive—something that was playing oldies.

After a few seconds, Rose asked, "Can we listen to NPR?"

I bristled. "Um, no?"

"Just because your dad owns this truck doesn't mean you automatically get to make executive decisions."

"I do when it involves listening to freaking NPR."

"Yeah, because wow, how super *uncool* to pay attention to what happens in the world."

I yanked the steering wheel hard as we turned left onto Vermont. "You said it, not *moi*."

"Forget it, you're such a brat," she huffed, rolling down her window and turning her head away from me. We didn't talk the rest of the ride, which was *fine by me*.

Driving through K-Town in a clunky food truck was no joke. No matter what time of day, traffic was always jammed, and my usual weaving, raging style was seriously cramped by both the cars and the unwieldiness of the giant truck. I didn't really mind; it was always fun to people-watch in traffic since K-Town was one of the few neighborhoods in LA where people actually walked.

There were professionals in business wear; teenagers in giant headphones and backpacks; grandmothers clutching hands of toddlers and children. All within the shadows of the skyscrapers and strip malls pushed up against one another. Koreatown was an LA neighborhood that told the city's entire history through its architecture—from 1920s apartment buildings with art deco iron lettering on top of the roofs to the neon, layered storefronts that arrived loudly in Los Angeles via Seoul.

I felt at home here, not only because I'm Korean American, but because it was a blend of old and new LA. I related to this future version of America that wasn't tidy but layered, improvised, and complicated.

We arrived at the butcher where I had to use my preschool-level Korean to order the beef rump and pork loin. The butcher grumbled under his breath the entire time, and I suspected he was criticizing my bad upbringing as he heaved slabs of meat over the counter.

Back at the commissary, we worked on prepping the food like my dad had showed us—marinating the meats, making the sauces, cooking the rice. Rose reluctantly let me take the lead with food since I had a bit more experience than her. But she watched every move I made with hawk eyes, memorizing everything I was doing like an android. It was annoying, and I felt self-conscious.

"Got that properly downloaded?" I grumbled as I washed my hands.

"It's not exactly brain surgery," she said, but I noticed that she still had that little wrinkle of concentration between her eyes.

I started the truck. "I can't believe my dad actually trusts us."

Rose rolled down her window and pulled on her sunglasses. "Well, he knows *one* of us is responsible."

"You are a delightful conversationalist, you know that?"

She didn't respond and we didn't speak until we drove into the office park.

And there was Hamlet, tossing that sign up in the air. This time wearing a dark green baseball cap, white T-shirt, and very well-fitting navy shorts. No socks and sparkling white sneakers.

"Hey, Hamlet!" Rose waved at him from the window before we even parked.

He waved the sign in return. "Hey! You're back!"

She glanced at me, her smile disappearing then reappearing as she turned back to him. "Yup! Actually, it's just Clara and me running the truck for a week."

"Whoa, really?" He walked over to us, the sign still held up high above his head. "Did Adrian go somewhere?"

Yep, going to let Rose handle this question. Ever the politician, she smiled and chirped, "Oh, no, he thought we were ready to try this on our own. You know, trial by fire and all!"

He threw his head back and laughed. Heartily. Like someone had told a joke, except no one had told a freaking joke.

Rose hopped out of the truck to walk up to him. As they talked, I rolled my eyes and put on my KoBra shirt and hat.

Then I heard an exclamation from Rose. "Wait a second, are you on Arcadia Prep's debate team?" She was pointing at his T-shirt, which said, in a big nerd proclamation: ARCADIA PREP DEBATE. She grasped his upper arm in excitement.

I stuck my head out the window.

He dropped the sign and grasped both *her* arms. "Yeah! Wait, you're that captain from—"

"Elysian High!"

And for some reason that elicited a huge bear hug from Hamlet. I felt a stirring of jealousy that startled me. Pardon, why was I jealous about this?

But watching the two of them lose their collective mind over recognizing each other from dorky-ass debate club definitely made me feel funny inside.

"You were *so* awesome at the semifinals this spring!" Hamlet said with both his hands held up in front of him in this bizarre way. I kept staring at him. Who or what was he reminding me of . . .

Rose *giggled*, and he looked at her with this toothy grin, his canines glinting again.

Canines.

Yeah, still reminded me of a Lab. His hands were held up in front of him, torso-height. Waiting for his treat.

Why did I find him attractive?

Watching the two of them wax poetic about debate club made me realize that I was being a total loser getting jealous *purely* because Rose was flirting with him. That was it.

I opened the order window and whistled sharply. "Rose! When you two debate dorks are done, maybe we could actually get to work?"

Rose glared at me, but Hamlet, of course, was unfazed. In fact, he trotted over to the truck. All that was missing was a Frisbee in his mouth. "Hey, Clara." He fixed his big eyes on me, dark lashes contrasting sharply against his skin. "So you guys go to the same high school, right?"

I slammed the cashbox onto the counter. "Yup."

"Not on debate team, though?"

"Literally would rather die."

He guffawed. If dogs could laugh, their laugh of choice would be the guffaw. "So, what are you into, then?"

I looked at him, cocking my head a bit. "Why?" I could see Rose stalking toward us, clearly annoyed that Hamlet was talking to me.

"Why not?" And there was something so matter-of-fact and weirdly intimate about that, almost a challenge. Daring me to be earnest in my answer. It didn't help that he was looking straight into my eyes with unnerving openness.

"I'm into walks on the beach, cupcakes, and kittens."

He laughed again, that guffaw. His incredibly straight, white teeth gleaming. "You're so funny."

I pressed my lips together, holding back laughter and a cutting remark. Because, to be honest, I had no idea how to react. Who *says* that?

"No, but really. You don't do anything?" he asked.

It was a rude question, but the way he asked it was so genuine. Or confused. Or something. And I felt like there was this giant spotlight on me that I wasn't ready for. Nobody ever asked me *what I did* at school. I was the class clown. Good for a laugh, and the leader of my merrymen, Patrick and Felix. But in the truck, all of that felt little. Not important.

"We have a customer coming," Rose said, shoving me away from the window.

I wiggled my fingers at Hamlet. "Bye."

He blinked. "Bye!" Then he bounded over to his spot on the corner.

Rose glanced at me. "Looks like someone has a crush."

I almost dropped the pitcher of water I was holding. "I don't have a crush!"

She shook her head. "Who says I'm talking about *you*?"

90

CHAPTER 11

SOMEHOW ROSE AND I MANAGED TO GET THROUGH our entire first day without a single fight. There was an incident where I hit her head by accident and she hit me back, but that was fine. I could tell it was just instinct.

Also, we were both *exhausted*. Running that truck with just the two of us was no joke.

At the end of the day, we both lurched out of the truck, one of the commissary lights flickering on and off in the dark lot. Rose lifted her arms and stretched them above her head like a little ballerina cake topper.

I rubbed one of my Docs onto my bare leg, scratching a mosquito bite I'd somehow acquired while inside the truck for eight hours. "Maybe since we didn't kill each other today, my dad will come back tomorrow."

Rose pulled out her phone, not even looking at me, the light of the screen making her face glow eerily. "Yeah."

All right, then. I gritted my teeth and was about to start my walk home but stopped when I saw a couple of guys walk by—shrouded in shadow, walking slowly, appraising us as they did so. I stared at them. *I see you.* And they kept walking. When one of them looked back at me, I kept my gaze steady. Creeps.

I sighed and turned around. "Do you have a ride home?"

She tried to look nonchalant, but I saw her glance down at her phone again, agitated. "Um, yeah, I mean my mom was supposed to be here."

"So you're gonna wait here alone?"

"Aren't you going to walk home alone?" she immediately countered. Her bravado would have been more convincing if she hadn't checked her phone again.

I pulled my sweatshirt tighter around myself. "Yeah, but this is my neighborhood, I know how to deal." I paused. "Plus, my dad makes me carry pepper spray."

Rose pulled something out of her shorts pocket and held it up. Mace.

I laughed. "LA kids."

"We know all varieties of pervs," she said with a wry smile. I smiled back, and then we looked away from each other.

I could hear her take rapid shallow breaths again. And this

time I wasn't so sure if she was breathing like that to get control—it didn't seem in her control at all.

"I'll wait with you, then." Before she could respond, I crouched low to the ground, my feet flat, my butt just an inch or so off the cement, pulling out my phone to avoid looking at her.

"How are you sitting like that?" Rose asked, bending over to look at my feet. "You're using your ankles as a seat!" She tried to copy me, but when she reached a certain depth, she fell over, landing on her butt.

I tsked. "See, even though you can touch your head with your toes, only Koreans can do this squat. It's called the kimchi squat for that reason." Obviously, any human could do this squat, but I liked goading Rose.

She scoffed. "Give me a break. You're making that up."

"Try it again."

Rose squatted down, but had to balance on the balls of her feet, so her butt was still a good foot off the ground rather than the near-hovering mine was doing. I could sense her concentration, her thighs strained in the awkward position.

"Ha! I've found the one thing Rose Carver can't do."

She stayed balanced. "We'll see about that." Looking down at her feet she said, "Also, it's true, I really didn't think you'd get suspended."

I almost fell over. "Are you *apologizing*?"

She laughed, an unexpected response that further startled me. "No, actually I'm not. Hasn't anyone told you that it's annoying when girls apologize all the time?"

"Good one."

"Also, don't think I'm stupid. I know that's why you've hated me and made my life as awful as possible since then," she said.

I shrugged, still crouched. "You deserved it."

"I admire your endurance."

"Thanks."

There were a few seconds of silence, a gusty wind kicking in. Rose steadied herself, and I looked at her. "That was only the first time I smoked, you know?"

That little wrinkle between her eyes showed up again, and she shook her head.

"This is lame, but I only did it because I decided I wanted to *rebel*." I didn't know why I was even saying this. It was like something needed to fill in the gap between being annoyed at someone for narcing and my relentless poking over the years. "A few weeks before that, my parents had this huge fight about me. As you've noticed, my parents aren't together anymore. My mom travels a lot for her job, so my dad's got sole custody."

Rose nodded.

"Anyway, my mom wanted me to take a break from school to travel with her, and my dad flipped. I was really pissed. I wanted to be with my mom, but, I don't know. I also knew it wasn't right, really? Anyway. The smoking. It was something I could control."

The wind made the trees around us creak. "I'm sorry, that sounds stressful," Rose said after a few seconds, giving me a tiny smile. "I know I apologize a lot. But maybe it's not a bad thing. Maybe it's considered a bad thing because it's something girls do a lot. Maybe it's actually something nice that keeps the world humane. It's a gesture."

Huh. I nodded. "Yeah. It's not always bad. And . . . thanks, I guess."

Headlights flooded the lot.

"Rosie! Sorry hon, Jessie's snake went missing!" Rose's mom yelled out the driver's side window of the sleek luxury SUV.

Rose sprang up, graceful as ever even on the verge of falling over. "Oh my God, Pizza went missing?" she yelped. "Did you find him?"

Her mom's hand fluttered out the window. "Kind of."

Disturbing. I got up, too. "See ya."

"Where are you going?" Rose asked.

I looked around. "Home?"

"We can give you a ride home," she said stiffly, the headlights shining behind her, her figure a silhouette.

"I live six blocks away; it's fine."

She shrugged. "Okay, but don't say I didn't warn you."

Uh, ominous much? I knew this walk, nothing would happen to *me*. As I skirted by the car, Mrs. Carver honked and I nearly flew out of my skin. Rose's mom stuck her head out the window again. "Get your butt in this car, Clara!"

I scrambled over and hopped into the back seat.

My dad's feet greeted me when I walked into the apartment—bare and propped up on the sofa arm. The rest of him was hidden

95

under a fleece LA Galaxy blanket, his hands and phone sticking out. There was a lump near him that was, unmistakably, a comatose Flo.

I slammed the door shut, making Flo yowl and causing our clock from the dollar store to rattle. It was orange and plastic and uggo beyond belief, but my dad had a fondness for it. I knew he liked it precisely because it was ugly. My dad had a sick need to adopt and foster rejected and unwanted things. We'd been at the register when he spotted it in the sale bin. In case it wasn't obvious, the sale bin at the dollar store was seriously like the crème de la crème of sadness.

What a pair we made.

"How's my darling daughter?" he called out from his reclined position, not even lifting his lazy head.

"Wonderful." I grabbed a carton of mint chocolate chip ice cream from the freezer. But there was only a small scraping left— with a fine layer of frostbite on top. "Pai! Can't you be on top of ice cream duty *for once*?" I said as I emptied it into the sink.

"You only talk to me to yell at me?"

Our stupid faucet had the water pressure of a gentle breeze, and it took forever for me to rinse out the carton before tossing it into our recycling bin. "Yeah, that's what you deserve."

Pai sat up on the sofa and looked at me, his arms draped over his bent knees. "So, it went just as terrible as I suspected?"

I leaned against the sink and looked at him. "Contrary to popular belief, I'm not *totally* incompetent."

"Good to know. So you guys did okay? You didn't text anything but barnacle photos."

Heh-heh. "You're welcome. And yeah, it was *fine*. I don't know what you thought was going to happen."

"Oh, I don't know. Maybe a *fire*." Flo wriggled out from the blanket and stretched before making her way over to me.

I bent down to scoop her up, kissing her white-dipped front paws. "Well, there was just that small grease fire."

"What!"

I laughed, making Flo squirm out of my arms. "You're off your game."

My dad harrumphed, settling back into the sofa. "Don't forget to tally how much you made in the Google doc." The KoBra had a Google doc shared between Pai, Rose, and me. Whoever was in charge of cash was supposed to fill in the day's total profits.

"Rose handled the money, so she's going to do it."

"Well, good job, Shorty. I'm proud of you for not killing each other and not burning the truck down."

"Such high expectations." I picked some cat hair off my shirt. "I feel like Rose has some issues that might explain why she's so annoying."

Pai adjusted his reading glasses and looked a little concerned. "Like what?"

"I dunno. Something. She's a little too stressed out all the time. And holding herself to some impossible standard." I yawned. "Anyway, I'm gonna take a shower. I smell like a walking barbecue."

As I headed upstairs with Flo close at my heels, my dad shouted out, "How was Hamlet?"

I stalled on the stairs. What was with everyone and Hamlet? "He's fine, why?"

"Just curious." The silence that followed was so heavy with insinuation that you could cut it with a pastry knife.

CHAPTER 12

HAMLET GREETED US WITH ICED LATTES A FEW DAYS
later when we were back in Pasadena.

It was already ninety degrees out, and I grasped the cold drink
gratefully. "Thanks."

Rose looked at the cup he was holding out with mild trepidation. "Um, thank you. But did you use whole milk?"

Hamlet glanced down at the drink, assessing it. "Yeah. Uh-oh,
are you lactose intolerant?"

"She's delicious intolerant," I said before taking a nice, long
swig from mine.

Rose shot me a dirty look. "I'm a dancer. I have to watch what
I put into my body." She looked back at Hamlet apologetically.
"But it's okay! I can just drink it." When she brought the straw

to her lips, it was almost in slow-mo, her reluctance clear in every micromillimeter of movement.

I grabbed it out of her hands. "For Pete's sake! *I'll* drink it. Hamlet, please make her something else." Sometimes Rose was such a contradiction—a bulldozing boss one minute, and someone fretting over hurt feelings the next.

But then, look at who was the object of her worry.

Hamlet's strong shoulders shrugged in his form-fitting mint green T-shirt. "Not a problem. Why don't you tell me what you want?" As the two walked over to his coffee cart, I watched them with irritation.

My phone buzzed in my pocket. It was a text from Felix: **Pool today?**

FOMO seared through me. Last summer, I had spent almost every day poolside with Felix and Patrick, reading crappy magazines at a community pool no one else seemed to know about. It cost two dollars for the day and always had hot lifeguards. Summer was usually sweaty make-outs, sunscreen, and sneaking into air-conditioned theaters.

Now it was about Rose Carver and grilled meats.

I had leveled down hard-core.

Working 😫

Felix texted back: **Ditch it**

Normally, I would. But when I glanced up at Rose and Hamlet, two earnest little citizens, I didn't feel like it. There were actual consequences with my dad if I ditched this time. And I needed to do a good-enough job to make it to Tulum.

Can't. Don't get sunburned on your scalp again. 🔥

I slipped my phone into my back pocket and tightened my apron. Time to get this party started.

When Rose got back to the truck, she was holding an iced black coffee.

"You live a joyless existence," I said as I stirred the rice in the pot, making it nice and fluffy. There was nothing worse than matted-down rice. She ignored me and sipped her drink in one long, loud drag.

The office park run went astonishingly well. I slipped easily into the cooking zone. Soon I knew how to get the lombo to the perfect crispness level and how many pickles to scoop out so that the juices didn't run into the rice. I was surprised by how little I hated this. Rose chatted easily with the regulars and grew adept at both taking orders and getting the food out at the pickup window.

When we were getting ready to wrap up the stop, Hamlet moseyed over to the truck again.

"Slow day?" I asked as I wiped down the counters.

He smiled, his eyes crinkling in the corners as he propped his arms on the low counter where people could place their plates to eat, cradling his chin in one hand. "Yeah."

He was just looking at me at this point. I stopped and stared at him levelly. "So, are you a gymnast or something?"

"A gymnast?" An adorable puzzled expression appeared on his face for a second.

"Yeah. You do all those flips and stuff."

A grin stretched across his face, quick and easy. "Oh! No, I used to do a lot of martial arts and stuff as a kid. But now I mostly box."

Totally out of my own control, my face flushed. I found this inexplicably hot. "Who boxes anymore?" I sputtered. "I mean, like men from the 1970s wearing sweatpants maybe." What *are* you saying, Clara.

But this made Hamlet crack up. Head thrown back and everything.

Rose popped up next to me, outta nowhere. "Where do you train?"

"At this gym in Chinatown."

"Cool! Do you compete?"

A little modest shrug. "Yeah."

To my surprise, Rose scrambled out of the truck and hopped over next to him on the pavement. "Show me some moves!" She held up her fists comically, a huge grin on her face.

It was cute, and I wanted to barf.

Hamlet laughed and stepped toward her, hands reaching out. "Is it okay if I touch your arms?"

WAS IT OKAY TO TOUCH HER ARMS.

She nodded, keeping it cool.

"Are you right- or left-handed?"

"Right."

He adjusted her arms so that her right fist was held up to her cheek and her left was in front of her face, positioned a little to the left of her nose. "Okay, keep your arms up like this at all times, protect that nice face." His voice took on an authoritative tone, and I resisted the urge to fan myself.

Even in this awkward new pose, Rose looked graceful. Then he adjusted her stance a little bit. I wanted to look away, but I couldn't.

"So, strike out at my hand with your left fist," he held up his right hand, palm facing out. "But take a small step with your left foot forward as you do it."

In one pretty, fluid motion, Rose gently punched, her body moving toward him.

"Awesome! That was good, but you can *really* hit me, you know," he said.

She made a face. "No way!" He assured her that it was fine, and while skeptical, she hit him harder the next time.

"Yes!" he cried out, giving her a high five. She was glowing. Brownie points via hot dude: a heady cocktail for Rose Carver, I'm sure.

I watched them go back and forth for a while, getting grumpier with every second, with every bit of physical contact between the two of them.

To squash down this unpleasant jealous feeling, I turned away and wiped down the griddle.

After a few minutes, Hamlet called my name. Argh. I looked out the window, and he motioned toward himself and Rose. "Do you wanna try?"

No. "No."

Rose rolled her eyes. "Come on! It's fun! Plus, you get to punch a dude."

Well. That was actually enticing. My hesitation was enough. Rose ran inside the truck and dragged me out. I stood in front of Hamlet, my arms crossed. He looked at me, head to toe, and I blushed. *What the heck, Clara. Chill!*

"So, you saw what I showed Rose, right?" He stepped forward but stopped, hesitating. "Um, do you need me to . . ."

Feeling extremely stupid, I held up my fists like Rose had. "Like this?" He nodded, and I was disappointed when he didn't adjust them for me.

"Okay, Clara. Hit me."

I looked at his face, so open, so encouraging. A sheen of sweat on his forehead, his high cheekbones. And I got incredibly self-conscious. My limbs felt clumsy and heavy, and I couldn't figure out how to move my feet properly as I reached out to punch him. When my fist hit his open palm, it was weak and sloppy. It didn't make the satisfying smacking noise that Rose's punch had.

I dropped my arms to my sides. "Cool. That sucked."

"No, it didn't! It was good!" Hamlet exclaimed, walking over to me. "Here, just spread your legs out a little more . . ." His voice trailed off and he kept staring at my feet. But I saw a blush creeping up the back of his neck. "Um, sorry, I mean . . ."

He was dying. I was dying.

Making a fool of myself in front of cute dudes was literally the opposite of my brand, and every molecule of my being was on fire right now. "Thanks, but we have to go anyway." I ran inside and hopped into the driver's seat. "Rose!" I barked as I started the engine.

She threw me an exasperated look, then shut the metal awnings that covered up the order and pickup windows. When she slipped into the passenger seat, I honked and yelled, "BYE, HAMLET!" Rose waved out the window. As we drove away, I saw Hamlet toss the sign up in the air in the rearview mirror, as if sending us off.

"What a total dork," I said.

Rose scoffed. "Clara. Who do you think you're kidding?" I opened my mouth, but she reached over and turned on the radio, cranking NPR. Loud. Then she sat back with her arms crossed. I was still so flustered by the whole boxing thing that I didn't bother fighting her.

We stopped by the commissary for prep and a little break as usual, then headed toward our next destination, a farmers market in Echo Park that was one of our weekly stops. The market was tucked behind a row of historic buildings, and it was starting to bustle. I parked the KoBra next to a few other trucks: a classic taco truck, an udon bowl truck, a grilled cheese truck, and a boba truck.

We parked and nervously started setting up—the air tense and both of us quiet in our own little corners. This would be the biggest crowd we'd served so far.

"Hey, are you Adrian's girl?"

I glanced out the window and saw a young white woman sporting a bandana and blond pigtails. "Yeah, hi. Clara."

She wiped her hands on her gingham-print apron before reaching out to shake mine. "Hi, Clara, I'm Kat, the owner of Gouda Done Worse."

Oh *my*. No, Kat, you gouda NOT done worse.

Keeping a smile plastered on my face, I shook Kat's hand. "Hi, Kat."

Kat grinned at me, and her eyes swept over the truck. "Adrian told us that you'd be manning the KoBra today. Pretty impressive."

Before I could respond, another blond girl who looked exactly like Kat stepped down from Gouda Done Worse. "Hi, Clara! I'm Kat's sister, Sarah!" Twins.

And then a man-bun-sporting Middle Eastern guy popped his head out from the udon truck. "Oh heeeey, it's the KoBra's heir!" For Pete's sake. Yet again, it was like *Mister Rogers' Neighborhood* up in here.

After some introductions with Rose, I realized very quickly that my dad had prepped everyone beforehand—there was this forced oh-so-casual nature to how they were all checking up on us.

And it was nice, because it got busy, fast. The truck grew hotter as we hustled our orders for a while. Then a familiar voice called out, ringing through the noise in the truck.

"Surprise, Rosie!"

I turned around to see Rose's parents and a little kid, who I could only assume was her brother, at the order window.

"Hey!" Rose said with a huge smile. "What are you guys doing here?"

Rose's dad's voice boomed into the truck, and to everyone within earshot. "We're here to see our gorgeous daughter at her first real summer job!" I could hear Rose's mom laugh.

Rose dropped her face into her hands, but she was still smiling when she looked up again. I wiped my hands on my apron and walked over to the window. "Hi," I said with a wave.

"HI, CLARA!" The kid waved back. "I'm Jessie!" He was wearing a Pikachu hat. And was about two feet tall with a lisp and missing front tooth. Basically, the cutest kid alive.

"Hey, Jessie, what do you guys wanna order? This is usually Rose's job, but she seems to have turned into a robot momentarily."

Jessie's eyes widened. "Wait . . . no, not really, right?"

I shrugged. "I dunno, we'll have to see if she reboots."

"Like when Grandma uses Windows."

I burst out laughing and nodded my head. "Yes, exactly like that."

Rose's mom smiled at me from under her large, stylish straw hat. She was wearing a breezy caftan cinched at the waist and strappy gold sandals—like she belonged in a fashion magazine spread titled "Look chic during your farmers market run!"

"Hi there, Clara. May we please get one lombo, one picanha, and two pasteis? Also, two lime sugarcane juices?" she asked.

"I want my own juice!" Jessie pleaded.

Rose's mom looked down at him. "Excuse me?"

He gulped. "I mean, please can I have my own juice?"

"Yes, you may. One for you, one for me. Daddy's going to drink water," Rose's mom said while pulling some cash out of her wallet.

I gave her some change. "Thank you, it should be ready in a few minutes."

Jessie came up to the window on tippy-toe, and Rose's dad lifted him so that Jessie was eye level with me. "Nice to meet you, Clara." Then he held out his hand.

I took the sticky little hand in mine and shook it solemnly. "Nice to meet you, too, Jessie."

Rose stuck her head out the window. "I can't hang out, un-fortunately. I have to work."

Rose's dad winked. "Got it, Rosie. We're here to support you in this new chapter of your life. Even if it is a punishment."

It was almost farcical except it was *sincere*.

"Okay, okay," Rose said before blowing her family a kiss and helping the next customer.

The Carvers sat at one of the picnic tables scattered at the market and eventually left with waves and cheerful good-byes.

I watched them walk away into the crowds, swinging large baskets full of produce. "Are you guys for real?" I asked Rose. We had a break from customers so I sat on the floor and took a swig from my water bottle. It was boiling in the truck.

Rose wiped her brow and adjusted the little oscillating fan so that it was aimed directly at her face. "Are you being a jerk?"

I pulled my shirt away from my chest, airing it out a little. "No, for once in my life, I'm being sincere. Your family is pretty cool to show up. Plus, Jessie's rad."

"Jessie can be 'rad' when he's not being a little know-it-all."

"Pardon me?" I held my hand up to my ear. "Did . . . did *you* call someone a *know-it-all*?"

Rose tossed an ice cube into her mouth and crunched it, making me cringe. "Believe it or not, I am *not* the worst in my family. Know-it-allness is a shared trait among the Carvers."

"Well, you definitely seem like a family of total brains."

She crunched the ice again, making my arm hairs stand on end. "Let me just say this one thing to explain the Carvers: we have a weekly dinner pop quiz."

I stopped fanning myself with my shirt. "Are you serious?"

"Yeah. About the week's news, like *Wait Wait . . . Don't Tell Me!*" She noticed my blank expression. "It's a weekly quiz show on NPR."

"Of course."

"Anyway, yeah. Every Friday evening, we invite some person over, like a city council member or teacher or something, and we do the quiz with my parents as the hosts."

I snorted. "Wild Friday nights with the Carvers."

She laughed. "I mean, I know how it sounds. But I actually like hanging out with my family." Her fondness was apparent in how she perked up when talking about them. Again, I felt a pang of curious jealousy. Rose's family kind of seemed like my worst nightmare. Or maybe it was the worst nightmare in some narrative about myself that I wasn't sure was totally accurate.

Another ice cube crunched in her mouth and I pointed at her. "*Don't!* That sound is the worst thing in *the entire world.*"

Rose rolled her eyes but tucked the ice cube into her cheek so that it bulged out. "Well, I'm sure my family seems super boring compared to your like, cool-dad life."

I made a face and fanned myself with a napkin. "Cool-dad life, oh my God."

"It's true! Your dad is so awesome."

"Please don't get a crush on him."

Her mouth dropped open slightly. "I won't!"

"Good." I took another sip of water.

Her eyes lit up. "Hey! Also, not to be a creep, but I found your mom online through the truck's Instagram account. What is her *life?*"

Whenever people found out about my mom, I wasn't sure what to feel—pride? Embarrassment? In most cases, I feigned ambivalence. So I shrugged. "Oh, she's a social media influencer. Or something."

Rose mulled that over. "That's her job?"

"I guess."

"How do you get a job doing . . . that?"

The words flew out of my mouth before I could stop them. "Extreme narcissism."

Her eyes widened in surprise and I laughed loudly. "Just kidding. She's really good at social media. And looking good in clothes. And . . ."

"Having good taste?" Rose ventured. I looked at her sharply for signs of sarcasm, but she seemed genuine. A sly expression crossed her face. "I mean, she must. She hooked up with your dad."

"ROSE!"

She cackled and the awkwardness quickly dissipated. I fanned myself with a paper plate and asked, "Are both your parents lawyers? I forget."

She nodded. "Yeah. My dad has his own law firm. My mom's a prosecutor. She got kind of big a few years ago when—"

"That police-beating case."

Rose raised her eyebrows. "Wow. You know about that?"

"It was all over the news, hello."

"Says the girl who hates NPR."

"I didn't say I *hated* NPR. It just doesn't exactly pump me up for work."

She smiled. "Okay, whatever. Anyway. My mom became this community figure. She got to meet Michelle *Obama*."

"I'm not even kidding, that's a life dream of mine," I said, my voice high with excitement.

"You and every human being who isn't garbage," she said. "Anyway, so that's my mom. She was on the cover of magazines; people wanted to interview her. And then there's me."

I frowned. "What about you? You're basically Joanne Jr."

She shook her head firmly. "I wish."

"Whoa. Rose Carver doesn't think she's good enough? What are the rest of us subpar humans supposed to do now? Might as well give up and jump off a cliff."

She crossed her arms. "I'm serious."

"So am I! You're basically on track to become the president of the United States of America."

I could tell she was pleased by that for a second. "The point is that there's a lot of pressure on black girls to be *better* than everyone else anyway. And then add to that the fact that my mom is who she is. You don't even know how aware I am of how I look and act *all the time*. I don't have the luxury of rolling out of bed and acting like a little jerk like you do every day."

"Thanks."

"You know what I mean. Like, I can't just run errands wearing cruddy sweatpants and not do my hair."

I squinted at her. "I understand what you mean, but you would still look like a celebrity doing a coffee run in *Us* magazine."

Someone rapped on the window. "Hey, are you guys open?"

Rose hopped off the counter and smoothed her hair back from her forehead. "Hi there, what would you like to order?"

Reluctantly, I dragged myself back up to the griddle, but before I turned it on, I made a sugarcane juice with less sugar and more lime, and filled it with ice until the plastic cup frosted over.

"Here," I said, holding it out to Rose.

She startled, then took it from me. "Oh. Thanks, Clara."

"And keep doing what you do. The first woman president has to happen in my lifetime, or I'm going to light this entire planet on fire."

Rose laughed, her teeth straight and perfect, and I turned back to the griddle to hide my own smile.

CHAPTER 13

"TODAY'S TEA HAS A LITTLE SOMETHING EXTRA FOR you. To celebrate your last day of manning up."

I took the mug from my dad. "You mean womaning up. But thanks." When I took a sip, my eyes widened. "Oh yum, horchata hybrid?"

My dad tapped the tip of my nose. "Bingo, Shorty."

Horchata was my favorite, and my dad usually added it to chai on my birthday. Today was the last day of me and Rose running the KoBra together, so I suppose he thought a celebration was in order.

But the difference between how I felt today and how I felt a week ago was so drastic that I myself couldn't really understand it. Instead of dragging myself out of bed and being filled with dread on my walk to the commissary, I was actually—excited? Looking forward to it?

Maybe it was because I knew we had passed the test with flying colors. My dad would definitely cave and let me go to Tulum, I was sure of it. I was in such a good mood that I cheerfully waved at two surly middle school girls walking by me. "What's her freaking problem?" one of them bitched to the other. I laughed.

As always, Rose was waiting for me at the truck, already prepping.

"Morning," I said as I climbed in. Rose glanced up from where she was wiping down the oven.

"Morning!" she greeted back. Then she stood up and wiped her hands on her apron nervously. "Um."

I kept looking at her when she wouldn't go on. "Yeah?"

She turned around and grabbed something off the counter and shoved it at me. "Here. In case you're hungry."

It was a small plastic bag filled with fresh fruit tossed with chili powder. "I know you really like that one fruit cart," she said nonchalantly.

Aw, Rose. So awkward at gestures of friendship. Taking it from her, I said, "Thanks. Do you wanna share? This is a lot of fruit."

She shrugged and tugged at one of her delicate gold heart studs. "Sure." I grabbed a couple of forks and handed one to her.

We ate the fruit in silence—one mango slice and melon piece at a time. Finally, I spoke up. "So, my dad says that since we did better than he thought we would, he wants us to keep going with limited supervision. So, three days out of the week we'll be work-ing alone." I glanced at her, gauging her reaction. Maybe she'd hate it?

But her face remained relaxed and she nodded. "Cool."

"So you're okay with it?"

She shrugged. "Yeah. I mean, even if it means our reward for surviving our punishment is the extension of that punishment."

I laughed. "True. Well, I think he's been excited to have some more time off the truck. He's taking this business course at the community college, and he wants to focus on the business side and getting his restaurant started. Finding investors and space and stuff. We can handle more of the day-to-day in the truck."

"Oh cool! I didn't know he wanted to open a restaurant?"

I nodded, wiping some chili powder from the corner of my mouth. "Yeah, it's his big dream. The KoBra is the first step toward it."

"That's so awesome!"

"Calm down, future Mrs. Shin."

Normally, that would have pissed Rose off—normally, that would have been my intention. But she snort-laughed instead, then coughed and looked down at the fruit. "Wow, that's spicy."

"Oh, you probably got a pocket of chili powder." I moved some of the fruit around until I found an area without too much of it. "Here."

"There's only coconut left?" She made a face as she poked around.

"Stop complaining, you ingrate." The words came out of my

mouth before I could stop them. Before she could react, I said, "Sorry, that came out wrong. I mean, actually it came out how I meant it. But I guess I don't need to say exactly what I feel all the time."

She looked down at the bag of fruit for a second before lifting her head to respond. "That's okay." Then she grinned. "Man, we're so good at this friendship thing."

I almost choked on my mango, laughing. "Yeah, we should do tutorials on it."

"Put it on YouTube."

"Bring on guests to show them how to awkwardly compliment each other."

We were both giggling so hard at this point that we had to put our fruit down. I kimchi squatted because my legs lost their strength and Rose joined me.

"Hey! You're doing it!" I said, pointing at her flat feet and balanced butt.

She twirled her arms up in the air, like a squatting showgirl.

"I practiced. Did you think I was gonna let *you* be able to do something that I couldn't?"

I pushed her over.

We got to the office park, and I honked in greeting to Hamlet, who saluted us, tucking his sign neatly under his arm.

As had become ritual, once we parked, Hamlet jogged over to us carrying a couple of iced drinks—a mocha for me and an iced coffee for Rose. "Thanks!" I said, taking mine with a wink. He blushed slightly. In return for our usual drinks, we gave him a plate of whatever he wanted.

"So, when are you going to throw Hamlet a bone?" Rose asked as we prepped.

My nose scrunched. "How did you know?"

She looked at me with a hand on her hip. "What? That he likes you?"

"What? No," I sputtered. "You said, throw him a *bone*. I mean, how did you know he's a Lab . . . ah, never mind." I fumbled with the cashbox, trying to remember the padlock code and messing up twice. I cursed and smacked the box with the palm of my hand.

She took it from me slowly, as if taking a bomb away from an unstable person. "Well, what *I* mean is that it's obvious he likes you. Are you into him at all?"

I squinted out the window into the sunny courtyard, watching him make a drink with gusto. Tossing cups into the air, whistling, grinning. Eyes sparkling, charming everyone's pants off.

Except mine. No, my pants were firmly on.

"He's not my type." I brushed by Rose and turned on the grill.

She laughed this smug little laugh that ended with a condescending shaking of the head. A specially patented Rose Carver kind of laugh.

"What?"

"So your type is not *that*?" She pointed out the window. Where Hamlet's thick black hair shone in the sun, arms tanned and flexing as he reached for a gallon of milk. And when he glanced up at us, his eyes crinkled into a smile before his toothy, white grin broke out. He waved.

Rose and I looked at each other and started cracking up. He cocked his head to the side, curious but smiling.

Labrador.

"He's adorable, and you know it," Rose said as she organized the cash—large bills under the tray, change and small bills sorted on top.

I leaned against the counter and pulled my hair up into a sloppy ponytail, a few strands escaping and falling loose around my face. "Like I said, adorable is not my type."

"Let me guess—you like 'em *naughty*."

"Ew. Who even says 'naughty'?"

Rose waved a hand in front of herself, lips pursed. "You know what I mean, bad boys. Like, high school Mr. Rochesters."

"Who?"

"Don't act obtuse."

I pulled the container of vinaigrette out of the refrigerator. "Oh, but actually I *am* obtuse."

"Clara!"

Something about Rose's exasperation delighted me. Always. I stirred the sauce with a wooden spoon, breaking apart bits of parsley, the scent of vinegar filling the truck. "And no, I'm not into Mr. Rochesters. One, I like men who aren't controlling-old-uncle types. Two, I'm not into brooding, either."

"So, what then? What's your issue with Hamlet?"

I placed the bowl of vinaigrette in the small fridge under the counter. "I don't have an *issue*. He's just—I mean, he's *your* type. Eager beaver overachiever."

She was quiet long enough for me to get nervous. *Did* she like him? A little bit of dread pooled in my stomach because even though I didn't take flirting with Hamlet seriously, the thought of not having him as an option bummed me out. Not to mention the fact that I actually liked being on nonhating terms with Rose. And I didn't know if I had the energy to be mortal enemies again. Especially over a *dude*.

But after a few seconds, Rose shrugged and smiled. "He's cute, for sure. But he's made it *so clear* that he likes you. I've got some pride, okay?"

I smiled tentatively. "Are you sure? Because, you should go for him if you want."

"Thanks for the permission," she said with an eye roll.

"It's not permission! Jesus, I'm just saying—"

She threw a dish towel at me. "I said no! He likes *you*! And honestly, the lady doth protest too much . . ."

I snatched the towel off the floor and waved it at her. "Can you not talk like that? I'm embarrassed for you."

Rose spent the rest of the afternoon speaking like a Shakespearean reject to every customer. Touché, humorless one.

Later that evening, we were closing up the truck when Rose's phone rang. "Hey, Mom," she said when she picked up.

A few seconds passed before she exclaimed, "What? Tonight? But I'm not ready!" I heard her mom's muffled voice. "It *is* a big deal! I'm not ready." They spoke for a few more seconds, with Rose's voice so quiet I couldn't catch the rest of the conversation.

After she ended the call, Rose pressed her forehead against the wall and started taking those shallow breaths again. I approached her tentatively, "Hey, are you okay?"

She nodded. "Yup." But then she kept her eyes closed.

"Rose. Seriously, are you all right? Sit down." I took her arm and pulled her over to the driver's seat.

I crouched down by her and just watched her, unsure of what to do. She seemed seriously freaked out, and I knew friend duty involved making her feel better, but *how*? I was about to tell some terrible joke when she looked up at me.

"I'm fine," she said, sounding embarrassed.

"Are you sure?"

She nodded. I wasn't sure if she wanted to talk about it, but it seemed like we should. I filled a cup with water and ice and handed it to her. "What do you have to do tonight?"

She took a sip before answering. "Thanks. And it's not a big deal." Which was *literally* the opposite of what she had said to her mom.

"You seemed upset." Understatement of the year.

Again, she didn't answer right away, and I picked at a spot of dried sauce on the counter. After some silence, she said, "Well, it's that we're going to have a senator over for dinner."

"What!"

"It's really not a big deal. She's friends with my dad and might write a letter of recommendation for me. I just, I didn't know I had to have dinner with her tonight." Rose picked at her nails again.

"Oh. I mean, *for me*, having dinner with a senator would be a big deal, but small potatoes when you're a Carver, I guess," I said.

She scoffed. "It's *not* small potatoes. I have to impress her tonight is *all*." Her voice was raised now. "This letter of recommendation is for an internship in the *governor's office* next summer! Only the most important internship of my freaking life!" She got up and paced back and forth in the truck, fanning herself off with her hand. "And I'm about to get home and have about five minutes to get this nasty grease smell off of me and be prepared to be informally interviewed!"

I glanced at the clock in the truck. "Well, how about I drive you home instead of to the commissary? I can handle closing up alone today. That should buy you some time?"

Rose stopped pacing. "Really?"

"Yeah. This sounds like a ridiculous dinner, but important nonetheless."

She laughed. "Nonetheless, huh? And you have the nerve to call *me* a dork?"

I started the truck. "All right, all right. Buckle up. We're about to weave through the 110, baby."

She opened the window and cleared her throat. "And thanks. I really appreciate it."

I raised the volume on the radio. "What?!" I shouted.

She shook her head.

"TELL ME WHAT YOU SAID RIGHT NOW! LIKE SHOUT IT!"

"YOU ARE SUCH A LOSER!" she shouted back as we hit the road.

CHAPTER 14

ON SATURDAY, MY DAD HANDED ME A PLATE OF EGGS Benedict drizzled with a sriracha hollandaise sauce. "So, I have some last-minute plans. I'm going out of town. Do you think you can handle the truck all weekend?"

I shoved a forkful of runny yolk and English muffin into my mouth. "Sure. Wait, you're leaving today?"

"Yup." He glanced at the clock. "In like, an hour in fact."

"Where are you going?" I asked as I added more sriracha to my eggs.

My dad plopped down on the stool next to me with his own plate of eggs. "Santa Barbara. Wine tasting."

I almost choked. "What? Who *are* you? Diane Keaton?"

"Yeah, I'm Diane Keaton. Surprise."

"Wait a second." I looked at him suspiciously. "*Who* are you going with?"

He cut his egg in half, the yolk oozing out onto the wilted kale and muffin. A giant forkful of egg went into his mouth, and he didn't answer.

"Pai!"

Many seconds later, he took a gulp of coffee and looked at me. "I'm going with Kody."

My brain quickly flipped through the Rolodex o' women from my dad's life until it stilled on one. "Kody the . . . ?"

"The drummer."

Kody was a Filipino American babe with a Patti Smith haircut and a raspy smoker's voice. My dad had dated her a couple of years ago, though, so I was confused. "Kody the drummer? Didn't you guys break up?"

He expertly cut the rest of his eggs, crisscrossing his slices so that each piece was perfectly bite-size. "Yeah. But we grabbed coffee last week and . . ." He shrugged. "You know how it goes."

"No, I don't. I'm a child."

A snort of laughter sent a piece of egg flying across the counter at me. I swiped it off my forearm. "Gross! If all these women only knew how disgusting you are at home."

I said "all these women" because, well, my dad had all these women. Which I understood—he was thirty-four and not hideous. I never made a big stink about it. Even so, he tried not to introduce me to too many girlfriends. "Don't want you to get attached," he always said. I think he might have learned that from watching sitcoms about single dads or something. The only thing that annoyed me was when he made jokes about being a hot commodity at PTA meetings. You'd think he was Don Draper waltzing into classrooms full of harried mothers desperately feeding him baked goods. And in what universe did he go to PTA meetings? Please.

My dad shifted uncomfortably on his stool. "Well, to be honest. I've been seeing Kody for a couple of months now."

"Really?" I racked my brain for when they could have had dates in the past two months. It seemed like my dad was home a lot in the evenings, so when did this happen?

As if reading my mind, he said, "She's been helping me out with restaurant stuff. Since before you guys started working on the truck."

"You sly dog."

He made a face. "Gross," he said, throwing the word back at me. I laughed. He looked over at me, nervous again. "So, Clara. I think we're a little serious? Kody and I."

Whether it was the words or the tone of my dad's voice, I didn't know, but my stomach flipped. "Oh, okay." I looked down at my eggs and tried to keep any trace of weirdness out of my voice.

"Yeah. Like, maybe more serious than anyone else in my entire life."

I glanced up then, my eyebrows raised. "What? No way."

"Yes way."

And the tells—the tiny pieces of egg, his foot tapping on the stool bar, his impeccably shaved jawline—were suddenly clear. He *was* serious.

"Pai! Why would you want to settle down now? This is like, your prime of life!" I held my fork up in the air for emphasis.

He laughed. "Okay, *sixteen-year-old daughter.* In case you couldn't tell, I was forced to settle down a long time ago." I blinked. Because even though my dad never, ever complained about being a young dad, I always wondered about his regrets. How his need to keep abandoned, sad things might apply to me, too.

Pai kept talking. "Anyway. Kody's older than me by a little bit, and she's thinking about the future, too. The crowd's starting to settle down."

Every week there was a new wedding invitation or baby announcement in the mail. Our refrigerator was crowded with them. Script fonts letter-pressed into thick paper announcing some hip wedding or a giant newborn's face, its hands in mittens and its face always froglike and never cute. I guess I always thought that phase of my dad's life was over. The thought of Kody and him getting married one day . . . having a kid? It was too much for my brain to handle.

I changed the subject. "Well, be sure to drink a lot of merlots or whatever it is people do."

He laughed. "Thanks. Aren't you excited to have some privacy for once?" He paused, holding *his* fork in the air for a second. "Privacy for reading books and finishing your knitting home alone, that is."

"Ha ha." I took a sip of tea. "You know I don't know how to read."

He pulled his Dodgers cap down over his eyes. "Well, just knitting then."

I smiled. He wasn't saying it, but this was a big step. Pre-cafeteria fire he was cool with leaving me alone for a night or two. But post-fire, he had been more watchful than he had ever been in my life. Leaving me alone was a gesture—to show that I was regaining his trust.

My dad and Kody headed off for Santa Barbara shortly after. "Enjoy those tannins!" I yelled from the balcony, standing barefoot on the metal railing as I leaned over and watched them drive away.

After working the KoBra that day, I had the evening free. I picked up my phone to see what Patrick and Felix were up to. But my fingers hovered over the screen, and I ended up texting Rose.

Let me guess: you're brushing up on constitutional law tonight?

She immediately texted back: **Ha. Are you enjoying the heroin den?**

You took the joke too far

Too accurate?

Yeah I draw the line at doing drugs that require accessories for them

I waited a second before typing: **How did the dinner with the senator go?**

I was searching for a senatorial-looking emoji when another text popped up. Mãe.

No Tulum??? 😫 😟 😡 🌴 ☀️ 🍹

Shoot. I guess my dad did tell her. I texted back immediately: I'm working on it! We're doing good on the truck—he'll cave.

K k got it. Make your eyes like this 😍. Your dad's a sucker for that kinda stuff.

I wanted to agree, to LOL, but I realized my mom didn't actually know Pai at all anymore. Current Pai was no longer the doormat of the past. Then I noticed the barrage of texts from Rose updating me on the senator dinner. She was excited because it went well. I had settled into the sofa and was texting with her when someone knocked. Flo jumped off my lap and ran over to the entrance, her nose poking at the space under the door.

"Clara!"

Felix? What in the world.

I dragged myself to the door. "What are you doing here?" The words were out of my mouth before the door fully opened.

He was spiffed up—his thick hair tousled just so, smelling good, and wearing his tightest black jeans. "You're coming with us." I saw Patrick's car idling on the curb.

I nudged Flo out of the way with my foot so she wouldn't escape. "What? Where?"

"Some party. Come on, we barely see you anymore. I'll give you five minutes to get ready."

"What, I don't look good enough?" My arm swept over my ripped white tank top and knee-length sweat shorts.

He raised his eyebrows and shot me a wolfish grin. "You always look good, babe."

"God." Felix was full of moves, and two years ago I had fallen for *all* of them. "Give me a second." I ran upstairs and got dressed in record time. I remembered to grab my cell as I was headed out the door, sending Rose a text: **Want to do something fun for once?**

"So then if you think of it that way, Tom Cruise is basically a *wizard*, transcending time and space."

I stared at the guy in front of me, then wrapped my hands tighter around the warm bottle of beer I was holding. Rose and I had been talking to this conspiracy theorist about Tom Cruise at this house party for a solid five minutes.

The guy licked his lips nervously, his fair skin getting paler by the second. "So actually, if Cruise—"

"I have to pee," I said, handing my drink to him as I grabbed Rose by the arm.

"Wow, I thought people got more stable once they graduated high school," Rose said as we headed out of the living room toward the kitchen.

"Paranoid people exist at every age," I shouted to be heard over the live band. Patrick had some sort of sixth sense for parties with a high ratio of hot dudes in bands. It had been hard to persuade Rose to come out, but I promised her cute boys and she had met us fifteen minutes later. Too bad we had been stuck with Tom Cruise Whiz.

It was stuffy in the apartment, so we went searching for some air through the kitchen. It had terrible fluorescent overhead lighting that was a harsh contrast to the cave feeling of the living room. Rose and I skirted by a group of girls in various denim cutoffs and cropped tanks while a tall man in a felted hat lectured them on something or another. They looked bored to tears, some of them even on their phones.

As we walked by the opining guy, I slipped into him, knocking his beer into his pinstripe shirt. "Watch it!" he yelped as he jumped away from me and wiped at his shirt furiously.

"Oh no. So sorry," I said, holding up my hands apologetically. The group of girls scattered immediately. *You're welcome.*

Rose laughed. "That was some good sabotage, Shin." I resisted the urge to create further disruption, my prank itch temporarily scratched.

"Thanks, Carver." I found a sliding door that led us out onto the balcony, which was miraculously empty. Taking a deep breath of fresh air, I asked, "Are we a buddy-cop movie now?"

Rose took a sip of her Diet Coke, which I had managed to find for her deep in the recesses of the refrigerator. "Carver and Shin. We need to have like, moments of culture clash."

"I'll teach you how to use chopsticks while you fumble and curse the entire time," I said as I leaned against the railing.

The sliding door opened then. Felix.

"Hey. You guys hiding out here?"

I shrugged. "This party is full of the most unbearable dudes."

Felix plopped down into a dirty plastic chair. "I know. Found out it's some band's apartment."

"Figures."

"But Patrick's interested in some guy, so I think we're stuck for a while." He clinked his bottle on Rose's can. Patrick and Felix had been surprised when I told them Rose was coming, especially because they had always been integral to Project Make Rose's Life a Living Hell. But despite the initial awkwardness, everyone was being civil.

I leaned against the balcony railing and looked over at the CVS parking lot that was adjacent to us. "Isn't Patrick's new boyfriend going to have a problem with that?"

Felix laughed. "Define 'boyfriend.'"

I took a sip of beer. "Speaking of significant others, where's Cynthia?"

"She had to work tonight."

My stomach rumbled. "Let's go visit her!"

Felix rolled his eyes. "She can't give us free food."

"Where does she work?" Rose asked.

I interrupted Felix before he could answer. "Why not?!" Cynthia worked as a server at a burger place whose theme was literally "island stuff." And getting us the occasional free meal was one of her finer qualities.

"Her new boss is a total dick." He glanced at Rose. "She works at Island's."

"Well, I'm starving and this party sucks. You guys want to go find some food?"

Felix shrugged. "Sure."

I looked over at Rose, who downed the rest of her drink. "Okay," she said as she wiped off her mouth. I liked Game Rose.

A few minutes later, we left Patrick at the party with the dudes and headed out toward Sunset, where I could practically smell the tacos. My favorite truck, Cielo Tacos, was only a few blocks away. On the way over, Felix spent the entire time talking about Cynthia and the fight they'd just had. I tried my best to be attentive, but honestly it took every ounce of willpower not to just say, "Dump her already." They had the same fight every week: Felix wasn't spending enough time with her. When in reality, his life pretty much revolved around her every move. It was tedious. If this was what being in a serious relationship was like, count me the eff out. Rose was being nice and making the occasional sympathetic comment so that I didn't have to.

A line had already formed at the truck. As I pulled out my wallet to see if I had enough cash, a guy approached me with a flyer in hand. "Food truck competition this summer!" he said cheerfully.

"No thanks, man," Felix said with a wave.

But I grabbed it. "Thanks."

The glossy card read *AUGUST 11—ANNUAL LA FOOD TRUCK COMPETITION* in hot-pink scrawl, the text laid over a photo of swaying palm trees. Under it:

The biggest competition in town! Winner takes home $100K. ALL trucks eligible, sign up on our website. Or just show up and enjoy some choice foods and local music.

Whoa. 100K?! Pai thought opening a restaurant was far off—like after I was married with children far off. Maybe it could be much sooner.

"What's that?" Rose asked, poking her head over my shoulder to read the flyer.

I handed it to her. "There's a food truck competition in August and—"

"ONE HUNDRED THOUSAND DOLLARS?" she screamed.

People were staring at us, so I stepped in closer to her and snatched the flyer out of her hand. "Dude, have some *chill*."

"Your dad *needs* to enter this!" she said, her voice back to normal decibel levels.

I started to nod but was struck by an idea. "What if we entered the KoBra but didn't tell him? It would be the *best* surprise if we won!"

Skepticism wrinkled her forehead. "Don't tell him? At all?"

"Yeah!" I was getting excited at the idea of hitting my dad with this kind of killer surprise. "Can you even imagine getting a check for that kind of money?"

Rose nodded slowly. "I mean, that would be so cool. And honestly, we're good at this now."

"I have complete faith in us," I said firmly.

That's when I noticed Felix staring at me. Arms folded, eyebrows raised. "What?" I asked, my arms also crossed over my chest, the tanned limbs protecting me against his judgment.

"It's just . . . wow. I've never seen you care about your dad's truck before."

Embarrassment flared through me. Felix always had this way of pointing out when people were trying too hard or being uncool. I had never been on the receiving end of it before.

"So?" I pushed by him to order my tacos.

"Nothing, jeez!" He held his hands up, all "Hey, now!" I hated when he did this. Made me feel like I was overreacting when he had clearly set me up for it. Typical boy gaslighting crap.

I folded the flyer in half and tucked it into my back pocket.

When I got home that night, I opened the laptop I shared with my dad. The apartment was dark except for the blue glow of the screen.

Folding my legs under me, I knelt down on the living room rug and stared at the application form I had filled out, the cursor hovering over the Submit button. A nervous flutter in my stomach made me pause. But then I imagined Pai's reaction when we won. How I could do something for my dad, for once. Fast-forward his dreams.

I clicked the Submit button.

CHAPTER 15

ON MONDAY MORNING WHEN I GOT TO THE commissary, Rose was lying down on the hood of the truck, sunglasses on, limbs splayed. "Good morning," I said, tapping her foot with an iced coffee I'd bought for her.

At glacial speed, she sat up with a groan. "Morning."

"What's wrong?" I handed her the drink.

She took the world's longest sip before answering. "I just had a two-hour barre this morning."

"*Two hours?* That means . . . you've been awake since, like, four a.m.?"

"Yup." She swiveled her long neck slowly, touching her ear to her shoulder, then dropping her head back to stare up at the sky. "I want to die."

"Why do you do this to yourself?"

Bringing her head back up, she took off her sunglasses and looked at me. "I love it, I guess."

What was it like to love something so much you woke up at four a.m. on your summer break to do it?

We got into the truck and buckled ourselves in—me in the driver's seat as usual. Rose glanced over at me. "Oh, I forgot to ask at the party. I heard you talking to Patrick about a trip to Tulum?"

I steered the truck toward the freeway. "Yeah, a vacation with my mom."

"Adrian's letting you go?"

As we waited for the light to turn green on the ramp, I drummed my fingers on the steering wheel. The morning was already hot, and I couldn't tell whether the dampness under my arms was from that or from the mere mention of Tulum. I stared at the little sign that said ONE CAR PER GREEN. It felt unnecessarily aggressive today.

When the light turned green, I stepped on the accelerator with force—making the truck lurch forward. A couple of metal bowls rolled around noisily in the cupboards. "Not exactly. It's still more than a month away, though, and I have plenty of time to prove my worthiness. He'll have to let me go."

Rose didn't react.

I took a breath. "I never get to see her. They don't get along, and I know my dad uses any excuse to undermine our relationship. He doesn't approve of her life choices."

Rose raised her eyebrows. "What? I doubt he tries to undermine your relationship. I mean, he's raising you; maybe he just feels protective?"

"I know, but . . . it's complicated."

A few loaded seconds passed. Rose was one of those people who could never feign indifference; her do-gooderly intentions emanated from her pores. She said, carefully, "When did your parents get divorced?"

Divorced. That was an interesting way to put it. "They were never married. My mom left my dad when I was four." The words came out before I could stop them. "I mean, she didn't just, like, *leave* with a suitcase overnight. It was a mutual decision for them to separate."

"Oh! Wow. That's a long time ago."

Weaving through traffic, I glanced at my rearview mirror before replying. "She and my dad met in high school—that's when she got pregnant, actually. They were both eighteen."

"Yeah, your dad looks way young."

"He is. They met in Brazil. Making my dad Korean Brazilian. American? Not sure. A lot of things. He was born there, his parents emigrated from Korea back in the day. My mom's also Korean Brazilian."

Rose nodded. "Hence the KoBra's fusion menu."

"Right. Hence. Anyway, after my mom got pregnant, my parents decided to move to LA. More economic opportunity, fresh starts and all. They thought they'd get married and raise me here. As an American citizen."

"Their families were cool with that?"

"Not exactly. My mom's parents pretty much disowned her. My dad's didn't love it, but they couldn't do much since my parents were both eighteen by then."

"Wow."

We drove through downtown, passing a solid line of bumper-to-bumper traffic on the opposite side. "Yeah. Dramatic. So they moved here, I was born, and then . . ." I trailed off, gripping the steering wheel. "Then, my mom went back to São Paulo before they ever got married."

I kept my eyes on the road, but I could *feel* Rose's stare. "She . . . moved back to *Brazil*?"

"She couldn't handle LA. I mean, it was a different country, and she was a teenage mom. Could you blame her for freaking out?"

Pity unfurled from Rose like ribbons. "I guess not," she said quietly. Even though I knew that Rose Carver, even if she got pregnant this very second, would stick to whatever plan she made until the end. But eighteen-year-old Mãe was not Rose Carver.

"How often do you see her?" she asked.

Our exit was coming up, and I pulled the truck into the right-hand lane. "It depends. She has to come to LA now and then because of her job. So that works out—I've seen her more in the past few years than ever. But it's been like six months, so I *really* want to go to Tulum."

"Six months! Holy crap. I can't imagine not seeing my mom

for that long," Rose said. Then she touched my arm. "Sorry. Not judging."

I pulled the truck onto the off-ramp. "No worries, I didn't take it that way. I know my family's not normal."

She laughed deeply. "*No one's* family is normal."

I drove into the office plaza. "Get out of here, your family is so blessedly normal."

After I parked, Rose got up and stood next to me. "Thanks for sharing that."

I took my seat belt off and fiddled with it for a second. "Um, you're welcome. And, hey. That was fun at the party. I'm glad you came out." We had worked together on Sunday after the party but hadn't talked about it yet.

"You're welcome," she answered primly. We made eye contact and cracked up.

"I mean, really I should thank you," she said. "As you can tell, I don't go out that much. I just spend so much time with my family. I forget I can go and have like . . . *friends*?"

I shook my head. "Sad."

"More fodder for our YouTube channel."

"You really need to stop saying things like 'fodder.' "

After counting out the change in the cashbox, Rose opened the order window. She glanced outside, then did a double take. "Whoa. Look at Hamlet today."

I peered over her shoulder. He was doing his usual embarrassing acrobatics with the sign. But he was dressed up. Wearing slim-fitting navy pants, a light blue button-up, and a gray-and-white striped tie. A tie. In ninety-degree weather.

"Who died?" I wondered out loud.

Rose elbowed me. "Rude. Also, he's wearing blue, not black."

"Yeah, but . . . why would you wear that?"

Before she could answer, Hamlet dropped the sign onto the grass and jogged over to the coffee cart. He ducked down away from view and then popped back up, holding two drinks.

I found myself smoothing back my hair as he walked over. Something about him looking so snazzy made me feel like a bag lady.

"Hey, Hamlet," Rose said cheerfully, taking her drink from him. I reached for mine, too, and my fingers brushed against his. "Thanks."

"You're welcome," he said, his eyes meeting mine for a second. I blinked and took a huge gulp of my iced mocha.

Rose looked at us, eyes twinkling. Oh no. She took a sip of her drink. "So, you look nice today."

Hamlet looked down at his outfit and put his hands on his hips. "Oh. Yeah? Thanks."

"What's the occasion?"

He looked up at me first, then looked back at Rose. "Well. Funny you should ask."

My mouth went dry.

"One second!" he said, then ran off toward the coffee cart again. Rose and I looked at each other in confusion.

He came back with his hands held behind him. Rose and I stared. After an eternity, he cleared his throat. "Clara."

Rose's eyes widened when she looked at me. I choked on my mocha. "Yeah?" I finally managed to squeak out.

He whipped out a bouquet of flowers and held them up toward the order window. "Will you let me take you out on a date this weekend?"

For a second, all that existed was that bouquet of light pink roses. Fragrant, extravagantly wrapped in pink-tinted cellophane, tied together with a thin white grosgrain ribbon.

Then I felt a poke in my arm. I blinked and looked up to see both Rose and Hamlet staring at me.

There was no way. I mean, this was *Hamlet*. No matter how cute the dude, he was *not* someone I would date. Like ever. I opened my mouth, ready with some kind of nice but firm rejection, when Rose kicked my ankle, out of Hamlet's view. Her eyes were threatening to murder me.

Jesus.

Hamlet was starting to sweat. He wiped his forehead with his crisp shirt sleeve. And that little gesture softened something in me.

"Sure." The word slipped out so easily that I almost gasped. I accepted the bouquet of flowers.

Nervousness instantly gave way to pure sunshine and rainbows. Hamlet grinned, his sharp canines sparkling. "Okay! Awesome! Here's my number!" He slid a scrap of paper over to me. It was creased and soft, as if it had been sitting in his pocket for a week. "Let me know what day works for you!"

Someone coughed loudly behind him, and Hamlet turned around to see a line of customers. "Oh! Okay, see you guys later!" Then he high-fived the guy behind him and ran off to his coffee cart.

I held the bouquet in my hands and glared at Rose. "Not a word."

She laughed and started taking orders.

CHAPTER 16

BY SATURDAY AFTERNOON, I HAD BITTEN MY NAILS down to nubs. Hamlet and I had agreed to have dinner, and for some reason I was nervous.

Nervous for a date with Hamlet Wong. Like, what was happening, universe? One, I'd been on many dates. No big deal. In my experience, guys hardly took the time to swipe on deodorant, so why in God's name should *we* sweat it? I barely bothered shaving my legs.

Two, this was Hamlet. I wasn't even into the guy. Biggest dork I knew second to Rose, and he's crushing on *me*, therefore this date would already begin with my having the upper hand.

And yet.

Because Rose and I had the day off, it was one of my dad's

solo shifts on the truck, and I was whiling the morning away in front of the TV with Flo grooming herself in my lap. Continuing my life's goal of watching every episode of *Supernatural*, the show that would not die.

My phone vibrated with a text from Rose: **What are you wearing tonight?**

I looked down at my sweats cutoffs and black tank covered in Flo's hair and Doritos crumbs.

Probably what I'm wearing now

I took a selfie with Flo and sent it to her.

Is that the same tank top you wear every single day?

How dare you this is my weekend tank

Isn't Hamlet taking you somewhere nice? You need to wear something cute for once in your life.

Cat hair necklace doesn't qualify as cute?

Sure, if you want to die alone.

That pretty much is my dream

I cackled and ate another handful of chips while she took a few seconds to text back.

Do you want help picking out your outfit?

Just say it—you're bored and need something to do

Actually, I'm wrapping up this meeting for the Future Leaders of Los Angeles and could head over after grabbing some clothes from my house.

Shaking my head, I texted back: **Come over then**

* * *

Rose arrived on my doorstep holding an armful of clothes.

"What *is* all that?" I asked as she stepped inside.

"Clothes befitting a first date," she said, her voice muffled by the pile in her face. She kicked off her strappy cobalt blue heels and dropped the clothes onto an armchair, making Flo jump.

At the sight of Flo, Rose let out an ungodly squeal and dropped to her knees. "Look at the kitty!" she said in a voice I had never heard come out of her mouth before.

Flo stared at her from under the coffee table, not blinking, her striped tail flicking to the side.

Rose beckoned her with clucking sounds, holding out her fingers. "Come here, kitty!" She glanced up at me, as I stood dumbfounded. "I wish we could have a cat, but my brother's allergic."

I watched her as she continued to cluck and make kissy noises. "So clearly this is the first cat you have ever seen in your entire life."

"Ha-ha." She stood up reluctantly after Flo made no move to come closer. Instead Flo sat there like a stone, staring at some random spot between Rose and the sofa.

I riffled through the pile of clothes. "Did it ever occur to you that you're like seven feet taller than me?"

"It did. That's why it's mostly dresses."

I held up a frothy mint green dress with white polka dots on it. "I see. Also, I'm not a cartoon mouse."

"Listen, anything's better than your situation right now." Rose gestured toward me with fluttery hands. "And that dress is super flattering on."

"I don't care if it magically gives me a Kardashian butt, this dress isn't my style."

Rose grumbled as she pushed me aside to look through the dresses. "You're incredibly stubborn. It's fun to be around." She held up a black dress with lace sleeves. "Try this one."

I appraised it skeptically. It was short and looked like it would be super tight around my thighs. I didn't mind my body, liked it in fact, but I also knew that I didn't want to spend all night worrying about thigh bondage.

"Just try it on!" She tossed it at me with exasperation.

I took it with a scowl. "Fine."

I was pulling off my tank when she yelped and spun around. "Clara!"

"What?" I tossed the tank onto the floor and pulled the dress on over my head. "Are you seriously squeamish about seeing me in a bra? Aren't you a dancer?"

Her back still turned, she answered with her hands on her hips. "Yeah, but I *know* those girls and we're in a changing room. Give me a little advance warning, I don't like to see random people's body parts all willy-nilly!"

I stuck my arms through the sleeves, my face hidden within the folds of the dress. "I'm not a *stranger*. Haven't you ever had *girlfriends* before?" When I popped my head out, I saw Rose turn around with a strange expression. "What?" I asked.

She shrugged. "I haven't."

"Haven't what?"

"Had girlfriends." She looked down at her nails, her snobby arched eyebrows at odds with her words.

I let that settle over me, thinking back to the Rose Carver I'd known since middle school. She was always in charge of stuff, in lots of organizations . . . but had there ever been a best friend or a group that I could actually connect her to?

When I thought about it, when was the last time *I'd* had a best girlfriend? Veronica Souza in sixth grade. We drifted apart when she went to private school in seventh grade, and soon after I had befriended Patrick and Felix. "I haven't had a 'bestie' in forever, too. Been hanging with my goons for too long," I said, tugging the skirt of the dress over my thighs.

She nodded. "They were nice." We both knew they weren't "nice," but I let the generic compliment pass. "The thing is, I kind of tell my mom everything. So I've never really needed a best friend."

Again, we both knew that was a weird statement, but I didn't bat an eyelash. "I can see that."

"I know you think I'm weird."

"Well, of course." I held up my arms, showing her the dress.

"That looks good on you," she said.

I looked down. The dress actually fit me pretty well and was comfortable despite the tightness. "Yeah, it's not bad."

Rose wouldn't let me get away with trying on just one, though. She even had me match shoes and hair styles to different outfits. I honestly couldn't remember the last time I had leaned in so hard-core to girlie stuff like this, and it was fun. I felt a giddiness settle into me and actually found myself saying, "That's so cute," about a freaking tube of lip gloss.

Finally, we settled on the perfect dress. It was a loose, short navy blue tank dress made out of comfy jersey material that felt like my favorite old T-shirt. Because the style was meant to show a peep of your bra, Rose made me trade my ratty black one for a bright lacy fuchsia one I had buried deep in my dresser.

I plopped down onto the sofa from the exhaustion of our makeover montage. "I'm starved."

"Not done yet."

When I glanced over at Rose, she was holding some kind of kettle-looking thing with a long chord. "What is *that*?"

"A portable steamer. I'm going to steam your dress." She hung the dress up on a sturdy curtain rod. I opened my mouth to make fun of the portable steamer but shut it. At some point, the mocking grounds were just too fertile, even for me.

"Should I order a pizza?" I asked while watching her meticulously steam the dress.

She glanced at me over her shoulder. "Oh. Um, is that okay? I wasn't sure if I was invited to eat here."

"Huh? Invited? You're already here." It hit me then, the depths of Rose's friendship void. Had she never just hung out, with no plans or schedules? "If you don't have anywhere to go, that is."

The steamer sputtered its last bits of steam and Rose shut it off. "No, I mean, I have plans later but not now."

I was confused by that answer. "So . . . yes, you want to get pizza?" The discomfort continued to weigh down the room.

"Sure." Phew. The most awkwardly earned pizza ever.

After I ordered through an app on my phone ("You have a Domino's *app*?" she asked. "I'm VIP," I answered, a fact that drove my dad and his fancy-pizza feels crazy), we sat around my living room, Rose spending most of the time trying to lure Flo over to her. Some progress was being made. Flo was now lying a foot away from Rose, licking her paws.

"When is Hamlet picking you up?" Rose asked as she lay on her belly, her hand reached out toward Flo, holding a small pile of treats. Flo sniffed the air for a second, her eyes focused on Rose, but the magical cat moment left as quickly as it came.

"I forget."

Rose looked up at me. "What! You don't remember what time?"

"Yeah, it was evening-ish."

"Oh my God." She sat up and pushed a lock of hair out of her eyes. "Check right now what time."

"It's fine! It's only like noon."

"First, that is alarming because it's two p.m. Second, what if you're wrong and he's picking you up in like thirty minutes?"

The doorbell rang, and I scrambled off the sofa. "Pizza time."

"Or it's Hamlet because your date is actually now."

I laughed. "You're nuts." It was the pizza, of course.

We settled around the coffee table with paper towels instead of plates. I folded a slice in half and took a huge, cheesy bite, watching Rose nibble hers, eating the pepperoni off her slice first.

"Are you nervous?" Rose asked as she held out a bit of pepperoni toward Flo. Flo bolted over and sniffed it, taking a little lick. Rose looked ecstatic when Flo took it from her, but then frowned when she just dropped it on the rug and walked off.

I laughed. "Don't take it personally. She only likes her own boring cat food, kibble from Costco. The finest palate." I took a large gulp of soda. "So, yeah, I am a *little* nervous about this date."

"I'm always super nervous before first dates," she said, picking up the abandoned pepperoni and wrapping it in a paper towel. "Sometimes normal, perfectly nice guys turn into total jerks on dates."

Wouldn't have taken Rose for a dating expert. "Do you go on a lot of dates?"

She shrugged, her shoulders lifting slightly. "Kind of."

"For someone with an Awkward Friendship YouTube channel, that's surprising."

Her eyebrows arched. "I might be awkward with girls, but I've got the whole boy thing *down*."

"I guess it helps when you look like *you*."

Rose took a sip of Coke. "Thank you." That was so very Rose Carver of her, but there was something refreshing about her just accepting a compliment. I had a hard time doing it—my girl-instinct was to deflect it, something that I was always working against.

"Are you dating anyone now?" I asked.

She sighed—the long-suffering sigh of a woman in hot demand. "Not dating, but seeing like three guys. I dunno, they're kind of . . . whatever."

"*Three?* Damn."

"Like I said, they're all whatever. But I like to keep my options open. I refuse to date anyone seriously right now."

"Distractions you don't need?"

She nodded. "Exactly." Eschewing the bottle of sriracha, Rose reached for the Tabasco instead and doused her slice of pizza with it. Legit. Before taking a bite, she looked over at me, suddenly shy again. "Have you had a boyfriend before?"

"Yep."

"Like, a lot of them?"

"Yep."

"How many?" Rose was so riveted that she didn't notice Flo slowly making her way toward her.

I thought about it for a second. "Um, I don't know, five?"

"FIVE? You've had five boyfriends?!"

"Don't judge!"

"I'm not! I'm just impressed." Flo sniffed Rose's foot. Rose still didn't notice. "I think I remember some of them . . . you were with Leo Nguyen this year, weren't you?"

A shudder passed through me. "Unfortunately. I found out he didn't brush his teeth."

Rose screamed, sending Flo shooting off to the kitchen. "Gross!"

"Yeah, I don't even want to . . . I mean, we made out so many times . . ."

She laughed so hard that she choked. I pounded her back and handed her a drink.

"Thanks," she gasped, waving her hand at me. "Anyway, wow. Totally gross."

"Agreed. So, what about you? Have you had boyfriends? I don't remember any rumors of you dating anyone at Elysian anyway." It was strange to know someone for so many years and not know them at all, I realized. The bulk of my Rose Carver knowledge was like the news feed of someone's life—only the obvious, visible stuff.

"Not really? I date guys, but never longer than a few weeks at most." She looked around for Flo, who was now lapping up water at her bowl in the kitchen. "I've never liked anyone enough. I like them at first. But something happens when I spend more time with them."

"You're over it?"

"Exactly. I don't know . . . when they like me too much I stop liking them?" Suddenly Flo plopped into Rose's lap. Rose's eyes grew wide, and she froze.

I raised my eyebrows. "See, Flo gets you. You only start liking them when they stop paying attention to you."

Rose laughed and pulled Flo to her chest, which made her yowl and jump out of Rose's arms—flouncing away with a swish of her finicky tail. "So . . . five guys. You didn't like any of them enough to keep them around longer than . . ."

"Six months," I finished for her. "My longest relationship. With Felix Rafael Benavides, believe it or not."

"Oh, I remember when you guys dated. You were like our high school's Brangelina."

I snorted. "Please. He wishes he were Brad. Anyway . . . yeah. I dunno, when it gets boring and too real, I bail. Who needs that? We're in high school."

"But you like boys enough to keep wanting them around," she said with a waggle of her eyebrows.

I waggled mine back. "Well, *yeah*." We both laughed.

"I can't even imagine liking a guy enough to call him my boyfriend, so you're preaching to the choir," she said, taking a sip of her drink. She looked at me. "But you know, why is it that we're supposed to feel bad about this part of our lives? Like, if we don't have a boyfriend, we're loser weirdos. If we date too much, we're 'sluts.'"

I chewed my fourth slice of pizza thoughtfully. "Maybe the truth is . . . nothing is weird about dating in high school. Everyone is different, and we need to stop reading so many magazines giving us dated-ass relationship advice."

She held up her cup. "Hear, hear!"

"Rose. Stop saying stuff like that."

"Cheers to that."

I threw a Parmesan cheese packet at her.

CHAPTER 17

AFTER ROSE LEFT (MAKING SURE I VERIFIED THE TIME of my date), I cleaned up lunch and took a shower. Confession: I hate taking showers. They're just so much time and effort. I have the thickest hair on the planet, and it takes hours to dry.

Once I was dressed, I swiped on some eyeliner—making a cat eye with a little swoop at the end. Then I grabbed a glittery teal eyeshadow and extended the end of the swoop. I blinked and looked in the mirror. There. Properly fancy.

I heard my dad's voice echo through the hallway. "Clara! He's here!"

Why my dad had to get home in time for my date was beyond me. Cosmic timing. I grabbed my mini black leather backpack and headed downstairs.

I stopped in my tracks. Oh boy. There was Hamlet at the front door, grasping yet another bouquet of flowers. My dad was holding the door open, and they both looked up at me at the same time.

"What is this, some teen movie?" I cracked, suddenly feeling so nervous that I almost tripped down the stairs. I saved it with a little jig, but their weird expressions confirmed that it was not a smooth move.

I stopped in front of my dad and pointed at him. "No speeches, no warnings, no anything. None of that paternalistic stuff."

My dad grinned and leaned against the doorway. "I'm paternal by biology, Shorty."

"You know what I mean," I said while pulling on my sandals, avoiding Hamlet.

Suddenly a bunch of flowers were in my line of vision and I sprang up, knocking them out of Hamlet's hands. "Sorry!" I bent over to pick them up at the same time he did, and we bonked heads. Ugh. What was *happening* to me? I was never this flustered! Hamlet managed to re-create the bouquet and held it out to me again, a lock of hair falling into his eyes.

They were a spray of white snapdragons. "Thank you. They're pretty," I said as I took them from him.

He flushed deeply, red creeping up from the collar of his crisp, white button-down shirt. The sleeves were rolled up, and the shirt fit him perfectly, paired with dark blue shorts that hit his knees. He looked like he was about to make an Asian cameo in a Nicholas Sparks movie. (Did they have Asian cameos?)

After I got the flowers in a vase, I rushed out the door with Hamlet, waving at my dad. "See you, Pai."

Before the door shut, I heard him holler, "Come home in time for breakfast!"

Now it was *my* turn to blush. What even. I couldn't make eye contact with Hamlet. I just flew down the apartment stairs.

When we reached the sidewalk, I stopped abruptly. "Did you drive?" I asked.

A car beeped in the street. "Yup," Hamlet said as he walked briskly toward the sound.

When we reached his car, I held up my hands. "Whoa, mama." The car in front of us was a slick white Lexus. "*This* is your car?!"

He held the passenger door open, pressing his lips together. "Yeah. Um, my parents overcompensate for not spending enough time with me."

As I slipped into the leather interior, I thought about how at odds Coffee Kiosk Hamlet was with this car. Who knew he was some rich kid? It annoyed me, and I felt uneasier with each passing second until he got into the driver's seat. I was never comfortable with people who had a lot of money. I knew I shouldn't care, but it was just one of those things.

"So, um, I didn't want to assume you would eat where I picked, so I made a few different reservations," Hamlet said, placing his hands on the wheel but not yet starting the car. "They are Three Leaf, Café Lola, or Hawkins & Post."

My lips curved up into a little smile. The trifecta of hipster restaurants. Hamlet trying his hardest. "Um, I guess we could try Café Lola? I haven't been to Highland Park in a while."

"All right, Café Lola it is!" he announced cheerfully as he headed toward the 110. Highland Park was north of us, between here and Pasadena, where the office park was. He tapped the steering wheel. "I've heard good things about this place."

"From who?"

"From . . . people."

I opened my window, letting in a gust of warm summer evening air. "Like real people you know or the Internet?"

He laughed, all ease. "Okay. I just read the Yelp reviews." Then I saw him shut off the AC with a near-imperceptible flick of his wrist.

"Oh, I didn't know you had the AC on, sorry," I said, rolling up the window.

"That's okay! The night air feels good!" Hamlet said, rolling down his own window.

Discomfited by his niceness, I opened my window halfway as some kind of awkward compromise. We passed the next couple of minutes in strained silence. Then Hamlet picked up his phone and swiped a few times and music blasted, startling me.

"Sorry!" He immediately lowered the volume.

After a few seconds, I felt this irritation creeping in as I watched Arroyo Park flash by my window. What in the world was annoying me so much? Then a male voice screeched.

I cringed. "Are we listening to IMAGINE DRAGONS?"

Hamlet grinned, glancing over at me. "Yeah! Aren't they great?"

"Um, yes." I tried my best to keep my voice neutral.

His smile faltered. "Well, I can change it," he said, fumbling for the phone while he kept his eyes on the road.

You are a butt, Clara. I took the phone from him. "Here, it's fine. You should concentrate on driving. Sorry, I've got the worst poker face." I snuck a glance at Hamlet, his profile lit from the side in two-second intervals by the streetlamps. His eyelashes were short but insanely thick, his nose straight, his mouth kind of perfect. And at the moment, he was chewing on his bottom lip, brow furrowed.

Pretty sure I was already ruining this date. "So, um, where do you live again?"

"San Gabriel." His eyes stayed on the road—the wild curves of the 110 were barely lit by the headlights.

I raised my eyebrows. "Whoa. The SGV. Pretty far out there."

"Yup."

Monosyllabic and Sullen Hamlet was unnerving. "I guess there's a lot of good Chinese food, though." *No duh, Clara.* The San Gabriel Valley had a big Asian population.

His expression basically relayed the same thing.

"We could use better Chinese food in Echo Park." The desperation was palpable. "Also Korean food. Actually, that's kind of my dad's dream—opening up a good Korean place in our neighborhood. Although, yeah, we're so close to K-Town that it seems ridiculous. But, it'll be like the KoBra, Korean with Brazilian influences." I found myself unable to stop speaking, wanting to fix the jerkiness of my behavior. Again, something I didn't usually care about, but suddenly did with Hamlet nearby.

My rambling worked.

"That sounds like a really good idea," Hamlet said, a little cautiously. "Your dad's a great cook; he could do it."

And while *I* knew my dad was good at what he did, hearing Hamlet say it out loud warmed me up from the inside. "Thanks," I said. Then flushed. "I mean, not that you were complimenting *me*, but you know what I mean . . ."

Hamlet laughed. "I love how you always have to point out awkward moments."

Jeez. "Wow, and you like to point out stuff in general."

"Yeah, I do!"

I couldn't help laughing, and he looked over at me with the biggest, most genuine grin I have ever seen on another human. Sheesh, this guy. We got to the restaurant and were greeted by the hottest woman I have ever seen in my life. I am a straight girl, and my jaw dropped as she led us to our table, her long black hair swishing above a tiny leather miniskirt. I glanced at Hamlet, expecting a drop of drool to be hanging from his mouth, but he was looking around the restaurant, oblivious to the supermodel in front of us.

Point one.

Hot Hostess sat us down at a tiny marble table, like one you'd find in a Parisian café or something. Our knees were touching. Hamlet made a few not-so-subtle attempts to space us out a bit more, but he hit the back of his chair on the one behind him—which was unfortunate because the woman in it was wearing a giant hat, which toppled off.

"Sorry!" he said, reaching down to pick it up. She yanked it out of his hands and turned around with a terse little "God!"

Hamlet flushed.

Yeah, I don't think so. The nervousness of this date melted away when faced with an opportunity to annoy someone who deserved it. I pulled a little leaf off the succulent on our table and tossed it over Hamlet's head so it landed on the brim of the woman's hat. Hamlet's eyes widened. I grabbed a small handful of leaves off the plant (sorry, guy, but you're tough, you'll recover) and tossed them one by one onto her hat. It was dark enough in there that neither she nor her friends noticed.

"Can I take your drink order?" A server popped up next to us, and I tucked my handful of leaves under the table. Hamlet let out a snort of laughter, and the server was unamused.

Hamlet fumbled for the menu. "Oh, let me see if . . ."

"I'm assuming no alcohol?" Unamused Server interrupted.

"Actually, lots of it," I said with a wink.

Still unamused. "Do you have an ID?"

"Yes, I do. I am a citizen of the United States."

Hamlet stammered, "Ah, ha-ha. Um, we'll start with water, thank you."

The server shot me a dirty look before leaving our table.

When I looked over at Hamlet, his head was dropped into his hands. I cleared my throat. "Sorry, this is what I'm like in public."

But when he looked up, I was surprised to see he was smiling. "You're so funny."

Again, just . . . announcing thoughts here. I reached for the menu so that I didn't have to respond. As I strained my eyes to read in the dimly lit room (a tiny tea candle was the only light at our table), Hamlet's phone rang.

He glanced down at it and looked up at me apologetically. "One sec, it's my grandmother."

Oh, a casual grandma call during a date. No biggie. He talked in a low voice, but I caught snippets of worried conversation.

I glanced back down at the menu. Everything was kind of expensive. I checked out the appetizers to see if they were any cheaper. Hm, the citrus salad or *literally anything else* for dinner? Choices, choices.

"Hey."

I glanced up to see Hamlet with an actual frown on his face. "What's up?" I asked uneasily.

"Sorry, but would you mind changing the date to . . . dinner at my grandparents'?"

Would I mind doing *what*? My face must have said it all, because he looked down. "Ah, never mind. Sorry, I think we'll have to do this another time. I've gotta get over there right now."

"Is everything all right?" I asked.

He sighed. "Probably. I don't know. My grandpa's grumpy because he's been sick a few days and insists on going out when he shouldn't. My grandma wants me home to distract him."

And I don't know whether it was the little smile or the worry in his eyes at odds with that smile that made me say, "Sure. Let's go there, then."

He gaped at me. "Really?"

"Yeah. This place gives me hives, anyway."

He laughed and scooted his chair out so quickly that he bonked into the lady again. Before she could say anything, he tucked his chair back in and said, "Sorry. Nice hat."

We rushed out of there, laughing.

CHAPTER 18

WHEN WE PULLED UP TO HAMLET'S GRANDPARENTS' house, I took in the suburban-ness of it all. The street was wide, clean, and flanked by uniform Aleppo pines and streetlamps. Everything glowed a bit pink and orange as the sun set, light bouncing off the dramatic range of mountains behind the neatly lined tract homes.

The San Gabriel Valley was almost as far east of LA as you could get. Everywhere in this valley you saw the San Gabriel Mountains, and it was probably the prettiest view in this otherwise concrete landscape.

Hamlet parked in the wide driveway. The yard and house were tidy, the lawn brown and dead like every other lawn by July. How had I even ended up here, at Hamlet's *grandparents'* house?

I didn't know what I was expecting on a first date with Hamlet, but it sure wasn't this.

As we headed toward the front door, Hamlet stopped to check the mail. Then he used his own set of keys to let us in. I looked at him curiously as we took off our shoes in the foyer. "You have the keys to your grandparents' place?"

He slipped off his Nikes. "Yeah, because I live with them?"

Oh.

"Hamlet! Hamlet, is that you?" A woman's voice echoed through the house, which smelled delicious. I sniffed the air. Sichuan peppers and sesame oil. And lamb?

"Yeah, I'm here!" he shouted back, then glanced at me. "I brought my friend!"

"Dinner's almost ready. Come over here!" Her voice came from around the corner and when we followed it, we landed right in the kitchen. His grandmother was at the stove, sautéing food in a large, nearly flat frying pan. She looked anywhere from fifty to seventy years old (Asian genes always hiding your true age!), small and sturdy with black hair tied in a low ponytail. She wore maroon track pants and a loose T-shirt that said STOP DRUNK DRIVING with an illustration of a cracked rearview mirror.

"Give me a small bowl," she said with her left arm extended, not even looking up at us.

Hamlet opened a cupboard and handed her a porcelain bowl. "Nainai, this is Clara."

She used the bowl as a ladle, scooping up some food in the

pan and sniffing it. "This is probably perfect." She looked at me. "Clara, try it and tell me if it's perfect."

Her English was precise, and her eyes shrewd as she watched me take the bowl. I glanced inside to see little pieces of meat with green onions and peppers. "Toothpick lamb?" I asked.

She looked impressed. "Yes, good job." She looked me up and down. "But you're not Chinese. Korean?"

I nodded before picking up a piece of perfectly charred lamb and popping it into my mouth. The taste of cumin and peppers instantly hit. *Mmmm.* After I finished chewing, I said, "Yes, I am. Well, my grandparents are from there. My parents grew up in Brazil."

She waved her hand in the air. "That's nice. How's the lamb?"

"So good!" I gave her a thumbs-up. "And I've had the lamb at Sichuan Dreams."

"Pft. That place sucks."

I choked. Hamlet ran across the kitchen to grab me a glass of water. I gulped it gratefully. "Sichuan Dreams doesn't suck!" I gasped. "Beloved food critic Stephen Fitch loves it, and everyone says it's the most authentic Sichuan in the city."

"Are those people *from* the Sichuan province? Because guess what, my family *is*!" She put her hands on her little hips and glared at me.

I frowned. "Well, it's *still good*."

"Clara, did your Brazilian parents not teach you to respect your elders?"

Hamlet swiveled toward her. "Oh my God. *Nainai.*"

She waved her hand at him dismissively. "This one's tough, she doesn't care."

I shrugged. "It's true. But also, my dad taught me to stick up for what I believe in. And I believe in Sichuan Dreams."

Hamlet's grandma rolled her eyes dramatically, turning back toward the stove. "Give me a break, that's the problem with you American kids. You think all your opinions matter. So annoying."

I laughed. "We *are* annoying." When I glanced over at Hamlet to see if he agreed, he was staring at me. A small smile hovering over his lips, eyes focused on me and only me.

Was it just me, or was this kitchen getting a bit too warm?

He glanced over at his grandmother then. "Whatever, Nai-nai. You're American, too. She was born here," he said to me.

"You think being born here seventy years ago is the same as being born here sixteen years ago, child? Stop bothering me and go check on Yeye. He wants to clean out the rain gutters with that back and those knees. Rain gutters in *July*!" She poked Hamlet with a long-handled wooden spoon. "Anyway, go tell him a story or something. He needs to rest if it kills him."

I was still giggling when I followed Hamlet upstairs. His grandfather was lying down in a spacious bedroom with high ceilings and sliding doors leading to a balcony. It was sparsely furnished, with a luxurious Persian rug and two large Chinese landscape paintings.

He was playing video games in bed when we walked in. On a huge TV that could be seen from space.

"Hi, Yeye." Hamlet bounded into the room and flopped down on the bed, making his grandfather groan and pause his game with a little *beep-boop* sound. "I brought my friend Clara to hang out."

His grandfather looked up at me with a smile. "Hi, Clara. Fun first date, huh?" Unlike Hamlet's grandma, his English was slightly accented. "Sorry you were forced to come here *unnecessarily*. I know Hamlet was looking forward to this."

Hamlet kept his eyes on his grandpa, his face a mask of *keep cool*. "Anyway. Why are you insisting on cleaning rain gutters? Nainai's about to put a tracker on you."

"You know I like to drive her crazy," he said with a wink.

Were Hamlet's grandparents *me*?

He continued, sitting up straighter. "It's not like I'm dying. Our rain gutters are *packed*. What if we have a summer rain?"

There was a second of silence before we all cracked up. Summer rain was simply not a thing here.

Hamlet and I chatted with his grandfather for a bit, then got pulled into playing a really creepy video game. It was so scary that I eventually crawled onto the bed next to Hamlet, making for some tight quarters. My knee brushed against his, and we sprang apart.

At one point Hamlet's grandma hollered at us to come down for dinner. The table was laid out with a platter of that yummy toothpick lamb (given that name because each little piece had a toothpick poked into it for easy eating), bowls of rice, a dark red soup with dumplings, and a pile of steamed pea shoots.

Needless to say, I ate a lot. His grandparents were hilarious—bickering nonstop while placing food on each other's plates. His grandpa even brushed a strand of hair out of his grandmother's face, gently and with such love, before launching into a complaint about the dumplings in the soup being too cold.

I sat next to Hamlet, but barely talked to him as I shoveled seconds, then thirds, into my mouth.

"I'm impressed by your appetite!" Hamlet's grandmother exclaimed at the end of the meal, nodding toward my absolutely pristine plate.

I looked down, a little sheepish. "I love to eat."

"Good," she said, getting up to clear our dishes. Her approval pleased me.

Hamlet jumped up from the table to take them from her. "Here, we'll do that. You guys go watch a show and relax."

"Thank you so much, everything was delicious. I'll have to share your lamb recipe with my dad," I said as I carried the dishes over to the sink.

"She never shares her recipes! Greedy," Hamlet's grandpa said with a belch.

Hamlet froze next to me at the sink so I whispered, "My dad and I have burp contests."

The chair scraped loudly against the linoleum floor when his grandpa stood up. "You're going to make your date do dishes?"

I held up a hand, already soapy. "He also said I'd have to do your laundry tonight, so . . ."

Both his grandparents cackled all the way to the family room.

"She's funny," Hamlet's grandpa declared, and I flushed with pleasure. The words to my heart.

Hamlet and I stood side by side washing the dishes, me scrubbing and Hamlet rinsing then drying.

"So, we have a dishwasher, but we never use it," he said at one point, gesturing toward it.

I nodded. "Let me guess, you use it as a dish rack?"

"Yes! I thought it was a Chinese thing?"

"It is very much a non-American thing. My dad still inspects every dish afterward, like he's trying to 'catch it' not working right."

He laughed. "Your dad's the best."

"I guess," I said, handing him a glass. "Your grandparents are pretty cool, too."

"You're probably wondering why I live with them."

I scratched my face with a soapy hand. "Oh, um, yeah, that did occur to me."

"My parents moved back to Beijing because their business was growing so much. That was a couple years ago. So now I live with these guys." He lifted his chin toward the living room. "Who aren't my real grandparents."

I looked at him. "What do you mean?"

"I mean, they're my parents' friends' parents. So, family friends, essentially."

Hm. I turned the water on a little more forcefully. "Oh, okay."

"I know that sounds weird to you. But my parents wanted me to stay here for my schooling."

"Oh, okay." It made me a little sad then, how he was working an entire summer tossing a sign up into the air, separated from his family. Driving a Lexus because his parents thought maybe that made up for the fact that they lived in separate countries.

With the last dish washed, I shut the water off. My hands were wet, but I couldn't find a dry towel.

"Here." Hamlet took one of my hands and then pulled up the bottom of his shirt to wipe it off. Then he took the other and dried that one, too.

What an incredibly sexy thing to do for a dork.

"Thank you," I muttered as I looked around at anywhere but his abs.

"You're welcome." Shirt was properly placed back in its usual position, and I felt a sharp sense of loss. RIP view of abs. "My grandparents *are* super cool, though. They're both retired NASA scientists and have lived here forever!"

I raised my eyebrows. "Wow, really? They do seem Americanized."

"Well, Nainai's from San Francisco. You know, her family's been here since like the gold-rush days."

"What!" I glanced at her small figure, hunched over as she cut pears in the living room. "That's so cool."

"Yup," he said. "And she met Yeye at Berkeley. He was there from China studying physics. After Yeye became a US citizen they moved here to work at JPL together."

JPL was the Jet Propulsion Laboratory in Pasadena. "Wow,

nerd love. That's pretty sweet," I said. I watched his grandparents sit back in their matching recliners as they started *Law & Order.*

"Yeah, it is," he said with a little smile. "Hey! Speaking of sweet, do you want to get *the best shaved ice ever?*"

I smiled. His enthusiasm was so contagious. "Sure."

We said bye to his grandparents, who sent me home with Tupperware containers full of leftovers. I was excited for my dad to taste the toothpick lamb. They waved us off from the front door.

"So, what would you pick for music, then?" Hamlet asked as we started driving.

I picked up my phone. "May I?"

He nodded, and I connected to his Bluetooth speakers. I scrolled through my music until I found what I was looking for. Some dreamy guitar and mellow electronic beats—it was a perfect match for the warm summer air whipping through the car.

I asked, "So, what's this shaved ice we're getting? Patbingsoo?" It was my favorite—Korean shaved ice topped with red beans and fruit.

"No, the Taiwanese kind, there's that new place . . . from Taipei?"

"I know that one. I've always wanted to try it!" I said with my hand out the window, feeling the wind hit my palm. Hamlet's enthusiasm *was* contagious, but also Asian desserts were my weakness.

We drove through the practically empty, wide streets of San

Gabriel, zooming by old 1960s diners-turned-Hanoi-chicken-spots and endless strip malls designed in faux Mediterranean style, landscaped with spindly palm trees. Hamlet pulled into one of the strip-mall parking lots, and we walked up to a small shop with neon lights that spelled out SNOW DAZE. There were people out the door for it.

"Whoa, busy," I said, looking around. "I didn't know the SGV had a nightlife."

He tucked his hands into his shorts pockets and puffed out his chest. "Well, a lot of us are Asian, and you know we stay up late."

I grinned. "True." People trekked here from all over LA to get the most authentic Chinese food because of the growing Chinese population in the area. There were so many regional specialties here that you couldn't get anywhere else outside of China—from northern Chinese Islamic dishes to brain-numbing Sichuan to Taiwanese desserts.

"Do you sleep before midnight? Like, ever?" Hamlet asked.

"Literally never."

He bounced from one foot to the other—I would have thought he had to go pee, except that he was doing it in this jock-ish way that I'd often seen him do at the office park. "Yeah, even when I had morning sparring last year, I managed to go to sleep at one a.m. every single night. Drives Nainai crazy."

"I feel you on everything but the physical activity part." My phone buzzed, and I looked down at it, surprised. I'd forgotten to check it all night.

How's it going??? 😊 Rose.

We had dinner with his grandparents

WHAT?

Hamlet was looking at me with that polite but kind of annoyed expression people make when you pull out your phone mid-hangout. I dropped my phone back into my purse and made a mental note to text her later. "It's Rose."

"Oh cool! Are you guys best friends?"

What a question. "Best friends. Er." I swished the skirt of my dress around a bit. "We don't actually know each other that well. We only started hanging out because of the KoBra." Our fraught history could be explained another day.

We moved forward in line so that we were standing inside the brightly lit shop. The walls were white and light blue, painted with cartoon foxes who were wearing scarves and making snowmen. A strange juxtaposition with everyone wearing shorts and flip-flops.

"So, if Rose isn't your best friend, who do you hang with at school?" Hamlet asked.

I surveyed the toppings. Mm, taro. "A few friends. These guys Felix and Patrick."

"Oh. Cool. You hang out with guys? That's awesome."

Hamlet was also studying the toppings, as if his life depended on it. I smiled. "They're just my friends. Felix has a girlfriend, and Patrick's gay."

His expression brightened considerably. "Oh, that's cool. I didn't think anything of it."

"If you say so." I admit, jealous Hamlet was kind of cute. Only because it was still the nicest, least gross male-possessive jealousy I had ever witnessed.

We ordered our shaved ice, which was served in huge tubs. Mine was flavored with cranberry syrup and topped with red bean, taro, and sesame balls. Hamlet's was plain with grass jelly. I made a face at it. "So healthy."

He shrugged. "I like it!" Then happily ate a spoonful. I got the feeling Hamlet never did anything if it wasn't out of a genuine desire to do it. Unlike most of the guys I had dated in the past, he was completely devoid of pretense.

"So who do *you* hang out with at school? A bunch of hot girls?" I asked as we sat down on the curb outside.

He guffawed. "Yeah, right. All guys. Mostly my D and D—" He stopped talking. "Um, these guys who I like to play basketball with."

"That's *not* what you were about to say."

"It was!"

I pointed my plastic spoon at him. "Dude, I know what Dungeons and Dragons is. Patrick and Felix used to be obsessed with it."

He laughed. "Okay, fine! Yeah, I mostly hang out with the D and D crew. They were the only ones who wanted to be friends with me when I first moved here. We've stuck together since."

"Were kids *mean* to you?" I asked, surprised. How anyone could be mean to Hamlet was beyond me. Did they also enjoy kicking bunny rabbits?

He shrugged. "Not exactly. But the Chinese American kids didn't connect with me; they had no interest in a FOB."

Fresh off the boat. A protective instinct came over me. Imagining Hamlet isolated in a totally different country made me want to walk over to his school and wreak some havoc.

"You're frowning." Hamlet interrupted my detailed revenge fantasy.

"Oh, sorry. Just . . . annoyed for you," I admitted.

His eyes met mine over his cup. "That's nice of you."

I tucked my hair behind my ear, to have something to do while he looked at me like that. "I'm just being a decent human." Hamlet had a way of making me self-conscious—at the earnestness of this conversation, at how much I found myself having to say.

But I was with King Earnest. And King Earnest was licking the ice dripping off the side of his cup, being meticulous and hot at the same time. I tore my eyes away. *Yeesh.*

"Yeah, you're decent," he said with a smile, teasing me.

I flushed but a thought suddenly occurred to me. "Are you going to go back to China after you go to college here?"

He scraped up the last of the shaved ice in his cup. "I don't know. I like America! A lot. But I also miss a lot of things back home. I don't know if I'll ever feel fully American like you guys who were born here."

A car's headlights beamed directly into my eyes, and I turned away from them, leaning in closer to Hamlet. "I get that. My dad's kind of like you . . . he's pretty Americanized now, but he also has mad Brazil and Korea pride."

"Who does he root for during the World Cup?" Hamlet asked, serious as he leaned in toward me, too. Our foreheads were almost touching.

"Oh! In this order: Korea, Brazil, then the US."

Hamlet pulled back and laughed. "That's what I thought."

I finished my shaved ice, and Hamlet took my empty cup and spoon to toss into the recycle bin. That gesture, these little things Hamlet did—they really got to me. So much so that when he walked back to me, I reached for his hand. He looked down at me in surprise as I slipped my fingers through his. The warm air blew through the parking lot, stirring up litter and dust, and we stood there for a second in the glow of neon signs. Everything felt right. I squeezed his hand. "Ready?"

We headed to his car, his steps buoyant as he kept my hand firmly clasped into his. "Thanks for the nice talk," he said, unlocking the car.

I let go of his hand, reluctantly, and smiled. "You're welcome?"

He opened my door, and when I slid into the seat, he leaned over, his arm draped on top of the door. "I just want to know everything about you." Astonished, I didn't answer, and he closed the door before I could react.

When Hamlet pulled up to the front of my apartment building, I hesitated in my seat, wondering if we should hug or something. But he put the car in Park and walked over to my side, opening the door. The little things.

"Thanks." We walked across the crunchy lawn, past the jasmine hedge. I could smell the fragrant jasmine blooms as we climbed up the stairs.

We reached my door, and I paused, the bag of leftovers bonking my leg. "Thanks for the ride and letting me meet your grandparents."

The corners of his eyes did that crinkly thing as he smiled. "Yeah, that's a rare privilege for only the most special of dates." His hands were in his pockets again. Everything about him right now was shy and unsure.

But I was sure about one thing. I wanted Hamlet Wong to kiss me.

"Have a good night, Clara." His voice was quiet. Low and sweet and real.

I glanced up from his hands to his face. That expressive, open face. "Good night," I replied.

He took a step backward but kept looking at me expectantly, as if he was waiting for me to go inside.

So I dropped the bag of food, took a step forward, and tugged him by his shirt until our hips bumped. "I want to kiss you. Is that okay?" I asked, my face tilted up toward his.

His eyes widened and his lips parted slightly. Then he placed a warm hand on my waist. "Okay," he murmured.

I got up on my tippy-toes to reach his lips, and brushed them over his. My eyes closed, I took in the scent of him—grass jelly.

His lips were soft, but they were quick to meet mine. He drew me in closer until our bodies were pressed against each other, one of my hands still clutching his shirt, the other wrapped around his neck, curled into his hair.

When we pulled apart, the blood rushed from my head into my toes.

Hamlet looked stunned. And adorable—his hair mussed and shirt wrinkled.

"Good night, for reals," I said as I grabbed the leftovers bag and unlocked my door.

I caught a glimpse of his face before I closed the door. Pink cheeks and a huge smile. "Good night!" he shouted.

"Oh my God!" I closed the door with a smile. It stayed on my face until I fell asleep that night.

CHAPTER 19

A PERSISTENT KNOCKING WOKE ME UP THE NEXT morning.

"*What?*" I yelled from under my blanket.

"I'm coming in!" my dad said before opening the door a crack. "Are you decent?"

"No, I'm in my lace negligee," I muttered. "Since when do you care if I'm 'decent'?"

My dad stepped inside. "I don't know, you were on a date last night so . . ."

I moved the blanket off my face. "Are you implying that Hamlet might have *slept over*?"

He shrugged as he leaned against the doorway.

"Okay, I'm not *you* in high school, so . . ." I sputtered.

"Burn, Shorty," he said with a laugh. "So, how was it?"

"Pai. Seriously?"

"What!"

"I don't wanna talk to you about my date!"

"Ooh, so it *was* a *date* date. So there's something to *talk about*."

I buried myself in my blanket again. "CAN WE NOT?"

"So it went well?"

Suddenly the memory of last night's kiss came flooding back. Night air laced with jasmine. The glow of the apartment lights throwing half of Hamlet's face into shadow. The taste of grass jelly. I giggled involuntarily.

My dad gaped at me. "Whoa."

"Can you *leave*?" I yelled, tossing my stuffed sriracha bottle pillow at him.

He caught it swiftly. "All right, all right. Have a good day, Shorty."

I dragged myself out of bed to give him a hug. "You too."

He made a face. "Get out of here, Morning Breath."

"*You* get out!" I pushed him to the door.

"Clara, can you slather me?"

I squinted up at Patrick. "Can you not say 'slather,' though?"

He handed me a giant bottle of generic brand sunblock. "That's what it is. Would you rather I say 'rub'?"

I got up and tugged on my baseball cap and sunglasses. "I'd rather not have to do this task." Patrick turned his freckled and bony back to me. His shoulder blades were sharp and delicate like bird wings.

The community pool was unusually crowded today. It was in the high nineties and scorching hot on the concrete. We had spread out layers of towels, but the heat still managed to seep through and I got the distinct feeling that, from space, we looked like little rotisserie hens gathered around a blue rectangle.

"Babe! Get in the water!" Felix shouted from the edge of the pool.

Cynthia made a face from under her giant umbrella. She had alabaster skin that turned into a third-degree burn upon contact with the sun. Between that and her inability to walk more than half a mile without complaining, I was pretty sure she was meant to live in a Victorian attic.

"I just showered this morning," she said with a sniff.

"So did I—who cares?" Felix said, exasperated.

After I finished smearing sunblock on Patrick, I put in my earbuds to avoid hearing the inevitable testy couple fight ahead.

When I swiped my screen to pick my music, I noticed a few missed texts.

Want to come over and hang out by the pool? Rose.

And then Hamlet:

I had fun last night. Hope you did, too.

What are you doing today?

I have the day off, too!

Didn't even give me a chance to answer any questions. His texts were as enthusiastic and rapid-fire as real-life Hamlet.

I looked around at the kids screaming in the pool as sweat and sunblock mingled together in one delightful skin soup. Heard Felix and Cynthia shouting at each other. Saw Patrick already dozing off next to me.

Guilt about ditching these guys chipped away at me with each word I texted.

To Rose: **Yeah sounds cool. Could I invite Hamlet?**

She replied: **O M G I'm gonna need the dirt later.**

I sent her a thumbs-up emoji. Then I texted Hamlet: **Hi. I had fun too . . . I'm going to Rose's place to hang out at her pool. Want to come with?**

COOL! Yes! For sure! And I just had practice in Chinatown, so I can be there like NOW.

I let out a bark of laughter at his enthusiasm and woke Patrick up.

"What's up?" Patrick asked from his face-planted position as I typed away furiously on my phone, figuring out logistics with Rose and Hamlet.

I considered asking these guys if they wanted to come, but I couldn't imagine all of us hanging out. Talk about motley.

"Gonna head home. Getting too much sun, I think."

"Are you serious? We haven't hung out in weeks."

Stuffing my towel and book back into my tote, I frowned. "That's not true. I hung out with you guys a few days ago, at Taco Bell."

"Oh. Well, it's just hard to see you lately, that's all."

He was right. Not only was I busy with the KoBra, but I didn't feel like spending all my free time with them anymore. The fact that I was ditching them to hang out with *Rose* would be considered totally bizarre. Because what they knew about Rose was so limited and wrong. I should know, because that's what I used to know about her, too. And now, well. I found myself wanting to hang out with her more and more each day. "I'll see you guys soon, though. Text me this Thursday when it's my day off, okay?"

He grunted in reply, his eyes already fluttering closed.

Hamlet picked me up at the pool, and we drove toward Rose's house up in the hills, a historic neighborhood filled with old Craftsman houses.

"This place is so cool!" Hamlet exclaimed as we drove up the hilly streets. "I never knew it existed."

"That happens to me all the time, and I was *born* here," I said as we pulled up to Rose's house, which had a huge porch, giant pine trees shading the property, and pretty bright green trim against the dark wood.

We were walking up the driveway when Hamlet stopped abruptly in his tracks.

"What's up?" I asked.

His eyes were hidden behind sunglasses, so I couldn't read his expression right away. "So, I don't want to be awkward, but the thing is, I've never had a girlfriend before."

I stood there, feeling the heat rise off the concrete in warm waves onto my bare legs. How did we go from first date to girlfriend talk? I kind of felt like I was being cooked alive. "Girl-friend?" The question squeaked out of me.

He stuck his hands into his shorts pockets and then took them out. Then put them back in again. "Yeah. What I'm saying is, I'm not sure how this works?"

Hm. I fanned myself with my hand. "Well, uh, we don't have to put a label on it or anything . . ."

"Oh. Okay. So you don't want to date *just* me?" He was smil-ing, but I could hear the hurt.

"No, I didn't say that," I said in a rush. Wait, did I want to date other people? Did I want to be *exclusive* with Hamlet?

Maybe. I wasn't sure. I just knew that the way he was look-ing at me right now was special, and I couldn't really handle the idea of him looking at anyone else that way.

I walked up to him and poked his arm. "I like you."

His smile transformed from forced to genuine, and I felt the wall of emotional defense so carefully constructed inside me start to chip away. "I like you, too," he said before poking me back.

"Okay then," I said, returning the smile. "Can we start from there?" Would he be all right with this? Something about Ham-let destabilized my usual assurance, which was built on my will-ingness to walk away. That willingness gave you power. With Hamlet, I wasn't sure if I could walk away.

And to my relief, he said, "Sure." Then he pulled me in quickly and kissed me on the tip of my nose. "Sorry, I've been distracted by your cute nose the entire car ride."

Oof. My heart fluttered as we walked up to Rose's front door.

She answered the door before we even knocked, wearing a long, gauzy, floral-pattern dress over a bathing suit. "Took you guys long enough to make it up the driveway."

Hamlet's telltale flush crept up his neck again, and I reached out for his hand instinctively. Rose glanced down at our clasped hands and smiled. "Well, well, *well*!"

I slipped past her, pulling Hamlet in behind me. "Calm down."

She closed the door. "I am calm. I'm so calm that I'm a clam."

Hamlet laughed, and I looked at him. "Are you going to encourage that kind of joke?"

"It's funny," he insisted.

I pointed at Rose and said, "Don't get excited. He thinks everything I say is funny."

We stood in her living room, which was bright and sunny—big windows; white walls; and soft, neutral-colored furniture set against gleaming hardwood floors. There was art everywhere, from oversize paintings with abstract shapes and bright color to little watercolors in delicate gold frames.

"Wow, your house looks like Pinterest," said Hamlet.

Rose laughed as she handed us towels. "Thanks, I think? That'll make my mom happy."

She led us out of the living room into the kitchen, which had a big open floor plan and more windows. You could see the pool from in here, sparkling and surrounded by colorful chairs and lush native landscaping. "My dad works from home nowadays, so he's upstairs. FYI, in case you guys were planning on doing it in the pool."

"Are you ten years old?" I screeched while Hamlet chuckled nervously. The words "doing it" being said with both of us so fresh in our dating made me feel queasy. I glanced at Hamlet to make sure he hadn't fainted. He was just the color of a tomato, was all.

My usual pool time consisted of dozing off and reading gossip rags, but with Rose and Hamlet, they wanted to be *in* the pool. Playing games.

"Marco Polo? Are you serious?" I asked as I stood in the shallow end, on my tippy-toes to prevent the water from touching my torso.

"Yes! And also, it's ninety degrees out, are you actually *cold*?" Rose asked, treading water in the deep end.

"This water is *freezing*!" I protested.

Hamlet swam over (shirtless Hamlet was always . . . well . . . just *well*) and stood up so that he was directly in front of me. Water poured off his shoulders, and I was so distracted that I didn't even pay attention when he said, "Sorry about this." A second later, he had hoisted me under the arms and dragged me out into the deeper part of the pool so that my body was now completely submerged.

I screeched, like a total wuss. But after three seconds, the water was warm and I stopped flailing.

"You are such a baby," Rose scoffed before dipping under the water to do a little backflip, as if to highlight the difference between us.

Hamlet kept one hand supporting my back. My bare back. "You good?" he asked.

I nodded. "Yeah." Then I touched his hip underwater, grazing it gently with my fingers. His eyes met mine, and this time his smile was slow.

"EH-HEM!" Rose splashed us.

We played Marco Polo with Hamlet as the seeker first. I hadn't played since I was a kid, and it was hard to get into at the start. I tried to escape out of the pool a few times, but Rose dragged me back in. She was about one thousand times stronger than me in every way. But when Hamlet, as Marco, found me and grasped my shoulder, I screamed and felt that very real competitive thrill. After that, it was *game on*.

By the time our third round was finished, we were starving so we padded into Rose's kitchen, dripping water on the tile floor. Rose pulled out cans of sparkling water, fruit, and cheese. "Admit it, you had fun, Clara."

I grabbed an apple and bit into it. "It wasn't the worst."

Hamlet immediately went into helpful mode, pulling out a cutting board and knife to start slicing apples and pears. This pleased me. One of my pet peeves was people standing around asking, "Can I help?" when they were secretly hoping they could just watch TV in the other room. Like those bums Felix and Patrick.

Rose and Hamlet, on the other hand, were a flurry of activity. I joined them, grabbing some glasses and ice for the drinks.

"Clara, have you told Hamlet about the food truck competition?" Rose asked as she sliced a large hunk of cheese.

The sparkling water hissed as it hit the ice. "I'm not sure . . ."

"No, you haven't! What is it?" he asked, his eyes on the fruit, careful in his deft and precise chopping.

"There's a big food truck competition in August with a *one hundred thousand dollar* prize," I answered.

His hand stilled as he looked up at me. "What?"

"I know, right?" Rose said. "So Clara, did you actually enter us?"

"Yup."

Hamlet was so excited he abandoned his fruit and walked over to me. "This is so so cool. Adrian hadn't mentioned it to me!"

Rose and I glanced at each other. I bit my lip. "Well, that's because he doesn't know."

"Whoa, why not?" Hamlet asked, his voice immediately dropping an octave.

I took a sip of one of the drinks. "Because I want it to be a surprise! Plus, I don't want him to stress. Worry about losing, you know?"

Rose said, "Well, I mean, there's a chance you can lose when you do anything. He's an adult. I'm sure he could handle the pressure."

I exhaled in irritation. "It's hard to explain to overachievers like you guys. Some people don't have confidence running through their veins since birth."

Rose frowned. "Yeah, that must be it. Not a highly effective combination of hard work and growing tough to failure."

I stared at her. "Are you saying my dad doesn't work hard?"

"No! I'm just saying that people who are 'fearless' have actually just failed a lot. It's not some preternatural characteristic I was born with." She looked for validation to Hamlet, who hesitated before nodding in agreement. "To me, that totally undermines all the work I've done to build this confidence."

Normally this kind of lecture from Rose would have annoyed me—having to be so serious about everything. But I had to admit that I had grown to care about the truck and wanted to succeed in this one thing, too. And was willing to take that risk of failing for once. Ugh, had Rose Carver's can-do-itness rubbed off on me?

I held up my hands. "Okay, okay. Remind me to never call you confident again."

A deep voice interrupted us. "Well, if it isn't a bunch of hard-working teenagers in the service industry!" Rose's dad walked in with a grin. He was wearing a blue T-shirt, jeans, and glasses, his imposing height instantly filling up the sprawling kitchen.

"Hey, Dad," Rose said with an embarrassed giggle. He gave her a kiss on the top of her head, then walked to the island and peered over Hamlet's shoulder. "Ooh, pears." He grabbed a slice, then looked at Hamlet. "Who are *you*?"

"Dad!" Rose exclaimed. "That is so rude."

"What! I'm being straightforward." His eyes twinkled with

humor before he turned toward Hamlet again. "I'm Jon, Rose's dad, in case you couldn't tell by her embarrassment."

Hamlet wiped his hands on his shorts. Which were damp. He didn't seem to notice, as he held out his hand to shake Jon's. "Hi! I'm Hamlet. I'm Clara's boyfriend."

The ice tray I was holding fell onto the counter. Rose gaped at Hamlet then at me. "What! ALREADY? You had *one date*!"

I took a deep breath. Dating Hamlet Wong was going to be a freaking trial for my chill.

CHAPTER 20

HAMLET WAS A FORCE TO BE RECKONED WITH. FOR THE next couple of weeks, he leveled all my normal boy barriers—texting me about everything (from making plans to sea otter gifs), showing up at the truck, and inviting himself to meals with my dad and me. That arm's length I required with boys was shrunk down to a millimeter.

Normally, I would have seen this as obnoxious behavior. In fact, I should have been running for the hills.

But no one had ever blown through my defenses like this. In my other relationships, I'd always had the upper hand. Even the most macho and controlling of dudes had never managed to push me out of my comfort zone. The only person on planet Earth who could get away with it was Hamlet. Because with him it wasn't entitled or pushy—it was just . . . Hamlet. Earnest and genuine in his interest in me.

That's how I found myself walking across a hot parking lot to the Chinatown gym where Hamlet boxed on Saturday mornings. It was a large space in an old warehouse—all concrete and sweat. The bay doors were open, and Hamlet was directly in my line of vision. Punching a heavy bag, his strong shoulders swinging, an intense expression of concentration on his face.

My thirst for Hamlet came in waves. And right now, it was a straight-up tsunami. Why was I so attracted to him in this state? I tried to override the archaic sexist wiring in my brain. The second he saw me, he stopped moving and grinned, the bag narrowly missing his face as it came swinging back at him.

"Hi." I pushed the black bag with the tip of one finger.

He leaned over, his thin cotton shirt stuck to him with sweat, and gave me a quick kiss on the cheek. "Hi." His lips hovered by my jaw, and I felt the hairs on my neck stand on end. "I'm just gonna take a quick shower, and I'll meet you outside?"

"Sure," I said, acting cool and feeling hot. I skirted the piles of shoes and boxing gloves as I left the gym and sat down on the hood of Hamlet's car, which was parked in the shade of an oak tree. A few minutes later he came out, shouldering his gym bag, hair damp and clothes crisp and sparkling clean.

"Ready for tacos?" he asked as he pulled on his sunglasses and stood in front of me.

I hooked my legs around his. "Always." Some whoops and hollers came out of the gym, and he blushed.

"All right, that's our cue to leave." He reached for my hand to help me down from the hood.

Hamlet and I were going to do a "taco walko," a walking tour of eastside taco trucks patented by my dad and me. Hamlet had admitted to Chipotle being his Mexican restaurant of choice and, when I'd finally recovered, I made a plan to remedy that.

At our third truck in Echo Park, he was shoveling a monstrous carnitas taco into his mouth and I was trying to capture it on my camera when a text from Rose popped up.

Hey, do you have plans today?

Taco walko hellloooo

Oh, whoops. Ok, nevermind!

I stared at the text for a second before texting back: **Why what's up**

Oh, nothing, no big deal.

Something about that nagged at me while Hamlet and I finished up our tacos.

"Who's texting you?" he asked as we dumped our greasy paper plates into the trash.

Hamlet had the ability to tell when I was agitated even when I was silent. Something that probably made his life really pleasant.

"Rose. I think she wants to hang out," I said apologetically.

He took out a little Wet-Nap from his wallet and handed it to me. "Cool, tell her to meet us for the movie tonight."

I took the Wet-Nap with nary a smart-ass remark. Hamlet's pockets were like a mom's purse. "Are you sure?"

"Sure, I'm sure. Unless you don't want to? I don't really

understand how close you guys actually are." He wiped his fingers off fastidiously with the Wet-Nap.

Good observation. I wasn't so sure either. Our friendship was so, for lack of a better word, organic. I shrugged. "Well, we're friends. And I don't hate hanging out with her."

Hamlet laughed. "That's Clara-speak for 'I like her.'"

I flushed because it was true and said, "Well, then let's invite her. Watching a movie in a cemetery will creep her out!"

We're going to watch The Exorcist at Hollywood Forever wanna come?

Not how I thought I'd spend my birthday, but why not!

Birthday! "Hamlet, it's her *birthday* today!"

His entire face lit up—he was Christmas Day and Disneyland all rolled into one. "Her *birthday*? I'm so glad we invited her then! We have to prepare!"

I pulled my dad's black Dodgers cap down lower over my head, avoiding the sun. "All right, calm down. Let me respond to her first."

I wished her happy birthday with some dumb bitmojis that were sure to infuriate her, then told her where to meet us.

A few minutes later, Hamlet and I were in a dollar store ransacking the aisles for the worst possible party favors.

I held up a tiara with tiny baby bottles attached. "What in God's name do you think this is for?"

Hamlet tilted his head, which was currently wearing a pink cowboy hat. "I have this *wild* suspicion that it's related to princess baby showers."

"What is wrong with people?" I put it back on the rack, frowning.

"We need to get this," Hamlet announced, holding up a SpongeBob piñata.

"What about SpongeBob SquarePants screams Rose to you? I am really curious."

He shrugged. "It doesn't. That's why it's funny?"

I laughed. "Actually, that's a good idea except we can't really do piñata stuff at the cemetery." We were headed to Hollywood Forever, an old cemetery where a bunch of golden-age movie stars were buried, like Judy Garland. Every summer they showed movies—their whole motto was "Watch the stars under and OVER the stars." Pretty messed up. And rad. Hamlet had never been before and neither had Rose, and I was excited to share it with them. That's the thing about having new friends—everything you like and do feels fresh again.

Again, I felt a flash of guilt for not inviting Felix and Patrick. Hollywood Forever was usually our thing. But I knew it would be awkward, and I didn't want to worry about everyone getting along. It'd been getting harder and harder to separate my social life between the two groups. Hamlet never said anything, but I'm sure he was wondering why I hadn't introduced them to him yet. But when I told Patrick and Felix about dating Hamlet, they didn't take it seriously at all ("TO BE OR NOT TO BE!") and thought I was just working a lot.

After the dollar store, we grabbed a cake at the grocery and some sandwiches at the deli counter. The best part of the cemetery movie screenings was that you got there early, staked out a spot, and had a picnic. Hamlet didn't need to know that this would be my sixth time going with a boyfriend. Sixth different guy. And when he insisted on blasting some dated pop music in the car, I couldn't help but marvel at how different from the others he was. How I didn't care that he had kinda bad music taste. How I liked how confident and assured he was in the things he liked because he was so free of judgment himself.

He tapped his hands on the steering wheel and sang along.

"Hamlet."

"Yes?" Without tearing his eyes off the road, he slid his hand up the back of my neck, his fingers pushing into my hair.

See, one second Hamlet's singing some dorky pop song and the next he's doing sexy stuff like this, and the juxtaposition of it all really got to a person. That person being me. Only me.

Before I could truly savor the moment, my phone buzzed. A text. I wriggled a little so that Hamlet would let go of my neck. He glanced over at me with a questioning smile. I smiled back and his eyes returned to the road and he continued singing. The text was from my mom.

Get a load of the hotel where we'll be staying in Tulum! 🌴😊📇☀️🏢

It was accompanying a link to a hotel website. I scrolled through the photos and groaned.

"What?" Hamlet asked.

I held up my phone to him, but of course he kept his eyes on the road. "My mom just sent me a link to the resort in Tulum. It's *killer*."

"Tulum?"

"Oh! I'm going to see my mom in Mexico next month!"

He lowered the volume of the music. "Cool, that should be fun." Hamlet knew the lowdown on my parents and, without his saying anything, I could tell he had some chilly feelings about my mom. Loyalty to my dad and all. It both annoyed and pleased me.

"I plan on flying out early enough to get back in time for the food truck contest. Best reward *ever* for my summer of the KoBra."

We turned into the parking lot for the screening, driving by the sidewalk filled with people waiting in line for the movie. Hamlet reached for the parking ticket at the entrance. "Do you really think your dad's gonna let you go since your punishment was for the *entire* summer?"

I texted my mom back with the heart-eyed emoji then slipped my phone into my pocket. "I have zero doubt in my mind. My dad always caves."

Hamlet grinned. "Well, you've got a way."

My heart flipped in my chest, and I resisted rolling my eyes at myself.

CHAPTER 21

THE SUN WAS STARTING TO SET, AND THE SKY WAS A
pale lavender and pink that I always felt was specific to a certain
kind of hot day in LA—when the sun had been so brutal for
hours on end that even the sky needed a minute to chill. So the
sunset took its sweet time, letting the light blue fade at a lazy pace
under the thick blanket of ever-present smog, and turning the sky
into a palette of hazy, desaturated pastels.

It was against this backdrop that we found Rose, an elegant
silhouette, waiting at the front of the line and clutching a lawn
chair.

"Finally!" she exclaimed when she saw us. "It's been murder
trying to hold this spot." Her eyes darted over to a group of

men behind her. "Do you think they'll be pissed if you guys get in?"

I assessed them in less than half a second. Not a threat. "It's just the two of us, and you were holding a place in line. We're not *cutting*." I raised my voice, challenging the bespectacled and short-shorted to have a problem with that. None of them said a word. Sometimes teenagers really scared the crap out of hipsters. It was like their tenuous hold on "cool" was exposed around the truly young.

Hamlet hastily stepped into line, then gave Rose a bear hug. "Happy birthday!"

She smiled, a little sheepish. "Thanks. Sorry to crash your date." Both of us protested with scoffs and waving hands, and it was a bit much.

"I had no idea you'd be here like an hour early to get a spot in line," I said, poking fun to mask feeling guilty about it.

"Did you actually think I would be able to relax knowing this was a first-come first-served deal?" Rose asked, her voice harried. "I'd rather be here yesterday than have to wonder if we'd get a good spot!"

I put my hand on her shoulder and replied, "I'm sorry for your life." Then I held up a huge shopping bag. "Despite that, we have some birthday goodies for you. Get excited."

Her eyes lit up. "You didn't have to! My family already did this whole birthday extravaganza earlier."

"What's a birthday extravaganza? Americans take birthdays

so seriously," Hamlet said while reaching out for my hand. Instinctively and comfortably. There was some movement at the gate, and Rose craned her neck to check it out before responding. "Oh, we went to get crepes at my favorite brunch spot and then my mom took me shopping. Then we got home to . . ." She trailed off for a second. "To uh, watch the Rose Birthday Movie."

I stopped chewing my gum. "What? What is the *Rose Birthday Movie*?"

The line moved ahead and I handed the tickets to the agent, still looking expectantly at Rose.

"Calm down, Clara. It's just a little movie my parents make every year—they make one for my brother, too—a compilation of videos taken of me over the years."

Hamlet took Rose's unwieldy lawn chair from her, a tiny chivalrous move that would normally irritate me, but I knew Hamlet would do that for a fellow male, too. For anyone. He said, "That sounds amazing. You guys are like a TV family."

"Thanks," she said. "For holding the chair, I mean. We're not a TV family, but I know it always sounds like that."

"To be honest, I was expecting something worse," I said as I shifted the shopping bag on my shoulder. "Two points to the Carver family for not being more embarrassing. In fact, that sounds sorta great." Rose looked pleased, and I was pleased she was pleased.

We moved into the cemetery, currently the only place in the

city with lush green grass. There was a winding path that took us to our destination, lit in intervals by torches. We wove between various tombstones—some modest brass plates laid into the earth, others ostentatious sculptures made of shiny black marble, and even the occasional cherub fountain marking the final resting place of some old rich person or another.

Rose glanced around. "This is really strange, you know. Watching movies around all these dead people."

"Hey, the dead need to be entertained, too," I said.

We arrived at a big grassy lawn spread out in front of a giant wall where the movie would be projected. I beelined for a good spot in the center and tossed a couple of blankets down. People started mad-dashing around us for spots. These movie screenings were like Black Friday sales for movie buffs—sometimes I feared for my life. If I died by Converse stampede, I'd be one pissed-off ghost.

I pulled out some miniature party hats the size of shot glasses. "We have to wear these."

Rose laughed and picked a mint green one with gold glitter trim. "Yes!"

I put a purple one on Hamlet, adjusting the gold elastic behind his ears. "So handsome."

"Wait, I want to wear the pink one," he said, reaching for it in the bag. "It matches my outfit better." He was wearing an oatmeal-colored shirt flecked with pastel fibers and dark brown shorts. I was learning that Hamlet was quite the fussy dresser.

Unlike me. I gestured down at my black denim cutoffs and ratty striped tank. "Give me that one, then. Purple will be stunning on me."

Once we were properly outfitted with tiny hats, I held up party blowers. "We have to get this out of our system now, or people will kill us during the movie." After handing them to Rose and Hamlet, I blew so hard into mine that the honk echoed throughout the lawn. People threw dirty looks at us.

"You love it!" I blew again.

Rose hid her face behind her hand. "Oh my God."

Hamlet blew into his, but at a moderate volume. "I don't want to get in trouble," he said apologetically.

I blew hard again. Rose flinched and sank down into her chair, separating her entire being from me. Hamlet laughed, and I honked and hummed in rapid succession along to "Happy Birthday."

Rose sank lower and lower into her chair, but Hamlet was laughing so hard his face matched the color of his tiny pink hat.

While he was recovering, I pulled out a small cake that had Transformers toys all over it. It said "Happy Birthday, Son!" on it. This time Rose burst out laughing. "What the heck?"

Hamlet placed candles in it, methodical and thoughtful in their placement so that they complemented the tiny robots and cars and things. I took out a lighter and lit the candles. "It's not like there weren't more appropriate cakes, but we thought this one provided the most entertainment."

"Good call," she said, a grin still plastered on her face.

We sang "Happy Birthday" to her, Hamlet in a low voice, kind of embarrassed the entire time. I, of course, sang with vibrato in a volume so loud that people around us starting joining in. By the end of it, there were, like, thirty voices wishing Rose a happy birthday.

She couldn't stop smiling after she blew out the candles. "Thanks, guys."

"You're very welcome," Hamlet said, already slicing the cake expertly. He handed her a slice on a My Little Pony paper plate with a plastic fork.

Although we were sitting there eating a Transformers cake off of paper plates with colorful ponies on them, there was a conspicuous lack of irony in this moment. It was something I noticed every time I hung out with these guys because I had become so used to a certain behavior with Patrick and Felix. Where everything was a joke, a mockery, a way to separate ourselves from feeling stuff for real. It was easier not to feel the real stuff—and Patrick the slacker was all about easy. Felix, he was so preoccupied with being cool all the time. And Rose and Hamlet? I watched them set up the Connect 4 we had purchased at the dollar store and immediately throw themselves into it, competitive and serious within seconds.

They were the opposite of that. They were all in.

When the movie ended, we headed to Hamlet's car. I held his hand in one hand and a lawn chair in the other.

Rose stayed close to us as we walked down the dark paths

toward the parking lot. She glanced around the headstones nervously. "I can't believe I just watched that movie in the cemetery. I'm *never* going to fall asleep tonight."

That night, at two a.m., I texted her a gif of Linda Blair's head spinning. I could practically hear her scream from miles away.

CHAPTER 22

THE NEXT WEEKEND, I STOOD IN FRONT OF THE FAN IN the living room, letting it cool off my face. Summer in our apartment was the pits. We only had one of those window air conditioners, and it barely kept the living room cool, let alone the whole apartment.

As we got more and more experienced with the truck, my dad let Rose and me each have some solo Sundays, since we only had one routine stop. And today, Rose was manning the KoBra. It was a rare day off together for my dad and me, and being hot and miserable was how we were spending it.

My dad was draped across the sofa like a rag doll, trying not to move. Flo hadn't left the cool porcelain of the bathtub in hours. We were like a Renaissance painting. Suddenly, my dad sprang up. "Ooh, let's get naengmyeon!" Cold Korean buckwheat noodles, often served with slushy, icy beef broth. The best and only thing to eat on a hot summer day.

My dad started to do an excited-for-food dance: pulling his cap down low and making weird, wobbly moves with his legs, while keeping his arms up at chest level.

I hated it so much that I loved it. He stopped dancing long enough to ask, "Hey, do you mind if Kody comes along?"

Yes.

But my dad's hopeful and nervous expression made me bite my tongue. And I never hung out with his girlfriends, so I knew it must be somewhat important. I plastered on a smile and said, "No, that's cool."

A half hour later, we were all piled into my dad's old rear-wheel-drive Nissan, still souped up from his racing days. You could hear us coming from a mile away. Kody had politely of-fered me shotgun, but my dad's quick warning glance stopped me from taking it. "No, you go ahead." I crammed myself into the tiny back seat instead, cursing her with every bump—my dad did not believe in suspension.

We pulled into a packed strip mall—storefronts crowded with neon lettering in both Korean and English, the parking lot manned by two valet guys who somehow made sense of the automobile Tetris. The icy-cold AC hit us when we opened the glass double doors into the restaurant. I shivered instantly and noticed the patrons huddled over their big metal bowls, also shivering in their shorts and tanks.

The smiling yet gruff hostess led us to our table, which was under a floating flat-screen TV playing K-pop videos. The table-tops were laid with paper place mats emblazoned with beer advertisements. "Hey, isn't this the actress you have the hots for?" I asked Pai, pointing at the dewy face on the mat, being a brat in front of his girlfriend. Maybe it was the hot day or the pressure of meeting Kody, but I couldn't stop myself.

He peered down at it. "Nah."

"Plastic surgery confuses all."

Kody laughed and I allowed myself to be pleased for .5 seconds. My dad threw the little paper packaging for the metal chopsticks at me. "Hey! Not everyone gets plastic surgery."

"Maybe not, but probably every *actress*!" This was a common argument between us. Because I was one step further removed from Korea, my dad always felt super defensive about Korean culture. I liked to tease him about it to rile him up—especially about plastic surgery.

Before my dad could answer, the server came over and asked for our orders. You had about thirty seconds to review a menu at K-Town restaurants.

"We'll get three mul naengmyeon," my dad said, pointing at the menu just in case his Korean wasn't quite up to snuff. "And one galbi." A meal with my dad was never complete unless we added *more* meat. In this case, grilled beef short ribs that would come out sizzling on a stone plate.

"Did you want to ask your *girlfriend* if that's what she wants?" I asked pointedly. Sometimes my dad could be such a dude.

He looked chastised for a second, but Kody put her hand on his arm. "Oh, it's fine. Adrian always orders at Korean places. And I order the sushi," she said with a wink at him. They exchanged this intimate look that made me wrinkle my nose involuntarily.

"You're a sushi expert?" I asked politely, taking a swig of some of the cold barley tea the server handed us.

Kody shrugged, her long brass earrings shaped like crescent moons jangling. "Kind of. I lived in Japan for a few years."

"She's fluent in Japanese!" my dad bragged.

Something about my dad's pride made my stomach clench a little. The only time he talked like that was when it was about *me*.

Our side dishes arrived—small bowls of white radish kimchi, regular cabbage kimchi, some potato salad with apple slices, and little marinated black beans. My dad and I dug into them, me going straight for the potato salad and my dad for the radish kimchi. "You can tell the quality of a Korean restaurant by its side dishes," my dad often said. Side dishes were always free, so it was impressive when a restaurant took care to make them tasty.

Kody picked up a slice of the cabbage kimchi. "So, Clara. Adrian tells me you're doing a great job on the truck."

"Yeah, we've been killing it," I said as I poked around the potato salad with my chopsticks until I found a slice of apple. I glanced at Kody. Maybe I could use her presence to my advantage. Pai might be in better spirits, or at the very least want to look nicer around her. "That reminds me, considering how well we've been doing, could I still meet Mãe in Tulum?" I opened my eyes as wide as they would go.

Pai looked at me, annoyed. "Really? You want to bring that up now?"

I had to give Kody credit, she was cool as a cucumber. We might as well have been talking about the weather, poking around the side dishes.

"Why not? I've proven my worthiness, blah blah blah."

Pai made a face. "Are you kidding me?"

Before I could answer, the server arrived with a tray holding three metal bowls of noodles, frosted over with the cold. Also on the tray was vinegar in a squeeze bottle and a little glass jar of Korean mustard. Before handing us our bowls, the server took out a pair of scissors from his apron pocket and cut the noodles— first left to right, then top to bottom.

To avoid my dad, I took the mustard and spooned a tiny dollop into the icy beef broth. If you put more than that, there was the danger of lighting your entire brain on fire. Then I squeezed a healthy amount of vinegar in and mixed everything around with my chopsticks. We were silent for a few minutes as we dug into our food, and when the plate of sizzling galbi arrived we attacked that too without speaking. For all my chattiness, I had been taught to respect good food and give it my full attention. When I was able to catch my breath after inhaling my noodles, I looked up at my dad. "I think I've proven myself. It only seems fair to let me go."

Kody slurped her noodles.

Pai put his chopsticks down. "That's the problem, Shorty. You were supposed to learn something from this—not just get it over with to meet your mom at some resort."

I couldn't believe it. He wanted to give me a lecture right now, in front of Kody. Who finally looked uncomfortable, by the way—picking up the bowl to take a sip of the soup so that her face was obscured from us. "I *did* learn something!"

"Oh yeah? What?"

Why was he being such a jerk right now? His combative tone immediately put me on the defensive. "I learned how to make a stupid pastel."

Pai was silent, his clean-shaven jaw clenched, his body very still. Kody moved toward him, and he immediately relaxed. Watching this interaction made me want to throw my bowl of noodles at them. Why did they suddenly feel so close together and me so far away? The table between us felt like an ocean.

He eventually spoke. "Yeah. So no, you're not going to Tulum."

"Pai!" The whine came out before I could stop it.

Leaning forward, Pai pointed a chopstick at me. "It's not just because you're being a little butthole right now. It's because your mom has *nothing* planned. Did she already book your flight? Because it would be really expensive this late in the game. No, she wouldn't even think about that. She has no concept of money or responsibility."

My face burned. Pai's feelings about my mom weren't a surprise, but I didn't want to hear them laid out in front of Kody, of all people. Suddenly I hated everything about her—starting with her shaggy haircut and ending with her on-trend black clogs.

"We didn't *plan* anything because you've been a total drag all summer, and I haven't had a *minute*," I said, keeping my voice low but feeling my anger build.

Kody paled, and my dad pushed himself away from the table. "I'm getting the check."

The ride home was silent, and as soon as we parked, I muttered a good-bye to Kody, jumped out of the car, and ran up the stairs to the apartment. When I got to my room, I pulled my curtains aside and watched Kody hug my dad good-bye and then get into her own car. The need to talk to my mom was overwhelming. When I called her, it went to her voice mail. I didn't do voice mail, so I texted her.

Pai is a hard NOPE on Tulum

I paced the room as I waited for her response. Minutes went by, the phone slippery in my sweaty palm. Phantom vibrations kept me checking it for a response.

Eventually my dad knocked on my door. "Clara."

I ignored him.

Another knock. "Open the door."

Dragging myself over to the door, I took a deep breath before opening it. "What?" I didn't look him in the eye.

He made a face. "Excuse me? You think you can be rude to *me* right now?"

"Why not? You were rude earlier!"

He raked a hand through his hair, agitated. "I'm sorry I called you a butthole."

"In front of Kody."

"Yes, in front of Kody."

"Butthole is reserved for family fights only."

He laughed, quick and low. "Yes, butthole is reserved for family."

I pulled at a piece of splintering wood in the doorjamb. "And I didn't like you talking crap about Mãe in front of her, either."

"Understood." He crossed his arms over his chest. "But you pushed me to it, Shorty. I wanted you and Kody to get to know each other, but you wouldn't let it happen. Instead, you kept insisting on this Tulum thing."

A tiny crumb of remorse rattled through me, but it wasn't enough to change my feelings. "Well, you've made your position clear. I texted Mãe to tell her I'm not going."

For a second, it looked like he wanted to apologize. But his mouth formed a line, the expression that made him look like a serious frog. "Listen, at the end of the summer, let's go somewhere. Someplace way more fun than a bougie beach. It'll be your reward for working hard all summer."

The sliver of wood I was pulling at pierced my skin and I hissed, pulling my finger back. My dad reached out and held my hand up toward the hallway light to get a better look. "Splinter. Let's pull it out before it gets infected."

I sat on the edge of the tub as my dad picked at the splinter with a pair of tweezers that he dipped in alcohol. As we both stared intently at the tiny line of wood under the translucent layer of skin on my index finger, my phone vibrated next to me. I glanced down and saw it was my mom, finally.

It was a simple, succinct 🙂.

CHAPTER 23

"WHAT'S THE DEAL? YOUR BOYFRIEND'S A MILLIONAIRE?"

I flipped down the visor in Patrick's car so the sun wasn't blinding me. It was Tuesday and I had the day off, so I'd invited Felix, Patrick, and Cynthia to a waterpark. That Hamlet's mom happened to own. It was going to be *real fun* having them all meet for the first time. Rose included.

I looked back at Felix to answer his question. "No. I mean, I don't know. But his mom bought this totally bizarro bankrupt water park a couple years ago and it's going to reopen next week. And we're allowed to try out the rides before it does."

Cynthia's frown was visible in the rearview mirror. "Didn't you say his parents lived in China or something?"

I pinched the bridge of my nose. CYNTHIA. "Yeah. They do. They bought it as an investment. Even Hamlet acknowledges it was weird, but apparently his mom always has these hare-brained schemes." I giggled, thinking about the last story he'd told me. "One time, she bought an American customer-service telemarketing office in Beijing but didn't realize until weeks into it that it was for sex toys." After a few seconds, I realized I was the only one laughing.

The water park was about two hours inland from LA, so it was going to be a long ride. Hamlet and Rose were meeting us there. Initially I was going to drive with them, but I'd felt guilty and told these guys I would ride with them instead.

The dead air in the car was making me have serious regrets.

But then we blasted Prince and all was well as we drove on the desolate 210 freeway, passing brown hills, tract homes, and endless gas stations and fast-food stops. At one point, we stopped for In-N-Out because no road trip was complete without it.

"So, is Rose your new bestie now?" Felix asked in a teasing tone as we dug into our burgers. I caught a hint of something else in there—a little hurt.

Normally I would have denied it in a heartbeat, paired with a grade-A scoff. But it wasn't really something I could deny. I'd hung out with Rose for about 80 percent of my summer break. And I liked doing it. I grabbed a fry off Felix's tray, earning me a glare from Cynthia. "Rose is cool."

"Are you serious?" Cynthia asked, her cat-eye sunglasses lifting on her face as she wrinkled her nose.

I sighed. "Yes. I'm serious."

Patrick shook his head. "That's messed up. Who's going to be your mortal enemy now?" Patrick was making light of it, too. But like with Felix, I detected some bitterness underneath. I took a bite of my burger, fending off that nagging feeling I'd had for weeks—that I wasn't sure how much I enjoyed hanging out with these guys anymore.

"Your mom," I replied with my mouth full. He laughed, and the awkwardness dissipated.

Full of burgers, fries, and milk shakes, we pulled up to the water park an hour later.

"Oh. My. God," I said as I stepped out of the car, pushing my sunglasses onto my head so that I could get a better look.

We were in the middle of absolutely nowhere. The desert. A scrubby mountain range loomed in the distance, shrouded by the smoggy curtain that took up permanent residence here during the hot months. We were in a giant parking lot that could fit an entire city's worth of cars. And spread out before us was an oasis.

Kind of.

A huge turquoise retro sign declared this place AQUA-TROPICA. A neat row of palm trees flanked either side, and behind the ticket booth you could see giant waterslides rising and dipping like pastel-colored snakes. Everything was very "Americana"—from the 1950s lettering on the signs to the paintings of happy blond families.

Hamlet and Rose were waiting for us out front. Rose was hovering under the awning, fanning herself. The heat here in the inland empire was no joke. It must have been triple digits, easy.

But my eyes were on Hamlet. And his on mine, with an easy smile matching his relaxed stance.

He had no idea he was entering the lion's den.

Wearing a robin's-egg blue baseball cap, white T-shirt, and navy swim trunks, Hamlet extended a hand to Felix first. "Hey, nice to meet you guys finally. I'm Hamlet."

Felix looked at the hand for a second. Raised an eyebrow. "Hey. I'm Felix." An almost imperceptible look of recognition passed across Hamlet's face. He knew Felix was an ex. But he kept his hand out, and Felix reluctantly shook it. My shoulders relaxed a little—this whole interaction was making me so tense.

Everyone else introduced themselves, and then we entered the park. A sense of foreboding followed me inside while Hamlet talked to some maintenance workers. He eventually waved us over.

"Okay, we're good to go," he said. "There are some rides we're not allowed to go on because they're not quite ready, but the rest should be fine. Our jobs are to test everything at least once to make sure it's going well." He grinned, waiting for an excited reaction that never came, except from Rose, who whooped.

Rose was sticking to Hamlet like glue, barely talking to everyone else. "So, there are workers at each ride? Just waiting for us?"

He nodded. "Yeah, I guess?"

"Like slaves," Patrick said as he snapped his gum.

What the heck, Patrick!

Hamlet laughed. "Wow, never thought of it that way since they're paid, but yeah, whatever." I squeezed his hand. One point Hamlet.

"Yeah, so no, not like slaves," Rose said drily. Patrick had the grace to blush.

I looked around. "Where do we even start?"

Hamlet stopped walking and let go of my hand to rummage around in his back pocket. He pulled out a colorful laminated map with various attractions and landmarks illustrated in a cartoony style. "Well, we're here," he said, pointing at the bottom middle of the map. "We could go in a circle, starting at the Rocky Rapids?"

"Sounds good," Rose said after a few seconds of scrutinizing the map. "That way we can make sure we don't miss anything."

"Wouldn't want to *miss* anything," Cynthia said, her red lips curved up into a smirk.

Before I could react, Rose leveled her sunglass-covered gaze onto Cynthia. "Excuse me?" Normally, I would have loved to see Cynthia wither under a Rose freeze, but I was hoping everyone would actually get along today. Hamlet, ever the diplomat, strode ahead, taking Rose with him. "All right, Rocky Rapids it is!"

There was a particular thrill in not having to wait in lines to go on a ride. A childlike giddiness took over everyone. For a few minutes as we ran laughing through the grounds, hopping over barricades, it felt like we were little kids again.

With the assistance of a stocky, barrel-chested Aqua-Tropica worker, we climbed into a large circular raft. "Thanks, Rodney," Hamlet said as Rodney pushed us off.

Patrick had both of his arms spread out on either side of him, the picture of ease. "Do you know *everyone's* names?"

"Pretty much. I've had to visit here a few times to help out since my parents are out of the country," Hamlet said with a shrug.

"That's nice," Patrick said. And he wasn't being sarcastic. I think it was becoming clear to him that Hamlet *was* nice. That he wasn't faking it, that—surprise, Patrick—sometimes people were genuine!

The raft tilted to the side a bit when I bounced hard on the seat, making everyone squeal and grab hold of the handles. Cynthia glared at me and I smiled, teeth showing.

Rocky Rapids wasn't as rocky as the name promised. It was mostly us floating along a "river" that snaked past various plasticky islands and real palm trees. Every once in a while, we passed through a waterfall, which made us scream as if it was unexpected each time.

By the time we finished, every single one of us was properly soaked. Cynthia looked irritated by it, her mascara running down her face.

Rose pointed at her eyes. "Waterproof. It's all about the waterproof." Cynthia furiously pulled out a compact and wiped at the streaks under her eyes.

We went on some more rides: Tsunami Bay, which had us

crashing around so hard in a giant pool that both Felix and I almost threw up; Death Drop, which was exactly what it sounded like, a huge slide that went down, almost completely vertically, into a "lagoon" with fake sharks floating around in it; and Battle Cove, a pool of calm water where we floated in doughnuts and bonked each other with foam noodles.

All of us were a little sunburned and soaking wet after a few rides. Cynthia was reapplying sunblock on Felix's neck, and Rose and I had ducked into the shade of a bushy palm. Hamlet pulled out his map. (I now understood why it was laminated.) "Okay, so next is Dueling Devils. Oh, this ride is *amazing*, two people can race each other!"

We followed him down one of the paths and stopped when Hamlet slapped his forehead. "Oh crap, this is one of the closed ones."

"What? That looks *awesome*, though," Felix said.

We looked over at the ride, which had yellow tape draped across the entrance and a sign that read CLOSED TEMPORARILY. The look that appeared on Patrick's face set off alarm bells. "Hey, I bet we could still sneak on."

Rose shook her head adamantly. "No. We are *not* doing that."

Hamlet pushed his sunglasses up onto his head and peered over at the ride. "Yeah. I don't think that's a good idea. It's cool. The next ride is the Beast, which is like a roller coaster—"

But Patrick was already scrambling over the fence with Felix and Cynthia close behind.

"Hey!" I yelled. But they ignored me, making their way to the other side of the fence in seconds. The one athletic activity we all excelled in.

Rose ran over to me. "Get your friends in order!"

Hamlet was already at their heels, and he nimbly hopped up onto the fence, leaning over the top. "You guys! Come on, it's not safe!" he yelled.

If I was being honest, there was a part of me that wanted to jump the fence with them, but one glance at Hamlet's worried expression squelched that compulsion. So instead I jogged over to the fence and hollered, "You *better* not get on that ride! I swear to God!"

Hamlet helped me up so that I could see them on the other side.

The three of them were already running to the top of the stairs that led to the giant tubular slides. "Come *on*, Clara! You know you want to!" Patrick shouted.

Felix was pushing Cynthia into one of the slides. Before he hopped in right after her, he pointed at me. "See you at the bottom!" Then he and Patrick jumped into their respective slides—their whoops audible as they whooshed through the pastel green and blue tubes, hidden from view.

"I'm sorry, Hamlet." I glanced at him

But Hamlet was already over the fence, running. "I'm serious—it's *not* safe!" he shouted as he headed toward the end of the ride, his legs moving so fast they were almost a blur. *Crap-crapcrap.*

In a few seconds, Rose was on the other side, too. She looked up at me and held out her clasped hands as a sort of stirrup. "Here!"

I used the stirrup as I hopped down, landing a little low and scraping my knee. Rose pulled me up. "Are you okay?"

"I'm fine! Follow Hamlet!" Both of us booked it, the hundred-degree sun scorching us as we sprinted after him.

We were stopped by an ear-piercing scream. Rose and I looked at each other in alarm, then ran even faster.

When we reached the end of the ride, I gasped. The slide ended at a giant pool, where it jettisoned people. A giant pool that was currently only half-filled.

"Oh *no*," Rose muttered. Hamlet was already in the pool, and I saw him bent over someone—Felix. Cynthia was sobbing, and Patrick was sitting waist-deep in the pool, looking dazed.

I ran over, and my heart hammered in my chest when I noticed the blood spreading like ink through the water. Surrounding Felix.

"Is he okay?" I asked, my voice shrill and unrecognizable.

Rose immediately jumped into the pool and helped Hamlet—grabbing the other side of Felix, who was limp but had his eyes open, dazed. There was a wound on his head, the source of the blood.

"Go get help," Hamlet said to me in a low voice.

"But, I—I don't have my phone!" None of us did; we'd left them in our lockers at the entrance.

"One of the workers can call," he replied, pointing at the exit gate. Then he looked over at Patrick. "Are you all right?"

Patrick nodded, but he was clutching his left arm, which was bent at an unnatural angle. I felt vomit rising in my throat.

"Clara." Hamlet looked at me again. I nodded and ran to the gate, finding one of the workers. After he called 911, I ran back to everyone, hoping that somehow when I returned everything would be different. That my friends were pulling another prank.

But Rose and Hamlet were sitting next to Felix, keeping his head out of the water. The sight of Cynthia holding her bundled-up tank top to Felix's head, soaked red with his blood, made me woozy.

Nope, it was all very real.

"Don't close your eyes," Rose said firmly. "Unless you want to die."

Cynthia sobbed, and Hamlet threw Rose an exasperated look. She frowned. "Well, it's a possibility!"

Patrick stood next to them, still cradling his arm. When he started to sway, I ran over and steadied him. "Hey, how about you get out of the water and sit down," I said.

He followed me, nary a wisecrack for once, and I helped him climb the stairs out of the pool. As I set him down on a bench, I heard sirens. Shortly after that, a group of medics were running in, some of the park's employees close behind.

Everything happened in a blur—Felix was lifted onto a

stretcher. Cynthia was okay but wanted to ride in the ambulance with Felix. After some inspection, a medic told Patrick he'd probably broken his arm and needed to go to the hospital, too.

Hamlet, Rose, and I followed them out into the parking lot. I walked alongside Patrick for a few seconds. I didn't know what I was expecting, contrition or an apology? But when they got into the ambulances without a word to Hamlet and Rose—both of whom had done everything to help them—I had to say something.

"Hey!" I shouted.

Other than Felix who was lying down, everyone looked at me. I took a deep breath. "I hope you guys feel better soon, but after this is all done, you owe Hamlet an apology."

Hamlet tugged at me. "It's okay, Clara. They're hurt—"

"Are you seriously asking for an apology *right now*?" Cynthia cried from the ambulance bench.

Felix put a hand on her arm. "It's fine, Cyn. She's right. Sorry about this, Hamlet."

"Don't even worry about it," Hamlet said with a grim smile. "Just take care of yourself, man."

Then the doors shut, and Felix's ambulance wailed off into the distance. Patrick's ambulance was idling, his injury not as serious. I walked over to him and he gave me a small smile. "Best summer ever." I didn't laugh. He sighed. "You're right, we were being jerks." He looked down at his lap. "But, I mean, it kind of sucks. Being ditched, you know?"

I bit down on my lip, suddenly feeling like I wanted to cry. "I didn't ditch you guys."

He glanced behind me at Rose and Hamlet, who were talking to the EMTs. "Maybe not. But you're going to."

Before I could respond, the medics closed up the doors and drove off, the ambulance growing smaller in the distance, leaving me caught between its receding lights and Hamlet and Rose.

CHAPTER 24

"CLARA, LOOK ALIVE!"

I startled and looked up at the TV. My player had just fallen off a cliff.

Hamlet's grandma threw her controller down in disgust. "I want to be on a different team!"

It was a few days after the water-park catastrophe and I was sitting on the carpet at Hamlet's, playing our usual Friday night *Space Pineapple Death Match*. Early on in this new Friday routine, his grandpa reluctantly moved the video-game console downstairs so that we could play group matches. I was distracted, and Hamlet's grandmother pulled herself off the carpet with a groan. "I'm going to get some snacks." She pointed at me. "You. Practice some more while I'm gone." Hamlet's grandpa heaved himself off a chair to follow her. "You're going to pick bad snacks," he complained after her.

We paused the game, and the second his grandparents had scuttled into the kitchen, Hamlet reached over and pulled me closer to him—both of our backs pressed against the sofa. He touched the tip of my nose. "What's up?"

"Your grandpa's kicking my butt, as per usual."

"No, I mean you seem off today. Is everything okay?"

I took a second to appreciate this Hamlet quality of checking on me. He was good at honing in on my feelings, and right now it was guilt about my friends ruining his parents' grand opening. My shoulder bumped his as I scooted closer. "Yeah, I'm all right. Did your mom pick a new grand opening date yet?"

He shrugged. "No, my parents have to figure out the lawsuit first."

Shame seeped into me. After the accident, Hamlet's mom had to decide whether to delay the grand opening since the accident was bad press—you know, "Teenagers Almost Die in Water Park." Before she could figure that out, however, Felix's parents were threatening to file a lawsuit against the park. Felix had reached out to me to apologize because his parents weren't backing down. I cursed Past Clara for not endearing herself more to Felix's parents when we'd dated.

And in the middle of all this, I couldn't get Patrick's voice out of my head: *But you're going to.* Everyone around me seemed to be noticing some sort of shift in me that I wasn't sure I was ready for.

Here I was spending a Friday night with my debate-club-president boyfriend at his grandparents' house. My debate-club-president boyfriend. And I already knew my weekend plans: I was going to get Ethiopian food with Pai and Kody (my idea—an olive branch after naengmyeon-gone-wrong) and *go on a hike* with Hamlet. And then work the KoBra on Sunday.

Over the course of the summer, my life really had become unrecognizable.

"Why do you like me?" The words came out before my brain could stop them—its squishy brain arms reaching out frantically while its "Noooooooo!" became an echo as the words flew farther away from its grasp.

I expected silence, the normal reaction to such a random and naked question. But Hamlet just chuckled and said, "Because!"

"Because why?" I couldn't stop. The need to see myself through Hamlet's eyes was overwhelming. I didn't feel like myself lately, and I needed someone else to confirm that I was, indeed, the same person. Or confirm that I wasn't.

He pulled his knees up into his chest. "Well, you're really funny."

What else was new. "So you're into clowns."

The joke got a belly laugh from Hamlet that it did not deserve. "Actually, I'm scared of clowns."

"Who *isn't*? The person who feels no fear in their heart when seeing a freaking clown in the flesh is probably a serial killer!"

Hamlet threw his head back and the laugh that came out of

his body immediately made me crack up with him. When he finally calmed down, he was wiping away tears. Tears. I smiled at him, and the tenderness that flooded out of my chest and into all my extremities caught me off guard.

I don't deserve him.

I blinked. "Okay, so what else?"

"Jeez. You're being so bossy about this."

"Your grandparents are going to take three hours making a fruit platter for us. We need to fill the time."

His head was still leaning back on the edge of the sofa, his arm draped casually behind me. But when he looked over, not smiling for a second, his eyes were serious and intense. They cut through me, blazing hot, and I was completely disarmed.

Keeping his eyes on mine, his fingers grazed my bare shoulder. "I like your freckles. The way you chew on your lips when you're annoyed." I rubbed them together self-consciously and he smiled. "And I like . . . how you dress. Especially when you wear your Docs with your little shorts."

I rolled my eyes. "Okay, pervo." But I was pleased—I always felt so sloppy and unkempt next to Hamlet. Whenever I first saw Rose in her carefully coordinated outfits, I wished that I dressed more like her.

"But I think what I like most," he said almost sleepily, his fingers playing with my tank-top strap, "is how you're different from me."

It should have been sweet, comforting—something like that. But instead, I could only think of how that chasm of difference between us had shrunk over the summer. How that bothered me for some reason. "Different how?" My needling knew no bounds.

"You know how. Everything! I like how sure of yourself you are. You don't do things to please other people."

"But you're confident, too!"

He scoffed. "Kind of. I'm always worried about, I don't know, being nice or something." He seemed a little embarrassed by that admission. But it was one of the reasons I liked him so much, too.

"You're kind," I said quietly, resting my face on his hand. "I'm not."

"What?"

I shrugged. "It's fine, one human being cannot exemplify all the good things in the world."

Instead of laughing, he frowned. "You are kind. You just don't like to show it. Like a cranky old man in a village."

I released a bark of laughter. "Get out!"

He sat up and ran a hand through his hair. Hair so thick I imagined combs shattered upon touch. "You are! You're like that cranky man who yells at children but then secretly mends their shoes."

"*What!*" I couldn't stop laughing.

"You're . . ." he paused. "You're all tough candy shell. When inside—"

"I'm oozy chocolate? Please."

Instead of responding, he leaned over, pulling me in so close

231

that our eyelashes practically touched. His lips grazed my jaw and then moved up toward my ear. "Yeah, chocolate. Melted."

Every bone in my body turned into liquid as I turned my lips to his. He cradled my head gently and kissed me softly. And then. Then he said, "I love you."

I stilled. My blood stopped coursing through my veins, my heart froze midbeat, my cells were suspended. I couldn't move.

Uncertainty passed over his face, his eyes still on mine. When I didn't react, he moved back a little, his body no longer touching mine.

Hamlet loves me. Hamlet LOVES me? Hamlet loves ME? My brain was malfunctioning, wires being crossed, indecipherable signals being passed back and forth, and I couldn't speak. I didn't know what to say.

"Don't let *me* interrupt."

Both of our heads swiveled to see Hamlet's grandma holding a tray of fruit in front of the TV. His grandpa was right behind, with a giant bowl of popcorn.

Hamlet blushed. "We were just—"

"Give me a break," his grandmother grumbled as she tottered back over to the sofa, walking between us and plopping herself down, the tray rattling on her lap. She glanced over at me. "This one is a bad influence, huh?"

I stammered, "What, why . . ."

"Eat some fruit. Cool off," she said, shoving the tray onto the coffee table in front of us. We both reached for the tiny forks poked into the pears and ate silently, not making eye contact with each other while the video game started up again.

That night, I looked through some old photos of Felix and me from when we dated. There was one of us hanging out in some parking lot. Felix with his arm draped lazily around me, both of us smiling in the harsh glare of the lights. I didn't remember that day, because days with Felix and Patrick always ran together into one indistinct blur.

Felix never said he loved me. Even though we cared for each other, and still did, it never got to that level. We liked a lot of the same things and were attracted to each other at the time. But Felix didn't dig past a certain depth, and neither did I. Hamlet, though? He was fearless in his digging, in his pursuit of something more meaningful.

Looking at these photos with Felix was bittersweet. The chasm between us from the water-park incident felt unbridgeable, and I wondered if Patrick was right. Were they being replaced?

I texted Patrick and Felix: **How are you guys?**

The conversation bubbles were immediate. But took forever. I frowned. It wasn't like them to take that much time drafting texts to me.

Patrick replied first: **Good. I requested a child's neon green cast.**

I laughed.

Felix replied soon after: **Okay. My parents are being over the top and keep checking up on me in the middle of the night to make sure I haven't died.**

I texted back: **Do they know you're past the danger zone??**

They think Jesus was punishing them for letting me date you.

The laughter felt good, and for just one evening, it was like old times.

CHAPTER 25

WHAT 😲 😲

I could feel the force of Rose's enthusiasm through her texts. For once, my energy level matched hers, my fingers flying on my phone as I texted back: RIGHT?????????!!!!!

I need to process this. Are you home? Can I come over?

It was Monday afternoon and both of us were off KoBra duty.

Yeah, come over

An hour later, we were sitting in my room, Flo in my lap while the fan rattled inches away from us.

"Nothing? You said nothing," she said, her voice flat.

I fiddled with Flo's collar, irritating her. One paw pushed my hand away. "Well, I was *shocked*. And then his grandparents came in the room!"

She groaned. "Hamlet, what the heck? Why would he say that with his *grandparents* around?"

"I don't think he was planning it. It just seemed to slip out."

"Either way, terrible timing."

"Agreed." I let go of Flo, plopping down backward onto the bed.

Rose propped her chin on the edge of my bed. "Do you feel the same way?" she asked.

I stared at the ceiling. "I don't know. I mean, yes, I like him. But . . . *love*?"

"I know. So serious."

"SO serious!"

The breeze from the fan lifted my tank top off my belly, making the fabric flutter for a second. "I feel like that guy in a rom-com who freaks out over the obviously perfect-catch girl having feelings for him. Like, why am I obsessing over a love declaration from a nice guy?"

"Rom-com main characters are old. You're sixteen. Love declarations are weird."

This was stressing me out, and my room started to feel oppressive. Rose seemed to pick up on this and said, "Let's do something fun today."

"Yes and yes."

Her eyes narrowed in concentration. "You know, there's a list of all the trucks entering the competition on the website."

I sat up. "And?"

"Maybe we can check them out. See what we're up against."

My mind took that suggestion and spun through other ways to make it more interesting, like prank roulette. By the time it landed on an idea, I was brainstorming.

"Is a wig completely necessary?" Rose asked, her voice low and skeptical.

I browsed through the wig bin at my favorite thrift store. "Is *anything* ever necessary?"

"Hi, Clara!" The woman behind the counter waved at me, her eyebrows drawn high and dramatically, her fake mole shifting on her upper lip as she smiled widely at me.

I waved back. "Hey, Erin!" I glanced at Rose next to me. "I've purchased many a disguise here."

"I am very much *not* surprised," she said, wrinkling her nose as she picked up a neon orange bob with her fingertips.

"We're spies today. We need to be fully covert," I said, eyeing an electric blue pixie wig.

She lifted an eyebrow. "Aren't we going for inconspicuous here?"

"No way. Just *unrecognizable*." I pulled the blue wig on and looked at her. She grinned and gave me two thumbs up.

Rose picked a long, wavy, blond-streaked wig with bangs. She looked amazing in it and I made her take a billion photos. As we sorted through the racks for clothes, she got more and more into it. Clothes were definitely her forte.

When we left the store, I was wearing a short polyester shift dress with geometric patterns. Very 1960s go-go girl. Rose was decked out in a long white caftan with little laced-up booties straight out of *Little House on the Prairie*. We both wore large sunglasses that obscured our faces.

Rose couldn't stop giggling, self-conscious as she drove us to the first stop: No Pain No Grain, a grain-bowl truck in Hollywood. Rose parked her car at a metered spot, and the sun beat down relentlessly on the tops of our wigged heads when we stepped out.

I tugged at my dress. "Ugh, should have considered the weather before choosing this piece o' crap unbreathable fabric!"

Rose was scrolling through an iPad. She had, of course, mapped out all the trucks and made a very thorough checklist. "Okay, so their specialty is making healthy, 'clean' bowls full of obscure veggies and various free-range or grass-fed meats."

"Sounds like the worst." I peered at the truck through my sunglasses. Their line was minuscule, and it was full of Hollywood's finest clean-eaters—mostly thin and most likely wealthy as well, judging from the menu pricing. Before Rose could protest, I jumped into line and targeted a young white woman with wavy red hair who was wearing a crop top and loose linen pants. "What's your favorite thing here?" I asked with a heavy vocal fry.

She glanced at my hair and then my outfit, visibly startled. Probably not the usual clientele she found at her ol' reliable grain truck. "Well, I usually go for farro topped with okra, black beans, and a sprinkling of gomasio."

"Interesting. Are you a vegetarian?" I asked.

Glancing around quickly, she leaned in a bit and whispered, "No. Between you and me, I don't actually think their chicken is free-range." Her eyebrows lifted.

I raised my own. Quelle horreur. "Are you for real?"

"For real." A firm, knowing nod. "But their veggies are grown in their own garden, and they're heavenly." I stored that fact away. Strengths: veggies. Weaknesses: chicken. We bailed before it was our turn to order, already moving on to our next destination, the Frank 'n' Frank truck, which served, you guessed it, fancy hot dogs. My dad and I both loved this truck, so I braced myself for some stiff competition. We surveyed the long line before us. It was peak lunch hour, so that wasn't surprising.

"Hm . . . this truck doesn't even give you options," Rose pondered as she glanced at the menu scrawled on the side of the shiny white truck in neon green. "There's, like, one hot dog, and you get grilled onions on it with various condiments."

I nodded. "Their hot dogs are freaking delicious, that's why. Why dilute the product?"

Rose stood there looking like a serious cult leader in her caftan. "Not too different from the KoBra, we keep it minimal, too."

"My dad knows his strengths," I said. Because we were both hungry, we grabbed a couple of hot dogs (Rose discovered she could actually get a vegan one, bleh) and sat down at a nearby bus stop bench shaded by a large magnolia tree.

"This is fun," Rose said between bites.

"You sound surprised."

She shrugged. "I never know what I'm getting into with you. And . . . I still don't get why we need to wear costumes, but whatever."

I pointed my hot dog at her. "Aha! You say 'whatever' because you know the costumes are purely for fun. And could it be that you're embracing *hijinks* right now?"

"Calm down, Clara," she said. "You're so annoying."

"I know," I said with a laugh. A bus pulled up, and we watched some people unload before it drove off, the exhaust fumes spewing some debris up into the air. I waved it away from my face. "Thanks for hanging out with me today." It was getting easier and easier to say things like that to Rose without having to crack a joke, too.

"Of course." She wiped the corner of her mouth with a napkin. "I know what it's like to need a distraction when you're worried about stuff."

I was hesitant before I asked, "So, is that how you cope with your anxiety?"

And to my surprise, Rose didn't shut it down. She fiddled with her straw. "Kind of. Sometimes I think it's just me being a worry-wart? I've always been this way. I worry about *everything*. And sometimes the dumbest stuff keeps worrying me, days and weeks after." A breeze hit us then, and it felt so good. She lifted her face up to it. "It's like this pitch-black field where I'm forced to walk, and I know there's a giant hole somewhere waiting for me. So I'm constantly thinking about it, when I'm going to drop into this pit."

That sounded like a literal nightmare, and it hit me then how seemingly perfect people were just as messed up as everyone else. I stayed quiet so she would keep talking.

"Sometimes, I can't . . . live in the moment. I'm always thinking of what-ifs and the terrible things people could be thinking about me." She looked up at me. "I always think everyone's mad at me. All the time. And it's like, I don't really care? But I do. It's hard to explain."

"You mean, like your parents?" I asked.

She shook her head. "No. I mean, yeah, of course I worry about what they think. But literally *everyone*. Like a stranger on the street. If I say something dumb to a barista, it bothers me for weeks. If someone doesn't respond to a text or e-mail right away, I'm convinced I did something wrong. I feel as if my brain's *trolling* me."

"Your brain is a jerk."

She laughed, the sound filled with relief. "It is."

"Do you want me to give your brain a talking-to?" I joked, but inside I felt a flare of sympathy and frustration for her. Rose's shallow breathing—it was a way for her to calm that troll brain down. I knew that dealing with something like this wasn't as simple as hanging out with friends to forget your worries, but I was glad to be that friend for her these days.

We finished up our hot dogs and headed to our next destination, a lobster-roll truck in Glendale. As far from the ocean as you could get in LA, but I guess things didn't always make sense.

CHAPTER 26

A FEW DAYS LATER, MY DAD HOPPED INTO THE TRUCK, where Rose and I were setting up for the day. "Ladies," he said, giving each of us a nod.

"Man," I said with an exaggerated bow.

Wearing a stiff new Dodgers cap, my dad rubbed his hands together. "All right, how did yesterday go?"

Rose grinned. "Great. We ran out of pork, so we stopped by the store and got more ingredients on the way back."

He gave me a little sideways hug in greeting. "Good job, my ladies."

"Please stop saying 'ladies.' Blech." I elbowed him in the side.

"And!" Rose exclaimed, holding up a finger. "We had our best day ever, money-wise!" She and I bumped fists, then did a little dance.

I looked at my dad for his equally celebratory reaction, but instead he had this strained expression on his face.

"Hello? Pai? Aren't congratulations in order?"

He ducked into the driver's seat before answering. "Yeah, definitely! All right, let's head over to Mid-City before traffic gets bad."

I glanced at the clock. It was almost five. Fat chance.

Nearly an hour later, we arrived at a craft fair set up on a big parking lot off Wilshire.

As my dad and I prepped the food, I glanced at him. "So, what's up?"

My dad kept his eyes on the green bell pepper he was chopping. "What do you mean?"

"Why are you acting all weird?"

He made a face but didn't look at me. "I'm not?"

"Yeah, you are."

He sighed. "Sorry. I just have a lot on my mind right now."

"What is it?" I asked, a little nervous. My dad rarely stressed out in front of me, and it only really happened when things were serious.

My dad finally looked at me. "The investor I was counting on for the restaurant just backed out."

I felt a knot form in my stomach. Growing up without much money, it was still an instant reaction—a wave of dread passing over me every time my dad worried about finances. "Oh no. What does that mean?"

"It just means that after all my work and planning this summer, everything may have to be put on hold."

I blinked. "Sorry, Pai. That sucks."

"What about the competition?" Rose piped up from the order window.

I whipped my head around and stared at Rose with huge eyes, telepathically telling her to shut up.

"What competition?" My dad glanced over at me.

Rose looked at me apologetically. "Sorry, I know you wanted to keep it a secret, but it could solve everything, right?"

A tiny flare of hope shot up into my chest. Maybe Rose was right. "Well, I wanted it to be a surprise, but . . ."

"Clara." My dad's voice was short with impatience. "What's this about?"

I looked at Rose and she nodded, her eyes supportive. I took a deep breath. "Well, there's this food truck competition on August eleventh—"

"I know what competition you're talking about," my dad interrupted, his voice clipped. "And no, I don't want to enter that."

"Why not?" both Rose and I yelped.

He tossed the bell pepper scraps into a compost bowl. "Because. It's a circus. I don't have time for it."

Since when did my dad have this attitude? I frowned at him. "What? What do you mean? What could possibly be the risk? If you win, you win ONE HUNDRED THOUSAND DOLLARS!"

"So what, Clara? Do you know how many trucks enter that thing? It's nuts, the chances of winning are so slim, and I don't want to go through that headache. Plus, the deadline to enter probably passed."

I felt Rose's eyeballs digging into my skull. "I already entered us," I whispered.

"What!" Pai yelled, making me startle and drop the spoon I was using onto the floor.

Rose immediately tried to de-escalate the situation. Something she probably learned in the Young UN Club or something. "Clara wanted it to be a nice surprise if we won, Adrian! It was—"

"I don't care! You did this *without my permission*! Are you two out of your minds?"

The silence that followed was like a vacuum—the air sucked out of the truck, my ears ringing with the absolute voidness of it all. Betrayal and disappointment were so heavy in my chest that I could barely breathe. It was unfamiliar, and I didn't like it.

"You okay, Clara?" Rose asked quietly, putting a hand on my shoulder.

I wasn't sure how to answer. No, I wasn't okay. And I wasn't okay with not being okay. My emotional investment in this truck came crashing down on me, as if to say, "Ha-ha, this is what happens when you care." I felt suffocated. By my dad's reaction to me trying to do something nice. By Rose's concern. By this stupid truck.

I tossed my cap onto the counter. "See you guys later." My voice shook, and it took all my willpower to not burst into tears as I stepped out of the truck.

"Clara!"

I ignored my dad's voice and walked rapidly toward the craft fair exit, and kept walking until the fair was far behind me, my face hot with tears.

Feeling disoriented, I looked around and noticed that I was headed west on Wilshire. My feet kept moving—past traffic and the big office buildings.

Before I knew it, I was at the La Brea Tar Pits. I hadn't been here since I was a kid. There had been more than one field trip to this ancient, bubbling mass of tar sitting smack in the middle of the city. I entered the museum grounds, the scent of sulfur hitting me as I walked by the lake of tar and the expansive lawns. When I stepped inside the museum itself, the cool, circulated air hit me. Air-conditioning in LA was almost healing; it made every place feel the same, a guarantee of something familiar.

I didn't move for a few minutes, letting the air cool off the fine layer of sweat on my face. Letting time slow everything down—my thoughts, my pulse, my anger.

After a few seconds, I paid for a ticket and entered the main exhibit hall. There were big informational displays about the last

Ice Age, showing dire-wolf skulls and animatronic woolly mammoths roaming the earth. Reading about long-extinct animals made me feel insignificant, which calmed me down.

My phone vibrated. I'd been getting texts since I started walking, but this time it was a phone call.

Hamlet. I picked it up.

"Hi."

"Clara? Are you okay?"

"Sure."

There was a pause. "Well, your dad told me about what happened. Where are you right now?"

I stood in the middle of a dark room, a timeline of ancient animals circling me on the walls, lit dimly. "I'm looking at ancient history."

"Huh? They said you guys were in Mid-City somewhere."

"Yeah, I ended up at the Tar Pits."

I heard a car turning on. "Please stay there. I'm coming."

"Hamlet. I don't need saving." I watched a group of little girls press their faces up against the timeline on the wall, gaping at the illustrations of saber-toothed cats being sucked into the tar.

"It's a billion degrees out. Are you going to *walk* home?"

Good point. "I can get a car."

"That would cost fifty bucks or something, give me a break. I'm coming—I'm actually not that far. Don't leave, okay?"

I sighed. "Fine. I'll be here."

We hung up, and suddenly I was very tired. I stepped outside into the lush atrium, found a bench next to a small waterfall, and lay down. Kids' voices mingled with the sound of tumbling water, and I took a deep breath. My eyelids fluttered once, twice.

"Clara?"

I woke up with a start. My neck hurt, and I was totally disoriented.

Hamlet's face appeared over me. "Hey."

Right. I sat up slowly, my legs stiff. "Hey."

He sat down next to me, his shoulder hitting mine. "Good nap?"

"Yeah, I give this Airbnb four stars."

He smiled. "I don't think you give stars for Airbnbs."

"Oh God, whatever."

His expression more serious, Hamlet looked at me. "What happened? Your dad didn't really tell me much."

"It's not a big deal."

"Kind of seems like a big deal. Like, this was very *drama*." He held up jazz hands.

"Well, you know how I entered us in the food truck competition?" He nodded. I continued, "Rose told my dad about it because he was bummed that an investor backed out of his restaurant plans. She thought he'd be excited, and instead he was a *total dick*."

"How so?"

Anger built up inside me, seeping out in tiny, toxic increments. "He got *mad* I entered the truck and said he didn't want to do it!"

Hamlet was quiet for a second. "Did he say why?"

"Just something about it being a hassle. I was so freaking disappointed." My voice trembled, and my eyes filled with tears.

He tucked a strand of my hair behind my ear, a gesture that instantly soothed me. "I understand."

The tears fell before I could wipe them. "Do you, though? He got me to care about this stupid truck, this stupid job—and then he let me down. So hard."

Holding my hand, he said, "Well, I don't think he meant to let you down. He must have his reasons . . ."

"He got me invested in this, and now I've wasted my entire summer." I thought of all my time on the KoBra with Rose, my summer spent away from my other friends to be with Hamlet. All these little threads holding this new version of me in place. A line appeared between his eyes, on top of his nose. His voice was quiet. "*Wasted* seems a little harsh."

And even though I knew why it stung for him, I felt a flare of frustration where compassion should be and I pulled my hand out from his grasp. This was just *so much*.

And then, I knew what I wanted to do.

"I'm going to Mexico."

His head snapped up. "What?"

"Screw my dad. Screw the competition. My mom wants me there so I'm going."

Hamlet's expression was incredulous. "Are you kidding me? How . . . And what about your punishment? Don't you have to work the entire summer to avoid suspension?"

"Who cares?" I felt the weight of the past couple of months

lifting off me in big chunks, making it easier to breathe, to be myself again. The threads loosening.

"Who *cares*?" His voice was loud now.

All around me, a thin, invisible barrier formed—a translucent thing covering every inch of my skin. I felt my expression slacken, my eyes turn into two cold stones. "You're being a drag, Hamlet."

Hamlet looked at me, his expression hardening as well. "You know what? You've asked me why I like you. I've given you reasons. I've even told you I *love* you." I flinched. He kept going. "And while you've never told me why you like me, I have my own theories—the main one being that you've surrounded yourself with people who enable this side of you, and I don't."

"What side of me?" My voice was acid.

"The side of you that can't handle being real, that thinks it's special not to care." He stood up and put his hands into his shorts pockets. "But, Clara, it's the least special thing about you. It's the exception."

There were so many comebacks that flew to my mouth, so many mean things I wanted to throw at him. But his words cut straight through my chest and into my heart. Before I could recover, he walked away from me, leaving me alone with a bunch of ferns and aimless koi fish.

CHAPTER 27

I EVENTUALLY GOT HOME AFTER THE MOST EXPENSIVE cab ride of my life and ran straight up to my dad's room. Ignoring Flo rubbing on my legs and still wearing my shoes like an animal, I grabbed the laptop off his desk and took it to my room.

During the ride home, I had stalked my mom's Instagram account, looking through her Stories to make sure I had her location right. She was staying at the Lotus Hotel and had arrived today. Perfect.

I opened the laptop and Googled "flights to Tulum."

The part of me that wanted to run after Hamlet, to call my dad—it was overshadowed by that familiar need to escape, to have some breathing room away from everything.

By the time my dad came home, I had purchased a one-way flight to Mexico for the next morning with my dad's credit card. I felt only a slight pitter-patter in my chest when I hit Finalize Purchase.

Consider it my summer bonus, Pai.

A few minutes after he got home, there was a knock at my door. This time, I ignored it. Flo meowed and I shushed her.

There was another knock. I turned up my music—lots of incoherent screaming with clanging piano. I let that do the talking.

I only turned it down when I heard his footsteps fade away.

To avoid feeling whatever it was I was feeling about my dad, I packed, focusing on how surprised my mom was going to be instead. I threw several bathing suits, shorts, and tanks into a duffel bag.

While I was loading up my phone with podcasts, there was another knock at the door.

"Clara."

Hearing him say my name almost shattered my resolve. I closed my eyes and concentrated on Mexico. The beach. Mãe.

"Clara, please. Let's talk."

I couldn't ignore him forever, so I spoke through the door. "Can we talk tomorrow? I need time." If I saw his face, I knew I would cave.

He was quiet for a moment. "Okay. Tomorrow. Did you eat?"

My stomach grumbled at the mention of it. "I'm fine."

"You should eat."

252

I smelled it then—kimchi stew. I took another sniff. And an omelet. "Maybe later."

"I'm not going to leave you a tray of food. No one died."

I almost laughed. "Whatever."

"I'll leave it on the stove for later so you don't have to look at my monstrous face." I heard him go downstairs shortly after that.

Later that night, when my dad was asleep, I crept downstairs and saw the stove light left on for me. The rice cooker was full and warm, and there was a small stone pot filled with kimchi stew, sitting next to a chunk of omelet wrapped in plastic.

I ate my food in silence, and in the dark.

The closest airport to Tulum was Cancún, and there had been no direct flights left that were affordable. So, after getting up long before the crack of dawn for a seven a.m. flight and taking an airport shuttle to LAX, many, many hours later I finally landed in Mexico at eight p.m. My phone was dead, so I could avoid hearing any voice mails or seeing any texts from my dad for now. He would have found the note I left on the counter for him hours ago.

I wondered if he would have contacted my mom. Probably. Would she be at the airport to pick me up?

Feeling like a shriveled corpse with greasy hair, I made it out of customs and into the fairly small but busy airport. Although I had met up with my mom plenty of times in various cities, this was my first time traveling to another country alone.

There was no sign of my mom. Okay, so maybe she didn't know I was coming after all.

Luckily, I had saved New Year's cash from my grandparents, so I had some money on hand for a cab ride. I went to the currency exchange desk and switched out my American dollars for pesos. *Next, get a taxi.*

Nervous, I walked to an information booth. My Spanish wasn't the best, but between growing up in LA and speaking some Portuguese, I'd survive. "Perdón," I said to the man behind the counter in a quiet voice, embarrassed already. "¿Dónde están los taxis?"

With a friendly smile, the young dude with short wavy hair and thick glasses pointed to my right and directed me in accented English. I nodded and said, "Gracias!" As I walked to the taxi stand, I glanced out the bank of windows to my left and stopped in my tracks.

What.

There was a storm raging outside—the palm trees bent, rain pouring in a slant, and everything blanketed in gray mist.

It had *not* been raining when we landed. The storm must have just started. What *was* this? My summer getaway hurricane?

After I grabbed a receipt at the taxi stand and waited in line outside, a cab was pulled up for me.

I slipped inside and took out a scrap of paper from my pocket. It had the hotel address, which I showed to the driver, an older man wearing a fedora and sporting a soccer jersey. He nodded and gave me a thumbs-up. "Okay!" he said.

"Gracias," I said in my quiet foreign-language voice, and settled back into the seat, the rhythm of the windshield wipers lulling me.

After a few minutes, the driver held out a phone charger. "¿Necesitas?" he asked.

"Oh, sí. Por favor." I hooked up my phone. "Gracias."

After a few seconds, my phone buzzed to life—alight with a flurry of texts from my dad, Rose, and Hamlet. I didn't open them.

We headed into the storm, and my stomach felt as tumultuous as the weather surrounding us.

CHAPTER 28

WE GOT ON THE HIGHWAY AND PASSED THROUGH Cancún—full of large, looming resorts that gave off eerily empty vibes during this storm. But after about an hour and a half, we turned onto a road that transported us from the busy, touristy, spring-break vibes of Cancún onto a more remote, low-key thoroughfare. There were people on bikes, even in the rain. Everyone looked less spring break and more yoga retreat. One side of the main road was jungle, and the other, just across the street, was beach. No large resorts here, just tucked-away "eco hotels" with discreet entrances off the main road. We pulled up to the Lotus Hotel—a small but elegant thatched-roof, two-story building with rustic wood columns. Despite the weather, the windows and doors were thrown open, with only gauzy white curtains separating the lobby from the elements. The driver helped me with my bag, and I thanked him.

As I hoisted the duffel onto my shoulder, I saw a figure run out from the entrance with a large white umbrella. It was a young guy wearing a polo shirt and khaki shorts. "Señorita, let me help you," he said as he took my bag.

"Oh, thank you."

He held the umbrella over me as we walked toward the hotel. The second we stepped inside, the stormy weather was muffled, even though we were basically standing in a glorified gazebo. Soothing music played, all flutes and chimes. Scattered between plush white furnishings were various bronze sculptures of elephants and tigers. Candles flickered everywhere, and I had the distinct feeling that someone was about to massage me right there in that lobby.

"Good evening. Do you need to check in?" a woman behind the front desk asked me. To her credit, she gave me and my dirty jeans and sweatshirt only the quickest once-over and managed to stay polite. Who knows how many children of celebrities had rolled in here looking as ratty as me?

"I'm here as a guest of Juliana Choi," I said.

The woman nodded. "Ah, are you the DJ for the party tonight?"

My eyes darted around. Was I being *Punk'd*? "DJ? Uh, no. I'm her daughter."

"Oh!" Her thick, sculpted eyebrows jumped in surprise. "Please excuse me. I wasn't told there was a daughter arriving . . ."

"It's a surprise," I said, beginning to feel nervous about this whole plan.

As she typed away, I wondered about this party. Did I pick a bad night to visit? She was hiring a *DJ*? My anxiety mounted with every tap of her keyboard, and I was about to drop my bag on the floor and text Mãe when I heard a shriek.

"Clara?"

I turned to see my mom running toward me, her arms raised and a huge smile on her face. And like every time I saw my mom, I was startled by how pretty and young she was. Petite in height, like me, but small-boned and delicate. Her long, highlighted brown hair was wavy and artfully tousled, spilling over onto a coral crop top that she wore with matching high-waisted shorts. A long, fringed, cream-colored robe was thrown over it all, and she resembled an exotic bird.

She embraced me in a tight bear hug as soon as she reached me. "I can't *believe* it!" she shrieked. I caught a whiff of some spicy perfume as she crushed her hair against my face.

"Surprise, Mãe," I said, laughing at her excitement.

Clutching my arms as she stood back, she asked, "What happened? Did your dad cave as you predicted? He texted me this morning, saying you were coming, but he wouldn't elaborate!"

I was about to answer when I realized something. "Wait, you knew I was coming?"

She pushed aside a lock of my hair and peered at my face, distracted when she answered. "Yeah, but I had no info on when you'd get here. I texted you to ask, but you didn't respond. I would have sent a car for you, silly." It's true—I had told my dad my plans but had purposely left out the flight info so he wouldn't try to catch me before I could get on the plane.

I also noticed that she said "sent a car" not "picked you up." I guess it wasn't surprising. My mom was *not* the kind of person to schlep over to the airport. She paid someone to fold her laundry for her. Macrobiotic meals were delivered to her home—her refrigerator was empty save for a few cans of sparkling water and iced coffee.

She nodded at one of the bellhops in the lobby and he came over, taking my duffel bag from me. There was something ludicrous about a well-groomed young man in a polo shirt holding my ten-year-old nylon black duffel with a giant rainbow-patterned patch that said DIE on it in huge letters.

"First, let's get you settled into your villa. It's *amazing*. You're basically *on the beach*, and the whole place is done up in *sheepskin*," Mãe said as she clip-clopped out of the lobby in her Greek sandals. My mother excelled at speaking in italics.

I followed her and the bellhop out into a courtyard, my wet Vans squeaking on the floors. "Wait, I get my own *villa*?"

Mãe looked back at me, winking over her shoulder. "Of course, do you think I'd make you share a room with me?"

While the idea of having my own "villa" was exciting, I was surprised by the simultaneous disappointment I felt—I had imagined spending tonight with my mom cozied into a giant bed watching *Real Housewives* and ordering room service, our usual hotel combo.

Instead, we approached a little hut with a thatched roof like the rest of the hotel, petite palm trees planted around its perimeter, a hammock swaying in the wind on a closed-off balcony. The bellhop opened the door, and we entered a room that was simply but stylishly furnished—all boho textiles and sheepskins tossed over rough-hewn wood pieces. There was a canopy bed tucked into a corner by a large window, the mosquito netting pulled aside, and a small sitting area with a love seat and coffee table. Another gauzy white curtain separated the room from the small bathroom with its bamboo-and-granite sink and rain showerhead.

It was probably the nicest room I would ever sleep in.

The bellhop left after my mom tipped him, and we were alone, finally. Unexpectedly, I felt shy. But my mom plopped onto my bed and pulled out her phone. "I'm gonna Story this, okay?" Pointing the phone at herself, her chin expertly tilted at a flattering angle as she lay down on the bed with her hair spread around her, she started speaking. "Guys. I had the BEST surprise of my life!" Then suddenly her face turned to its normal expression, and I knew the camera was pointed at me.

It's not like I wasn't used to this—my mom had been recording every minute of her life for the past few years—but I still felt ambushed. I pretty much knew what I looked like—a bedraggled mop with half my makeup rubbed off. My hands flew to cover my face instinctively.

Mãe laughed and went back into selfie mode. "That's my daughter, Clara, and she's feeling *uncharacteristically* shy. Best surprise EVER!" The words echoed back as she watched the video a few times before uploading it. She sprang up from the bed. "So, I gotta get ready for this poolside party thing. Meet me out there in a few?"

"What poolside party thing?" I asked, already staring longingly at my bed.

Her hands fluttered dismissively. "Oh, it's part of this whole tastemaker retreat."

"Wait, what? What retreat?"

She made a face and laughed. "Clara. That's what all of this is. I'm here as part of a retreat with other social media taste-makers."

My heart thudded down into my feet. "Oh. I guess I didn't know."

"Didn't I mention it?"

The fatigue from the travel hit me so hard then that I almost fell over. "Maybe you did? I don't remember."

"We'll still have fun! I'll just have to do a few events here and there."

The idea of being trapped in a resort full of social media

tastemakers made me want to scream, but I forced a smile. "Cool. Give me a sec and I'll meet you out there."

As soon as she left, I pulled out my phone, connected to the hotel's Wi-Fi, and took a deep breath. I had avoided this long enough.

After a couple of rings, my dad answered. "Clara?"

Out of *nowhere*, a tidal wave of homesickness rushed over me, filling my lungs. I couldn't breathe.

"Clara? Can you hear me?" he repeated.

I nodded, stupidly. Realizing he couldn't see me, I cleared my throat. "Yeah. Hi."

"HI?! IS THAT ALL YOU HAVE TO SAY RIGHT NOW?"

Something about his yelling calmed me down. I understood this; this was familiar.

"YOU WENT TO ANOTHER COUNTRY WITHOUT MY PERMISSION!"

Pause.

"HOW IS THAT LEGAL? WHAT HAS THIS COUNTRY COME TO? OH, BETTER NOT LET IN REFUGEES, BUT SURE, HEY, LET A MINOR FLY TO CENTRAL AMERICA!"

Pause.

"ARE YOU LISTENING TO ME?!"

I cringed. "Yes, I'm listening."

His breath came out in angry huffs. "Well? What do you have to say for yourself?"

"Young lady."

"What?!"

"You forgot to add 'young lady.'"

Another pause.

"Clara, I swear to God, I'm going to—"

"Kill me?"

"You know. Maybe. Maybe I'd murder you. My own child."

I started to laugh then, but then the laugh got weird and garbled and filled with tears. I managed to say, "I was so mad at you."

Pai's silence made me squirm. Finally, he responded, his voice tired. "I know. But, you have to wonder, was this reaction perhaps a *tad* disproportionate?"

"Nah. Seemed about right."

He sighed. "Clara. This is insane. You're in deep trouble when you get home, you realize this, right? Like, this is *way* worse than the fight with Rose. You're going to have to work on the truck your entire senior year to make it up to me."

The mosquito net got caught in my hair as I paced in my room, and I tried to pull it out with one hand. "I know. And I'll pay you back for this ticket. And everything else. But, I just . . ." With a quick yank, my hair was released. I straightened out. "I needed to see Mãe."

"You needed to see Mãe, or get away from us?"

He didn't have to clarify who "us" was. Hamlet's and Rose's unread texts practically weighed my hand down. I didn't answer, and when enough seconds had passed, my dad changed the subject. "Well, Shorty, how are you? How was the flight? How's *Tulum*?" The last word dripped with a faux frou-frou accent.

I sat down on the bed, my back against the fluffy pillows. "The flight was fine. I watched three movies."

"Whoa, which ones? Wait, let me guess. The new Marvel thing, the new Pixar thing, and a documentary about the financial crisis of 2007."

"Are you *psychic*?!"

We both laughed, then an awkward silence settled between us. "So, how's your mom?" he asked.

I stared at a large spider that was making its way across the wall next to the window. "She's good!" Could he hear the effort it took for me to be chipper? "And this hotel is, as you would say, *the bomb*. My villa is on the beach."

"*Your* villa?"

"Yeah, I get my own. Isn't that cool?"

The judgy pause on the other end made it clear that *no*, it was not cool. But he replied with, "Yeah! So what have you guys got planned?"

I turned on the ceiling fan when I realized how hot and sticky I was. "Well, I just got here, so not sure. There's a party tonight or something, so we're going to that."

"A *party*?"

"Pai. Calm down. It's one of the events for this retreat thing."

"Oh. So she told you about that?"

My dad's relief didn't go unnoticed. "You knew about it?"

I felt his shrug over the phone. "Yeah. Jules told me about it a while back." *Jules.* It was moments like this that reminded me that my parents had actually known each other at one point in their lives. Really well.

"Wait," he said. "Did *you* know?"

Ugh. When you were a kid with parents who were divorced or separated or whatever it was my parents were, you were stuck in this annoying diplomatic purgatory—always wondering if you were saying something to get the other parent in trouble. "Yeah, I knew," I lied again.

"I'm surprised you were still hell-bent on going, then."

I took my time responding because, had I known, maybe I wouldn't have been so quick to hop on a plane to get here. With my dad's credit card. In the middle of a fight with my boyfriend. "It's going to be fun. Once the storm passes, I'm going to work on my tan."

"Right, that storm. I saw that when I checked the weather report. Did your flight get in all right? When did you land?"

My dad and I talked for a bit longer—I told him the details of my flight, which he actually wanted to hear. Suddenly, I realized the rain had stopped. And that there was live music playing outside.

"I think I should go now," I said, reluctant to interrupt our conversation. "Party's in full effect."

"Okay. Well, enjoy yourself, because you're grounded forever once you get back."

I would have laughed except I knew he wasn't joking. "I will. I'll buy you a puka-shell necklace."

He laughed then. "Looking forward to it." A beat of silence. "I told Hamlet and Rose where you were."

Another wave of homesickness hit me. "I'm pretty sure I broke up with Hamlet. And Rose is probably mad, too."

"I don't think so. They were both worried about you."

I blinked, my eyes tired. "Is it okay if we don't talk about them right now?"

"Sure." He sighed. "Can you do me a solid, though, and call Hamlet? Or text him? Or something?"

The room was growing warmer. I fanned my face with my hand. "Maybe. I don't know."

"And, I noticed in my lovely airline receipt that you didn't buy a ticket back home yet. How long are you going to stay there?"

I stood up and moved the phone to my other ear so I could examine the thermostat. "I don't know."

"Lot of thought went into this plan of yours."

"Well, I mean, it's not *forever*."

"Oh good!" I heard Flo mew in the background, and I missed her so much.

"Talk to you later, Pai."

"Later, Shorty. Also: one week max, got it? You need some downtime before school starts."

A week. That seemed like forever and not enough at the same time. "Okay."

A pause. "Love you, little girl."

I swallowed the lump in my throat. "Love you, too, Pai."

When we hung up, I stared out the window at the beautiful people who had started to gather in the courtyard. Time to put my game face on.

CHAPTER 29

WHEN I STEPPED OUTSIDE, THE AIR WAS COOL AND THE sky was filled with stars. The storm had left everything drenched and sparkling—palm trees, the woven hammocks in everyone's villas, and the slick stone paths leading from the rooms to the lit-up courtyard.

Strings of twinkly lights and torches made everything glow. Perfect Instagram lighting, apparently—every single person out there seemed to be snapping Stories or photos on their phones. Beautiful moments never happened unless you uploaded them first.

I'd been to plenty of these kinds of events with my mom, and I'd dressed for the occasion. Knowing that I couldn't match these people with their outrageous clothing budgets, I went with "teenage minimalist": black cutoffs, my Docs with black ankle socks peeking out, and a white cotton T with the sleeves rolled up. I hadn't had time to shower, so I leaned into my dirty hair by adding more product to push it back from my face, the tousled strands tucked behind my ears.

Eyes appraised me as I wove through the crowd—everyone was probably wondering if I was that teen fashion blogger, or a YouTube star.

I found my mom pouring some kind of bubbly drink into a delicate wineglass, surrounded by people. She'd had a wardrobe change, too. Still wearing the fringy robe, she had switched into a long, silky black dress with a leg slit a mile high. She was barefoot and her hair was done up in an artfully messy topknot. What glammed up the entire outfit were her bright pink lips on a glowing, otherwise makeup-free face. When I noticed these things about my mom, I couldn't tell if it was admiration I felt or irritation.

She looked up with the glass and her eyes met mine. "Clara! Finally!" she exclaimed. "Everyone, meet my perfect daughter. I mean, *look* at her."

Gazes zeroed in on me. You could see some faces registering my age and doing the math. Others skimmed over me, head to toe, trying to figure out what I was trying to do with my outfit. Some smiled warmly at me.

"Cool intro, Mãe," I said drily before smiling at everyone. "Hi, I'm Clara."

Here's the thing: when you act confident, even when you're nervous, people relax and stop scrutinizing you.

"I didn't know you had a *child*, Jules!" A Latino man wearing the tightest shorts I'd ever seen pushed my mom playfully on the shoulder.

She handed me the drink, and I happily accepted it. "Well, I do, Jeremy. She's my one and only." Pouring another drink for herself, she looked up at the mini crowd held in her thrall with a huge grin. "And Clara is *amazing*. She flew out here and surprised me!"

"Get *out*!" This time Jeremy pushed me, and I had to laugh.

"It's not a big deal," I said before taking a sip of the drink, the fizziness pleasantly traveling down my throat.

A blond white woman wearing a tropical-print romper pointed her drink at me. "Said like a true cool teenager. How old are you?"

I glanced at my mom before answering. "Sixteen. Seventeen in a couple months."

Her eyes widened, metallic blue eyeliner meeting meticulous eyebrows. "Wow! Jules, when did you get pregnant?"

The familiarity didn't seem to faze my mom. She rolled her eyes. "Kendra, I was so young. God . . . I was basically *her* age. Can you even?"

"Babies having babies," Jeremy said with a disapproving cluck. Everyone cracked up, and the music thrummed through the night air, making everything feel funny and good and clever. Or maybe it was the champagne.

"Who's the dad?" Kendra asked.

Mãe perched herself on the edge of an armchair, the twinkly

lights creating a soft halo around her. "He was my high school boyfriend, Adrian. Meu Deus, Adrian was *so hot* back then."

I groaned. "Grossss."

She laughed and pulled me over to her. "Sorry, filha, but it's true. He was good at *break dancing*." Everyone laughed, but it wasn't unkind. Like a nostalgic we-get-it kinda laugh. "Anyway, I got pregnant, and the rest is history. Adrian's done a fantastic job helping raise this daughter of mine in LA."

Helping raise? Something needed to be corrected there, but I felt like it would be awkward to react, so instead I took another sip.

And I continued to drink—people kept offering me shots and various frosty cupped drinks with fruit in them. At one point, my mom and I did a near-perfect choreographed dance to "Baby One More Time." When Jeremy claimed that he was swim team captain in high school, I pushed him into the pool, only to dive in soon after. Soaking wet, I peeled off my shirt and wore it as a turban.

And I knew all this because people there recorded every single moment.

Sunlight streamed through the mosquito net, and I blinked. My mouth felt like it was filled with cotton, my head was throbbing, and there was something happening in my stomach that I had to stay very still to ignore.

There was a vibration near my leg. I grasped for my phone with the most minimal movement possible. *Do not barf. Do not barf. Do not barf.*

When I peered at the screen, the clock said eleven a.m. And there were about a billion texts from Rose and Hamlet. Now a prisoner in my hungover body, I finally decided to read them. I opened the ones from Rose first.

Yesterday:

Adrian told me you left for Tulum. He's kidding right?

HOLY CRAP YOU DID IT

How could you do this to your dad? TO US? The whole deal was we had to work all summer or get suspended when we get back. You BETTER not have messed this up for us.

Clearly we were never friends.

I hope you drown in the ocean.

This morning:

You know, for some reason I lost sleep over that last text to you. I don't want you to die but I wouldn't mind some severe injuries.

My head throbbed behind my eyes as if in response, but I still had to smile at these texts.

I wanted to read Hamlet's next, but first I needed some water. There was a bottle of Perrier in a gift basket from the hotel and I chugged it, almost choking in the process. Stupid sparkling water. I managed to drag myself to the bathroom, splashing my face. When I glanced in the mirror, I startled. If a raccoon became a ghost and then dipped its head in grease, it would have looked like me.

Feeling like The Worst, I picked up my phone again to read Hamlet's texts.

Yesterday:

I'm sorry about our fight. Can we talk?

Ok, I understand if you need time.

Wait. Adrian told me you went to TULUM???????

Because of our fight? Or your dad?

Either way, WTF CLARA! Can you please text me when you land? I just checked the weather for Tulum and there's a storm coming??

All right looks like there were no plane crashes today. But I also checked to see if anyone was abducted or murdered in Cancun and its surrounding areas and looks like no. So that means you're alive. I guess I'm relieved.

Today:

Uh. Have you seen your mom's IG? Who is that guy in the tight shorts?

I almost dropped my phone. Last night came back to me in quick flashes. *Ugggghhhhh social media influencers!* I wanted to respond to Rose and Hamlet, but I needed to shower. To clear my head.

An hour later, I managed to make it to the hotel café, essentially a long balcony filled with tables lined alongside the beach. My mom was already there, wearing a large straw hat and sunglasses, nursing a giant cup of coffee. I sat down between her and Kendra, who was drinking a *Bloody Mary* of all things. I held back a gag.

"Morning, filha," Mãe said, giving me a kiss on the cheek. "Want some coffee?"

I took her mug gratefully. "Yes, please."

Kendra clinked my mug with her Bloody Mary. "You were a total star last night. My DMs are *crazy* this morning. Everyone wants to know who you are!"

That made me cringe. "Oh God."

"Oh, yes. I got an earful from Adrian this morning," my mom said with an eye roll. "Thanks for getting me in trouble, friends."

Kendra laughed. "You're always welcome. Anyway, Clara, you have to join us for the *activities* today," she said, her round, mirrored sunglasses showing my grimacing expression reflected back at me.

I looked at my mom, who grinned and dug into a plate of eggs. "Oh yeah. You're coming."

"What are these *activities*?"

Kendra answered, "First, we're going shopping. There are a few sponsored posts we have to do with local boutiques. Then we're hitting up a spa. Lunch at a resort later. Then back here for a yoga class and chill before dinner."

I shrugged. "Cool, I'm in."

Mãe squealed. "I'm so glad you're here!"

With my headache subsiding and the sun shining, I couldn't help but smile and agree.

CHAPTER 30

TULUM HAS ONE LONG MAIN STREET, AND IT'S WHERE you can find a lot of the boutiques, cafés, and restaurants. It was a very sleepy town that had somehow, in the past few years, become wildly popular.

Riding a sleek new beach cruiser, I glanced at the squad I was with. Jeremy and Kendra had joined us, along with a few others: a photographer who traveled the world taking photos of fancy hotels, a stylist for celebs, someone who ate a lot of fancy food, and an interior designer. My mom and Kendra were both fashion influencers—meaning they wore free designer clothes and took lots of photos and collaborated with designers sometimes. Jeremy was an architect who also happened to be a model.

The day was sunny, but there were dark clouds on the horizon. Apparently, it was the rainy season, so the weather was temperamental. We had already hit up a few boutiques where everyone had gotten free stuff (including me! A pair of insanely overpriced leather sandals and a straw hat—both of which I decided to wear immediately) and taken a thousand and one photos.

We were on our way to the spa at yet another eco resort. I found a lot of this stuff really over-the-top, but at the same time I couldn't deny that it was a pretty sweet deal. Getting paid to shop and relax? To eat fancy food and stay at posh boutique hotels? Okay!

"That hat looks fab, Clara Shin!" Kendra shouted to me from her bike, snapping a photo and making her bike teeter precariously for a few seconds while doing so. I couldn't believe none of them had eaten it while filming and riding. It was bound to happen, right? Bonus points if caught on camera. I was almost willing to do it for them.

While everyone else had been glued to their phones all afternoon, I decided to leave mine back in my room. One, international roaming charges were no joke. Two, avoiding Hamlet and Rose.

I popped a wheelie, making someone behind me scream with fear. My mom called out, "You better not hurt yourself on this trip, or Adrian will kill me!" He would, but it was my dad who taught me all the tricks on my eighth birthday. I felt another wave of homesickness, but the kind where I wished my dad could be here to experience this with me. I couldn't remember the last time he traveled anywhere by plane. He would have foodie-fainted over the ceviche we'd had at the party last night.

A couple of spa staff were waiting for us at the entrance that was shaded by tall palms. They took our bikes (bike *valet*?), and we entered the white adobe-style building. After getting signed in and bundled up in plush robes, we got our various treatments—everything was planned out for us: first, a dip in the various pools. I stayed in the cold one, sweaty from the bike ride. Then we got hot stone massages in individual huts outside. I made sure to stick close to my mom. I didn't want to be rubbed down while naked next to a stranger. Then it was time for a facial. My face was glowing afterward, and I felt like an angel. When everyone was in the saunas and steam rooms, I went poolside and took a nap. Throughout everything, we were served bottled water with slices of lemon and various fruits. My mom took a Story of me with an orange slice covering my teeth as she asked me a bunch of questions, cracking up the entire time. I also let her take photos of me with cucumbers on my eyes, even though apparently that was a spa cliché and no one really did that anymore.

By the time we got back to the hotel, I was pooped from pampering. Everyone seemed to feel the same and went off to their villas to relax until the yoga class.

My mom and I lay back in lounge chairs facing the Caribbean Sea, each with a coconut in hand. People actually did that here. I was hoping for a sunset, but Mãe told me we were facing east. She said we could have dinner on the jungle side tomorrow to watch it to the west. As a warm breeze drifted lazily over us, I glanced at my mom and smiled. "Today was fun."

She rolled over onto her side to look at me. "Right? I'm so glad you made it, meu bem." When my mom wasn't around her posse, she used Portuguese mom-expressions like "meu bem."

"Me too." And I was.

"How's everything going, then?" she asked, taking a sip.

I shrugged. "Fine."

"Really? Then how come Adrian was totally panicked when he called me yesterday?"

My head swiveled toward her. "What! You told me . . ."

"Girl. I was lying. Where do you think you get your skills from?" She flipped her hair to punctuate the point.

I shook my head. "Of course." The sky darkened, and someone lit the tiki torches around us. "Well, I kind of . . . left without telling Pai."

"What?"

"Yeah."

"How did you pay for your ticket?" Incredulity made her eyes huge.

Picking at the lemon yellow cushion on my chair, I took my time answering. "I know Pai's credit card number by heart."

"Meu Deus," she breathed, making the sign of the cross on herself. "I can't believe you're still alive."

"I know. It was . . . impulsive."

"Ya think?" she said with an exaggerated American accent.

"What made you do it? You wanted to come here that badly? *I* could have convinced your dad!"

Someone came by to offer us mango slices. We dutifully took some. So delicious, it hurt. After chewing, I responded, "Well, see, I entered the KoBra in a food truck competition. It was supposed to be a surprise for Pai because the reward is *one hundred thousand dollars*." Mãe whistled. "Yeah. Exactly. But then Rose accidentally told him about it—"

"Who's Rose?"

I exhaled impatiently. "My friend from school who had to work with me on the truck."

"Wait, your *friend*? Adrian told me you guys got into a huge fight and that's why you had to work on the truck in the first place?"

My hand fluttered between us. "Yeah, we hated each other, but it's cool now. *Anyway*. She told him about the contest, and he *freaked out* and got mad. At *me*!" I looked to her for confirmation on how horribly unfair it was.

She frowned. "Why?"

"I have no clue! I mean, he was in a bad mood because an investor backed out for his restaurant."

"Clara." My mom looked at me with exasperation. "Maybe he was just in a bad mood, and it wasn't the right time to tell him the news about the contest?"

I ate another slice of mango. "Maybe. Either way, he got mad and that made me mad." Suddenly my words sounded absurd coming out of my mouth. The monumentalness of my dad's offense became so small as I sat here on a beach in Tulum. I tried to figure out why, at the time, it felt so big. "It made me mad because . . . I finally cared about this stupid truck. And I was trying to help—that money could be the final piece he needs to open his dream restaurant! And, and . . ."

"You were disappointed?" my mom asked. She was stirring her coconut water, the question casual. Perfunctory, even. But it zeroed in on everything.

The ocean and sky were the same color now. I stared at the reflection of the moon on the water. "Yeah. I was disappointed." And it was the first time I had been that thoroughly disappointed. It's easy not to be disappointed when you're always wading in the shallow end of feelings. Patrick and Felix never disappointed me. I glanced at my mom.

Neither did she.

"Hey, so your dad also told me you were dating someone new?"

The subject change caught me off guard. "Oh. Yeah . . . I mean, I was? I'm not sure what the deal is now. I fought with him, too, before I left," I said sheepishly.

"Wow, Clara. Burning everything *down*," she said, spraying herself with some mosquito repellent. "What's his deal?"

Hm, Hamlet's deal. How to explain this guy? "Well, he works at this coffee kiosk at one of our stops. Which he doesn't really have to do because his parents are rich. Like, they own skyscrapers in China rich." My mom nodded knowingly. I'm sure she knew every variety of wealth in her line of work. I continued, "He was born in Beijing and moved to LA when he was little, but his parents moved back for work, so he lives with some family friends. They're cool. And he goes to a different school but is the same grade as me. And . . . that's where our similarities end." I had to laugh.

"What does he look like? Is he cute?" Right down to business, my mother.

"He's your basic . . . hot."

"Basic hot?"

I squinted. "No, he's more than that. I mean, he's definitely hot. But there's nothing basic about him." I swallowed the lump that was forming in my throat talking about him. A buildup of guilt, remorse, and *missing*. "He's driven and kind. A boxer."

"Ooh."

"Yeah. There's a lot of 'ooh.' "

My mom whipped her phone out. "Can I find him on your Insta?"

"Yeah. He's there."

I craned my neck to watch as she scrolled through my feed. "Oh!" she exclaimed, pointing to a photo of him holding Flo up like a prize fish. "Is that *him*?"

A surge of happiness coursed through me just seeing his face. "Yeah, that's him! Hamlet."

She glanced up at me. "Excuse me?"

"Don't ask."

"Well, he's *cute*. What's the problem? Why did you fight?"

It's the least special thing about you. The words still hurt days later. "Oh. You know. The stuff people fight about."

Before she could respond, Kendra and Jeremy were running down the beach waving to us with big, sweeping arm gestures. My mom waved back. "Looks like yoga's starting," she said, getting up. She held out her hands to help me up. "Well, don't be too sad, Clara. High school romances, who needs them, right? There are so many guys out there, and they'd be lucky to date you."

It was the nice, mom thing to say. But a small part of me wanted her to push me, to challenge my reasons for wanting to end things with Hamlet. But I knew, for my mom, high school romances didn't work out. And she'd been keeping herself at arm's reach from those kinds of intense feelings ever since.

I trailed behind her as she ran toward her friends. A reminder of teenage mistakes, of the ephemeral nature of love.

CHAPTER 31

DAYS PASSED IN A RELAXED AND PAMPERED HAZE.

I'd wake up, take a morning yoga class with my mom or Kendra or someone on the beach, have a super-late brunch at the hotel, then spend the afternoon helping my mom take photos of herself at some destination. One day it was ancient ruins (which was rad until someone almost fell off a ledge taking a selfie); another day it was sailing to an island where we had a picnic spread out for us with, like, antique flatware. Evenings were always spent back at the hotel—dinner, drinks, hot tub. Repeat.

And in all that time, I had sent one text to Hamlet: **Thanks for checking in. I'm good. I just need time. Talk soon.**

He had responded with a thumbs-up emoji, which in Hamlet-speak was a low-key "F-you."

I had apologized to Rose but I hadn't heard back yet. It would have worried me more, except it was easy to bury that stuff deep in the back of my brain, prioritized way below the sand in my bathing-suit bottom or the mosquito bites on my ankles.

But one morning I woke up and just didn't feel like doing yoga. Instead I wondered what Rose, Hamlet, and my dad were doing. Because my dad was respecting my time with Mãe, I hadn't really talked to him, either. How was the KoBra doing? Was Rose still working on it? Did Hamlet win his boxing tournament last weekend? Was it still hot in LA? Did Flo miss me?

So I told my mom I was going to take the day for myself. I borrowed her iPad because I had dropped my phone into the ocean yesterday, and it was on the fritz. I slathered on sunscreen even though the day was overcast, packed my backpack with water and the iPad, then hopped on my bike.

Shuttled off from one activity to the next since the day I arrived, I hadn't had time to explore on my own. I was pretty tired of all the restaurants and businesses on the main drag, so I decided to explore the small side streets today.

The instant I turned left onto the first random street, the vibe completely changed. Everything was slower, quieter. I saw actual children playing in the road. There were homes and businesses, but spread far apart, and the buildings were older, less finished.

Time passed as I rode leisurely around these little roads and soon the sun came out—beating down on my new straw hat. Sweat trickled down my temple, and I pulled over to have some water. As I guzzled out of my bottle, I noticed a small wooden sign with an arrow pointing down a sandy path shaded by overgrown tropical greenery. Vines and ropey limbs tangled up to create a dense corridor.

Well, why not? I walked my bike down the path, swatting at the occasional mosquito. After a few minutes, the plants gave way, and I was standing on a pristine white beach. But in the middle of it was a tiny hut and plastic tables scattered with chairs. Nothing matched, everything looked like it came from someone's porch.

I loved it.

"Hola," a woman greeted me warmly as I walked up to the hut. There was a counter, and I could smell food cooking in the back.

I smiled and waved. "Hola." Then I glanced around to see if there was a menu.

Catching my searching expression, the woman said, "No menu here. We cook what we have!"

Sniffing the air, I was down to eat whatever they were serving. "Okay, sounds good." She told me to seat myself, and I sat down at the table closest to the ocean. There were some people in the water. It seemed like you could plop down at the beach here and eat or just hang out.

The setting was perfect and quiet and peaceful. And yet . . . the antsiness I'd woken up to was still there. I pulled my mom's iPad out of my backpack, slipping it from its designer leather sleeve. I really wanted to see what was going on with the KoBra.

Opening up the browser, I planned on stalking the Twitter

account first, but my mom's e-mail popped up. I was about to close out of it until I noticed a folder labeled CLARA on the sidebar.

Probably all of our e-mail correspondence archived. Oh boy, there would definitely be some hilarious gems in there—like the epic diary entries I'd sent her in middle school when I hated all my friends. I clicked on it, excited to go down memory lane.

But the e-mails weren't from me. They were from Pai.

What? Were these, like, child-custody-related e-mails? I knew I shouldn't, but I clicked on the latest one, which was from a few weeks ago.

July 24
To: Juliana Choi
From: Adrian Shin

Jules,
Does Clara know this Tulum trip is for work? She seems to think it's just a vacation for you two. Mind clearing that up so she's not so pissed about not being able to go?
-Adrian

I frowned. Okay, clearly my dad was waiting for my mom to tell me. Which she never had. I scrolled down and skimmed the e-mail subjects. My dad had been sending them regularly for years, it seemed. I clicked one from six months ago, in February.

February 10
To: Juliana Choi
From: Adrian Shin

Jules,
Clara's sad about her breakup with that loser
whatshisname. Thought she could use some Mom time
when Valentine's Day comes around. Probably less
awkward than me talking to her. Give her a call, okay?
-Adrian

Whatshisname. My dad's least favorite boyfriend of mine,
Leo, he of the no teeth-brushing. He always called my dad "bro."
Although he wasn't the love of my life, I had been pretty bummed
when we broke it off. So it was nice when my mom called. We
had Skyped while watching the least romantic movie we could
think of on Valentine's Day. (*Blackfish*—nothing kills romance
like a documentary about animal cruelty!) I had chalked up the
timing to Mom instincts.

I went even further back, to two years ago.

September 3
To: Juliana Choi
From: Adrian Shin

Jules,
Hey, I didn't hear back about whether or not you can make
it to Clara's birthday this year. Here's the wish list I promised

of things she wants. She's going through a spectacular phase in puberty of hating everything, so this was a serious undertaking.

- *The Bell Jar* by Sylvia Plath
- A Venus flytrap
- A neon sign shaped like a cat
- New pair of Vans, high-top black ones
- Colored pencils
- Something called "primer." I think it's makeup??
- Pasta maker

True mystery, our daughter.

-Adrian

My breath caught in my throat. I got every single thing on my birthday list that year. From my mom. My dad took me to the beach, and I remember thinking my mom was so much cooler than him. How she was so good at knowing exactly what I liked. He had let her take all the glory for the presents.

Always.

I went as far back as ten years ago in e-mails and found birthday lists then, too. From my dad to my mom, every time. Dozens, hundreds of e-mails. Reminders for my mom about school recitals and upcoming visits. Photos of me on the first day of school in slightly bizarre outfits. Horrible class pictures. Holiday and birthday photos when she couldn't make it—posing with the gifts she sent. Updates on my health, including medications I was taking when I got sick. Every lost tooth noted. The first day of my period and the sheer panic that came with it. Questions about birth control and makeup and clothes.

This folder was a record of my entire life.

My food arrived: a whole grilled fish with buttery rice, beans, and a fresh salad. I looked up and the same woman from behind the counter looked concerned. "¿Estas bien?" she asked.

I touched my face; it was wet with tears. Good God. Crying in public was my new thing now? "Yes, I'm fine! Just allergies." She gave my shoulder a little pat, and I stared at the screen for a few seconds before shutting it off.

When I took a bite of the food, I immediately thought of how much Pai would like the seasoning. Sitting there eating fish on a white sand beach with a cool breeze drifting over me, more than ever I wished I were on the KoBra—enclosed in an over-heated truck with my dad and my best friend.

CHAPTER 32

WHEN I GOT BACK TO THE HOTEL, MY MOM WAS GETTING her hair and makeup done in her villa.

"Clara! You're just in time. I'm about to start this interview for *Pleat and Gather*," she said as a stylist tugged viciously on her hair with a curling iron.

I plopped onto her bed. "What's *Pleat and Gather*?"

"You don't know *PLEAT AND GATHER*?" she yelped, whether from incredulity or pain, I couldn't tell. "It's only the biggest fashion website, kiddo. Anyway, wanna stick around?"

"I have no life obligations, so sure." I was a little dazed from my afternoon snooping, and passively watching my mom get interviewed seemed like a great idea at the moment.

The interview took place outside, where my mom lounged on

a pale pink sofa, the white sand beach and sparkling blue ocean as her backdrop. Her hair fell in waves over her tanned shoulders, and she wore a long white linen dress with thin spaghetti straps, her legs tucked under her casually. She looked like a fancy mermaid.

With a camerawoman behind her, the interviewer—a young Mexican blogger with a bleached-blond bob named Teresa—started asking Mãe questions.

"We're here with influencer and tastemaker Juliana Choi in gorgeous *it* destination Lotus Hotel in Tulum." *Gotta get that product placement.* "Jules, as her fans like to call her, does it all with her four million followers—travels the world, sits in the front row of every major fashion event, and collaborates with designers to add that *extra*. She's also a mom to a very chill teenage daughter who's here with us. Can you *even?*"

Luckily, I was sitting in a chair behind the camera woman, so they couldn't swing the camera over to me or anything. Nonetheless, I still felt uneasy being discussed. My mom winked at me, and I was sure her fans would love that authentic private moment between mother and daughter.

"So Jules, tell us about your creative journey."

I resisted laughing.

Mãe settled back into the patterned cushions. "Well, since I was a child, I was always drawn to beautiful things. I grew up in Brazil, surrounded by lush tropical landscapes, and that sensibility still informs me." I couldn't help but wonder—informs *what*? Social media people always talked about "creating content."

It seemed like a catchall to legitimize careers built on taking photos of yourself in aspirational settings. But people loved it, so who was I to judge? Also? My mom grew up in São Paulo, a huge city that I wouldn't exactly describe as "lush." She continued, "Not to mention the cultural influences—Catholic icons, the people, the food, the rich layers of diversity."

Teresa nodded intensely. "*Yes*, girl. So inspiring." Huh? She barely said anything! Didn't "journey" mean talk about actual events? But Teresa moved ahead. "What was your childhood in Brazil like?"

I knew what it was like. Her parents struggled financially running a small grocery store and were so strict and religious that my mother grew up feeling stifled and alone.

"Wild and free," Mãe said with a laugh. *Huh?* "You couldn't ask for a more magical childhood. Children played on the streets. I'd be fed by the street vendors and I ran amok. It was just so *liberating.*"

It was hard for me to keep a straight face as she kept talking about this magical childhood of hers. My mom had *hated* her childhood—it was what drew her to my dad, their common ground. I knew my mom was probably lying because the reality was so depressing, and this wasn't exactly a probing profile by the *New Yorker*, but still . . . It was so disingenuous it made me itchy.

"Speaking of liberation, do you have any plans to 'settle down' and work for a designer? You'd be great at branding," Teresa said.

A little wrinkle appeared between my mom's eyebrows. "I

adore all the designers I've collaborated with. But I'm not sure if I could ever pick a city in the world to live in for that long, you know?" Teresa nodded in firm agreement. "I love . . . *the world*. Discovery. I get to meet different people every month or week. I guess if most people are trees—putting down deep roots—I'm like an air plant?"

"Amaaaazing," Teresa declared, her eyes closing worshipfully. I was trying not to laugh. Leave it to my mom to pick an of-the-moment hipster plant to compare herself to.

Suddenly Teresa was looking at me. "Let's get real and talk about being a mother! How did you find time to raise such a great kid *and* follow your dreams?"

My skin tingled waiting for her answer. Because for sixteen years I had managed to gloss over, in my own memories, how absent my mom was. It felt like she was there because my dad made sure of it. She never missed a birthday call, gift, or holiday. But she wasn't actually there.

"I was really young when I had Clara," Mãe said. She took a long pause. "Obviously, right?" she said with a little laugh. Teresa laughed. She had a way, my mother.

"When I moved to LA with her dad, I was so lost," she said. And there it was. A genuine moment. "I thought that if I was a teen mom, I had to give up on my dreams. But, with Clara's dad's support, I was able to strike out on my own."

If I was being resentful, I would say that was an understatement. My dad's support? He raised me.

But everything about my mom—her uncomplicated ambitions,

the superficial friendships, never leaving her comfort zone—it all reminded me of . . . well, me. And I understood her.

I just didn't want to *be* her anymore.

As she continued the interview, a rosy revisionist history of our past, I snuck back to my villa and booked a flight home.

CHAPTER 33

"DID I DO SOMETHING WRONG?"

I looked up at my mom while I packed a few hours after the interview. "No! You didn't. I promise. It's just time for me to go back home. I left a lot of things hanging."

She sat down on the edge of my bed and nodded. "I got that feeling. Is it about that boy, Hamlet?"

I smiled. Hearing his name said by my mom was sweet. I liked her being in the loop. "Yes. But also the KoBra. Pai. Rose. I let people down." I willed my voice not to waver as I threw my new sandals into the duffel.

Mãe was quiet as she watched me pack. "I'll miss you." And even though my mom could be astonishingly clueless and self-absorbed sometimes, I knew I would also miss her.

"Me too."

"You'll miss you, too?" she joked.

I cracked a smile. "Good one."

"I know." She crossed her legs, turning herself into a tidy, folded little mermaid person. "So, why are you in such a rush?" I was catching a red-eye tonight to make it to LA by morning.

"Because the food truck competition is tomorrow." I wasn't sure if I could pull it off—I had e-mailed Rose and she'd responded immediately, saying she'd figure out a way to get the truck and meet me at the competition. I could tell she was still a little mad, but she seemed as invested in this contest as I was.

"Whoa. Bold move. Adrian was against it, right?"

Ignoring the nervous flutter against my ribs, I nodded. "Yep. But I still want to go through with it."

She squinted at me. "That's new."

"What, this?" My hand drifted up to the little silver hoop in my left ear cartilage, pierced a few months ago.

"No. This . . . drive." She paused and I was self-conscious. I hated that I wanted my mom to think that I was cool. "I like it," she said. "It suits you." The second person to say these words.

I tried to hide my pleasure by making a face, crossing my eyes. "I have so much drive. The *best* drive. Huge."

Mãe cracked up. "Well, good luck, minha filha." It was both optimistic and ominous.

After saying my good-byes to the social media squad that I had grown rather fond of, I got into a car headed to the airport.

My mom popped inside to give me one last hug. "See you soon, filha. Te amo."

"Love you, too, Mãe." I was usually so sad when we said our good-byes—never knowing when it would be that I'd see her next. And it wasn't that I wasn't sad this time. It was just that there was a lot for me to look forward to outside of this good-bye. Real life.

As the car drove away from the hotel, the sky rumbled and fat raindrops splashed onto the windshield. I tried not to read too much into the timing.

The flight back home wasn't too bad, even though the grandma next to me farted steadily the entire time. At least it was direct.

Bright eyed and bushy tailed after two hours of sleep, I swept through customs in record time and ran down the long LAX corridor lined with colorful subway tile.

I only had a few hours until the food truck competition started. It was going to be nuts since my phone was still broken and I would have to grab a cab and hope Rose was all set up.

The international terminal exit had a row of people waiting for their loved ones.

A very large, very neon yellow poster caught my eye. It said: MY GIRLFRIEND. And the person holding it was flipping it around his head, much to the annoyance of everyone near him.

My smile hurt my face it was so intense, and I ran toward

Hamlet. When I reached him, jostling people and apologizing along the way, he dropped the sign and closed the distance between us in two big steps.

We were so close that I could see the bit of sunblock left smudged and white on his cheek.

"I'm sorry," I blurted out.

He frowned, and for half a second my heart stopped. Then he leaned over and kissed me. Kissing Hamlet felt like coming home, for real. I stood up on my toes to deepen the kiss, my duffel smashed between us. When we finally broke apart, he smiled down at me, all tenderness. "I forgive you." Just like that. Hamlet was the least complicated thing in my life.

"That's it?"

He picked up the poster and tapped my butt with it. "Lucky you."

Suddenly it occurred to me—"How'd you know I was coming?"

He turned red. "Well, I might have talked to your mom."

"What?"

He took my bag from me, trying to distract me from what he was about to say. "Well, when you left I started following her on Instagram and, uh, well, she messaged me yesterday to tell me you were coming home. She wanted someone to be here to pick you up."

That's when I noticed Hamlet was wearing a KoBra T-shirt. "What's that?"

He grinned. "I'm going to help at the competition today."

Something warm bloomed in my chest. "You are?"

"Yeah. Why do you think I'm here? We have to *haul.*"

Minutes later, we were sprinting toward Hamlet's car in the parking garage. "We still have three hours before the competition!" he yelled, glancing back at me as he ran with my duffel carried easily over his shoulder.

We threw everything into the car, slammed on our seat belts, and peeled out of the parking lot. I braced myself against the dashboard and laughed. "Dang, James Bond."

He immediately slowed down and glanced over at me sheepishly. "Sorry, I just got caught up in the moment."

"I'm not complaining!"

"Well, it's not safe," he grumbled, pulling on his sunglasses primly. I shook my head but couldn't keep the smile off my face.

We got onto the freeway, starting our long trek to the competition. At the moment, we were on the westernmost side of town, near the beach, and the competition was a good twenty miles away at Griffith Park. I looked at the time nervously. "I hope the traffic gods are on our side today."

"Don't worry, I know all the best ways to avoid traffic," he said firmly. "The question is, what the heck was your plan? You were going to steal the truck and take it to the competition? Just you and Rose?"

"Well. Yes."

"Oh my God."

"What?" I stuck my chin out.

"It's just . . . the worst plan, that's all."

Hamlet drove across three lanes until we landed in the Express-Lane. I looked at him in surprise. "You have a FasTrak?"

"No."

"I'm really into this Jason Bourne side of you."

Again, he slowed down. "Don't get used to it. Is your seat belt on?" he barked.

"Yes, sir," I said with a wink, which only flustered him further.

We flew by some gridlock, but I kept my glee to myself. There's this LA curse—if you actually express your smugness at passing traffic, you will immediately hit some. It happens every single time.

"This is going to be the best surprise!" Hamlet exclaimed, slapping his hands on the steering wheel happily. "Rose kind of hates you right now, though. Just FYI."

"I'm counting on it." The thought of being stuck in that stuffy truck bickering with Rose filled me with the most intense relief. I found myself missing the weirdest stuff lately.

And, like with Hamlet, I knew the first thing I needed to do when I saw her was apologize.

We were quiet for a few seconds, long enough for the car to be filled with a huge elephant. His love confession and my non-reciprocation. I chewed my lip down to bits trying to decide if this was the right time to bring it up.

Hamlet's phone buzzed with a barrage of texts. THANK GOD! I picked it up gratefully. "Rose is freaking out."

"Ignore it," he said, speeding up again.

"You got it, Bryan Mills."

"Who's *that*?"

"You know, Liam Neeson's character from the *Taken* movies?"

He shook his head and turned on the radio. Loud.

The rest of the drive was quick—there was no traffic, and we found a parking spot in a secret lot that Hamlet knew about. I found this competence very attractive.

Taking a few trails off the main path shaded by ancient live oak trees, I could hear and smell the trucks before we arrived. They were parked in a giant lot bordered by the gnarled old trees and gently sloping hills of brush. As we got closer, my nerves finally caught up with me and I was filled with trepidation.

When I saw the KoBra, I took a deep breath. *Here we go.*

CHAPTER 34

ROSE STARED AT ME, FROWNING.

For normal friends, it would have been a moment ripe for a hug. But I was me and she was Rose. So we stood there awkwardly without speaking. I punched her arm. "Hi."

She punched my arm back. Hard. "Hi."

"Sorry for leaving you," I said, the words whooshing out of me. And I was surprised by how easy and natural it was. Words that usually had to be yanked out of my insides with a crowbar.

Her delicate chin quivered. I was mortified. Seeing Rose cry would be like breaking the seventh seal to bring on the apocalypse or something.

"We can talk about that later," she said, her voice steady. Before I could answer, I spotted my dad in the doorway of the truck.

What! What was he doing here? The happiness that flooded me in that moment almost knocked me off my feet. Never had I been happier to see that lucky Dodgers cap.

I looked over at Rose and she smiled. "Surprise!"

"Adrian?" Hamlet exclaimed from behind me.

But my dad kept it cool. He leaned against the truck's doorframe and crossed his arms—the birthday tattoo visible on his forearm. "Well, well, well."

Looking at my dad in his truck—a culmination of decades of blood, sweat, and tears—the e-mails I'd read yesterday flashed through my mind, paired with the strongest memories of my childhood.

The day my mom left, the feeling of her hair pressed against my face and the wetness of her tears immediately forgotten when my dad scooped me up in his arms and took me down to this very park we were standing in. Putting me on the little train that traversed through creeks, horse stables, and trees. The worst day turned into a magical one.

My first day of kindergarten, the first time I'd been truly apart from my dad and left with strangers. He let me wear his old Bone Thugs-N-Harmony T-shirt, tied into a knot at the waist, and the animal charm bracelet my mom had mailed me for good luck. When I wouldn't stop crying, he stayed parked outside the school, within view of the window all day—missing his first day at a new job and getting fired.

Being picked up from a sleepover in fifth grade when all the girls circled around me and asked me why my dad was so young and was he really my brother and where were my *real* parents. My dad pounded on the front door of Lily Callihan-Wang's house so hard that the entire family woke up. He bought me a McDonald's hot fudge sundae on the midnight drive home and we sang along to TLC's "No Scrubs."

My dad's expression as he sat in the doctor's office with me as I got a shot for a bacterial infection, wailing. Not being able to tell if it was his palm that was sweaty or mine as he grasped my hand, so tight.

My dad's expression, again, as he read the instructions on the back of a tampon box out loud to me as I lay curled up in fetal position on my bed, torn between laughter and tears.

And his expression, now. I realized right then—how disappointed you could be when you were all in with someone. When you cared so deeply. How your heart could break, so precisely and quickly.

But I'd always known that. Ever since my mom left my dad, left us. And everything since then had been an attempt to keep myself so far away from all that. Anything real, anything difficult to hold on to.

As I stood there surrounded by three people who had the ability to do just that—crack my chest open to all the disappointment and difficulty and grief—I knew I still wanted it. The risk of the bad stuff was so worth the good stuff. People who would be there for you even when you messed up and behaved like a little jerk? They were the good stuff.

My fear that my dad would move on without me, with Kody or whoever else, seemed so absurd then.

It was hard to keep the emotion out of my voice. "I'm back."

"I see," Pai said, cool and distant.

I took a deep breath. "And I'm the worst person. Do you still want me as your daughter?" The words came out choked, garbled.

His posture relaxed and he smiled, somehow sad and happy at the same time. "Sure, Shorty." He stepped down from the truck and when he reached me, I hugged him fiercely.

"I'm sorry," I said into his shirt, the tears dropping rapidly—they'd been at the ready since the second I saw him. I heard Rose and Hamlet tactfully walk away from us.

His chin rested on the top of my head, and he wrapped his arms around me, too. "I know."

"I'll never do anything like that again."

"I canceled my credit card, for one thing."

I laughed a little, snot running down my face. "I overreacted. I was just disappointed and it was hard and Mãe was easy."

He pulled back and rubbed the snot off my face with the dish towel from his back pocket. "Yeah, she has a way of making everything seem simple."

I looked at my dad's face—the one that resembled mine, but with a straighter nose and darker eyes. "The thing is, I didn't like it? It was fun at first but, ultimately . . ."

He smiled that crooked, knowing smile. "Unsatisfying?"

That was it. "Yeah. Missing something."

I heard a sniffle from somewhere inside the truck. Whether it was Rose or Hamlet, I really couldn't say.

"Don't ever do that again. Got it?" He poked my forehead.

I scowled but nodded. "I won't. I don't want to let you down again. Ever."

"Well, you will." He tucked the towel back into his pocket. "But that's okay. I'll be here."

There were two faces looking out at me from the windows on the KoBra. Rose wiped her eyes, and Hamlet was openly crying. Oh my God, we were a freaking mess!

My dad rubbed his hands together. "Ready to do this?"

"Yes! But wait, why did you change your mind?"

"You have a persuasive, annoying friend," he said drily, glancing at the truck.

As if on cue, Rose stuck her head out the window, her eyes miraculously dry. "Okay, cool! Everyone's happy and made-up— we only have an hour and a half until judging!"

My eyes widened at my dad. "Can we do it?"

He nodded, jaw slightly clenched. "Yeah, let's do this."

We scrambled into the truck. My dad tossed a KoBra T-shirt at me, and I started unbuttoning my flannel to put it on.

"CLARA!" Three voices shouted at me. I looked up to see everyone with their backs turned toward me.

"Calm down, puritans," I said while pulling on the T-shirt. "Hamlet, don't pretend like you don't love it."

There might as well have been a giant anime sweat drop over his head. He laughed nervously, looking at my dad. Pai made a strangled noise and banged the pots and pans around. "When Clara's done stripping, let's make our game plan," he said.

We immediately kicked into gear. Pai and I were in charge of meats, Rose was in charge of rice and sides, and Hamlet was tasked with drinks and assembly. The truck grew warm once we had the grill and burners on, and an unpleasant sense of panic washed over everything as we scrambled.

And then suddenly: "Ten minutes until judging!" Hamlet yelled.

My dad and I looked at each other. I'd never seen him so nervous. I tried to distract him as I stirred the sauce with a whisk. "So, do you know how the judging works?"

He nodded. "I did my research while you were gone. In ten minutes, they'll be coming up to the trucks, one by one, and trying our food. Did you know Stephen Fitch is a judge?" His voice almost squeaked.

"I did. That's why I entered us. We're basically custom-made for that man. Inventive cuisine unique to the LA immigrant experience? Check and *check*."

And then our ten minutes were up. My dad rushed around to make sure the dishes looked perfect, adding touches here and there. Wiping off the edges of the plates with a towel and peering down at each one with hawk eyes. I went over to where Hamlet was pouring drinks and moved a cup closer to his ladle so it wouldn't drip. He looked at me, his cheeks flushed from the heat and the excitement. "Thanks."

I winked at him. He turned redder, and I gave him a quick kiss, pressing my cool lips to his hot mouth.

"Hey, you two! No kissing while handling food!" my dad shouted.

And then an air horn blared somewhere outside, making me cover my ears with both hands. Someone spoke into a megaphone: "Time's up! Judges will be coming by."

We looked at one another nervously. I fanned my face with a plate. Rose smoothed her hair repeatedly. Hamlet picked up a pen and spun it on his fingers. My dad took a long swig of water from a Tupperware container.

After a few minutes, I stuck my head out the window to see where the judges were. There were about twenty trucks in this competition so this was going to take *forever*.

My dad cleared his throat. "Well, everyone. I just wanted to say thanks. Thanks for helping me this entire summer, even if you were forced. And thanks so much for this." He glanced at me. "I never would have done it if Clara hadn't signed me up. She was right about that."

I fanned myself with a paper plate. "I'm always right."

"And humble," added Rose.

Hamlet threw an arm around my dad. "You're welcome, Adrian, although all I did was help today."

My dad threw me a sly look. "You've helped in other ways."

For Pete's sake.

Suddenly, there was a rap on the window. We froze and Rose came to her senses first, rushing over with a huge smile, ready to charm. "Hi there!"

I scrambled to the stove and took the food out of the oven where we had stuck it to stay warm. My dad and Hamlet ferried the plates over to the window, and Rose handed them drinks.

"Here you go," my dad said. "I'm gonna hop out to explain what you're eating there." We watched as my dad stepped out of the truck and shook hands with the three judges. One was the food editor for a local magazine, one a restaurateur from France, and the other was food critic Stephen Fitch. I held in a squeal at seeing him in person. Pai gave them the rundown on the menu, then stepped back to let them eat the food.

The food editor, a tall Japanese American woman in her fifties, took a bite out of the pastel, and her eyes lit up. The muscular, bearded Frenchman ate a forkful of the lombo and chewed thoughtfully, giving nothing away with his expression. And Stephen Fitch dug into the picanha with gusto, his eyebrows raised as soon as the spice hit him.

A pool of sweat was practically gathered at my feet. I turned away and drank some water to distract myself. Rose did the same. Hamlet kept his head close to the window, watching everything.

Finally, we heard them thank my dad and move on. We got out of the truck and joined him outside. The afternoon sun was dropping lower into the sky, and the hottest part of the day had passed. A jazz band was playing not too far off and a breeze rustled the leaves of the eucalyptus trees.

We sat down, tired and relieved to be done. With the judges still making the rounds of the next few trucks, we had a minute to cool off and catch our breath. It was then that I realized I was starving. I went into the truck to plate some food, and we ate in amiable silence. The last twenty-four hours of emotional turmoil had caught up to all of us, it seemed.

Another air horn blare startled us. The voice came over the megaphone again, "We have a winner! All contestants please meet in the middle of the lot for the announcement!"

Gah! We ran to where everyone was gathered. The crowd was filled with nervous energy, and I looked over at the line of people next to me and squeezed Hamlet's hand really hard. *Please, please, please. For my dad. He deserves it. Please.* I didn't even know who I was pleading with.

The hopeful expression on my dad's face was unbearable, so I looked at the judges lined up in front of us instead. Stephen Fitch picked up the megaphone and cleared his throat before speaking. "Thank you so much to the contestants this year. As predicted, this was a really difficult task. The food of this city is better than ANY OTHER CITY in the world!" Everyone cheered. "It represents the beating heart of LA: the people." I felt myself choking up—thinking about how my dad's love for me had always been tied to food. How I identified with my city through the different flavors of the cultures brought over here by families around the world. By brave people like my dad.

And it hit me then—how much home mattered to me and my dad. How it had kept us anchored through so much uncertainty.

"And so let me just cut to the chase. The winner of this year's LA food truck competition is—Chili Today, Hot Tamale!"

CHAPTER 35

I DROPPED HAMLET'S HAND.

The winners were screaming and jumping up and down. Some were in tears. I'd be in tears, too. That was a boatload of money.

My dad took off his cap, ran a hand through his hair, then walked toward the truck. Rose cried, "What! That hunk of junk won over *us*! Completely unfair!" Several people looked over at us. Oh my God, Rose was the sorest loser on this *planet*.

My dad came over, put a hand on her shoulder, and said, "Hey. That's enough, Rose." She looked like she wanted to argue, but one look at my dad's crestfallen expression made her stop. When he walked to the truck, she followed him.

My chest hurt witnessing this sadness, and I turned to talk

to Hamlet. But he was a few feet away talking to Stephen Fitch. When Hamlet caught my eye, he waved me over.

"Are you Adrian Shin's daughter?" Stephen asked me, his wire-rimmed glasses sliding down his nose a bit.

I nodded, not able to speak for a second. "Yeah. Yes. I am."

"Your dad's food is just excellent," he said enthusiastically, reaching out for my hand. "I want to talk to him. Can you introduce us?"

Trying to remain cool and collected, I brushed a lock of hair away from my face. "Oh sure. Uh, he's in the truck. Follow me, please." Out of view, I shot Hamlet a *look*. His eyes were wide and he mouthed, *What's happening?*

I shrugged and hurried ahead of Stephen to warn my dad.

"Pai!" I hollered as soon as I got to the truck.

He looked up from wiping down the counter, his expression grim and irritated. "What?" he snapped.

"Stephen Fitch would like to speak to you," I said. "That's *all*," I hissed quietly, nudging him in the ribs.

"What?" Confusion clouded his features as he peered outside. Then he paled. Wiping his hand hastily on a towel, he stepped outside and I followed.

Rose, Hamlet, and I stood off to the side as they talked.

"Hi, Adrian. I'm really sorry you didn't win the competition," Stephen started. My dad held up a hand like, like "No problemo!" Please.

"But I wanted to say, you're doing something really special here. That pastel, the combination of flavors! Truly inventive."

"Thank you," Pai said, rubbing the back of his neck, suddenly shy.

Stephen handed him a business card. "If you're still interested in opening up a restaurant, I'd love to talk about investing. What you said about your Brazilian and Korean cultures—that was fantastic, and it's exactly the sort of thing that is integral to the food scene here. I'd love to set up a time to talk."

A very quiet, very long squeak came out of Rose, and I held back from dragging my hands down my face and screaming.

"Yes! Of course! Thanks, man," he said, holding out his fist. Stephen glanced down at it, then smiled, giving him a bump.

When he left, we remained cool for about .5 seconds. Then jumped up and down. Hamlet ran over to my dad and lifted him up.

"Ohmygodohmygod!" I screeched. I had zero chill and zero cares about it.

Rose paced in circles, beside herself. "Your investor problems are solved! Just like that! And what if he features you on *The Weekend Feast*?"

"What's that?" Hamlet asked, excited before knowing why.

"An NPR show about food!" she exclaimed.

My dad held his hands up. "All right, you guys. Let's remain calm. You don't know if he'll invest yet!"

But hope was making me buoyant. "Don't say that! Think positively!"

The three of them stopped moving. They exchanged glances then laughed. As one. One laugh unit.

"What?!" I asked, testy and defensive.

My dad shook his head. "You sound like . . ."

"Me," Rose finished for him. "You sound like a total try-hard." Her tone was like mine, flat and rude.

I flushed. "So?"

"It's a good look," Hamlet said with a wink. My own moves being used against me made me flustered, but I couldn't help but smile. So big my cheeks hurt.

We went back to the truck and cleaned up, everyone considerably less glum than before. When I noticed that the sun was setting, I had an idea. I hopped into the driver's seat. "Grab a hold of something," I announced as I lurched the truck out of the lot, finding the main road in the park.

"Clara! The four of us can't ride in this thing," my dad said, bracing himself against my headrest.

"It'll just be a few minutes, hide yourselves from cops," I said as I adjusted the rearview mirror. Rose threw herself into the passenger seat and put on her seat belt frantically. "Where are we going?"

"You'll see."

We followed a road that led us out of the park and up into the hills. A few minutes later, Hamlet popped up next to me, leaning against my headrest. Squinting into the tunnel we were headed toward, he asked, "Are we going to the observatory?"

Ugh, Google Maps boyfriend! I didn't answer, instead taking

us up the hills until we reached the parking lot for the Griffith Observatory. Since it was a Saturday evening, it was completely packed. I drove by the lot and instead went farther up the hill, to an area I knew we weren't really allowed to drive into—it was more of a hiking trail.

Rose sniffed out disobedience quicker than a cop. "Clara, we're not supposed to drive here."

Again, I ignored her. There was nothing obstructing us from driving on the dirt path. It was just wide enough. And finally, we reached the spot I was looking for. An old stomping ground of mine—a dirt lookout with the hillside behind us, and a view of the city in its entirety in front of us.

I parked and got out of the truck, climbing onto the hood and then the roof. I called down, "Come up!"

They joined me one by one. And by the time we were lined up on the roof, the sun was very low in the sky. To the left was the observatory—my favorite place in the entire city. Most people knew it from *Rebel Without a Cause*, the beautiful art deco architecture with the three domed buildings, the middle one housing a telescope that could view distant planets. It had a planetarium and exhibits inside, but my favorite thing about the observatory was the view. You could see all of LA from here.

What tourists usually came to see was the Hollywood sign, which was directly to the right of us, larger than life. Iconic but completely meaningless to me, to be honest. People who were born and raised here didn't see LA with the same starry eyes. It was just home, and the Hollywood sign did little to stir any feelings in me. But I did feel something when I looked down at the city stretched below us.

From this vantage point, you could see downtown to the left, Dodger Stadium a little farther north of it, a sprawl of suburban areas, the main drags that crisscrossed the entire city—Wilshire, La Brea, Santa Monica. And on a clear day like today, you could see a glimmering strip of the Pacific Ocean to the very west of us.

When you saw the city like this, everything inside you slowed down. Relaxed. It wasn't that LA was perfect, or some immigrant utopia. Like other good things in the world, it was deeply flawed, and on some days you sat parked on the 110 surrounded by buildings you couldn't see because of the smog, and you hated it here. It could be relentless and lonely. But it was also where my dad had built his life, where so many people had. It was a place where you could grab Brazilian Korean food in the park where Walt Disney dreamed up Disneyland. But more important, it was home. And I related, deeply, to a home that was a little messed up, but ever-evolving.

And as the sky turned a light lavender on the edges, pale pink in the middle, and then a deep orange near the horizon, you, gratefully, felt your littleness in the universe.

I looked over at the KoBra crew and felt so grateful for the small part of the universe I had.

We watched the sun set, quiet with our own thoughts. My head tilted back and my eyes closed as a cool breeze drifted over us. Summer was ending, I guess. It felt good, and it felt sad. I knew that things wouldn't be the same with Patrick and Felix, and I was okay with that. I glanced at Hamlet and Rose, their gazes straight ahead, the last of the day's light shining on them. It was startling how I felt about them now, how fiercely they mattered to me.

Yeah, I was okay with a lot of things.

When the sun dipped behind the hills, my dad jumped off the hood. "We should go before we actually get into trouble." At the word *trouble*, Rose booked it after him.

I grabbed Hamlet's hand before he could follow. "Wait a sec." I watched Rose disappear into the truck, then looked up at Hamlet. It was dark, but my eyes adjusted and I could see his features perfectly. I had his face pretty well memorized now. Like the streets in my neighborhood, the pages of my favorite books. "We need to talk about what you said to me last week, before I left. Um, how you love me." I was grateful for the darkness, hiding my blushing cheeks.

He took a deep breath. "You don't have to—"

"I know. And I'm not ready to say it back." Relief poured out of me, a weight that had been filling the parts between my bones finally lifting. "Is that okay?"

He blinked a couple of times, looking down at our feet. I held his hands firmly, and my palms were dry for once. After a while he looked at me and, while there was some sadness in his eyes, I believed him when he smiled and said, "Yeah, that's okay."

I squeezed his hand. "But you have to know . . . I've never said that to anyone before. Except my parents."

"Really? What about *all* those ex-boyfriends?"

I lifted my hand up to the base of his neck and wound my fingers into his thick hair. "I never loved them. In fact, I never liked any of them as much as I like you. I think that's why I freaked out. Not because you said you loved me. Just understanding the extent of my actual feelings for you. It's really new."

His eyes softened. His whole face, the edges of his body—they softened. Everything. "You like me more than them?"

I leaned my forehead against his. "Yeah. So much more."

Catching my belt loops with his fingers, he drew me closer to him and said, "All right. I guess I'll have to be patient. We'll live on Clara Time. Not Hamlet Time."

And then he lifted my chin, gently, touching his lips to mine. The kiss was sweet and full of promise. Like him. When he let go, I felt a lurch in my chest that told me Clara Time was going to catch up to Hamlet Time real fast. And when he climbed down from the roof, I took one last glance at the view—lights sparkling in the inky-blue night.

In this huge city, there were three people in this truck who mattered a lot to me. I'd protect that little part of the universe for as long as possible.

ACKNOWLEDGMENTS

MY FIRST THANK-YOU ALWAYS GOES TO MY AGENT, Judith Hansen, fiercest champion for any creator lucky enough to have her in their corner. I'm so grateful for your guidance and wisdom.

Endless gratitude to my editor, Janine O'Malley, and to Melissa Warten for their expertise and good humor while forming an actual book from this pile of swear words. Thank you to Margaret Ferguson for helping me shape this story in the very beginning and for everything before that. Thanks to the FSG/Macmillan team, including Elizabeth Clark, Brittany Pearlman, Joy Peskin, Jodie Chester Lowe, and Karen Ninnis.

For the research and eyeballs needed on this book, I'd like to thank Lisa McCune of Scratch, Louis Quezada of Border Grill,

Suzy Yu, Alice Fanchiang, Cat Fanchiang, Chengzhe Zhou, Sophie Xiao, Charmaine Ou, Ben Zhu, Adi Alsaid, Lilliam Rivera, Nemuel DePaula, Nina Khatibi, Fernando Encarnacao, and Jennifer Li.

Thank you to Derick Tsai for being the Josh Lyman of my book life. Thanks to Willard Ford and everyone at SSG for turning me into someone who can fight with more than just her words. Thanks to #RetreatYoSelf. Bless our frosé and In-N-Out. Thank you to Rilo Kiley for letting me use your perfect words.

Thanks to all the librarians, booksellers, festival organizers, and lovely readers whom I've met over the years. Your support and kind words have meant the world to me.

So much gratitude to early readers Brandy Colbert, Sarah Enni, Morgan Matson, and Amy Spalding. You weren't just readers but my lifeline during the wildest year ever. Keeping with this metaphor—thank you to Robin Benway, Anna Carey, Kirsten Hubbard, Alex Kahler, Elissa Sussman, and Zan Romanoff for keeping me afloat in our fair city.

Infinite 🖤 to the Bog: Leila Austin, Alexis Bass, Lindsey Roth Culli, Debra Driza, Kristin Halbrook, Kate Hart, Michelle Krys, Amy Lukavics, Samantha Mabry, Phoebe North, Veronica Roth, Steph Sinkhorn, Courtney Summers, Kara Thomas, and Kaitlin Ward. Special shout-outs to Somaiya Daud, Laurie Devore, Kody Keplinger, and Stephanie Kuehn for the #accountability on this book. Thank you, hags.

It's no surprise that families matter a whole lot in my books.

Because mine is always there, filling the pages, even when you can't see them.

For all the love and support, thank you to Kristi Appelhans, Tony Appelhans, Kira Appelhans, Tom Watson, Oliver Appelhans-Watson, Leah Appelhans, and Nate Petersen.

Thanks to my sister, Christine, for being the most reliable person in my life. I couldn't have done anything this year without your help. Even if I had to hear *Frasier* at midnight. Thanks to my parents for doing so many things right that I've only noticed and appreciated with time. For supporting everything I've ever wanted to do, minus going to sleepovers.

And thank you to my husband, Christopher Appelhans. I wrote about falling in love in LA because of you. I write everything because of you.

GOFISH

QUESTIONS FOR THE AUTHOR

MAURENE GOO

What did you want to be when you grew up?
For the longest time I wanted to be a journalist, like my mother. She used to do live broadcasts of American current events from an audio mixer set up in her bedroom in LA, which were then aired in Korea.

When did you realize you wanted to be a writer?
I always loved reading, but didn't write my real first piece of fiction until I was in ninth grade. Our assignment was to make up our own Greek myth and I wrote one that I thought was brilliant at the time. My teacher's impressed feedback was that first high I felt from having someone read my work.

What's your most embarrassing childhood memory?
I have many, many embarrassing childhood memories. One of them was in seventh grade, I was padding my bra with random bits of stuff I found (cotton, socks, etc.) and the cotton pad wriggled out and fell out of my shirt while I was talking to some boy. I don't THINK he noticed??

What's your favorite childhood memory?
One time my family and I went camping and our tiny blue tent flew up in the air and got caught in a pine tree. The camping

trip had been pretty miserable because of the heat and mosquitos but when that happened—it was this moment of hilarity mixed with magic, and my cousins and I still talk about it to this day.

As a young person, who did you look up to most?
On the surface, my parents. I was a Goody Two-Shoes. But deep inside, I was obsessed with celebrities and wanted to be perfect and adult and cool like them.

What was your favorite thing about school?
I loved reading and arts and crafts.

What were your hobbies as a kid? What are your hobbies now?
Honestly, all I did as a kid was read books. I hated sports and spent endless hours in Stoneybrook, Connecticut, with the Baby-Sitters Club. As an adult, reading is still a big hobby, but I've now welcomed sports into my life. If I'm not reading, I'm usually boxing.

Did you play sports as a kid?
Not really—I took tennis and swimming lessons but nothing ever stuck. I hated being bad at things. And I was bad at sports.

What was your first job, and what was your worst job?
My first real job was out of college, working as a sales person at the Gap. My worst job was this temp position I had one day in a literal mail room. The people who worked with me were, like, dead inside, and we had to listen to a static-y radio all day long.

How did you celebrate publishing your first book?
So not glam: I was online all day thanking everyone. But I did have a really good dinner out with my husband. I remember all the food: risotto with peas, champagne, and banana pudding for dessert.

Where do you write your books?
During the day, I get all my writing done in coffee shops with friends. In the evening, I'm home in my office.

What book is on your nightstand now?
Too many books: *If You Leave Me* by Crystal Hana Kim, *The Boneless Mercies* by April Genevieve Tucholke, and *City of Light, City of Poison: Murder, Magic, and the First Police Chief of Paris* by Holly Tucker.

What sparked your imagination for *The Way You Make Me Feel*?
I had three ideas in mind when I started this book: 1) a summer job story, 2) an enemy-to-friends story, and 3) an LA story. Once I figured out that Clara's dad owned a food truck, I realized I could do all three things in one fell swoop. What better, um, *vehicle* could force two enemies to become friends while traversing Los Angeles? Also, Clara came to me first: A prickly, emotionally closed-off girl who I would have been intimidated by in high school. I asked myself, what's *her* story and what sequence of events would change her?

What challenges do you face in the writing process, and how do you overcome them?
I get easily distracted. My brain knows *exactly* how many seconds I have until a deadline and makes me suffer. So,

just getting in the zone and starting is the hardest part. Getting off the Internet is key, as is writing with friends to hold me accountable.

What is your favorite word?
If favoritism is measured by embarrassing overuse, then my favorite words are *little* or *just*! But my whimsical answer is *ephemeral*.

If you could live in any fictional world, what would it be?
I know a lot of people want to live in the world of Harry Potter, but Hogwarts is kind of my nightmare. Your life is *always* in danger! So, I'm going to go with the Prince Edward Island of *Anne of Green Gables*. I know it's a real place, but I want to live in *that* version of it. So darn pleasant.

Who is your favorite fictional character?
I will always love Ramona Quimby. What a truly special, real kid she was.

What was your favorite book when you were a kid? Do you have a favorite book now?
A book I read over and over again was *Little Women* by Louisa May Alcott. And I probably read every BSC book about 864,560,987 times. Picking a favorite book now is near impossible, but *Cloud Atlas* by David Mitchell is consistently up there, as is *White Teeth* by Zadie Smith and *When You Reach Me* by Rebecca Stead.

If you could travel in time, where would you go and what would you do?
This is always hard for me because I love certain periods of history but know that they were actually disgusting and full of

pestilence and racist, violent people . . . *however*, if I could be isolated from that, I'd love to visit the Wild West or New York City during the Gilded Age and just *live* there. Nothing noble like stopping wars or anything!

What's the best advice you have ever received about writing?
The first panel I ever did was with the late and wonderful Ned Vizzini. And he could sense all my insecurities as a debut author and told me afterward, "Just be yourself and honest and your readers will find you." I think about it all the time.

What advice do you wish someone had given you when you were younger?
To keep doing things even if they are hard or you're bad at them. It'll be rewarding in the end, and you're tougher than you think.

Do you ever get writer's block? What do you do to get back on track?
Sure. I am very easy on myself—I take a break for as long as I feel like (even if on deadline!) and let myself "fill the well": I watch TV, read graphic novels, go out with friends, etc. I try to fire off other parts of my brain and I can usually start writing soon after. Forcing myself to write during a block never works.

What would you do if you ever stopped writing?
I would probably read a whole lot more and do more design work.

If you were a superhero, what would your superpower be?
Speed. I'm so impatient and wish I had more hours in my day.

Do you have any strange or funny habits? Did you when you were a kid?

I have to wash my feet every night before bed, no matter what. I also do this little morning run toward my cat's scratch post with her every morning. If I don't do it, I feel like my day is going to be unlucky. As a kid I had some compulsive habits, for example I had to count syllables on my hands when people spoke (I could only stop when the sentence was a multiple of five—your entire hand or both hands).

What do you consider to be your greatest accomplishment?

The obvious and honest answer is being a published author. I never even dreamt that this could be my job when I was a kid. The other corny answer is being a good friend. I'm a sap.

What do you want readers to remember about your books?

I want them to remember the characters warmly—that's how I felt about my favorite books when I was younger. They were like old friends. I would also like readers to remember that they laughed while reading my books. Out loud and with actual joy.

What would your readers be most surprised to learn about you?

That I wouldn't be able to recognize a Drake song if my life depended on it. Is that surprising, though?

LUCKY is the biggest Korean pop star on the scene, and tomorrow is her debut on *The Later Tonight Show* in America. Jack is a budding photographer, on assignment for the tabloid job he keeps secret from his parents. When Lucky and Jack run into each other at a hotel, nothing will ever be the same.

Keep reading for an excerpt.

CHAPTER ONE

LUCKY

WHEN YOU HAVE A FACE THAT'S RECOGNIZABLE BY AN entire continent, you have zero room to make mistakes.

Especially onstage.

I gazed into the screaming crowd, lights blinding me and the sound of my voice faint through the headset. The nonstop roar made it impossible for me to hear my own voice.

Once during a performance, when I threw my body into the outstretched arms of my backup dancer, the tiny microphone had shifted under my curtain of hair, and my voice cracked during the most dramatic moment of my hit single "Heartbeat."

It was the crack heard around Asia. Endless video loops of that moment were played on the Internet—some superimposed with cartoon rabbits and added screechy sound effects. My favorite one showed an animated pane of glass shattering at the exact moment of the voice crack. It was so masterfully done, I laughed every time I watched it.

My management label didn't find it funny, though. They saw it as a lapse, an imperfection on an otherwise perfect K-pop star.

That lapse was what I was thinking about as I stood on a stage in Hong Kong. The final stop on my Asian tour.

There was something about the vibration in the air, though—the currents of excitement filling in the spaces between me and the crowd. It was why I did this. Whatever I had been feeling days or seconds before I stepped onstage—like worrying about messing up again—all of that disappeared when the crowd's energy slipped under my skin and into my bloodstream.

Ferocious adoration by way of osmosis.

My silver stiletto boots were planted firmly in a wide stance, and my feet were killing me as per usual. I had this recurring nightmare of my boots chasing me around a parking lot. They were human-sized and ran after me in never-ending circles. My managers insisted on me wearing the same boots when I performed—my "signature look." Over-the-knee boots that stretched up the long expanse of my legs.

I was tall. Five foot ten—a veritable giant in Seoul. But there was no such thing as "too tall."

As I went through the familiar steps of the choreography for "Heartbeat," I managed to ignore the pain shooting up from the balls of my feet, the perpetual wedgie from my booty shorts, and the long strands of my pink wig sticking to the sweaty sides of my face.

Because I could do this choreography blindfolded, with two broken legs. I'd done this performance hundreds of times. At a certain point, my body moved on its own, as if on autopilot. Sometimes when

I finished performing "Heartbeat," my head hanging at an odd angle because of how the dance ended, I would blink and wonder where I had been for the last three minutes and twenty-four seconds.

When my body took over like that, I knew I got the job done. I was rewarded for the absolute precision with which I executed my performances.

And today was no different. I finished the song and looked out into the crowd, the screams of the fans piercing through me as I returned to my body with a *whoosh*.

I was finally done with this tour.

Backstage, I was immediately surrounded by people: my makeup artist, stylist, and head of security. I plopped down into a chair while my wig was adjusted and teased and my face dabbed with oil papers.

"Don't get rid of that dewy glow, though," I cracked to Lonni, my makeup artist.

Lonni pursed her lips. "You're seventeen, you don't need to be dewier. Also? Oil slick is not 'dewy.'"

Hmph. I let her continue mopping up my grease-face.

The back-up dancers stumbled backstage, a group of men and women in nondescript, sexy black outfits. I jumped up from my chair—making Lonni tsk in exasperation—and bent at the waist.

"Sugohaess-eoyo!" I said as I bowed. "Thank you so much." I always made sure to thank them in both Korean and English because the dancers came from all over.

They had suffered with me during every single practice and stop and never got any of the glory. My appreciation was genuine, but it was also expected. K-pop stars always had to be gracious.

They bowed and thanked me in return, sweaty and exhausted. "You killed it, Lucky," one of the dancers, Jin, said with a wink. "You were almost able to keep up with me."

I flushed. Jin was cute. He was also off-limits, as were most boys in my life. "I'll land that turn one of these days," I said with nervous laughter. They all shuffled off, going to their hotel together. I watched them with envy. Would they be hanging out in someone's room, eating cup ramen together?

No matter. My feet were going to crumble into dust. I plopped back into the chair.

A hand patted my back. "Hey. You too. Sugohaess-eo," my manager's assistant, Ji-Yeon, said. Ji-Yeon always told me I did a good job after performances, like a proud but stern older sister. She was a tiny rabbit of a young woman, her full-cheeked face obscured by edgy blunt-cut bangs and giant glasses. But she was a powerhouse who got things done.

She scrolled through her ever-present phone. "We're going to do a meet and greet for about an hour, so be sure to drink some water."

"What? A meet and greet?" I had stopped doing those a couple years ago. They were more for beginner pop groups. Once you reached a certain level, it got unwieldy.

"Yeah. Since it's your final show, we thought it would make a good photo op." She handed me a bottle of Evian.

"So, I'm going to be here for another hour?" I tried to keep the whininess out of my voice.

"It'll be fast. In and out. Do you not want to do it?" Ji-Yeon asked, peering over her glasses.

Don't be lazy. I shook my head. "No, it's fine."

"Okay, good. Now, let's get you out of this outfit and into something more comfortable for the fans," Ji-Yeon said with a slight twitch of her nose, making her glasses shift up and down on her pale face. "Except the shoes, of course. Gotta keep those on."

Of course.

Minutes later, I was sitting behind a table signing albums, posters, whatever the fans had brought with them. And even though I had wanted to crawl into bed mere minutes before, the excitement of the fans zapped me with a familiar energy. Interaction with them was so rare lately.

"Can I get a selfie?" I looked at the girl with braces and a pixie cut and was about to say yes when my head bodyguard, Ren Chang, stepped in front of me and shook his head.

I threw the girl an apologetic look before the next fan approached me with a poster to sign.

In the early days, I had wanted to give a hug and speak to everyone who had waited in line to see me. But the bigger my fan base grew, the more nebulous and faceless they became. I battled the instinct to give canned and wooden responses. "Thank you for coming," I said with a smile at the older man as I signed his poster with a fat black Sharpie.

He nodded, not making eye contact with me. But his hand grazed mine when I returned the poster, and he got in close. I could smell the meal he'd had, feel the heat of his body. Without missing a beat, Ren pushed him back with a firm hand. Again, I smiled apologetically at the man, even though my entire being recoiled. Most of my male fans were perfectly fine—but there was an overeager, sweaty subset that approached me with an intensity that frightened me. In those moments, I still had to act gracious. Always grateful for what I had.

The line was cut off eventually and I stood up and waved and bowed to the crying and cheering fans. They roared when I threw out a peace sign and I was whisked away through the back door.

The second I stepped outside, the paparazzi and fans descended. Camera flashes, voices yelling out my name, a crush of humanity.

Ren and a few other bodyguards closed in around me like a protective membrane. When people pushed against them, the force made the circle of security undulate as we moved through the narrow alley toward the van.

"*Lucky, I love you!*" a girl screamed. My instinct was to look toward the voice, to say, "Thank you!" But doing that would open the floodgates. I learned my lesson a long time ago.

Instead, I looked down, watching the steps of Ren in front of me. Keeping my eyes on his firm footsteps slowed my racing heart, gave me focus. I liked having something to focus on. Otherwise, I would spiral into sheer panic at the thought of being trampled, enclosed by a million people who all wanted a piece of me.

My guards slowed down, and I glanced up. The car was near, but people were blocking it. The police had arrived and the energy was feeding on itself—that stage of mania where absolutely no one had control. Where grown men with huge arms fought back teenage girls with dazed expressions, helplessly watching as the girls climbed over them as if they were trees, feral and hungry.

My heart raced, my palms grew sweaty, and a wave of nausea came over me.

"Stay close," Ren said in a low voice, stretching a thick arm across my torso.

"Like I have a choice?" I asked, my voice raspy from overuse. Feeling annoyed at Ren for no reason.

"Or you could get trampled," he replied mildly. Ren was my dad's age but had the fitness level of an Olympian. And the sense of humor of a Triscuit.

So I kept close—and within seconds, fresh air burst through the circle, breaking through the wall of bodies to reach me.

My heart resumed beating back to normal and I lifted my face up to the bright Hong Kong skyline. It flashed at me for a second before I was tucked safely into the van.

The first thing I did was take my freaking boots off.